FARSHIFT

CHRONICLES OF A WAYLAID WORLD

A novel of semi-fiction by
MJ Carambat

Cover art by
Alex Harvie

Farshift, Chronicles of a Waylaid World

Cover design by Alex Harvie

ISBN: 978-0-615-37893-0

Printed in the United States of America
November 2013

"All that we are is the result of what we have thought. The mind is everything. What we think we become."
—*Buddha*

"Not only is the universe stranger than we imagine… it is stranger than we *can* imagine."
—*Arthur Eddington*

Table of Contents

PART III

Foreword

A few words on semi-fiction:

Semi-fiction is a seldom-used literary term meaning a blend of fact and fiction, usually addressing a taboo or controversial subject. However, *Farshift* is neither taboo nor controversial; it is simply a chronicle of some very unusual events, both fictional and otherwise, of a world that no longer wants to be found.

Most of the dates, people, and places in this book are remarkably accurate. Sometimes truth really is stranger than fiction, in this case, really, really strange.

Much of what is in this book has been recovered from under the sofa cushions of time, having first been lost, discredited, or diabolically stricken from the public record. Every effort has been made to ascribe to the facts as accurately as possible, leaving it to the reader to determine if the details are true or to wonder what the heck the writer had been putting in his tea.

That said, *Farshift* brings together many of the mysterious, forgotten, and enigmatic events of our past, explaining them in bold, unexpected new ways. This eccentric alternative history illuminates hidden connections to seemingly unrelated events in our past.

For example, what caused the massive explosion in Tunguska in 1908? What happened during the solar eclipse of 1919? What actually occurred at Roswell, New Mexico in 1947, and why do aliens seem to have a thing for cows?

As the reader gains piece after piece of an enormous jigsaw puzzle—one that reveals a remarkably surprising picture of our history and our future—it will blur the line of what is bizarrely real and what is simply fiction.

- M.J. Carambat

Prologue

[Tunguska Region, Siberia – May 20th, 1927]

"Over here *c…c…comrades.* Southern Swamp is just over r…r…ridge," said Aleksei, in a remote Siberian dialect, barely recognizable as Russian. Professor Kulik often had trouble understanding their fifteen-year old guide, and now, with the boy's teeth chattering in the blistering cold, the Soviet scientist wasn't sure he heard him correctly.

"Wait for us, Aleksei. We are coming," shouted Kulik to the nearly frozen youth. "We are finally there, yes?"

Unable to proceed any further by canoe, the small expedition had traveled on foot for days, hacking their way through difficult entanglements of fallen trees and branches.

Kulik sat down and brushed the snow and debris off his beard. He hadn't bathed for days and was miserable and exhausted. His research assistant, Anya, sat down next to him and put her pack down, glad for the rest.

"Professor, look at trees." Anya motioned towards the ridge where hundreds of rotting, fallen trees angled towards them on the ground, obviously the result of a huge explosion further up. Neither scientist expected to see such incredible devastation from what was supposed to be a meteorite impact.

The villagers' stories described an enormous fireball falling from the sky nearly twenty years ago. The impact caused a bright flash and a shockwave that flattened huts and knocked people unconscious. When they awoke, they found shattered trees blazing around them, their ears still ringing from the great noise of the explosion. The ground shook violently and fierce thunderstorms raged over the apocalyptic scene for days. Until now, none of the locals dared visit the cursed impact site, believing it to be a visit from their vengeful god, Ogdy.

At the top of the ridge, Aleksei suddenly dropped to his knees. He was stammering again. From what Kulik could understand, he was pleading for mercy.

"Proshchat…Ogdy…Proshchat!" whimpered the frightened boy.

"What is it Aleksei?" asked Kulik coming up the ridge. "There is nothing to fear from swamp…"

Kulik's words caught in his throat. Stretched out before him lay a surreal landscape, amazingly unchanged over the past nineteen years. Instead of finding a crater, Kulik saw charred trees stripped of their branches, standing upright like telephone poles. The soft earth heaved outward from the center in giant waves, forming concentric rippling patterns. Dotting the scene were peculiar shallow holes from ten to fifty feet in diameter, filled with murky water.

Something shimmered like glass at the bottom of the misshapened valley. He turned to Anya and pointed. "Do you see a flash? There, near center?"

"Da, Professor. Could it still be meteorite after so many years?"

"No, it cannot be. Perhaps meteorite exploded in sky. Look, there is no crater. Yet *something* is there."

Aleksei was still on his knees with his eyes downcast, sobbing.

"Aleksei, please get up. It is surprising, but not to fear. Nothing is supernatural about meteorite impact." Kulik helped the boy to his feet.

The boy regained some of his composure. "Dis…dis sort of thing, you see mu…much Professor?"

"No, not at all. This exceeds wildest of expectations. Our discovery will shock world. This is largest meteorite impact in recent time."

Kulik patted the boy on the back and sent him to help Anya set up the photographic equipment as he took notes and made sketches.

"Look down there, it still flashes like mirror," said Anya, holding up a pair of binoculars.

Kulik took the binoculars and looked for himself.

"Astounding, we must go down."

They spent the better part of the morning making their way down the ridge into the frozen marsh. By noon they finally reached the center of the bog and spread out to search the pocket of twisted landscape.

It was Anya who found it first. She couldn't believe what she was seeing. She excitedly called out to the others.

Kulik and Aleksei ran to her. They saw what she had found, a fist sized rock, shiny as glass and black as ebony. It was unremarkable except for one thing—it was floating about two feet above the ground.

[PART I]

Chapter 1, Philolaus

Edington woke suddenly in complete darkness. Heart pounding, he quickly found the soft, reassuring glow of the radium dial of the pocket-watch lying on his nightstand. The time was 2:30 a.m., or at least that was what he thought he saw as he blinked at the small, blurry shapes. The little brass watch had been a going away present, given to him almost a year ago, shortly after he had turned sixteen.

Looking around for the larger and more visible glow of the Nixie tube clock recessed in the wall, he tried to shake off the nightmare. It had been about falling again. It was always about falling, falling forever, into a deep abyss.

The Nixie clock failed to present itself, as did any other light in his room. *So the power is out again. This is becoming ridiculous.* Sam Edington would normally be the last person to stir up trouble in the little town. He was young, straight out of the science academy and just an apprentice. Not many people would take him seriously. But then again, three power outages in a row would cause concern in the most dauntless of colonists.

He swung his legs out of bed and ran his slender fingers through his short, brown hair. *Well, I might as well take a reading while I'm up and the lights are out.* He took the observatory key off his nightstand. Nighttime power outages did have one advantage, albeit only for astronomers, an unparalleled view of the night sky. Gone would be the bright haze near the horizon caused by the town lights. There would be nothing but clear skies all the way down.

Edington was the apprentice to the Chief Royal Astronomer of the Porter Observatory in the town of Parifeldie. What this actually meant was that he did all the work and his supervisor, Professor Almos, received all the credit. This was something Almos did without even a second thought. *Actually, Professor Almos does many things without even first thoughts,* mused Edington. He groaned at the prospect of another day of dealing with the man. *The old bastard does what he wants when he wants to do it; my feelings aren't worth two bits.*

Not that the professor was useless; he was actually quite a brilliant astrophysicist. However, the social graces and common sense that most people take for granted apparently were waylaid to make room for the voluminous store of mathematical and scientific data accumulated in Professor Almos's head.

Be that as it may, the professor's mannerisms could be unbearable at times. Just watching the old curmudgeon go by with his chaotic head of white hair, unkempt beard, and handlebar mustache would set Edington's nerves on edge.

"Run those calculations again, Sam. You must have done something wrong," Almos said yesterday during the last cosmic reading.

He had run the calculations five times at this point, and he flushed with anger. "Sir, I can run these numbers until Helios explodes, but that won't change the outcome. There's nothing wrong with them."

Professor Almos angrily took the stack of papers from his hands. "Give them to me, boy. I'll do them myself," he said, storming off to his office.

Later that day, when the observatory posted the numbers in the square, the figures Edington had derived were still there, yet no apology was forthcoming from Almos.

Nor was he the only one bestowed by this singular lack of courtesy. Professor Almos was an equal opportunity annoyer. He was disliked by all members of observatory staff, and usually sat alone in his office, stewing over his facts and figures.

"Crikey! I don't see why you put up with it," said his best mate, Ayden Howell, a security watchman at the observatory. "Sam, you must go home every night and repeatedly thump your head on the wall! How many whacks does it take to keep from showing up with a loaded pistol every morning?"

"About twelve times seem to do the trick," he said with a smile. "At least that's when I start losing consciousness. Really though, working under Almos isn't that bad once you pack up your self-respect in a suitcase and ship it off to Flitwick."

"Flitwick colony?" inquired Ayden. "Right good choice, what with them losing luggage more than the other five colonies combined."

He had chuckled at that. Ayden always had a way of cheering him up, even when the professor was involved.

The professor was riotously annoying, but you could not question his qualifications. Never would the observatory have a more prominent and talented Chief Royal Astronomer.

Parifeldie had the largest, most modern observatory on Philolaus. It was no surprise that Almos accepted the observatory position offered to him nearly thirty years ago. After all, he had been instrumental in the original detection of the planet's presence ten years prior.

Under his guidance, Edington had learned valuable skills as an astronomer and as an astrophysicist. If it were not for the man's confounded temperament, he would have truly loved his job, power failures and all.

He made his way through the dark trying to find the door. The meager light from his pocket-watch moved slowly through the air bouncing like a firefly. The wooden floor was cold beneath his bare feet, now that the furnaces were not working. He wondered how much the outage had affected the town this time. There was going to be hell to pay in the morning, and make no mistake. He would not be the only irate colonist in the town meeting hall that afternoon.

Reaching the solid brass door to the outside hall, he gripped the release lever and pulled hard. Ever since the frost season, the door's release mechanism had been sticking with a vengeance. With a shudder, the lever gave way and the complex arrangement of clockwork valves and manual hydraulics unsealed the door and it swung open into the hallway.

His room was one of many in the dormitory beneath the main observatory dome. Each room in the dormitory had only one door. The rooms were built like those in a Royal Navy battle cruiser, and they even reeked of the same disinfectant and polish. Further down the hall was a communal lavatory with the same complicated door.

The reason for the sealed doors was not for security, although they certainly provided it. This was for protection from the odd weather.

Philolaus did not offer much in hospitality. Unlike their home world of Archænis, this planet had little to no animal life. Daytime was sweltering, and as night quickly fell, the temperature dropped to a frigid level.

Mostly a quagmire, there was little usable land for farming and colonization. High plateaus towered hundreds of feet over the sweltering jungle foliage. Differing in size from a few thousand feet to a few hundred miles wide, the plateaus contrasted strangely with the jungle below. Seen from space, they dotted the planet like a myriad of green islands on a sea of darker greens and blues.

Of the hundreds of plateaus surveyed, six were capable of supporting human habitation. In only a few years, the strange new world hosted a small colony on each of them. While the colonies of Windemere and Cogstead were still barely outposts, the town of Parifeldie had become the largest community on Philolaus, supporting well over a thousand people.

Although Archænis' planetary meteorologists had known of the fierce winds, they did not know about the deadly vapors they contained. The marshy lowland jungles contained noxious gases that were heavier than the air high above in the plateaus. During the wet season, the moisture in the air kept the vapors subdued, so the colonists knew nothing of the danger until the first serious windstorm.

Nearly half the population of Pennymoor, the first colony, perished in a short, but deadly storm.

Recently however, Edington knew that death to the vapors was a rare occurrence. Every room on every building on every colony had an airtight seal on its doors. Windstorms were difficult to predict, and there would be little time to find shelter when the alarm sounded.

Bugger…I won't have any warning at all with the power out. Hmmm…at least I'll die with my head full of stars. Protected only by his thin nightshirt and shorts, he grimly felt his way down the hall.

Being of slight build and light on his feet, he barely made a sound as he made his way to the stairs at the end of the long corridor which led up to the observatory platform. The door to the observatory was a hatch in the ceiling at the top of the stairs. Written on a bronze placard on the door were the words:

PORTER OBSERVATORY-PLATFORM B.
Authorized Personnel Only.

He produced the key from his nightshirt pocket, unlocked the door and pushed it open. The heavy wooden portal swung evenly to the side and rested on a catch inside with a loud click. He peered into the darkness above. He had been up here during outages before, and he knew that once he opened the dome there would be plenty of starlight to see by. Until then, the dome would be in total darkness and he would have only the faint amber glow of his watch to assist him.

Even though he practically lived up here, it was easy to get turned around in the large circular room. Using the hatch as a base, he walked towards the wall that housed the mechanism that opened the observatory dome. Feeling a little too confident, he walked briskly to the wheel platform, not noticing a chair someone had left in the middle of the room.

"Victoria's creaking corsets!" he exclaimed, as he toppled over, sending the chair skittering into the darkness, wheels clattering. A crash sounded followed by the noise of breaking glass as the chair finally came to a rest somewhere on the other side of the room.

"Just brilliant," he muttered. "What idiot left his chair in the middle of the room?"

Suddenly, a sick dread filled his chest as he realized what the sound of breaking glass could have been. Yesterday was the day they were cleaning the new primary mirror from the telescope in Platform A, and they were using the equipment in Platform B to do it! If the chair had somehow broken that extremely expensive mirror, Almos would be more than livid. He would have had him deported back home in disgrace with more than his dignity missing.

Limping a little, he carefully completed the distance to the apparatus that opened the dome. He had to know what he had hit with the chair. Quickly, he turned the big brass wheel to let in some light. It was almost as tall as he was. It turned easily, but it took many revolutions before the shutter would be entirely open. At last, a crack of starlight filled the room as two large doors in the domed ceiling slid noisily open.

A symphony of stars in a velvet black sky filled the opening as he turned. The scene never failed to amaze him. He could see so many more stars here than he could back home. The edge of an enormous purple and green nebulous cloud filled most of the horizon, filled with tiny hot stars, usually too dim to see over the town lights. Now, they seemed close enough to touch through the thin exotic atmosphere. He would be studying that enigmatic mass quite closely tonight.

With the room much brighter now by the starlight, he cautiously stepped down from the wheel platform to see what he had broken.

The chair had indeed gone careening directly into the workbench area where they kept the cleaning and calibration tools. Eyes traveling downward, he surveyed the workbench. Yes, they were working on the mirror here. Yes, there were the mirror transportation packing materials from Platform A, and yes, he saw with a sinking feeling, there was the cast iron mounting cell with the mirror removed.

Expecting the worst, his eyes traveled down to the floor where the chair had landed. They fell on a pile of broken glass. However, upon looking closer, he sighed and smiled with relief.

On the floor, shining in the starlight, were many small shards of glass from the large carafe that the collision had dislodged from the huge, bulky contraption that made Almos's foul tasting coffee every morning.

No one liked the noisy, steam driven machine nor did anyone except Almos enjoy the coffee it produced, but the codger had insisted on hauling the infernal device up here to be near his office. It was shipped to the planet at an exorbitant cost and had special ducts installed to evacuate the steam lest it damage the sensitive equipment in the observatory. Almos loved his coffee machine and had it make him several cups of the noxious brew every morning.

Professor Almos will have my head if he goes without his coffee this morning, thought Edington as he quickly replaced the carafe with a spare from the supply closet.

Molly Arden pushed herself away from her computer screen. The cursor blinked back at her expectantly, looking surprised that the roller coaster ride had suddenly ended. Molly had been typing for a very long time. *What time was it anyway? Nearly 3:00 a.m.? I've got to get some sleep.* She yawned, saved her file, and closed her laptop. With a click, the screen went dark, and she got out of the wicker chair.

Not a bad start, quite good, actually. Still stiff from sitting down so long, she undressed for bed.

She drew in the fresh air coming through the hotel room's open patio door. An unseasonably cool tropical breeze whispered into the room as she changed into her nightgown. Shivering a little, she quickly ducked beneath the soft, warm covers. Overall, it had been a very good day's work.

Rarely had she been able to write so many pages when just starting a new novel. Even stranger, this was her first attempt at writing science fiction.

She remembered how her father would drag the whole family to Star Wars and Star Trek conventions. Molly and her mother would loiter by the jewelry and fantasy tables while her father argued in Klingon with the vendors. Recently, she had lost count of how many fantasy conventions she had attended now, not as a fan, but as someone fans came to see.

Working on the book while vacationing in Costa Maya, however, was a pleasant fringe benefit. She needed to thank her agent, Ellen for suggesting the place. The quaint Mexican resort was beautiful.

Ellen had, in fact, been there herself during the honeymoon of her short, disastrous first marriage.

"Molly," Ellen had argued, "you've been doing the same fantasy books for five years. Don't get me wrong, there's nothing wrong with the sales, but as your friend, I think you may be burning yourself out. You've spent so much time in that *Dragon's Keep* universe of yours that you've forgotten that there's more to life than just writing books. You're nearly thirty years old. You need to take a break. Get out and meet someone!"

Ellen had hit rather uncomfortably close to the mark. Her mother had been saying much the same thing. But lately, Molly's love of writing had made her reclusive. It kept her shuttered away in her apartment, immersed in a fantasy world of magic and adventure. She used to be much more outgoing until she started writing the blasted *Dragon's Keep* novels.

As the series progressed, the fantastic world she envisioned had gotten smaller and harder to write about. With the popularity of her books and the expectations of millions of readers, writing had become less of a joy and more like a burden. The last book, *Dragon's Keep: Book 4* was still selling well, but had nowhere near the popularity of the first book in the series. It was still one of the year's best-selling books, but Molly knew that it was not her best work. The series was burning her out and she had tired of it. Her writing had stopped being a passion and had simply become a paycheck. Writing was normally an exquisite joy, but over the past five years she felt as though she was missing something.

Rekindling the dying embers of her once adventurous spirit, she took Ellen's advice. But she decided to retreat not so much in the literal sense as in the *literary*. She would vacation in a world that had never written about before, a world that had nothing to do with dragons.

The story she had just been writing came back to her. It was such an odd little world. She had no idea where it had all come from; she still couldn't believe how much she had written. In addition to the strangely obsessive compulsion to write so quickly, there were a few things about the story that bothered her.

I mean…am I really expecting my readers to believe that my characters don't have batteries or flashlights? A space-faring race, albeit somewhat Victorian in period, should at least provide for an emergency weather siren that doesn't fail when the power goes out. Ridiculous. She closed her eyes and drifted off to sleep.

Chapter 2, Cops and Robbers

"We've got him now. There's nowhere he can hide," shouted Corporal Carvalho as he chased the suspect through the narrow, twisting streets of Brazil. "That's a blind alley, *amigo*. You might as well give up now and save us all a chase."

Carvalho had been in the *Policia Militar* since he was sixteen years old, and chasing people through the streets of Tijuca was nothing new. He had lived in the area most of his life, and he knew it better than most of his *companheiros*. The other three soldiers in the chase finally caught up with him as he slowed.

"He's got nowhere to go, unless he can walk through solid rock," he told his breathless soldiers.

The twisting, inclined alleyway that the suspect had run into was bordered by the plastered brick walls of apartment complexes on either side, which ran right up to the sheer face of the mountain behind them.

The alley served as a channel for the volumes of water that came down from the mountain during Brazil's short but heavy deluges. The effects of years of runoff had dug a deep, cracked, and buckled concavity along the length of the narrow concrete path.

He stepped easily around the broken bits of concrete and motioned for the others to follow. Unshouldering their MP5s, the soldiers advanced up the narrow alley to arrest the man that had just robbed the Banco Real a few blocks away in broad daylight.

He did not know or care how the crime was committed. That would be the job of the *Policia Civil*. All he knew was that the suspect was about average height, had black hair, tan skin and was running away with a large bag of loot. That pretty much described more than ninety percent of the people in this part of town and did not make his job any easier.

Luckily, Carvalho's barracks were in the same part of the city as the bank. They had constructed several guard towers above the walls surrounding the barracks, which took up an entire city block. One of these guards had blown a whistle and shouted a warning as the suspect ran past.

The corporal's job was simply to apprehend the suspect and bring him in for questioning. After that, he would take the rest of the day off at the corner bar, the local *botequim*, putting down a few beers.

He turned the last corner and saw the suspect with his back turned, facing the wall of the mountain.

"Turn around slowly," he said, raising his gun. "There's nowhere to go."

Now that he was closer, he could see this man was not a local. He probably wasn't even Brazilian. For one thing, he looked strangely at ease even though they obviously had him trapped. He was muttering something quietly and had one of his hands on the wall. *Was he chanting*?

"Who are you praying to, *amigo*? God may forgive you, but the *tribunais* are a tougher lot to convince."

The man stopped chanting but did not turn around.

"Drop the bag and face me."

Instead, the man gave him a quick wave and said simply, *"Tchau."*

Silently and without hesitation, the thief walked straight through the wall of the mountain and disappeared into the naked rock.

"Mercda!" Carvalho cursed.

He immediately sent a hail of bullets from his machine gun into the face of the mountain. The other soldiers opened fire as well. The sound of shattering rock and ricocheting bullets was deafening in the narrow alley.

"Para! Para!" commanded Carvalho over the noise, shouting for his men to stop.

As the dust settled, it was obvious there was no hidden passage in the rock before them. Tiny craters of bright white rock pigeon-holed the bleak, gray surface of the mountain where the bullets had hit.

He walked up to where the man had been and touched the now quite warm surface of the rock. He considered testing the rock further with the butt of his rifle, but changed his mind. *What would that prove, other than how much of a fool I am?* Never in his long years as a solider had he seen anything like this and it scared the hell out of him.

"*Meu Deus,*" he said backing away slowly.

Wide-eyed, he found himself standing in the alleyway alone. His men had beaten a hasty retreat down the alley, spooked by the thief's unnatural exit. His own heart was thumping wildly, but he fought back the urge to run. There had to be a rational explanation for this.

As did much of the population of Rio, his grandmother had an unshakable belief in demons and spirits. She had died penniless in the *favela* where they lived, leaving him orphaned and alone, and no amount of spiritual superstition would change that. Life in the slum had taught him the harsh reality of life quickly, but he managed to scrape out a living until he looked old enough to join the military police.

Spirits, magic, and mediums were just foolish nonsense. He always thought that those who believed in a sixth sense must be lacking somewhat in the other five. However, considering what he had just seen, he was having second thoughts.

It's got to be a trick or an illusion of some kind. He looked the alleyway over, trying to find some sort of clue. All he found were rocks and garbage. At last, the eerie silence got the better of him, and he decided to catch up with his retreating companions. They would be probably steadying their nerves at the local bar. He couldn't blame them; he was sure there would be much drinking in the *botequim* tonight.

Ananmaya was lost. He had never shifted so much mass before, for such a long time. The adventure in Brazil was stretching him in ways he had never dreamed, and now he felt he might have gone too far. The matter manipulation left him buried deep in the mountain with absolutely no way to get his bearings.

Brilliant. I'm adrift in a sea of stone with no paddle. Everywhere he looked was inky blackness. The plan was simply to shift inside the mountain and hide for an hour or so, then step back out after the authorities had left. He hadn't counted on the local yokels to start blasting the mountainside with machine gun fire.

With his body now shifting at high speed at the subatomic level, his atoms possessed the infinitesimal void spaces between the particles of the rock, intelligently altering trajectories to avoid collisions. With this new intelligence imparted to his particles it made him practically frictionless but not impartial to gravity. He would have sunk into the ground if he had not also remembered to shift his gravity as well. He discovered he would need this trick after accidentally sending a pair of scissors, a flowerpot and a very surprised hamster to the center of the Earth when he first began practicing matter shifting.

What he had not considered was that his forward momentum, combined with the shock waves of the bullets from the automatic weapons, would send him careening deep into the mountainside. Somehow, he had slowed to a stop. Now he was lost, with hundreds of feet of solid rock in any direction. Trying not to panic, he considered his options.

The manipulation had taken a good deal more effort than he had expected. The rapid movement through the rock must have required tremendous amounts of energy to orchestrate all of those billions of tiny near-misses as his atoms pushed through the rock. Although he was never fully aware of what each atom was doing individually, he could feel their drain. At this point, he could not perform the most trivial of manipulations.

Like an astronaut in free fall, he could flail his arms and legs as much as wanted, yet go absolutely nowhere. With no friction, he had nothing to push against, so trying to swim his way out was out of the question. He tried to remember his training.

* * *

"Sit still and concentrate," said Bhuvanesh, his mentor and friend from back home in India.

Bhuvanesh was an itinerant magician performing magic in the hot, pungent bazaars of Chandigarh when they first met. Living as a street-wise youth, Ananmaya had already known the score. These magicians used various trained animals and sleight of hand to convince the tourists to cheerfully part with their spending money.

However, as young Ananmaya watched, this man was doing something quite different. He was not accepting payment for his services. He simply offered advice and sent people on their way. Smiling and animated, he was much less reserved than a real swami would have been. Most swamis simply did not speak at all, so profound was their usual repose.

In stark contrast to the old, quiet, sedate swamis of the village, this man was much younger. He had a close-cropped beard and moustache of dark hair, with streaks of white on the sides. His green eyes were bright and clear. He wore a green tunic and a white sash turban, common garb for men of his profession. But most remarkable were the incredible feats of levitation and magic he would perform. At times, he would make borrowed items disappear and reappear in unexpected places. Large crowds would gather around him when he performed these acts. Then, oddly enough, he would just stop what he was doing, pack his things into a bag roll, and walk away, ending the show for the day.

Ananmaya had seen him three times in the past week, each time in a different location. Word of the amazing man was beginning to spread; however, his appearances were lessening. He knew the next time he saw him he would have to talk to him. His chance came a week later as Bhuvanesh was packing up his bag for the day.

"You're like me. Aren't you?"

Bhuvanesh met his eyes with a steady gaze. "We are all like someone, I expect. In what way are we the same little one?"

He paused, gauging his next question. "You can make things disappear, and it is not a trick."

"Of course it's a trick. Everything is a trick in one way or the other. What you mean to say is that you simply do not know how the trick is done."

"But I know how it is done. I have done it myself and so have you. I know that look in your eyes before it goes. I know what it means and what you are doing. I cannot be wrong in this. You ARE like me."

Bhuvanesh moved in close to Ananmaya and held his gaze. "Can you prove this, little one? Make this pebble disappear."

Ananmaya looked at the rock in his hand and hesitated. He had used his power only a few times before. His expression fell as he remembered how it had brought him nothing but misery

Hard to control, and barely understanding what he did to cause it, he had inadvertently made his older brother disappear in a fit of jealousy when he was only ten years old. His father, a cruel and lazy man, who came home drunk more often than not, relied heavily on his eldest son's income after their mother had died.

When Ananmaya tearfully explained what had happened to his father's favorite son, the man flew into a rage and beat him severely.

His son's ability to make things disappear didn't surprise the horrible man. Smaller items had gone missing before, and the boy always seemed to be at the center of the disturbances. Once, during a rockslide, a large boulder had come bounding down the mountainside, rolling directly towards their cab. Traffic pinned them in on the steep mountain road, and they couldn't move. However, before it could crush the small car, it simply vanished and no one could explain where it had gone.

His father tried many times to capitalize on his son's unique abilities, but the infuriating boy couldn't control them in any meaningful way. No amount of punishment could make him perform on demand. With the primary source of income gone, he decided to send young Ananmaya to the neighboring city of Chandigarh to polish precious stones. At least the meager weekly income from the harsh labor would keep the rum coming.

When the crowded bus arrived in the bustling city, Ananmaya chose to take his chances in the streets, rather than face the cruel fate his father had set before him. His brother had often been an arrogant ass, but he had also been occasionally kind and supportive. He had loved him for that and he deeply regretted what had happened. He never forgave himself for what he had done.

Bhuvanesh put a hand on the downcast boy's shoulder. "Never mind. I can see your power has brought you pain."

"So, you believe me?"

"Yes," said Bhuvanesh. "The gift has brought me great pain as well, but also, great joy. Everything in the universe is so. There must always be a balance between the good and the bad."

Bhuvanesh explained that he had made many terrible mistakes. He had paid high penalties for the abuse of his power. This included the loss of his family as well. Since then, he had worked hard to seek out others with the same abilities to teach them not to make the same mistakes he had. He did this by playing the role of the animated bazaar swami and magician. He would perform just enough magic to get people talking. This would attract larger and larger crowds. As his popularity grew, he would have to move on, lest he face a closer inquisition of his powers.

For the most part, no one truly believed in magic. Even the tourists knew there must be a trick involved somehow. Only someone with the same talent would appreciate the trick for what it was. He hoped with each village he visited that someone would come forward one day and call him out on it.

"Are there many others like us?" Ananmaya asked, during a quiet evening under the shade of a mangrove tree at the village edge.

"Sit still and concentrate! There will be time for more discussion after you see what I want to show you."

Bhuvanesh picked up a leaf and asked him to describe what he saw.

Ananmaya studied the green mangrove leaf in his hands. It was smooth on one side and rough on the other. The narrow leaf was wide at the bottom and tapered to a point along a lengthy line running down the middle. Not sure what else he wanted him to see in the rather plain leaf, Ananmaya said simply, "It's just a mangrove leaf."

"Correct," said Bhuvanesh. "But, you held the leaf for just a short time. Surely, you could not have looked at it very closely."

Raising the leaf to his eyes once more, he attempted to study the leaf once more. However, Bhuvanesh took it from his grasp and put it into his pocket.

"Sorry. That is all the time you have. Now, do you think you can remember much about the leaf?"

He didn't think he could. *It was just a leaf, like the myriad of others on the ground. It was green and leafy. What else was there?*

Bhuvanesh picked up several other identical leaves off the ground and put them into the pocket containing the leaf he had just taken. Then, taking them out one by one, he placed them on the ground.

"Which one was your leaf?"

Without hesitation, Ananmaya picked up the third leaf from the left.

"Good! What made you pick this one?"

"Because that was my leaf," said Ananmaya, somewhat confused.

"But they are all identical. How did you know this was yours?"

"Because that was the one I studied. It's *my* leaf," Ananmaya said, somewhat annoyed at the question.

Bhuvanesh laughed. "My friend, you may not know this, but most people would not have been able to do what you just did. You would be able to find your leaf in a tree full of leaves. You have lived with this gift your whole life, so it is second nature to you. You must never assume that everyone else experiences the world as you do. Now I will show you something you probably did not know you were capable of."

Hiding the leaf, he asked, "How many lines branch off from the center line on your leaf?

"Twelve."

"Which branch is longer than the rest?"

"The second from the bottom on the right."

"How many smaller lines branch away from this one?"

Ananmaya thought for a moment, remembering the thin, filament-like lines that permeated the leaf as he had turned it around in the sun. There were hundreds of the tiny veins on the leaf. *How could he expect him to know how many touched the line in question?* Before he could argue, however, he found himself answering, "twenty-seven."

"Very good! Now, which of these is the shortest?"

This is ridiculous. The last number couldn't have been right. The strange thing was however, that he *knew* he was right.

To the question at hand, he thought about the leaf and a picture of this section appeared in his mind.

"The shortest is the third line from the top on the left."

"Excellent! Can you tell me how many cells are across this line?"

"Six," said Ananmaya, blinking in astonishment. A picture of the leaf, as if seen in the microscope he had at used once in school, appeared in his head and he was easily able to distinguish its cellular components in the picture in his mind. This was more than just imagination.

Bhuvanesh stopped asking questions. "You are now past the visible and seeing the invisible. You will see things you have never seen before. Things known to science, and things best left unknown. Using this technique, you will be able to see the fundamental building blocks of all matter in the universe. This is where your power comes from and it is crucial that you understand it."

His head had reeled at those words when he heard them for the first time. Could he truly have the power to know, implicitly, the physical makeup of everything he touched? How could he not have known about this ability before now?

Bhuvanesh had simply said that he had always had this power, but it had lain dormant, mostly unused in his subconscious. Without the visual exercise, he could have gone through his whole life not knowing the nature of his ability. He would be adrift, his strong passions causing chaos everywhere he went.

"You must learn to become a master of your emotions. With such a powerful gift, strong emotions can produce unexpected consequences."

Unexpected consequences? He knew all about unexpected consequences. Until now, his unpredictable gift had been more like a curse.

"Do you really think I will be able to control it?"

"With emotions as strong as yours, my friend, anything is possible. Now let us find some lunch. You look half-starved."

Chapter 3, Costa Maya

Molly woke up lazily to the sound of music coming from the beach. The Hotel Tierra Maya where she was staying was a small, privately owned resort near the small fishing village of Xcalak.

Her room was the best in the house and overlooked the beach. She had come during the off-season in February, and not many people were there to fill the quaint hotel. Yawning, she looked through the big, white louvered doors she had left open the previous night to view the beautiful Caribbean coast.

She had hoped to catch the sunrise, but working late had caused her to miss it. She needed the rest. She deserved the rest. This was a vacation after all.

The beautiful white sands outside and the thatched roof huts were something straight out of a travel journal. *Places like this really do exist. This is too good to be true.* She always suspected the beautiful photos of white sand beaches and palm trees always had something to hide. As if behind the photographer, you would find a busy, dirty city full of loud noises, honking cabs, shouting pedestrians, and littered streets.

She considered what she would do with her day. *Let's see, will I do laptop on the beach, or laptop at the ruins?*

She was serious about this new book. For her, writing was as much fun as body surfing was to the young, tan men down on the beach. She closed the wide louvered doors. *Too much distraction down there, maybe I'll visit the ruins.*

She read about the ancient Mayan Chaccoben ruins in the travel brochure on the plane. They sounded fascinating, and best of all, they sounded quiet. *At least at the ruins, I'll be out of this room and in the sun.*

Before she'd leave, she'd take a morning bath. A small, old-fashioned claw-foot cast iron bathtub and nightstand furnished the small room. No hotel embossed tiny bottles of shampoo or body wash here. Just a big thick slab of oddly colored soap in the wire tray and warm, inviting water.

She tried to remember the last time she had taken a proper soak. She had been taking quick showers in her New York apartment for so long, that the slow, quiet bath had felt both strange and relaxing to her.

Towel wrapped around her tangle of long dark hair and wearing her robe, she got the rest of her things together and prepared for the long, bumpy tour bus ride out the ruins. She heard the roads were not always in the best shape, especially after the late hurricane season. But maybe she could get some work done on the bus.

After piling her notes and her laptop into her backpack, she packed in a quick lunch. She looked around the room for anything else she would need. *Um…something other than just this robe would be nice.* She put on a pair of white shorts and a plain green t-shirt and tucked in the pendant that she wore everywhere. She had gotten it as a present from her mother on the day her first book made the bestseller list. It had been in her mother's family for years, and she treasured it dearly.

She completed the ensemble with a thatch hat she bought on the way to the hotel. It looked decidedly "touristy" but she was after all, going on a tour. What was the point of hiding it? Did people genuinely think that the locals rode tour busses? Shouldering her backpack, she left her room to find the next bus to Chaccoben.

An ancient ceiling fan spun lazily in the rafters of the small lobby, lending a stuttering beat to the music coming from the beach. The parking lot outside looked positively barren. She pulled out her itinerary. According to the tour schedule, the bus should be here by now. She decided to inquire at the front desk.

The attendant was reclining back in his chair, with his feet on the desk. He was reading the local newspaper. "*Perdón, senor,* when does the tour bus arrive?" asked Molly using the few Spanish words just about every American picks up from high school. Putting down the paper, the man met her gaze.

"Ah! Ms. Arden! *Beunos Días, señora*! I trust your night went well?" asked Juan Carlos, putting his feet down and standing up out of his chair.

"Quite nice. Thank you," she said, amused that even so far from home she was still easily recognizable.

"My son reads your books. I've seen the first two *Dragon's Keep* movies, but he tells me the books were much better," said Juan.

"That's very nice of you," said Molly, who very much had the same opinion.

"In fact, I've got a copy of book four right here," said Juan reaching under the desk. Molly had been fingering the pen in her pocket, fully expecting what was coming next, which of course it did.

"My son would be thrilled if I got this autographed for him. Could you do me this honor?"

"What's your son's name?"

"Juan. He is probably out there on the beach playing *fútbol* with his friends from school."

She looked out over the parking lot to the beach. *Almost the same age as my Edington,* she mused, thoughts returning to her book. She had to get back writing that story; it was calling her.

Opening Juan's book to the first blank page, she wrote:

"To my good friend, Juan.
Keep dreaming, but always with your eyes wide open."
- Molly Arden

She handed the book back to Juan Carlos. "I'd appreciate it if you and your son would keep my vacation here quiet.

I'm trying to focus on a new book, and was hoping for some anonymity."

"*No problema, señora.* There aren't many people on the coast right now anyway. You should have nothing but sunsets and margaritas to keep you company."

Molly looked again to the empty parking lot. "So I've noticed. Is the tour bus still coming today for Chaccoben?"

"Oh no. Not today. There aren't enough people in the hotel to justify the trip. I'm sorry, Ms. Arden. You should have been told about the revised schedule."

She probably had been told when she checked in to her room, but she must have missed it. At the time, she was excited about getting out of New York to a place she had never visited. Also, she was itching to write the story that had been bouncing around in her head on the flight over.

"Let me see what I can do," said Juan, picking up the phone to call a cab. Then, having a better idea, he put the receiver back down. "Chaccoben, you say? My son has a friend that lives in Pedro a Santos just east of there. He is always looking for an excuse to make the long drive up the coast to visit her. He brings her the latest news from the village, and she usually sends him back with a sack of her grandmother's tortillas. What else they do, I don't want to know."

"I couldn't possibly ask that of you," said Molly, rethinking her plans for the day. Maybe the beach would not be a bad alternative.

"No trouble at all and a lot nicer than a ride in one of our local cabs. Look! Here he is now."

A dark skinned youth sauntered into the hotel with a towel over his shoulders and a soccer ball under one arm. His muscular chest and legs were wet with sand and sea salt. Walking over to the front desk, he did a double take at Molly.

Staring at her in disbelief, he stammered, "*Sabes quién eres?!*"

"*Si, Juan.* She knows who she is, but she doesn't speak much Spanish. Ms. Arden checked in yesterday. Look, she has signed your book." He passed the book to his son.

"*Muchas gracias!*" said Juan Jr., passing a fingertip over her signature on the inside page. He quickly switched to English. "I have all your books, Ms. Arden! I just received this one last week and was going to start reading it tonight."

She smiled at the boy's honest enthusiasm; it was a nice change. More often than not, zealous fans could be a little creepy. Like the time a year ago when a man followed her into the LaGuardia bathroom, to get a *private* autograph. To this day, she always wondered what became of the wreck of a man she left in the stall, doubled over in pain.

"Juan, I need you to take Ms. Arden to Chaccoben. She wants to visit the ruins," said his father. "You can visit Adriana if you wish, but later you must pick up Ms. Arden and bring her back here. Do you understand?"

"Anything you need, Ms. Arden! I am your servant. When do you wish to leave?"

"Are you sure you want to drive all that way, Juan? The morning has only just started," said Molly, not wanting to be a burden.

"It's only a few hours or so. No problem at all. I have been there many times. Adriana will be glad to see me. Let me get cleaned up and then we'll go. *Está bien?*"

The boy looked earnest and trustworthy, so she finally agreed.

A little later, they were in the surprisingly new truck owned by the hotel, heading up the coastline. Juan turned the radio off so she could enjoy the quiet. She began typing on her laptop.

"The roads get a bit bumpier when we turn west," said Juan. "I do not think you'll get much done. Do you work all the time?"

"Not normally. I am on vacation after all. However, right now, I have something that simply cannot wait to be written down. I've got to strike while the iron's hot."

"Is there something wrong with your computer?" he asked, not understanding the euphemism.

"Sorry, what I meant to say is I have to write this down before I lose it. Sometimes my stories write themselves. If I don't pay attention, they might go somewhere else to be written," she said with a smile.

"You are writing a new book then?"

Well, not as long as I keep talking to you, silly boy, she thought. Juan was considerate, but the silence in the truck obviously made him uncomfortable and talkative. She was having a hard time getting into her book with all the starting and stopping.

"Juan, how much time do we have before the roads get bad?"

"About an hour."

"How about you let me work for an hour or so, then we can talk, ok?"

Juan thumped the steering wheel with his fist. "*Estupidez!* I am sorry, Ms. Arden. I'm ruining your vacation and your new book. I've just never been near someone so famous before."

"That's okay, Juan. I've never been driven to see the sights by one of my fans before. But I do need to get this down before Chaccoben, ok?"

"*No problema,* Ms. Arden. I understand."

So, with the promise of an hour of blessed silence, she dived into her book.

Chapter 4, Professor Almos

Edington slowly swung the telescope around in the cold night air. The giant copper cylinder felt cold to the touch. It responded hesitantly and required a little more effort than usual. The towering thirty-foot length of the reflector tube weighed over a ton, yet was counterbalanced to make manual adjustments possible by even the slightest of astronomers—which Edington was. *Well, I expect that any machine, as well as most people, need a little coaxing on a cold morning.*

This morning he knew exactly what he was looking for. The horizon was brilliant tonight with the blue-green smoky mists of the nebulous cloud touching the northern horizon. With the town lights out, he could observe the anomaly with dazzling clarity and get a much more accurate reading on its size. It looked much larger in the sky tonight than he had expected. He had a frightening thought. *Maybe it wasn't just larger. Maybe it was closer.*

The anomaly had been growing at an alarming rate. Even with the lights on, the colonists were beginning to suspect something unusual was in the sky. As dark as it was tonight, anyone looking out of their windows would see the full horrifying extent of the enigma in the northern horizon.

The daily posting of cosmic readings had become a recent requirement by the town council in response to the appeals of concern from the colonists. Other colonies on Philolaus were doing the same thing and the readings were consistent. The anomaly was indeed growing and changing. As it grew, a horizontal rift appeared in its middle, splitting the cloud into two halves. The deep black rift contained thousands of tiny stars. The nature of these stars is what Almos and Edington argued about constantly. *Those stars were trouble. Why hadn't Almos listened to me last week?* The argument still echoed in his head.

* * *

"I tell you they are moving!" said Edington for the third time.

"Balderdash," said Professor Almos with a grunt. "Stars don't move that fast and they aren't planets. You aren't accounting properly for our slow rotation and refractive atmosphere. Re-check your calculations. You are missing something."

Edington was not about to go over his numbers again. It had taken him most of the morning to work out the totals from the previous night's measurements. The old man had stayed up late with the astronomers last night, peering over their shoulders, making everyone nervous. He had been just as difficult with them as he was being now. No wonder why he needed the coffee machine so much—the man never slept.

Apparently, Almos needed yet another cup. Shuffling over to his contraption, he demanded it make him another cup of the foul liquid. Depending on the machine's morning temperament, this could take some time. Making coffee usually involved lots of banging and loud shouting. Edington took the opportunity to go outside for some fresh air, and to get away from the impossible man.

He escaped through the hatch leading down out of the observatory platform. Making his way down the last flight of stairs, he came into the observatory lobby. As usual, his friend Ayden was at the front desk. He was signing in a group of students and a teacher who had hiked up the mountainside for a morning field trip to the observatory.

Ayden held out the checkout clipboard for Edington to sign.

"Making for the pub again?" asked Ayden with a smile, noticing the scowl on his friend's face.

"A little early for that, but I'm sorely tempted. I'm just going for a walk down the mountain. I think I need some fresh air."

"What you need, mate, is a good rope, a deep lake, and a solid alibi," said Ayden with a wink, taking back his pen from the teacher who quickly rushed the students into the complex.

He grinned at Ayden's dark sense of humor.

"Anything you want to talk about?"

"It's just more of the same. Almos thinks he knows everything and that everyone else is stupid. We spend most of our time doing the same work over and over because he doesn't trust our results. Then, he gets all buggered because we aren't completing the day's agenda on time. He's worn everyone out trying to meet his impossible demands. I had to get out."

"Won't he notice you are missing?"

"Probably not. He thinks I'm at my desk, reworking figures. I have already worked them three times. I am not going to do it again."

"What's the problem with the numbers?"

"Well, it's about the anomaly. We've seen some strange effects that can't be explained. For example, it's growing exponentially. If it keeps going at that rate, it will fill the sky in less than a week. Also, the stars inside the rift appear to be moving."

"Moving?" asked Ayden. "As in like, shooting stars?"

"Oh no, not that fast. They are too far away, and their movement is just barely perceptible. But they appear to be spreading out, moving away from each other at a fantastic rate."

"And you are sure about this?"

"Quite. I've done the calculations three times," said Edington in disgust. "It will all be posted this evening in the town square. I think that is why the old geezer is giving us hell. It's his neck on the line if the conclusions aren't correct."

"What kind of conclusions?"

"Unfortunately, the kind only Professor Almos is qualified to give," said Edington apologetically. "We should all know more in the next few days. Anyway, I'm going out, Ayden. Do you need anything from town, if I make it that far?"

"No, my shift is over at noon. I'll grab some lunch then. You have a nice walk. I'll cover for you if Professor Almos comes looking."

"Thanks," said Edington, stepping outside.

* * *

Although he would never admit it publically, the anomaly seriously worried Professor Almos. What had started a few days ago as just a vague haze in the sky was now turning into something that he could not explain.

To add insult to injury, now his coffee machine was refusing to work, no matter how much he fiddled with it.

"You infernal beast!" he exclaimed, giving the coffee machine a swift kick.

The machine made a burbling sound and happily continued not to produce coffee. Made of cast iron and bronze, the huge coffee machine was virtually indestructible; and it appeared to be enjoying the attention, as if enjoying a massage.

"Confounded machine!" he shouted, giving up and storming down the stairs to his office.

At the sound of the trap door slamming shut, the coffee machine made a pinging sound and a trickle of black liquid began smuggly dripping into the carafe.

The boy was right, of course. Those stars are moving, and they are moving fast, too fast. Almos sighed. He could not explain this and not knowing things made him irritable. It made him feel helpless; a feeling he had not felt since leaving his unhappy past back on Archænis, a past that pained him to remember.

He had not spoken to Viktor in years. Discourse with his brother had become upsettingly painful since the bittersweet success of their *Farshift* project over fifty years ago. However, the man's insights had repeatedly proven invaluable in situations like this. He would give some thought to contacting Viktor again. In any event, it would be nice to check in on the family.

In the meantime, he had come to the conclusion that one of two things was happening in the sky: Either the anomaly was growing, or it was getting closer. Even more disturbing was that the rift was displacing their stars. It was as if something had taken a knife to the ethereal curtain and sliced it open to reveal another universe beyond; and the gash continued to unravel and widen.

He had fielded three telegrams already from other observatories on the planet. They all wanted the Chief Royal Astronomer's opinion on the matter. What could he tell them? That the universe was coming to an end?

He simply did not know for sure. The town elders needed an answer and the great Professor Almos would have to give them one soon. After all, they would not even be here if it were not for him.

He had discovered this world—a planet exactly what their ancient stories and texts said it would be—Archænis' twin on the opposite side of the sun.

The idea of a planet of near identical mass, existing without notice exactly on the opposite side of their sun, had been the stuff of imagination and historical fiction. However, never-ending war had taken its toll on their barren home planet, and soon, it would be unable to support its inhabitants. In order to escape, they were considering all possible options, even the fantastic.

They governments on Archænis temporarily set aside their disagreements and formed an interplanetary colonization initiative. They sent several ether probes to the newly discovered planet. Weeks later, the probes returned with their tiny reels of film waiting to be developed. The photos revealed a startling planet, similar in size, but radically different in appearance. Expeditions to the mysterious planet were mounted and the first colonists followed soon thereafter.

Travel to Philolaus would not be difficult because of their new ether ships. With the discovery of a large cache of Leviton ore, a rare mineral on Archænis that had the phenomenal property of inherently repelling gravity, breaking their ties to Archænis' surface became an easy process.

Almos sighed. Had they left the confines of their home planet only to face an even more dangerous threat? Why was this happening *now?* Surely, they were seeing the anomaly on Archænis as well. There were too many questions and not enough information to provide the answers.

Why had he accepted the position of Chief Royal Astronomer on this outpost world anyway? At the time, he had told himself it was for the prestige and notoriety, but he knew that was just an excuse. He had really been running away from a tragic event for which he could only blame himself. He had saved his family, but he could not save himself.

So now what was he supposed to do? He could not hold off the council for much longer. The colonies were in trouble, and people were starting to fear the worst. He needed to buy some time; maybe Viktor would have the answer.

In the meantime, he could say he was waiting on confirmation of the effect from Archænis. The postal ether probe would not be here for another week. That would buy him some more time to investigate further, and confirmation from the home world would be useful in any case.

Until then, he would deny confirming anything apocalyptic. No point in making people worry about things they had no control over. That apparently was his job.

Chapter 5, Shifters

Ananmaya was finding it hard to breathe. He had been trapped inside the mountain for too long. He was starting to run out of air now that he had stopped moving through the rock. It was like trying to breathe through a wet sponge. Soon, there would not be any air at all, and then where would he be? He would become just another geological curiosity for archeologists to discover in the distant future.

Maybe the little item he had stolen, now tucked away in his satchel, would be around as well. That would cause a stir in the future scientific community. He did not have the time to think about such things. He needed to focus his mind to get out of this stupid predicament.

He knew he did not have enough power to invoke a new manipulation. He was already maintaining two others: one keeping him in coexistence with the rock around him, and the other keeping him from joining his unfortunate hamster at the center of the Earth. Gravity nullification used much power, but he did not intend to release it. Letting gravity take hold of him would get him moving again, but quite in the wrong direction.

"There are always at least two solutions to every problem," his teacher had advised. "The easy way, and the best way. The easy way is always the quickest to conceive. With persistence, a better option will always present itself. Never trust your first solution."

That's fine, if you've got the time. Unfortunately, that's in short supply. Right now, I'll be happy with whatever pops into my head.

To make things worse, the stolen box in his satchel was vibrating wildly. Apparently, the artifact it contained didn't like its new molecular disposition at all. After shifting into the mountain, he almost had to leave it behind, which would have been unthinkable. Through sheer force of will, he had finally gotten it to cooperate. He wasn't quite sure how he had managed it. He would study the box and its contents more closely when he got out of this.

Wait a minute! The artifact is the key to getting out of here. He reached into his satchel and felt for the box's smooth, flat surface. Using his fingers, he felt for the light indentation that marked the lid. This was insanity, but he had no choice. Slowly, carefully, he slid the lid back just a little.

Immediately, the box rocketed upward, inside the satchel, as the artifact pushed hard against the lid of its cubical container. The satchel nearly yanked his arm out of its socket as he struggled to maintain his grip. Eventually, his weight slowed the initial acceleration, and they rose steadily through the mountain.

His breathing became easier as he moved swiftly through the rock, clearing his head. It was actually working! He was finally rising out of the oppressive darkness. The power of the small artifact amazed him. He hoped the stitching in the old sack would weather the injustice it was subjecting it to.

As he rose, he wondered if he thought about his next move. He needed to travel north. The police would be looking for him now, so he would have to keep a low profile. In addition, the owners of the box he carried would be sending people after him as well. The stunt at the bank would probably be in all the afternoon papers and the *oGlobo* news show.

The superstitious class of people in Brazil would be eating this up. He would be the talk of the city. *I probably already have my own moniker by now, something like "o fantasma,"* he mused. *Oh well, so much for being inconspicuous.*

He had not meant to be caught in the vault; it was not supposed to have gone like this. No one would have known he had been there, not even the owners of the rarely visited safe deposit box.

Unfortunately, the worst had happened. The bank manager and his client had walked into the supposedly empty vault, and had found Ananmaya there, rifling through the contents of box number twenty-eight. Explanations quickly broke down and the manager took the client outside, and shut the vault door, locking Ananmaya inside, while he called the *Policia Militar* to report the intruder. Once the door closed, Ananmaya simply left the way he came in, shifting through the wall, taking the box with him. The client saw Ananmaya passing on the street and not believing his eyes, he told the bank manager who quickly reopened the vault to see if he was still inside. By then the police had arrived, and everyone saw that Ananmaya was no longer present. Then the chase had started which led him to where he was now, all because of unlucky timing. He would have to be much more careful.

The temperature dropped dramatically, which meant he was getting closer to surface. He knew that the crushing pressure of the mountain created a temperature gradient that got cooler as he rose. He had learned a great deal many more things in the ten years since he discovered what he could do.

After learning much from Bhuvanesh, he still needed to know more. He could not afford a proper higher education, so he audited classes to gain knowledge. He soon became a nuisance to the trade colleges in India and bounced around from one to the other. Somehow, Bhuvanesh found textbooks for him, which he devoured late into the evening. He sat in on lectures, asked questions and posed problems that confounded the experts. Using public computers, he scoured the Internet and joined discussion groups. No matter where they found themselves, his ceaseless education followed.

Bhuvanesh had been like a father to him. They made a comfortable living performing in the streets, sometimes traveling as far as Nepal looking for others. Oddly, Bhuvanesh did not like to speak of other shifters. However, after much persuasion, he finally admitted that there had been quite a few people like themselves throughout history.

"Who has come before is not important now. Do not discuss this any further," he said tersely. "Focus on your lessons. Your education is the most important asset you will ever need."

The visual exercise Bhuvanesh had taught him provided amazing insights into the mysterious quantum world that any physicist would have given his right arm for.

Always curious, Ananmaya would take countless objects apart in his mind. He would start with the object, and then began visualizing separate components all the way down to the subatomic level. The numbers and concepts that would present themselves in his mind automatically amazed him. He had to learn advanced calculus and Euclidian geometry to have some of the math he needed to comprehend what his mind was doing intuitively. The more he learned, the more he knew he would never fully be able to understand everything of which he was capable.

However, now he had most of the vocabulary to help describe the most fundamental subatomic particles he was able to see. Yet, he understood them in ways no quantum physicist could ever comprehend. He knew all the current theories on the nature of the universe. However, he knew from personal observation which ones were true and which were false. All this by the time he was just 20 years old.

Dr. Suess had inadvertently summed up the nature of the universe quite well with his "Cat in the Hat" books. Suess' ubiquitous cat wore a tall, striped hat that contained twenty-six smaller and smaller duplicates of himself, each under a matching striped hat. He called them Cats "A" through "Z," However, this last cat, Cat "Z," was something special. Inside his hat was something called *Voom*. And oh, what a power *Voom* had. It was more powerful than all the other cat's abilities combined. To Ananmaya, this was a perfect metaphor for how he saw the basic building blocks of the universe.

Matter was built up of smaller and smaller particles, but eventually, you did reach the smallest particle possible, the nucleus of an atom. Then you entered the subatomic. At this point, you entered multidimensional quantum physics, where matter breaks down into particles with fewer and fewer dimensions. Eventually, you got to the single dimension quantum element called a string, something with infinite length, but no height or width. Yet this would only be cat "Z" in the Suess analogy. Like *Voom*, he knew that this particle was made of something wondrous and powerful. If you were to take away that last dimension, nothing would remain except the "concept" of a string. In other words, a thought.

This meant that all matter was made out of something as intangible as thought. Shifters operated on this level. They could "rethink" matter into any state just by concentrating.

He became a quiet expert on string theory and quantum mechanics, yet without any formal training or credentials. He hid under a well-known alias on the Internet and in scientific circles, although he never gave talks or lectures in public. He traveled extensively and had identities in several countries. When they nominated him for the Nobel Prize one year, he had to kill his online persona and effectively disappear. Like Bhuvanesh, he could not afford to live in the public eye, so he retreated to Brazil where no one could find him. He had chosen Brazil because of something fantastic Bhuvanesh had shared with him. That something was now in the bag hovering above him.

Suddenly, light exploded around him. Ananmaya squinted and tried to blink away the blinding afternoon brilliance. He was out of the mountain, yet still rising. He was breathing easily now. The humid tropical air was thick with the smell of bananas. With his vision returning, he looked down and saw the edge of the city receding far below him and the dense jungle covering the mountainside. He felt dizzy and a little sick. He had never been fond of heights and now felt a wild sense of vertigo. He solidified himself, and his previously rock-dulled senses returned to him with a start. It was like jumping into a freezing pool right after getting out of a hot tub.

The sun was already beginning to set behind the ridge of mountains in the distance. He had lost track of time during his entombment in the mountain. Besides the queasiness of hanging from a satchel suspended a few hundred feet over the Brazilian countryside, he also realized he was famished.

He had not had anything to eat since leaving his temporary home in the favelas, and this escapade had taken a lot of his energy. He gradually allowed gravity to regain a hold on his mass and he descended slowly to the ground with the satchel still pulling madly above his head. Once on the ground, he quickly closed the lid and the hot little object began to calm and cool.

The jungle was broken in places by steep, rocky, grassy fields. Luckily, he did not have to pick his way too far through the jungle to find a path to one. The small, sticky bananas he found in the jungle were not very tasty, but they had calmed his hunger for now.

Coming out of the dense undergrowth, he made his way to the far edge of the wide grazing field he had found. There were many crisscrossing goat paths on the mountain, most of which led down into the city below. Hiking his satchel onto his back, he walked briskly down the closest trail.

Chapter 6, Chaccoben

Molly looked up with a start. The truck leapt through a pothole, bouncing along the road.

"Sorry, Ms. Arden. This is where the roads get worse," said Juan. "We have two seasons here, the rainy season and the road construction season. They are always working on the roads."

Hurricanes often ravaged the poor tourist destination, often undermining the government's best efforts to provide adequate highways. The road they were on now was a tribute to this depressing fact.

Molly felt carsick. She closed her laptop and looked out the window. They were approaching what looked like a dump for discarded concrete and masonry. As they got closer, she began to see little ramshackle buildings. Many structures of concrete and thatch were in various states of construction along the sides of the road.

"Welcome to Pedro a Santos," said Juan, slowing down.

She looked down the street; she could easily see where the buildings ended, and the scrubby mangroves took over. *You would literally miss this town if you blinked,* she thought.

They passed by a small building with a big knobby tire in front. Painted on the tire in rough white letters was the name of what appeared to pass as an auto repair shop in this part of the world. Various unrecognizable parts hung from wires in the open window, where a bored mechanic was reclining in the shade, casually drinking a soft drink. Street vendors were selling pineapples and coconuts on the side of the road. The vendors were smiling broadly, and children played and waved as the truck rumbled through the town along the dusty road.

Modern satellite dishes were on top of most of the huts behind the shops and stalls along the roadside. They looked extremely out of place in the face of so much obvious poverty. Molly wondered if these people had their priorities straight. *Then again,* she thought, *probably most Americans would probably abandon a daily meal rather than miss an episode of their favorite soaps.*

"Juan, how long have you lived here?"

"Oh, I don't live here, I live in Xcalak. Our family has lived there for several generations. Most of us are fishermen. My uncle Tomas has a nice boat. We sometimes take the tourists out to the reef. I could never live out here, so far from the beach. Adriana only stays here because of her grandmother. Her parents died in Hurricane Dean, so she still lives here. There is nothing out here, which is why she loves it when I visit. You wouldn't mind seeing her would you?"

"Not at all. Is she a *Dragon's Keep* fan as well?"

"Not really, but I've taken her to a few of your movies, and she knows how famous you are. She won't believe this. We'll just stop by and pick her up on the way to Chaccoben. We're only a few miles from the site now."

Pulling off the road and parking beneath a trumpet tree covered in creeping vines, Juan pointed out her grandmother's house.

It's bigger than my New York apartment, thought Molly.

It was a small two story, brick and mortar construction with a thatched roof. A teenage girl was sweeping the front patio.

She looked up and shouted *"Juan!"* Then, frowning at Molly in the front seat, she said in English, "And who is your friend?"

"Adriana, you're not going to believe who I've got with me," said Juan getting out of the truck and walking over to the other side. "Remember those *Dragon's Keep* movies? Well, this is Ms. Molly Arden, the writer!" He opened the door and let Molly out.

Molly blinked in the afternoon light, stepping down from the truck. Apparently, she did not have quite the effect on Adriana as Juan had hoped.

Adriana ran over to Juan and hugged him. She looked past Molly into the truck. "What have you brought me Juan? I haven't seen you for weeks!"

"Adriana, this is Ms. Arden. She's the writer I've been telling you about. She is going to be staying at the hotel for a few days. I thought you would like to meet her. We're going up to Chaccoben, and thought you might want to come along."

"*Buenos días,* Ms. Arden," said Adriana coolly. Then, turning to Juan, she said in Spanish, "I haven't seen you for weeks, and you come here with another woman instead of bringing me my present? And why would I want to go see those stupid rocks? I grew up here, remember?"

"I just thought you'd like to meet someone that was famous. Look, she signed my book." Juan showed her the inside cover of *Dragon's Keep: Book 4*. "She's on vacation and would like to see the ruins. Since your family once owned the land they were on, I thought you'd be able to show her stuff not on the official tour."

Molly could not understand much of the conversation, but as many of the gestures they were making were in her general direction, they obviously were talking about her. When Adriana looked as if she was going to use her broom to reinforce her arguments with Juan, Molly interrupted. "Maybe I should just wait in the truck. I think I may be upsetting your girlfriend."

Juan blushed, "Girlfriend? Oh no, she's not my girlfriend."

WHACK! Down came the broom followed by several Spanish expletives. Adriana chased Juan around the truck with the broom. Molly got back into the truck to watch the scene from a safer location. But by then, they had taken the fight inside the house. Everything was oddly quiet for a while, and then the front door burst open and both Adriana and Juan came bounding out. They were closely followed by what Molly assumed was the grandmother, now brandishing the broom and shouting at them both to get out.

Juan and Adriana were now smiling and holding hands as they ran up to the truck. Apparently, Juan had smoothed things over or simply survived long enough to allow Adriana's anger to burn out on its own. Juan opened the driver's side door, and let Adriana get into the back seat of the cab. He climbed in after her and started the truck.

"Sorry about that, Ms. Arden. We can go now, and Adriana would be happy to show you the ruins."

Molly took a glance at Adriana in the rear-view mirror. "Thank you, Adriana. Are you sure it's okay?"

"My grandmother is trying to take a nap. I've got some free time now. *No problema.*"

It took only another ten minutes to arrive at the Chaccoben archeological site. Juan parked the truck and everyone got out. Molly grabbed her backpack and made sure the laptop was settled. There were several thatched open stalls just north of the parking lot. Adriana said those were for tourists and sold Mayan calendars, masks, and other souvenirs. These shops were empty now and were closed for the season.

Juan paid the entrance fee and gave Molly a full-color map of the site. It was an artist rendition of what the original complex would have looked like nearly two thousand years ago near the height of Mayan civilization.

The complex was large and covered nearly seven square miles. The excavation of this site was relatively new, even though people had known about the area since 1972. So far, the archeologists had uncovered only four of the many multi-tiered structures in the complex; dirt, rock, and trees still buried the rest.

The groundskeepers had kept the wide pathways around each of the structures clear of weeds and debris, but the jungle encroached on all sides. Only a few visitors were wandering around the excavations taking pictures. The air rustled through the tall trees lining Molly's path. The place was peaceful, and best of all quiet.

Perfect, she thought, as they came around a large temple. She had spied a bench beneath a tall and shady tree. She unslung her backpack and sat down. Somewhere she had a ham and cheese sandwich packed in there for lunch.

"I think I can take it from here, Juan. I should have enough battery power to write for another two or three hours. Can you pick me up then?"

"Sure, Ms. Arden. The park doesn't close until five at any rate. We'll go back to town but will be back soon to get you. Enjoy yourself," said Juan.

"Do you know what tree you are sitting under, Ms. Arden?" asked Adriana.

Molly looked at the strange, bright green tree next to her. It was tall and had branches extending at right angles in its bow. Odd little spikes protruded from the trunk near the base where thick roots gripped the ground.

"No, what is it?"

"It's a ceiba tree. The ancient Maya revered this tree. It represents the afterlife. The roots represent the nine lords of the underworld, and the branches above represent heaven. The trunk is what is in between, which of course is where we are now. They believed that when someone died, their soul must first go to the underworld before they can continue to heaven.

"However, if they died in a sacrifice, their soul went directly to heaven without having to endure the lower journey. Thus, it was a great honor and only virgins were worthy of sacrifice at the altar at the top of the temple," said Adriana.

Looking up at the restored ruin, she saw where she was pointing. "It's a good thing the practice hasn't continued," said Molly, looking at the grim stonework.

"Yes, but there aren't any more virgins anyhow," said Adriana with a smile.

Molly laughed. It had been over a year since she had last been intimate, much less even dated anyone, but she felt it safe to say that she would no longer qualify for the *honor* of being a Mayan sacrifice.

Why hadn't she ever settled down and gotten married? She was already in her late twenties, and she was not getting any younger. It had been such a whirlwind life since she had been published. The stories had demanded so much of her, this new book especially so. Here she was in the middle of paradise, but all she could think of was getting back to Edington's strange world.

"Mrs. Arden, would you like to see something not on the guided tour?"

Molly eyed her sandwich hungrily, but the offer intrigued her. Lunch would have to wait a little longer. "What do you mean?"

"My grandfather owned this property before the government purchased it, and the excavations began. When I was little, mud and rocks covered everything you see. The jungle was deep and thick, but many paths ran through it. I used to spend my time pretending to be an explorer. I found all kinds of things.

"My grandmother descends directly from the Maya, and she knows this place better than I do. When I found something, I would take it to her, and she would always know what it was. One day, I found a big mound of dirt, not part of the temple complex you are in now. My grandmother said there must be an artificial structure inside, reclaimed by the jungle. This is because there are no natural hills in Costa Maya, but it was odd to find one so far from the main complex.

"I still do not think anyone else knows about it. Do you want to see?"

"Come on, Adriana, let's go back to town. Ms. Arden has a book to write. We're taking up too much of her time," said Juan.

"But she will like it. There's a stella stone in front with some very intricate carvings."

Much as she would like to tour this fascinating and ancient city, Molly felt her book calling to her. "Thanks Adriana, but I must get back to my book. You guys go have fun. I'll be fine here."

"Well, if you change your mind and want to see it, just go down those steep stairs over there. The path into the part of the city where the Maya elite lived is easily marked. When you reach the first structure, turn north, into the jungle. You should not have to go far before you reach a huge gum tree. You will recognize it from the X's carved into its trunk from when the natives used to sell gum to the Spaniards.

"Look to the west when you reach the tree, and you should see the ground dip down sharply in just a few meters. There used to be a very deep sinkhole there, but I think it dried up and filled with rocks and dirt, making it sort of a valley. The mound is in the middle of the little depression. I think this is why no one has found this structure before. The depression has hidden its height," said Adriana.

Molly did not intend to go traipsing through the jungle, but she thanked her for the idea anyhow. The young couple left, leaving her alone on her bench in the shade. She opened the paper bag containing her sandwich and had her lunch. A few early season tourists were milling around, taking pictures, and for the most part were being respectful and quiet. There was an air of reverence here, like being in a museum or a library. Suddenly, a distressing beep from her backpack broke the silence.

Damn, she thought, realizing what the beep meant. She would have to get out the spiral bound notebook and her pencil, as her laptop would soon be useless. The low-battery indicator blinked red at her from inside the backpack.

Damn. Damn. Damn. The outlet she had left the charger plugged into at the hotel must have been defective.

The laptop had spoiled her; she only resorted to handwriting when absolutely necessary. Because she was quite out of practice, her handwriting was atrocious. She sometimes had a hard time deciphering everything she had written later. This had not always been a bad thing, as the slower pace allowed her to write more thoughtfully and carefully, but it was always such a bother. Typing was so much faster and easier as long as the blasted laptop had power.

She reflexively looked around her for a power outlet. Apparently, some habits were hard to break even in the face of such incredible improbability.

Surely, there must be an outlet right there on the side of the pyramid. How else did the ancient Maya power their Christmas lights? The idea of one of these ancient, foreboding temples lit up with festive holiday lights and topped with a fully decorated tree made her chuckle.

The laptop had just enough power to pull up the notes she had made during the trip up here. She soon caught up to where the story had left off.

Okay, Edington was just finishing up his flashback about Professor Almos a few days prior, and would be finally taking those cosmic readings before the morning sun came up. Flipping open the notebook to a blank page, she put her pencil to paper and began to write.

Chapter 7, A Waylaid World

Edington peered through the telescope lens. Hairline wires inside the eyepiece superimposed a grid-like pattern onto the night sky. Using this reticule, he would take his measurements. Later the following afternoon, others would run the complex mathematical equations needed to derive substance from the numbers. Normally, the thin black lines were hard to see against the night sky, but not tonight. Tonight, the sky was brilliant with stars and nebulosity. He quickly found what he was looking for and took his measurements.

He was studying an odd hourglass-shaped constellation in the new sky near the center of the anomaly. In particular, he studied the three stars in a line, which were in the neck of the hourglass. This constellation was easy to find in the anomaly, and he often used it as a basis for comparative analysis. The constellation also had a large and brilliant stellar nursery just below the line of stars, easily visible to the unaided eye. Although quite beautiful, the nebula did not offer much to him in his field of study, but he enjoyed looking at it all the same.

During his shift with the telescope, he would often find himself returning to this object. There was something so peaceful and majestic about this part of space that reminded him of home.

Before the anomaly had appeared, the *King's Crown* had dominated that part of the sky. It was easily the most recognizable constellation in the night sky. Even young children knew how to find it, and anyone with half an imagination could see it. Five stars created the zigzagging points in the crown and two stars below formed the base. Between those two stars was a large stellar nursery, much like this new one he examined now. Although quite different in appearance, both nebulas gave him the same sense of awe and wonder.

The sheer unimaginable magnitude of something that could be the birthplace of stars astounded him. This feeling never left him, and was what drove him to become an astronomer. Now, the familiar constellation was gone, completely replaced by the anomaly and the new stars it brought with it. He was saddened by its loss, but also excited by the discovery of the new stars, stars never seen by anyone until now.

You aren't the "Jewel of the King's Crown," but you are quite a satisfactory replacement, he thought, studying the new nebula more closely. It was larger than it was before, and he could make out details he had not yet seen. He could just make out four small stars in its center forming a rough rectangle. He fingered the lens-locking ring. *Maybe there is time to switch lenses and get a higher magnification.* He turned away to pick up another lens off the table.

He glanced through the round windows surrounding the domed ceiling. A faint glow was starting to appear on the horizon in the east and soon there would not be much of anything to look at. There would be time later to study the new nebula. What he needed to do now was to examine the faint fringes of the anomaly to determine its current size, shape, and structure.

Finding where the edge of where the anomaly stopped and real space began was problematic at best. However, in these dark skies it would be much easier. Moreover, by taking the readings so close to sunrise, he would have the readings a good four to six hours recent for the morning crew.

Holding his notepad to catch the starlight, he sketched the basic shape of the cloudy mass stretching across the sky, leaving room to pencil in measurements next to the sketch. The anomaly had grown well past the point of being visible in its entirety in the eyepiece, so he had to *walk the grid* from one end to the other in a slow pan to calculate its size. Even without doing the complex math, he knew it was still growing fast. It would fill the sky entirely in little over a week.

The sky along the eastern horizon was turning a deep crimson as the sun came up. He yawned and put his notepad down.

That's about all I'll get tonight, he sighed, removing the reticular lens from the back of the telescope. The wind had picked up and was whistling through the slotted opening in the dome. He returned the telescope to its stowed position and winched the dome shut with a loud clang. Looking through the round windows in the dome, he saw the crimson horizon had changed to a murky yellow-gray light filling the observatory with its dim hue. The scrubby mountainside plants were waving in the howling wind outside, and dust was starting to form in the air over the plains.

Suddenly, the trapdoor slammed open loudly.

"Damn it, boy! What are you doing up here?" shouted Professor Almos, poking his head into the dark observatory.

"I…I was…working," stammered Edington.

"In a power outage? Where is your mind, boy? Don't you realize there's a storm coming? We need to take shelter immediately."

Almos held the door open just long enough for Edington to stumble down the stairs. Together they made their way down the hall by the light of the candle Almos carried.

"There's no time to reach the dormitories. You will have to come with me."

They turned down the corridor that led to the astronomer's quarters and offices. The corridor door was already open. They found Almos's office and went inside. The professor sealed the door shut with a hiss.

Edington did not know what he was more shocked to discover; that he had almost died in a windstorm, or that he was in the Chief Royal Astronomer's office. No apprentice had ever been allowed to visit this level of the observatory tower, much less be allowed in the Chief Royal Astronomer's private office.

Throughout the academy, rumors had abounded about what the higher offices of the observatory tower contained. Common belief held that the Chief Royal Astronomer held secrets not known to the public, important secrets, secrets concerning the nature of the universe and everything in it.

These men held the keys to safe navigation of the ether, and without them, ether travel was a risky gamble. They guarded their secrets well and always kept the door connecting this level to the central staircase locked.

Professor Almos must have heard the dome clang shut, and he had rushed to the observatory level, disregarding the safety rules, leaving doors wide open as he ran. The open corridor door alone could have sentenced to death any of the five junior astronomers living on the lower level. He felt flushed with the weight of that responsibility. Although indirect and unintentional, his decision to use the telescope tonight could have killed people.

Almos was glaring at him in the darkness from a big upholstered chair.

"You almost killed us both tonight, boy."

"I'm sorry, sir," said Edington, not sure what to say, but knowing he was in trouble.

"Would you mind explaining to me what you were doing up there?"

Edington wasn't about to let him know that he had made this nocturnal excursion several times during other outages; no sense enraging the old man further.

"I thought that, with the power out, I'd have a better view of the sky, sir. I was already wide awake, so I just thought…"

"No, you didn't. You did not think at all. With the power out, the storm siren cannot function. Did you think of that?"

"Yes sir, I know, but the windstorms are so infrequent. I thought I would be able to see one coming from up there in the observatory. And we need these measurements. The sky was incredible tonight, sir. Nearly perfect viewing with no sky glow to contend with."

"That was a stupid risk, boy."

Although he had to admit, the boy had imagination and courage. Taking advantage of a power outage in such a manner was something he would not have thought of.

Suddenly, a brass telegraph pad on Almos's desk began tapping out a coded message. Even during a power outage, the telegraph could still receive messages as the sender powered it from the other end. The little electromagnet in the pad opened and shut a lever, creating sets of clicks and pauses that every astronomer could interpret and understand.

Almos quickly turned to write down the message.

NO RESPONSE FROM OUR LAST COMM. POWER OUTTAGE? STORM TO LAST FOR 30 MINUTES. CONTACT US WHEN POWER RESTORED. CASUALTIES? - FLITWICK

This was the second message coming over the telegraph tonight. The loud tapping from the first report is what woke Almos in the first place, twenty minutes earlier.

After realizing they were in another confounded power outage, he had fumbled for a lucifer, lit a candle and decoded the first message, which had been a windstorm warning from Flitwick colony. Right after writing it down, he had heard the sound of the dome closing on Platform B above his office. "Who in blazes is up there at this hour?" he had thundered. Without a second of hesitation, he bolted out of his office and ran upstairs to the observatory platform where he found his apprentice at work in the dark room, oblivious to the coming windstorm. He had no choice but to bring the boy here.

"*Blast!* It is going to be a long storm," cursed Almos, nearly knocking over his ink pot.

At least the council won't be thinking about the anomaly this morning, he thought. *After this, they may even have a few deaths on their hands.* It was inexcusable to have not invested in the proper maintenance of the town's power generators. It was only a matter of time before something like this was going to happen.

Edington was dumbstruck. In the dim candlelight, he could see many books and devices on the shelves around him. Some he recognized, but most he did not. There were books and papers everywhere. There were half-erased equations and diagrams scrawled on wooden black boards, and a complete model of the known solar system hung from the ceiling. The coffered walls were a deep mahogany color and looked worn with age. There seemed to be an overabundance of furniture in the room making it seem much smaller than it was.

A large circular window with wrought iron trimming overlooked the darkened town below. The wind outside was howling. The panels of glass were thick and created a rippling effect as his view shifted. Discarded cups were everywhere, stained with the remnants of what only could have been Almos's coffee. Eventually, his eyes returned to the professor who was still glaring at him. Edington immediately felt uncomfortable again.

"I'm trying to decide what to do with you. You are well aware of the rules, aren't you?" asked Almos, with a serious look.

"Yes sir," said Edington.

The rules concerning the safety of the colonists were enforced by immediate deportation back to Archænis. The rules required colonists to stay hunkered down and stay put during power outages, as there would not be enough time to take shelter without the early warning system. If you didn't get yourself killed by being outside in a windstorm, you would be sent on the next ether ship home for reckless endangerment.

He was grateful to the old codger for saving his life, but he would rather be dead than sent home this way. Nevertheless, he felt his dismissal was imminent.

"I'll begin packing my things as soon as the storm passes."

"Yes. That is a possible ending for this situation. But shall we entertain another?" said Almos. "Your passion for your work is commendable and I would not like to waste it. You show great promise and may someday find yourself in charge of your own facility. I have no intention of sending such a mind home to be killed in a mindless war." He lit a pipe and relaxed a little. He looked exhausted.

Edington's parents were farmers, and they had sacrificed much to send him to the academy and then later to apprentice to Professor Almos. Over the years, Edington had written to his parents, but never had a chance to visit much less even speak to them. To show up on their doorstep in disgrace would be unbearable.

"What do you suggest, sir?"

"Sam, I'll be blunt. I need you to lie for me."

"Lie for you, sir?" asked Edington, not quite believing what he just heard. Equally shocking was to hear the professor call him by his first name. Surely, he could not be serious; was he really going to blackmail him this way?

Almos began rummaging in his desk and came up with a pile of papers which he put on his desk. His tired, wrinkled face looked years older in the candle light. "A few days ago, I came to a conclusion concerning the anomaly. I know what it is and what it will do. I hold in my hand the results of my analysis."

Almos had taken loose sheets off the top of the stack and was offering them for Edington to read. As he took them,

Edington glanced at a string-tied bundle of yellowing papers that had been in the stack beneath them. Written on the cover sheet of the bundle were the words, "FARSHIFT PROJECT."

Almos apparently had noticed his lingering gaze, and he quickly returned the parcel to his desk drawer.

"You are probably wondering why I have not shared this information with anyone. There are forces at work I do not completely understand and as such, I cannot offer any course of action to take. Thus, needlessly worrying the colonists would not help anyone."

Edington could not make out much in the dark, but he could see a timeline drawn on one of the sheets Almos had given him an exceedingly short timeline.

"Am I to understand this graph represents the size of the anomaly over time?"

"Quite."

"Yes, but according to this, the anomaly will not just fill the sky, it will be the sky in just a few days.

"Don't act so incredulous. You are well aware of the speed of its growth. Your confounded numbers during the recent events have had you suspecting the same thing for days," he snapped, taking away the papers.

It was true of course, but he never thought he would hear Almos admit it. This disheveled, tired old man was no longer the pompous infallible scientist he had known with comic dislike. Now, he actually felt sorry for the old geezer in this beaten state.

"So, all this time, you've known?" he asked.

"Yes, yes. I have been deliberately making you and the others run in circles. I did of course need verification of the data, but any fool could see the thing was growing rapidly," said Almos, putting down his pipe and leaning forward. "What you have to understand, Sam, is that I need to buy time. It is too early to release this data without having a plan of action."

"Why are you telling me this *now?*" He was getting angry. "Why don't you take this to the council and let them decide whether or not we deserve to know that the end of the world is coming?"

"Stop being so dramatic. You don't know any more than I do about the final outcome of this development. So far, there have not been any adverse effects from the anomaly."

"No adverse effects? What about the loss of a thousand star systems?" asked Edington incredulously? "Surely they have seen this from Archænis by now. What do they have to say about it? Have you received the post from yesterday's ether probe?"

"There was no ether probe from Archænis yesterday," said Almos quietly. "There will not be any more probes from Archænis. *Ever again.*"

Edington sat down on one of the many chairs in the room. The silence hung in the air for a few moments before Almos spoke again.

"From my projections, I discovered we must have lost contact with Archænis nearly a month ago when all this started. With no ether probe yesterday, it confirmed my suspicions."

"But the anomaly is well beyond the edge of the solar system. It's in deep space!"

"If you read my report you would understand. It is not an object. It's not moving. It's not expanding towards us. Matter simply cannot move that fast. What we have been observing is an illusion. In fact, the anomaly is already here. It originated here.

"An immense spherical rift has encapsulated our planet, and much of the space around it. This sphere is transporting us out of our universe and into a new one. What we have been calling the anomaly is actually a fractured opening in the sphere's surface as it falls back upon itself. We maintain a link to our own universe only within this shrinking bubble. As the fracture widens, its spherical surface refracts the starlight, much like a lens. This explains why the new universe appears to be getting closer. As our old universe disappears into the breach, it is lost to us forever.

"As you know, the fracture is quite extensive and growing. Eventually we will be utterly adrift, alone in this new universe. Simply put—we are being abducted."

Edington didn't quite know what to make of all this. *Why was he so sure they were in no danger?*

"If this thing casts us deep into the ether with no sun, we'll freeze to death in just a few days!" he exclaimed.

"Oh, there would be much worse cataclysmic events than that. The lack of gravitational pull that Helios had on Philolaus will cause tidal forces that will wreck the planet, well before we lose our heat," said Almos.

"We must leave then, before it is too late!"

"Stupid boy. It is already too late. We are already inside the bubble. There is nowhere to escape *to.* Leaving the planet would just give us a better view of the inevitable." He grunted.

"So, you are just going to ignore it?"

"Look, there must be intelligence behind this. The process is too organized and too precise. No known natural phenomenon could have caused this. And if there is someone wielding such incredible power, they could have killed us easily with much less trouble."

"Are you suggesting this is the work of our science? Could one of us be behind this?"

Professor Almos hesitated for just a moment before answering; he could tell from his eyes that the old man knew more than he was going to tell.

"Perhaps, but I suspect a higher order of intelligence is also at work here. This is something from outside our experience, but I do not believe we are heading for a disastrous end. Yet, I do not expect that we will never see Archænis again."

"Well in that case, you can't exactly send me back home to face trial now, can you?" said Edington with a smile.

Almos smiled. "No, I suppose not, but I could still make your life difficult with the council. But I don't think I will need to do this. *Will I?*"

"So, you want me to keep quiet on this. This is what you want me to lie about?"

"Yes. When you make your readings, stabilize them. Make it look like the anomaly is slowing down, possibly reversing. Then I can go to the council with positive news. As far as they know, we are still in our own universe. The anomaly is still invisible during the day, and as it stretches mostly across the horizon, its full scope is not visible except from high vantage points."

"So, when do we tell them? When the sun disappears?"

"We do not tell them. We pretend to be as confused as they are. There is nothing we can do except keep hysteria down to a minimum. In just a few days, there will be plenty to go around. In the meantime, we can give them some hope, albeit a false one."

"That is by far, the worst plan of action I have ever heard."

"Do you have a better one?" retorted Almos.

"It just seems more like a plan of *inaction*," said Edington.

"Look son, I'm doing the best I can with what we have to work with. I'm trusting you with a great deal of information here. Please trust me in return. There's really isn't anything else we can do," said Almos, his eyes downcast.

Edington was warmed by the trust the old codger was putting in him. He had never shown anything resembling camaraderie before. The anomaly had changed the man. He looked positively humbled.

"Well, there is one thing we can do. When the windstorm passes and the power comes back, let's go have some of that awful stuff you call coffee," said Edington. "I'm obviously not going back to sleep tonight."

Almos's downtrodden expression brightened, as if a cloud had been lifted. He smiled at his apprentice. "An excellent suggestion. But, I expect you will first have to replace my broken carafe."

Chapter 8, The King's Crown

Molly shook her hand out; it was not used to so much manual labor. Likewise, neither was the pencil. The formerly sharp point was down to a woody nub and would not be good for writing much more today. Molly dug around in her book sack looking for her sharpener, which of course she had not thought to pack. Neither did she have another pencil. She had been writing for just over an hour, yet she looked in amazement at the number of pages she had filled. Writing this book was getting easier and easier yet the world seemed against her wanting to write it. Every time she worked up momentum in the story, something would happen to bring her out of her reverie.

This is why writers lock themselves in cabins in the middle of nowhere. No distractions. But hadn't she taken this vacation for exactly the same reason? Wasn't she here on this bench in the middle of nowhere to be alone with her story as well? *No, not really,* she thought. She was here to get away from *there.*

There was where *Dragon's Keep* was born, where it grew out of all expected proportion and made her life so spectacularly complicated. *There* was where she woke, wrote, ate, paid bills, and slept. *There* was a place where everything was easy and familiar. Too familiar, too predictable, and as of late, too mundane. She had exhausted all the inspiration she was going to get from *there.*

Looking at the ancient, multi-leveled, stepped pyramid in front of her, she felt disjointed. She felt totally out of place in this foreign and forgotten world.

She felt such loss for these people. This was such a tragic and violent end for a nation with such an obvious love and aptitude concerning art, science, mathematics, and astronomy. Who knows what they would have accomplished without all the bloodshed and greed in their history? Then again, maybe those things are what compelled them to achieve such academic heights.

Even now, war did have a way of accelerating progress in both science and the arts. Warfare had even influenced the great Leonardo Da Vinci. Many of his remarkable sketches were of early tanks, canon, helicopters, and other instruments of war.

Awe, tragedy, and loss, all in the last ten minutes. Ellen was right. Vacations did have a way of resetting the brain.

She stood up to stretch her legs. Looking at her watch, she noticed she still had a solid hour to kill before Juan and Adriana would return to pick her up.

She took a walk around the main temple and admired the perfect stonework. She wanted to take a closer look, but the public could only inspect the lower levels.

Hmmm, she thought, looking in the direction of the ruin of homes of the Maya elite. *Hadn't Adriana said there was an undiscovered temple somewhere in that direction?*

Feeling a rare adventurous urge, Molly walked into the area looking for the markers Adriana had pointed out. The foliage was not too thick, and she soon found the ground to be sloping downward at a shallow angle. *I must be walking on the edge of the valley caused by the old sinkhole,* she thought, looking for the telltale gum tree with the X's carved in its bark.

She found it soon enough and turned west as Adriana had suggested. The ground sloped more steeply now. Working her way down into the bowl shaped declivity, the rising slopes disoriented her, and she lost her view of the path. She considered turning around, but the ground soon leveled off and she arrived at the base of a huge mound of dirt.

It did not look much like a temple. It looked more like a large hill covered with boulders and scrubby trees. Here and there, stones that looked more like bricks were sticking out of the dirt. One of them, larger than the others, had odd markings on it, and she knew this must be the place. This must be the stella stone Adriana had mentioned.

She walked completely around the mound to get an idea of its size. It must have been about eighty feet on each side and half that in height.

Maybe if I climb it, I can get a better idea of where the way back to the main temple plaza is, she thought, not wanting to get further lost in the strange little valley.

She grabbed a vine and started climbing the hill. There weren't many large trees growing on the mound, so she didn't have to clear anything particularly difficult out of her way. Near the top, she stopped under what must be another Ceiba tree. Its roots had shattered a few of the stone bricks beneath it, creating jagged fissures in the stonework. It was strangely quiet and disconcerting up here. However, the silence was not empty; somehow, it pulsed with energy. She could feel it from her head down to her toes. She reached down and put her hand on the ground expecting to feel the vibration. There was none. Confused, she stood back up.

Suddenly, with a snap, the ground beneath her gave way. In a shower of dirt and rubble she fell through a hole in what she thought had been solid ground. Grasping for a hold on something as she fell, she found purchase on a root from the tree. Closing her eyes and gripping the hairy, brittle root, she slid down a few more feet before stopping with a jolt.

Dirt and rocks were still raining down on top of her, and she felt for sure a large stone would soon be joining the party, but none came. She opened her eyes and realized she was only a few inches above the floor. Letting go, she dropped the remaining distance and caught her breath.

Letting her eyes adjust to the darkness, she found she was in a small room, about ten feet square. A shaft of light from the hole above her head streamed into the chamber.

I must be in a room near the top of the pyramid, she thought in wonder. *It's a good thing this chamber isn't terribly deep or I might not be able to climb out.*

An overwhelming sense of power was in the room. She could feel the vibration all around her. It reminded her of a sensation she had on a cruise a long time ago as a little girl with her parents. They were on the return trip to California when her parents decided to have dinner at one of the nicer restaurants on the ship. Although outrageously expensive, her mom had insisted on dining there. She wanted to see the sunset, and the elegant restaurant had a magnificent view. Located at the very back of the boat and near the waterline, the wide windows commanded an unobstructed view of the unhurried, receding ocean.

However, because of the dining room's location, this meant it was directly above the main engine compartment. The ship's designers had taken much care to dampen the sound of what must have been a deafening noise in the engine room below. Most people hardly noticed it. However, Molly could still remember feeling the intense, vibrating hum of the powerful engines, as she enjoyed her meal and watched the sunset with her parents.

She marveled at the small, forgotten room of which she had fallen. The Maya did not typically build rooms inside their pyramids. Most temples were solid all the way through. She knew that much from the Chaccoben brochure. The little brochure was quick to point out that there were no hidden chambers filled with gold or mummies in the center of the Mayan pyramids.

Therefore, this building must have been significant, perhaps not a temple pyramid at all. Being so close to the city for the elite, it might have been a structure built for someone important. Maybe it was a vault or improbably, maybe even a tomb? She shuddered at the latter idea, and tried not to think of the possibility of a Mayan mummy being in here with her.

As her eyes adjusted to the dim light coming through the hole in the ceiling, she began to make out details in the room. It was empty; that much she was sure. However, near pristine decorations covered the walls. All the original, colorful hues seemed perfect. There were intricate carvings everywhere, even on the ceiling.

The scenes on the walls depicted a battle. She could see the invading tribe attacking with deadly spear-armed warriors. The defenders, easily outnumbered, were still holding fast, protecting their city. Strangely though, the city did not look Mayan. The city had buildings with dome-shaped roofs, and there were towers with tall spires. Here and there, odd hieroglyphs dotted the scene.

Molly looked up at the ceiling that had a celestial sky carved and painted onto it. The scene on the ceiling did not look like any part of the night sky she knew, although as old as it must be, the sky might have looked different back then. But what did she know? Molly had only done some preliminary astronomy research for her book, but she was not a professional astronomer.

Suddenly, she caught her breath in both surprise and fear. There was something in the carved alien sky she did recognize. On the ceiling, near the hole she had fell through, were seven stars forming a crown shaped constellation with a lapis lazuli jewel in its center. Shrinking away, she realized it looked exactly the way her Edington had just described it.

Chapter 9, The Observatório Nacional

Carvalho was annoyed. His beer had gone flat and warm in the hot sun. He had been staring at the glass for over an hour, and he still had no answers.

The story he and his soldiers had told the sergeant yesterday had not been well received. Assuming they had concocted the fantastic story to cover their own ineptitude, the sergeant took Carvalho and his men off active duty and sentenced them to a two-week leave without pay.

So now, he was having a few *cervajas* while he still had some change in his pocket and thinking hard about what had happened.

The *Policia Civil* had investigated and filed a cursory report. Carvalho knew they would simply shelve the case, yet he pressed them to pursue it further. Of course, they did not believe his report. Nor was he able to count on the other three soldiers to collaborate his story. Since being put off duty, they were not speaking to anyone. No one wanted to go chasing after ghosts. No one, except him.

He knew what he had seen. Although he could not explain how the man did it, he knew now there had been a man, not a ghost; why would a ghost want to rob a bank? The bank was the key. He would do a little private detective work of his own. After all, now he had the time.

He had showered and was now wearing regular street clothes over his muscular build. He got into his car and drove to the Banco Real, which was just a few miles from his apartment.

He found the bank manager to be congenial, and eager to learn of any news concerning the theft. "Did you catch him?" asked the bank manager.

"We don't know where he has gotten to, but we have a good description, and should be able to track him down soon if he is still in the city," he said, putting away his identification. "What exactly did he steal?"

"I honestly do not know," said the manager. "We do not require our clients to describe the contents of their safe deposit boxes, and they have elected not to tell us."

"Of course. Can you tell me who owned the box?"

"Yes, we were told to be as cooperative as possible with the police. The box belonged to the Observatório Nacional. Their offices are in the old São Cristóvão district."

He knew the place. "How long have they had a safe deposit box here?"

"From what I understand, it has been at this branch for nearly fifty years. The bank has changed names a few times, but the box has never been opened. No one comes to see it."

"Who else might have known about it? Are your employees allowed in the vault?"

"We only allow senior staff to escort clients into the safe-deposit vault. We remove their box with their key and leave the client in privacy to view its contents. They ring a buzzer when they have finished."

"And no one came to see this box recently?"

"No, no one."

"*Obrigado.* That's all I need for now," said Carvalho turning to leave.

"*De nada,*" said the manager. "Let me know if you catch him."

Carvalho caught a cab to visit the Observatório Nacional. From the cab, he called the observatory to set up an appointment with the director.

"*Desculpa, Corporal.* Dr. Mariconi is out of town until tomorrow afternoon. May I help you?" said the receptionist.

"Out of town? Why? Where?" he demanded.

"Dr. Mariconi left a week ago without leaving any details. I only have his calendar to go by. He has a staff meeting tomorrow that he has not told me to cancel, so I assume he would be back by then. You will have to speak to his assistant, Dr. Pinotti. Would you like me to transfer you to him?"

An hour later, Carvalho was sitting in Pinotti's office arguing with the man. Pinotti was much older than he and beginning to go a little bald. As he spoke, the corporal thought he detected the hint of an odd accent, perhaps Central American?

"I have already told the police everything I knew," grumbled Pinotti. "At the time, they did not seem very interested, so why have they sent you?"

"If you could tell me a little about the stolen item, perhaps we could do more. For now, you have told us nothing. The thief left millions of reals in the vault and only took this one item. Why would he do this?"

"The artifact was an important historical relic. It was unique and priceless. It has been in the observatory's care for over eighty years. During the military *coup d'etat* in 1964, someone at one of the banks the observatory does business with moved the box to the Banco Real for safekeeping. It had remained there until yesterday when your people managed to lose the thief who ran right past your very gates."

"I led that pursuit. I am the one that lost him," admitted Carvalho. "I'm investigating this on my own as no one at headquarters is taking my report seriously."

"What? What do you mean? Why wouldn't they take this seriously? Someone has stolen an irreplaceable artifact, and nothing is being done about it?"

"What do you expect? You will not describe your stolen artifact to us, and we have a thief that can walk through solid walls. What can anyone do with that?"

Pinotti sighed and picked up an old theodelite off his desk and studied it. It looked heavy and had a dull copper finish, as did the twenty or so other instruments it in the display cases downstairs.

The stolen artifact had been like the theodolite, one item among many, lost in the sea of antiquity. It had been one of thousands of items the museum owned. Until someone stole it, they had not even known it existed much less what it was. When the bank manager called, Pinotti was surprised to find that the museum had owned a safe deposit box at that branch.

Curious, he did a little digging and found the paperwork that paid the small yearly fee for the box. A special fund, which only the director had access, had paid for it. It was the same fund that provided for maintenance of a peculiar lab in the United States—a secret lab known only to a select few, which included Pinotti. The artifact must have something to do with the lab at Niagara, he had speculated.

At a dead end, he brought his concerns to the director directly. Unfortunately, besides a few details about the artifact's container, Dr. Mariconi had not been able to discover what the little box contained at all. However, they found unexpectedly that Albert Einstein himself had requisitioned its safekeeping as a personal favor during his second visit to Rio in 1930.

Pinotti decided he did not want the young, smug corporal to find out that they had only recently learned about the artifact, so he changed the subject.

"What's this about walking through walls?" asked Pinotti, looking up from the theodolite.

"Exactly that," said Carvalho. "I have friends in the *Civil Policia*. I know they did an insurance investigation for the bank. There was a camera recording the vault door. There is nothing on the video that shows him entering or leaving. Normally, I would think there was tampering involved with the camera, except for what I saw him do in the alley."

Just remembering what had happened made the hair on the back of his neck rise. "After a long chase, I saw the suspect walk into the side of a mountain."

"That must have hurt."

"You misunderstand me. What I mean to say is one minute he was in front of me smiling, and then with a quick turn, he disappeared into the mountain, like a ghost. He probably did the same trick in the bank vault."

Pinotti blinked in surprise. "Surely not, Corporal, a trick of the light. You obviously have a skilled illusionist on your hands. But it is only that, an illusion. I suggest you lose your superstitious notions, find this man, and recover our artifact. If you will excuse me, I have work to do."

He was getting nowhere with this annoying little man. "Look, if you want to recover your precious artifact, you should help me. I want to find this person as much as you do. I need to know how he did what he did. I am not fond of mysteries."

Pinotti studied the corporal for a few moments. He seemed to be trying to make up his mind about something.

"The artifact is a part of the director's private collection. It is not even on the official roster. Einstein brought it to the observatory in the 1930s and gave it to Dr. Mariconi's predecessors for safekeeping. The artifact is inside a box about ten centimeters on each side. The box is highly magnetic. This is all I can tell you. Honestly, Corporal, I am a very busy man, and your little unofficial investigation has taken up much of my time. I really must ask you to leave."

Feeling that Pinotti was still holding something back, he reluctantly got up to leave. "Before I go, just one more question. Why has Dr. Mariconi left Rio?"

"Dr. Mariconi left over a week ago on observatory business. He is also making inquiries of his own concerning the theft. I will tell him you stopped by when he returns," said Pinotti. "*Bom Dia, Corporal.* Do shut the door behind you."

"Thank you for your time," said Carvalho, exiting the room.

The man obviously knew more than he was saying. Playing a hunch, he lingered in the hallway outside Pinotti's closed door. He dropped to one knee and listened near the vent near the bottom of the door. A few seconds later, he heard a murmured conversation.

"Hello, Dr. Mariconi?" Pinotti was speaking on the telephone. "Yes sir, it's me. I have important news concerning the artifact. I think a shifter may be involved in the theft."

Ananmaya was surprised that no one seemed to be looking for him. Earlier this morning, he woke to find his larceny of the previous day had not even made the morning paper. Even now in the afternoon, there was no news of the theft. He felt relieved, but a little nonplused.

Nevertheless, he showered, shaved, and changed his clothes, deciding to keep a low profile. No sense in tempting fate. Looking around one last time at the place he had called home for several months, he left the tiny one-room shack and made his way down the twisting, steep dirt road. He walked slowly, wishing the bus depot were closer. He was tired and had not slept much. He traveled light, carrying only the worn and tattered satchel that contained everything he owned here, including the box from the bank.

The box was an enigma. All last night he had resisted the urge to open it. Exactly as Bhuvanesh had said, the artifact resisted his attempts to perceive it using his mind. The box was made entirely of magnetite; that much he was convinced. It also was not empty. There was some air in there and he had perceived the outline of the object displacing it. However, what the strange artifact was made of eluded him. It was as if there was a small hole in space where it should be. It was an eerie sensation to Ananmaya, one of which he was wholly unfamiliar.

The arduous trips down the mountainside favela, and then to the bus depot took longer than he expected. He barely had time to purchase a ticket and board a bus to São Paulo where airport security might not be quite as vigilant. The trip should only take a few hours, and with luck, he would get a flight out of the country from there. Taking a seat and putting his satchel on his lap, he again tried to focus on the box inside.

Visually taking apart the satchel, then its contents, and then the box was easy. His mind was well accustomed to the mental exercise by now. The artifact inside, however, was another matter entirely. With it, there was nothing to take apart, just a void space where the air around it described its ovoid shape.

Frustrated, he tried again. *If it is keeping the air away from it, it must exist and have mass, so I should be able to perceive it,* he thought. Still nothing. Eventually, with his eyes closed, and tiring with effort, Ananmaya took a short nap in his seat.

San Paulo did not look any less busy at night. Hectic traffic flowed around the bus like leaves in a stream. The drivers were treating the lane lines merely as friendly suggestions. A three-lane road was often four, sometimes five cars across. Taxis zipped around slower cars through escape routes even Houdini would have found perplexing. Strangely enough, the lumbering, noxious bus made decent time to Guarulhos airport.

He had some difficulty purchasing his ticket. The woman at the desk was surprised that he did not have any luggage other than his carry-on and that he wanted to pay cash. "Most people purchase international tickets online; they are usually cheaper and faster. No one pays with cash," said the attendant, suspiciously eyeing the large wad of reals Ananmaya was holding.

He quickly made up an excuse. "Someone took my luggage by mistake when we unloaded the bus. My tickets were in there, along with my credit cards. Cash is all I had with me in my satchel. Luckily, I kept my passport with me as well," he dug into the bag and handed it over to the attendant.

She looked it over critically, turned to her computer, and gave it back to him. "I can't refund you for your other ticket you know. In fact, I can't even find it in the system under your name."

"Look, my mother is dying of cancer in New York. She only has a few days left. I do not have time to argue with you or try to find the bastards that took my stuff. I will pay whatever it takes to get a ticket tonight. Just get me on the *damn* plane," said Ananmaya hoping this ruse would work.

A little relieved, the attendant peered at her screen and scowled. "The only thing I have is a flight leaving for Miami in an hour. You will have to purchase a connecting flight from there. If you were willing to wait until tomorrow, I could…"

"I'll take it," he interrupted, handing over the wad of cash.

He hoped he was prepared for customs security. He could not afford someone looking too closely at the box. He did not want to imagine what would happen if someone opened it under the wrong conditions.

He had planned for this, and thought he had the best way to handle it. Obviously, a sealed box made of magnetite was not going to make it through the metal detector. It had to go with the satchel through the x-ray machine. He simply did not know enough about the artifact to risk messing around with its molecular structure again. He had been lucky in the mountain.

He could shift it into an alternative quantum state to make it disappear, but that always had unexpected consequences. For some reason, he had no control over when or where objects chose to return, and he hated doing it. Moreover, he might only be able to make the box go, leaving the artifact behind, uncontrolled and in the open, another potential disaster. No, the best thing would be to modify the machine itself.

Walking up to the security arch, he put the satchel on the conveyor belt of the x-ray machine. Holding to the edge of the bulky device, he took off his shoes and put them with his wallet and his watch in a little tray on the conveyor.

As his belongings began their slow journey into the depths of the machine, Ananmaya concentrated, murmuring phrases under his breath. The timing for this had to be perfect.

"*Anda logo!* Come on, already! You are holding up the line," said an angry little man behind him, tapping him on the shoulder.

Ananmaya ignored him and maintained his focus. He would only need a few seconds more. When his things appeared at the other end of the machine, he stepped through the metal detector and went to retrieve the satchel.

"*Seu idiota,*" said the man, taking his place behind him, angrily putting things down on the conveyor. As the man turned, he noticed a bald patch on the top of his head.

"Is this your bag, *senhor?*" said a security guard holding Ananmaya's satchel.

"Yes, is there a problem?" he asked surprised. His mind raced. *Had the trick failed? What would he do now if it did? It was stupid to attempt this. There must have been a better way.*

"Would you mind showing us what's inside this?" asked the guard, reaching into the bag and pulling out a bundle of clothing.

By now, a few other guards had slipped in behind the first. *They were like vultures hovering over a kill,* he thought, getting concerned.

He took the bundle and opened it for the guard, revealing an antique, tin cookie box. He took a breath and tried not to show his relief. He had totally forgotten about the tin. Opening it revealed a letter from Bhuvanesh and a collection of folded papers. There were also newspaper clippings, some photographs and few coins from India. He had kept the old, ornate box as a reminder of where he came from, an anchor to his past.

"*Obrigato,*" said the guard inspecting the lot. "You're fine. Please gather your things and move along. *Boi Noite.*"

Ananmaya put everything back in his bag, put on his shoes, and walked to the departure gate. Scarcely believing his luck, he thanked Ganesh and found a seat in the waiting area by the gate.

I'm finding new ways to use my power every day, he thought, thinking about what he had just accomplished. *I could make a fortune doing special effects for Hollywood without all the expensive computers and expertise.*

At the security gate, he had needed a quick solution to fool the guard into not seeing the box appear on his display. Luckily, it was a standard monitor and not a flat screen; that would have been a much more complex operation. All he had to do was change the state of the screen phosphors making up the image of his box as it moved along the conveyor. This way, he did not need to mess with the box or its contents.

A still image would have been easy, but this picture was moving. He had to make constant adjustments to keep the box hidden until the satchel made it completely out of the machine.

The impatient fool behind him had almost ruined the effect. Never outright vindictive, Ananmaya had nevertheless left the little man a gift for his trouble.

"Last call for flight 1055 to Miami," announced a voice on the loudspeaker. Lost in his thoughts, he hadn't noticed that the gateway was almost empty. Last in line, the attendant processed his boarding pass and he boarded the plane. He hoped the flight would be serving an early dinner as he was starving. This would be a long, relaxing, eight-hour flight; a welcome change to the excitement of the past few days.

A commotion was going on at the front of the plane. He looked down the aisle and saw the flight attendant arguing with one of the passengers. "I'm sorry, senhor, your boarding pass has you in coach, not in first class. You must find a seat back there."

"I've tried to tell you there has been a mistake. I purchased a first-class ticket, and that is what was printed on it just an hour ago. Someone has switched tickets with me. I can't explain how," said the man, his face turning red.

"I'm sorry sir, but you must take your seat. We have already closed the door and are starting our taxi to the runway," said the flight attendant.

"There's no such thing as a seat 'Z' anyhow!" said the man contemptuously. This is obviously a misprint. I have no intention on spending this grueling flight in coach because of your own incompetence."

"And we have no intention of holding this flight and inconveniencing a hundred passengers because you will not take your seat. Please don't make me get the air marshal." By now, everyone was staring at the little man whose face was beet-red with anger.

"After we are airborne, we can discuss this further," the man said through clenched teeth, turning towards coach. He trundled down the aisle, looking for an empty seat. Unfortunately, the only empty seat was right next to Ananmaya who was trying not to look at him.

"Oh great, it's you. You are the one that is afraid to go through metal detectors," said the man sitting down in a huff. "I can't believe these people. This is preposterous. They do not know whom they are dealing with. Someone is going to pay for this."

Ananmaya decided this might not be a relaxing flight after all.

Chapter 10, The Dzolob

"Ms. Arden? Are you okay? You look like you've seen a ghost," said Juan, coming down the path with Adriana holding his hand.

"No, I mean, yes. I'm fine, just a little shaken," said Molly, picking a twig out of her hair. "I had an accident and fell down. But I'm okay."

"You look terrible. Your nice clothes are ruined!" said Adriana noticing all the dirt stains. "Were you buried alive?"

"Almost," she said sheepishly. "I found that ruin you told me about; or I should say, it found me. I was standing on top of it, it opened up beneath me, and I fell through. I was just able to climb back out and get back here. Did you know about the little room inside the ruin?"

"What do you mean?" asked Adriana, confused. "Sometimes, the ruins shift and leave small cavities filled with rubble. Did you fall into one of those?"

"This was no accidental cavity. There is a small square room at the top of that pyramid, and it is filled with paintings and carvings," said Molly. "I fell through a hole in its roof."

"That doesn't make sense. None of the pyramids here had any rooms built inside them. They are solid structures," said Adriana. "If there's a carved room in there, that ruin is the find of a lifetime. I have to see this. My grandmother will be thrilled when we tell her."

She excitedly began walking towards the steep stairs that led down to the village for the elite. Molly and Juan followed close behind.

"Shouldn't we tell the curators of the complex first?" asked Molly, barely keeping up.

"Ms. Arden, we would prefer you keep this between us," said Juan. "Adriana's family owned this property before the government forced them to sell it. They have never been on good terms with the current state of affairs. Let's wait and see what her grandmother has to say, okay?"

"Well, I suppose so," said Molly taking Juan's hand as he helped her down the last flight of stone steps. She was thinking more about the constellation she had seen than about the local politics. *What was going on here?* Nothing made any sense. This had to be a wild coincidence, but somehow she did not think so.

"Adriana, were there astronomers here at Chaccoben?"

"Oh yes. The stars were their guides. Knowing how to read the night sky to predict the seasons was privileged information that gave the priests much of their power. Knowing when to plant and harvest crops was a key to Mayan survival. Why do you ask?"

"Because, along with the other carvings on the walls in that room, there is a very detailed fresco of the stars on the ceiling. And although I'm not a professional astronomer, I don't recognize any of the constellations in that sky," she said, not entirely truthfully.

"I must see this for myself. It sounds fascinating," said Adriana, completely ignoring a "Do Not Enter. Park Personnel Only" sign. "This way is faster. Follow me."

The trail took them a little deeper into the jungle which was filling with long shadows as the sun set on the horizon.

"Look at the time, Adriana; the park is closing in just a few minutes. We need to go. You can come back tomorrow with your grandmother," said Juan. "Let's get to the truck. I've got to get Ms. Arden back to the hotel."

Adriana slowed her pace and stopped. "Shhh. I hear something," she said, motioning for the others to stop.

"What is it?" hissed Juan.

"I don't know. Talking, I think."

Juan listened for a moment but did not hear anything. "Adriana, we're not supposed to be here."

"Neither are they," she snapped, pointing over the edge of a steep ravine, which the trail turned and followed.

Molly looked down into the valley and recognized the gum tree with the X's carved in its bark. A little past the tree was Adriana's hidden mound, except that now, there were two people at the top. One was reaching down and helping the other out of the opening she had made earlier. He was holding something in his hand.

"What are they doing?" whispered Molly.

"I don't know. They don't look like tour guides or other park personnel," said Adriana. "They may be tourists, except why would they be out here? No one knows about this but my nana and me."

Adriana was right. These people were clearly not locals. *They were like her,* Molly thought. Their light skin stood out noticeably against the darkening jungle. Although, they wore black, somewhat military-looking clothes. They carried hand held radios, which one of them unholstered from his belt and began speaking into. In his other hand, he was holding what they had found and turning it in the receding sunlight. Suddenly, she knew what it was.

"My pendant!" she yelped, unable to stop herself. She put her hand over her mouth, but it was too late. The two men had stopped and turned in their direction.

"*Mierda,*" said Juan taking their hands and turning to run. "*Vamos! Vamos!*"

The men shouted something as they raced through the jungle. Molly's heart was pounding, and she could not clearly hear their demands, but they sounded emphatic.

Did they have guns holstered on those belts? She didn't know or want to find out. She bolted through the jungle, half-running, half-pulled by Juan and Adriana.

When they reached the base of the stairs up to the temple complex, they stopped for a moment to catch their breath.

"We've got to get out of here before they make it out of the valley," said Juan, panting.

"Who are they?" asked Molly gasping. She was bent over, hands on her knees, trying to recover from the unexpected sprint. She had not realized how out of shape she was.

Adriana was laughing. She did not appear tired at all. "Look at you two. You look like scared rabbits."

Juan gave her an exasperated look.

"Look, they couldn't possibly make it up the ravine to the path. It is too steep. It's not too bad to climb down, but going up is difficult. I was going to take us out the other way through the ancient village. Even if they run, it will take them at least fifteen minutes to get here," she said smiling.

"They had radios," said Juan scowling at her. "That means they have friends nearby. We need to go now."

Adriana's expression changed quickly. "Oh, right."

They made their way directly to the parking lot and found Juan's truck. Only two other vehicles were there so late in the afternoon. One was a jeep with the park emblem on it. The other was a blue sedan, obviously a rental car. They clambered into Juan's truck.

"Was that blue sedan there when you pulled in, Juan?" asked Molly.

"I don't remember. But there were a few other cars here when we pulled in, so I don't think my truck would give us away."

They quickly climbed in and Juan tore out of the parking lot.

Molly thought she was probably just being paranoid; why would anyone be after them? What had they done wrong? Those people were probably just curious tourists that had followed her to the mound, and were having a look on their own. *Strange looking tourists though.*

"If it is all the same to you, Juan, I'd like to speak with Adriana's grandmother myself before we go back to the hotel. I've got an idea about that ruin; let's call it book research."

Turning to Adriana she asked, "Do you think she would be available to speak with me?"

"She does not normally receive many visitors except the occasional student or researcher, but I think she would very much like to hear about this. She's not an archeologist, but she is very knowledgeable about this area's history. It is her life's work. She would love talking to you."

* * *

In the time it took to drive back to Pedro a Santos, things had calmed down. The whole affair seemed silly now, and they were laughing about it. Molly was smiling and picking leaves out of her hair when they arrived at Adriana's house.

Molly helped bring in some groceries that Juan and Adriana had picked up earlier. Setting the bag of vegetables on the table, she noticed how cool the house was compared to sweltering heat outside. She could hear the dramatic dialogue of South American soaps on the television in the kitchen.

"*Nana!* We're home. I have some friends with me," called Adriana.

From the kitchen, Molly heard an answer in Spanish, and an elderly woman came shuffling out of the kitchen. The first thing Molly noticed was her enigmatic green eyes. They spoke of years of experience and wisdom, yet looked youthful somehow, like a rebellious teenager trapped in an old woman's body.

Surprised at seeing Molly, she said, "Honestly, Adriana, the house is a mess. You should have told me we would be having more guests today." She put the dish towel she was holding into a pocket in her apron.

Holding out her hand to Molly, she said, "*Hola.* Are you a friend of Juan's?"

Taking her wrinkled hand, Molly said, "Hi, my name is Molly Arden. I'm staying at the resort where Juan works. I'm very pleased to meet you Mrs…I'm sorry, I didn't catch your name."

"My name is Naum Cohuo. But you can call me Naomi as most people have trouble with Naum. My parents named me after my grandmother. Hmmm. Arden, Arden, why is that name so familiar?" the little old woman looked at the ceiling for a moment. "Ah! I have it!"

She put her hand into another pocket in her apron and pulled out a paperback book. It was another copy of *Dragon's Keep: Book 4*.

"I found this in Adriana's room, and I haven't been able to put it down. It is very good. I recognize you now from the picture on the back of the book. You are the book's author, aren't you?" she asked.

Molly was stunned; she couldn't quite believe this. "Yes, Yes, I am. Do you read fantasy?"

"Ms. Arden, I read a great many things. At least when the *telenovelas* aren't on," she said smiling.

"*Mi Dios.* Where are my manners? Would you like a cup of coffee, Ms. Arden? You look as if you could use one."

Molly looked at her disheveled state self-consciously; she genuinely looked terrible. She could use the caffeine to help focus her thoughts.

"Yes, please," she said. "And if you have a moment, I'd like to talk to you about Chaccoben and the Maya. I've had an interesting, but very confusing day."

A little later, Molly and Naomi were in the kitchen talking about her recent adventure. Naomi seemed more interested in the hidden chamber than in the men at the mound.

"I saw illustrations everywhere. They were very literal, and they seemed to tell a war story," said Molly taking another sip of the rather strong coffee. "But what surprised me the most were the stars on the ceiling. They were in an odd configuration. I couldn't recognize any of the constellations."

Naomi was quiet for a long time. "Do you realize you may have stumbled upon the greatest Mayan discovery of the 20th century? From what you describe, this chamber could hold the key to understanding the lost Mayan language; we still cannot read many of the Mayan glyphs. If these illustrations are as literal as you say, this chamber could be a Mayan *Rosetta stone.* It needs to be studied and protected."

"What about the odd buildings on the walls? What about the sky on the ceiling?"

"Who knows? Perhaps the whole structure was an art gallery, and you saw the fruits of one man's imagination. There could be more rooms inside the structure with many more such designs. There is much we still do not know about my people."

"Oh yes, Adriana mentioned you were a direct descendant of the Maya and somewhat of an authority on the subject. You must have many stories. What can you tell me about their interest in astronomy? It was probably just a coincidence, but I saw something in that sky that unnerved me. Did they ever mention a crown shaped constellation before? A crown with a jewel in its center?"

"A crown?" Naomi thought for a moment. "I don't know. The Maya obsessed about knowing the future; they studied the heavens for clues. In doing so, they advanced in astronomy, mathematics, and other sciences. They were also obsessed with time. Even now, the Mayan calendar is the most accurate calendar we know of. In fact, there's one hanging on my wall over there."

Naomi pointed to a circular disk hanging over the stove. Blockish glyphs circled a figure in the middle that was bent under a heavy load.

"The fellow in the middle represents one of the deified carriers of the calendar in the procession of an age. The transition from age to age moves humanity from one stage of growth to the next. We have completed the fifth and sixth ages, which were a period of about 20 years. The sixth age supposed started in 2012. Surely, you remember all the talk about the Mayan calendar predicting the end of the world?"

Molly had of course heard the foreboding rumors, but not taken any of it seriously. People were always predicting the end of the world. Revelation, Nostradamus, and Edward Cayce, were just a few of the sources people commonly cited. She considered the Mayan calendar as simply the latest in a long list of false alarms.

"Sure, but you can't seriously believe any of that, can you? I mean, nothing happened."

"Well, I don't think of it the same way as the media, but I believe it did happen," said Naomi a little tersely. "Oh course, it wasn't Armageddon. The world didn't come to an end, but it's a time of great change. We call this time a *K'atun,* a time without time. It's a time of truth, reflection, and change, a crucible test where we will find out what we as a race are capable of and what we can become.

"Already, we are seeing significant changes in the environment, economics, society, and religion. People are changing in ways unprecedented in human history. Some of the changes are slight, but some are profound. Whether we believe it or not, we are changing. The change is not something to be feared, except by those afraid of change."

Naomi leaned forward conspiratorially, a twinkle in her green eyes, "My people believe some will develop talents beyond all comprehension in preparation for the new age. The human race will be bestowed with amazing gifts; we will evolve to a higher level."

Ok, thought Molly. *This is where I get off.* The conversation was getting a bit too weird. Naomi obviously believed all this, which meant she was either crazy, or heading in that general direction.

She looked at the titles of the books on the shelves around them. Most were about Mayan legends. On more than one she saw the name "Naum Cohuo" printed on the spine below the title. Most were large, encyclopedic references; some were parts of larger sets. This woman was a published and highly proliferate author.

Naomi followed her gaze and noticed Molly's obvious surprise. "Ms. Arden, we are very much the same; we both have a love of writing. However, I have never dabbled in fiction. I have dedicated my life to the study of the Maya. These books are my life's work and my people's history."

Molly remembered her first impressions of this little town and felt sorry for judging it to be inadequate in some ways. These people were pioneers, not refugees. They were scraping out a living by taking advantage of the one natural resource they had to work with—the natural beauty and history of Costa Maya. She reminded herself never again to judge a book by its cover.

"I'm somewhat of a respected authority on the Maya. As such, we travel extensively, mostly in the Yucatan. Adriana goes with me and to help with my research."

"She certainly knows a lot about Chaccoben."

"She should," laughed Naomi. "She was born there! Before Chaccoben became an official archeological site, it was farmland. Everyone knew about the ancient city and the mounds, but no one had any interest in spending money to dig it out. Adriana and her family lived on the property and loved it. She was born in a small farmhouse, not far from where you had your accident. She's never been happy about her family having to sell everything to the government."

"Do you really think the room I found is that important?"

"Extremely. If I were younger, I would go there right now and sneak under the fence. Chaccoben was one of the last cities standing. That room could shed some light on what happened to the Maya. No one knows all the reasons why the Maya disappeared, but warfare played a crucial role. In the end, war stopped being about conquest, and became campaigns for total annihilation.

"They conquered and destroyed the cities, hunted down and murdered the people, and even poisoned their sources of water. The marauding armies then moved to other cities, repeating the holocaust. That scene you saw could describe one of the last great battles."

"But what about the stars? How do they fit into all this? I know it sounds weird, but that crown looked exactly like a constellation I just described in my new book. It was exactly as I imagined it, down to the jewel in its center. I'd swear I'd never seen it before today."

Naomi thought for a moment, and then pulled out one of her books. She flipped back and forth through the pages. "No, it's not in this one. Maybe this…" she put the book down and pulled out another. "No, not there either. Let's try this," she pulled out a small, tattered book that looked like the spine was hand woven.

"This is a collection of stories my grandmother passed down to me. It has been in the Cohuo family for many, many generations. Eventually, I will pass it on to Adriana, and she will add to it the stories she has been told."

She carefully opened the book and began looking through the pages. There were hand drawn sketches everywhere. The book was more like a haphazard scrapbook, compared to the precise and professionally bound works Naomi had published.

"These legends may or may not be true, and none of them can be verified, which is why many of them are not in the mainstream history of the Maya. Many Maya families still live in the Yucatan highlands and Belize. Most have books like these. Finding the same story or even a slight variation in those books lends validity to the authenticity of the tales. I have spent much time convincing them to share their stories with me."

"Why wouldn't they share them with you? You are Mayan too, aren't you?" Molly had no idea that there were still entire communities of Maya living in the Yucatan.

"Most Maya live under an unsympathetic government that wouldn't hesitate to pull their reservations right out from under them. They've been fighting to save their way of life since the invasion of the Spanish nearly five-hundred years ago. I am afraid they are not doing very well, and most live in poverty. Understandably, they are very protective of their customs and traditions."

Naomi, turned to a page in the book covered with odd symbols. "Ah! I think I have it."

"What is it?"

"Well, it's silly really. There is an old legend in my family that my grandmother told me, which until now I had quite forgotten. It is a detail concerning Hanub Ku and the four-world myth. Have you heard of this?"

Molly shook her head. "I'm afraid I don't know much about Mayan history other than the things I've learned today. This is my first time here."

"Well, it is an obscure myth. To put it simply, Hanub Ku is the creator of all things, even our gods. The legend says that he populated the Earth with people from other planets that had become uninhabitable or destroyed. At regular intervals, cataclysmic events forced Hanub Ku to remake the world, each time taking humanity to a higher level.

"According to this legend, we are currently in the third age, with the fourth to come after this K'atun. These ages are longer, but correspond somewhat to the ones outlined in the Mayan calendar."

This sounded more like a modern science fiction story than a three-thousand year-old myth. Molly smiled at the memory of her dad watching his favorite late night sci-fi movies. Apparently, the idea of aliens and space travel was thousands of years old.

"In many of our carvings, some beings have little star constellations carved above their heads. This helped describe what race they were and from where they came. Most of these carvings depicted the Pleiades or Sirius constellations, but some were completely unknown. I believe your crown constellation may have been one of them. Look here. Is this it?" she showed her the book.

Molly looked at the illustration in the book, and her heart skipped a beat. There was the seven star crown with the jewel in the center above the drawing of a man with a spear. She was getting excited. This was getting stranger by the moment. She nodded in amazement.

"I remember my grandmother telling me a story about these people; they called themselves the Dzolob. They came to Earth from outside our world during the second age and oppressed the Maya. They called them the offenders because they desecrated many of our traditions and started the practice of blood sacrifice to reach the gods.

"The second deluge destroyed most of the Dzolob but Hanub Ku had protected the Maya. They were able to force the remaining Dzolob back to from where they had come."

"The ancient carvings have represented the Dzolob using the constellation Sirius and a few others, one of which was your seven-star crown.

"Very little is known about the race, but they were jealous of Hanub Ku's attention to the Maya. A more modern legend even states that they arrived hurtling asteroids from space into the Mayan cities of Lemuria and Atlantis, sinking the two continents."

"Atlantis was Mayan?" asked Molly with surprise.

"Well, some believe so. There is evidence in our texts to suggest Mayan influence at least. In our early history, the Maya considered themselves the whole of mankind—Hanub Ku's chosen people. This close relationship with the supreme deity is what the Dzolob craved, and they were willing to do anything to get it, including blood sacrifice."

"So, they were trying to impress this Hanub Ku so he would give them what...power?" asked Molly, trying hard to understand this.

"Hanub Ku is power, but without form. He is the only god without a description; he is known only by this symbol." Naomi pointed to a rug hanging on the wall with an intricate pattern in its center. It looked a lot like a spiral galaxy.

"Hanub Ku is more of a concept than a god, a concept of unity, balance, and truth, like the yin and the yang. The embodiment of our gods was only one of his various aspects. Hanub Ku's heart and mind are the center of the universe and by gazing upon this concept one can transcend the barriers of perception and time, creating gateways to other worlds. This is what Dzolob priests tried to achieve in many horrible and murderous ways."

"Did they succeed? Were they able to travel to other worlds?"

"The carvings you described may provide a clue. We do not know where the Dzolob came from or how they got here. But they did have the ability to travel here from outside our world, so that spoke of some success with their methods."

Molly looked out the window and noticed it was already dark outside. Her stomach rumbled letting her know her dinner was overdue. *How much of this poor woman's time had she taken up today, and what had happened to Juan?*

"I'm sorry, Naomi. I did not realize how late it was. I should probably be getting back to my hotel. I never meant to..."

Naomi touched Molly's hand. "Ms. Arden, we were obviously meant to meet today. Whether you believe it or not, you are now part of Hanub Ku's plan for his people, and I am grateful that I am playing a part as well. Things are going to start moving quickly, so you should be prepared. There is more to you than you realize. I want to give you a phone number."

She reached into her apron and pulled out a small pad of paper that had a small pencil tucked away in the coil of wire at the top. After writing down a number, she handed Molly a folded piece of paper.

"If your story takes on any other unexpected coincidences I want you to call this number. They may be able to help."

Molly took the number from her quizzically. "Who are they?"

"Last week I spoke with a man who was doing research in the area. I am often consulted about the local history. We spoke at some length about Chaccoben, but what struck me most about the man was his accent."

"Was he an American, like me?"

"No, quite the opposite. I think he was from somewhere in the northern Yucatan. He had a charming voice. I enjoyed my conversation with him. His friends, however, were a different story."

"What do you mean?"

"He had a few men with him. He said they were his expedition team. They were rude, impatient, and unpleasant. I just assumed they were just hired hands, but he said they were all volunteers doing work for a historical society. They also ate all of my oranges."

"What were they looking for?"

"Mostly, for details concerning the temple complexes. Apparently, I did not have what they wanted. In some respects, they knew more than I did, which was surprising. Before they left, he gave me a phone number and said to call if there were any more significant discoveries in Chaccoben.

"Look, this may all be just a big coincidence, but if you keep having these experiences they might be able to help. Be careful though; you do not want to waste these people's time."

Molly thanked her. Just then, Juan and Adriana walked in from the other room.

"What have you two been talking about?" asked Juan. "I don't know many things that can keep Naum from her *telenovas*."

"Adriana can catch me up on the soaps," said Naomi. "That's what you two have been doing, right—just watching television?"

Adriana blushed. Juan looked at the floor and studied it as if it were the most interesting thing he had ever seen.

Molly cut the awkward silence. "So Juan, your dad must be wondering where we've gotten off. I am sorry I have kept you out so late. We have been here for hours. Are you ready to go?"

"Ready when you are, Ms. Arden," said Juan.

Juan gave Adriana a hug and a peck on the cheek as she put away the groceries that were still on the table.

Adriana offered Molly a few bananas and whispered, "Thank you for coming. Juan rarely stays so long. Please come back soon."

She smiled and thanked her for the snack.

During the drive back to Xcalak, her stomach rumbled. It had been a long day, and she had missed dinner. She peeled a banana but was too tired to finish it.

She did not have much sleep the previous night, and it was catching up with her. As the truck rumbled along into the Mexican moonlight, she drifted off into a deep and welcome sleep.

Chapter 11, A Fire in the Sky

"Order! Order!" shouted the mayor over the noisy crowd in the town hall. Irate colonists had packed the sweltering hall this morning. To make things worse, half of the slow-turning, cast iron ceiling fans were not moving at all. A long, ribbon-like driving belt snaked through the fans, squealing loudly against the recalcitrant hubs of the spinning blades before returning to the electric motor outside. With so many people in the cramped room, the heat was getting unbearable.

Mayor Stanton lowered the gavel and wiped the sweat from his brow. He began fanning himself with the papers on the podium in front of him. The ceiling fans above creaked and whirred all too slowly. The colonists were angry, and the heat was not helping.

Being mayor was not always easy, but he had a job to do and did not let things like simple discomfort distract his attention from the important issues. There had been two near deaths in the town last night during the outage. A family had inadvertently left the seals on their windows open as they slept. Sadly, one of the victims was a child, and the other was her mother.

Doctor Panavi treated them in their home after other family members had discovered them in the morning. It was doubtful if they would recover. If they died, they would be the first deaths due to the windstorms in over ten years—all because of the infernal generators.

Power outages had plagued the town because their thermopile generators were the oldest on the planet. The electric generators took advantage of the dramatic temperature shifts the planet went through every day and night. With no moving parts, the towering thermoelectric piles normally provided a steady, reliable flow of current created by the wide temperature differential.

However, the constant heating and freezing eventually cracked the copper alloy fins and they needed replacing. Several of the twenty-four, two-storey piles were no longer functioning at all. Moreover, the additional load placed on the remaining piles accelerated corrosion in the plate junctions, substantially reducing their efficiency.

The Town Power Authority had cobbled together parts from the broken piles to keep the others running. Power rationing policies had been in place for years, but what the town needed were new generators. Only the mayor and the TPA knew the full extent of the problems, but they could do nothing because of the lack of supplies.

"How many of us need to die before they send us new generators?" yelled Elmer Norris, the town plumber, and neighbor of the recently stricken family. He was met with shouts of agreement from the rowdy crowd.

"And where is the last ether probe? It's a week overdue. Where is our shipment of parts and supplies?" asked Elspeth Dodds, a general store keeper. "The last probe returned with barely enough parts to fix one of the piles. When can we expect Archænis to take our complaints seriously? Surely, now they will see…"

"Please, Ms. Dodds, we are doing everything we can to resolve the problem. In addition, what has happened to the Kavanaughs is tragic. We will send an ether probe to the home world this afternoon," said Mayor Stanton. "Maybe now they will prioritize our power array situation."

"That will take months! Launch the HMS Calliope *now*. Send a real person to Archænis, and have them bring back what we need. We can't live like this any longer."

More shouts of agreement.

"Yes! Launch the Calliope."

"Put it to a vote!"

That was ridiculous, thought the mayor. The Calliope had not been in space for nearly thirty-five years. Each colony supposedly maintained their ether ships as emergency lifeboats, in case anything disastrous happened. However, the colonies had grown so much, that the provision became outdated and unrealistic. The Calliope was more of storage silo than ship at this point. Also, the volunteers maintaining her were far from experienced ethernauts.

Captain Forrestal was well into his eighties by now, and he would be in no condition to operate the gigantic ether ship. They would also have to assemble and train a new crew, which would take even more time.

The other four council members were nervously talking amongst themselves behind the podium, considering the idea.

"I don't see how we could send the Calliope; we can't afford the provisions," said a pretty woman with long blond hair.

"Mrs. Farlow, that is the least of the problems we face," said Quinn Mandic, the town engineer. "It will take some effort to get the Leviton chamber working again; we have already scavenged much of it. However, I might be able to work out something. Perhaps a ship should be sent."

"Professor Almos, what is your opinion on launching the Calliope? Should we be doing this or not?" asked George Hastings, a rotund councilman who did not look particularly happy. He was sweating profusely, creating small puddles on the table in front of him. Apparently, he had invited his shirt to breakfast that morning, and it had gotten most of it in his rush.

"Leaving Philolaus will not solve anything, Mr. Hastings," argued the professor. "It would take weeks, and there's no guarantee of supplies from Archænis. Also, a surprise emergency visit by one of our ether ships would send the wrong message. We do not want to give them the impression that we cannot handle things on our own. No one wants to see martial law imposed here."

Impressed, Edington watched the old man quickly taking control of the situation. No one, not even the mayor, opposed him. In many ways, Almos led the council and the mayor was just a figurehead. Mayor Stanton of course knew this, but had enough sense not to admit it. Putting Almos in the town council helped spread the blame if things went pear shaped.

Edington was near the back of the room with his friend Ayden. He wished he could tell Ayden that there would be no more support from Archænis and that they truly were on their own. All this talk about sending for help was so much wasted air.

Almos continued, "I suggest we contact the other colonies over the telegraph and repeat our request for aid. I know they are also strapped for resources and have already given us as much as possible. However, if we run a complete inventory of all the disabled generators in the colonies we may be able to make a planet-wide catalog of reusable parts. This would benefit everyone, not just the town of Parifeldie. I have already spoken with the TPA concerning this, and they are working on the details. We should form an inventory committee to expedite the process. This is something we can do now."

"Professor Almos has moved for the creation of a TPA inventory committee. Is there a second?" asked the mayor.

Someone quickly seconded the motion, and it passed.

There was still a lot of grumbling but most of the crowd dispersed, making the room significantly less crowded.

He is trying to make us more self-sufficient because he knows there is no more aid coming, thought Edington.

However, he knew that no amount of ingenuity and recycling would sustain them forever. Copper, brass, and other metals were exceedingly difficult to come by, and the colonies would collapse without help or some other dramatic change in their predicament.

"It's almost lunch time," said Ayden glancing at his pocket watch. "You want to go to the pub? It looks as if things are quieting down here."

"Sure," said Edington, turning to leave.

"Excuse me, Mr. Edington, but could you take the podium for a moment, please?" asked the mayor, noticing him by the door. "I read the observatory's figures you posted this morning and wanted to ask you a few questions."

"Yes sir," said Edington, wishing he could have avoided this. He took a seat next to the others. Almos gave him a nod.

"Your numbers this morning show a significant decrease in the anomaly's size. However, other observations across the planet are reporting an alternative view; most seem to think it is still growing. I have discussed this with Professor Almos, and although he agrees with your recent findings, I don't quite understand his reasoning. Could you shed some light for us on this new development?" The mayor took a seat and offered him the podium.

Edington took a nervous glance at Almos. He got up, took his place and cleared his throat.

"Yes sir, um, of course," he wasn't anywhere near as skilled as Almos in public speaking, and would have preferred to be anywhere else at this point. He was sweating now, but not because of the heat.

"Well, um, the last cosmic readings are more current. I took them this morning right before the windstorm," murmuring began at the mention of the storm. "Additionally, I was able to take very accurate size and distance readings since the town lights were out. The sky was exceptionally clear. I got a clear fix on the anomaly. From what I can tell, it is much smaller than we imagined. Atmospheric haze was contributing to previous measurements, which made the edges less defined."

"So you are saying the previous numbers have had it a size or two larger. That doesn't mean it's still not growing, does it?" inquired Mr. Quinn.

"Um, not exactly sir. I is definitely *not* growing, because…um…" stumbled Edington.

"Because of the red-shift dilation measurements," added Almos, coming to his rescue.

"Yes, right," said Edington with relief. "We measure the light coming from the stars, and it tells us the speed the direction the stars are moving. I was able to get a very accurate fix on this last night, and it is hardly moving at all."

In actuality, he had spent so much time looking at the pretty nebula in the strange hourglass constellation that he did not have time to take any spectrometer readings that night. Also, the photographic plates used in the process would require more than a few hours to develop and be scrutinized. He hoped no one here knew that. He cursed Almos for making him lie in front of all these people.

"Who cares about some ridiculous cloud in the sky?" asked Mr. Hastings. "What we need to focus on is getting the power situation remedied."

"Yes, Mayor, can we work on getting the TPA committee underway?" asked Mrs. Farlow.

The mayor looked curiously at Edington for a moment, then at Almos. He seemed to be about to say something, and then changed his mind.

Sighing, he agreed. "Very well. The developments in the anomaly can wait for now. You may go, Mr. Edington. Thank you for your *interesting* testimony."

Stepping down, he made his way through the room to Ayden. He hated to do what he just did. He was not used to lying in such an outrageous fashion.

Almos owes me big for this, he thought grimly. *My reputation is on the line. They are going to run me out if they ever learn that I falsified the numbers.*

"Come on, Mister Edington," said Ayden with a grin. "Let's nip off for a pint. You look like death warmed over. Did you get any sleep last night?"

He had told Ayden about almost being caught in the storm, but not about his conversation with Almos. Knowing the truth about the anomaly was a heavy burden. He wished he could have been like the others, innocently oblivious to the imminent danger.

"I got a little sleep, but not much. I was busy putting this morning's report together. Normally the morning shift does it, but Almos had me do it personally."

"You certainly have changed your tune about it," said Ayden. "I'm not complaining of course. That thing in the sky puts the willies up me. I was just surprised by the change, is all."

They walked down Edgar street to the little town pub which also served as a popular lunchtime hangout. Edington wiped the back of his neck; it was incredibly hot today.

They found the crowded bar much cooler inside. At the bar, they ordered a light lunch and a few beers and took a seat near the sturdy wooden window. They drained the mugs before they hit the table.

"Do you think Almos's idea for an inventory committee will do any good?" asked Ayden.

"I do not see what choice we have. I do not think the Calliope is in any shape to fly, and I doubt Archænis will be very sympathetic. That was kind of the idea for sending colonists here. Philolaus is an untapped planet, supposedly burgeoning with new resources. They expect us to be helping them by now, not the other way around," said Edington. "No one expected the planet to be so stingy with her valuables."

"Look, you know my dad. He's a good bloke. He can tell you first-hand how difficult mining is here. Beside the fact any decent amount of metal ore is down there in the bleeding jungle, it's also very deep, and straight down. These outcroppings we live on are solid basalt, and you can't make much out of basalt," said Ayden.

A bar attendant brought them their orders and two more pints of beer.

Edington wolfed his food down. He had not realized how hungry he was. Being up all night, he had worked up an appetite. He also had not eaten breakfast, unless he counted Almos's coffee as a meal, which it nearly was.

"*Blimey, Sam!* What's the rush? The food here isn't that good!" said Ayden, suspiciously eying a piece of barley cake, and then popping it into his mouth.

He barely heard him as he stared out of the window. People were running in the streets. Distantly, he thought he heard children crying.

"What the blazes in going on out there?" asked Ayden, speaking through a mouth full of food.

Edington shrugged his shoulders. "Well, we did have a big windstorm last night; maybe another octo got loose and is wreaking havoc."

Octopods were the only large indigenous animal life on the planet. About the size of a small child, they normally lived in the jungles below, in the upper leafy branches of the tall, broccoli-like trees.

Covered in a light fur, each of an octo's eight arms had several round patches, which contained thousands of tiny hooks that would stick to almost any surface. They could climb anything, including the near vertical cliff faces. Not terribly intelligent, but extremely curious creatures, they presented themselves to the colonists soon after their arrival. They were harmless enough, and made decent pets, as long as they were kept away from the vapors.

"Too right, mate. You remember our Juni?" asked Ayden. Then, not seeing recognition on Edington's face, he continued, "C'mon, sure ya do. We must have been about six or eight at the time. That octo took your hat and put it high up on top of the grain silo. You cried for hours until the wind finally blew it down. You and Juni never got along much."

"Right. Now I remember. What ever happened to that scamp?" asked Edington.

"She was getting old, and we had to leave her outside most of the time in the backyard because she was acting funny. Once, we forgot to bring her in during a windstorm, and she got caught in it. I must have been twelve or so."

Living high in the treetops, octopods protected themselves from the dangerous vapors. However, they ran to higher ground during windstorms. In a mad frenzy, they would scale the cliffs and invade the colonies, lashing and thrashing, making piercing squeals. To keep the animals out, the colonists had constructed a strong perimeter fence, and this worked most of the time.

"What happened to her?" asked Edington finishing off the last of his chips.

"Well, in the morning, we found the garden destroyed, and half the backyard fence ripped out. My dad and I followed her trail. We found her all right. She was dead, lying in a ditch. We buried her later that day. She was gonna die soon anyway, she was very old. But I hated to see her go that way," said Ayden, drowning the sad memory with his beer.

Looking closer at the mayhem outside, Edington noticed some of the people were open mouthed, staring at the eastern horizon. Because of his vantage point, he could not see what everyone was looking at.

Then, someone outside screamed. More people began running. People in the pub were crowding the window now, trying to see what was going on. They looked panicked, like frightened animals.

Suddenly, a siren rang out. But it wasn't the usual series of warning blasts telling the people of Parifeldie to take cover and seal themselves in their homes.

This siren had never been used except for the occasional drill, which Edington was sure had not been scheduled. This siren called for immediate evacuation of the entire planet!

"Bloody hell!" shouted Ayden, jumping up, nearly knocking over the table.

The shocked patrons crowded the door, everyone trying to get out at once.

"Nobody panic. There's no need to…please, don't! *Oi you*, Put that down!" said the barman trying to keep someone from throwing a heavy chair through the window. He was too late. The window smashed apart. The chair and most of the glass ended up on the ground outside.

"Right, you daft bastard. You're gonna pay for that," said the barman pushing up his sleeves, and coming out from behind the bar. Suddenly, the siren blasted again, and everyone went wild trying to get out of the pub.

Stunned at the speed things were happening, Edington pushed his slim body through the door, which panicked patrons had jam-packed.

He turned to see if Ayden had made it. Ayden was busy helping people through the busted window, which was now an exit. Apparently, he had been the one who had thrown the chair. He was now helping the barman over the sill. He didn't exactly look grateful, but he accepted the assistance.

"Come on, Ayden! We've got to get to the ship!" shouted Edington, joining the mob of rushing people in the street.

"But I thought…you said…it's not…functional," panted Ayden, catching up to him.

"Dunno. Maybe the mayor will tell us what to do when we get there. It's the designated grouping area anyhow," said Edington still running.

He turned to see what they were running from. Glancing over his shoulder as he ran, he saw something that stopped him in his tracks. Ayden collided with him, and they fell together in a heap.

"*Crikey!* What did you do that for?" exclaimed Ayden angrily, pushing Edington off him. Then his mouth dropped open as he saw where his friend was staring. "*Cor*…what is that? What does it mean, Sam?"

Edington was at a lost and said nothing, for coming up over the eastern horizon was a *second* sun, as big, bright, and hot as the one above it.

"You've got a fever," said Juan, moving his hand back to the steering wheel.

"Uhhh...what?" mumbled Molly, groggy with sleep and feeling very confused.

Why was she so hot? She could feel her shirt sticking to her back. *It's hot because of the two suns. No, wait. What two suns?* They must have been in the dream she just woken up from. She tried to remember more about the dream before it receded entirely into the shadows of her waking thoughts.

Suddenly, the last few moments of it rushed back with vivid clarity. She felt the fear of the colonists rushing to their ship. Her heart was pounding in her chest, in time with Edington's as he saw the huge yellow ball of fire rise into the sky.

"Oh my God. They're all going to die!" she exclaimed, sitting up quickly, and almost passing out from dizziness.

Juan nearly skidded off the road. "Whoa! Ms. Arden! Are you ok?"

Molly looked nervously at the night sky, which was full of stars with a full moon on the horizon. She took a quick reality check. *Ok, I am in Costa Maya, on vacation. I'm in the truck, on the way back to the hotel after having a very strange day.* Her head ached.

The only problem was that her mind didn't believe it. Molly's eyes kept returning to the sky, expecting to see something else up there. *What? Two moons? No, two suns. Yes, that was it, two suns. That's why it was so hot. Why else would she be sweating?*

All of a sudden, she felt sleepy again, and had to fight to stay awake and keep her eyes open. She lost the fight, as the dream came back to her, the swinging sign over the town pub, the creaking fans in the town hall, Ayden's pet octopod, the blast of the alarm siren.

A decidedly shocked looking boy was staring at her with wide-open eyes. He had pulled the truck over and was shaking her. "Ms. Arden? Ms. Arden? Can you hear me?"

"Uhhh huh," she said slowly, "Juan?"

"Yes, it's me! You have a high fever, and you were staring into space and mumbling. I'm sorry, but I was getting worried. I've been trying to wake you for five minutes! You need to see a doctor," he said with obvious concern.

Five minutes? A fever? She had a fever? That must be why she felt so hot. The dream must have incorporated the fever into the story as she slept. But somehow it felt more like the other way around. The dream was so real, so vivid. She had dreams often of her worlds and characters, but nothing like this. It was as if she were there, running alongside them, feeling what they felt.

"Thank you Juan, but I think I'm okay. How long have I been out?"

"Well, you talked in your sleep about half an hour ago, and then you got agitated. I could feel the heat coming off you. You were burning up, so I tried to wake you. You shouted something, and I nearly ran us into the ditch.

"When I pulled over, your eyes were open, but you were not seeing me. I didn't know what to do, so I shook you. You need to go to the hospital."

Molly held her head in her hands. *Was she going crazy? What was this all about?* She was way too involved with this story and what was happening in it. Sure, many books could bring her to tears, but this was a story of her own making. Like tickling yourself, it was rare to be so emotionally moved by something that was your own.

Maybe the stress of the past few months was getting to her. Fantasy and reality were getting difficult to separate. A visit to the hospital might not be such a bad idea.

"Ms. Arden, I'm sorry, but you yelled something when I woke you. Who is going to die?" asked Juan nervously.

Wiping her face, she felt a little more like herself. The tears had taken away most of the fear she had felt in the dream. Being reminded of her waking outburst embarrassed her.

"I'm sorry. I was just dreaming, Juan. Sometimes I dream about the characters in my books. This one was more like a nightmare though. I'd prefer not to talk about it."

Juan looked relieved. "For a moment there, I thought something had possessed you or something," Juan reached out and touched her forehead. "That's strange. I think you've already broken your fever, you are much cooler now. How do you feel now?"

How did she feel? That was a difficult question to answer. It was as if her emotions were on a roller coaster ride. Her head felt as if it had been through a garlic press.

"I've got a bit of a headache, but I'm okay. I don't think we need to go to a hospital. I have some aspirin in my bag. I must have caught a local bug or something. It will probably go away in a day or so."

"Yeah, that happens a lot to tourists here. Didn't anyone tell you not to drink the water?" he asked with a smile.

She felt this had nothing to do with being sick. But there was no sense worrying Juan about something she didn't understand herself.

"We're only a few miles from the hotel anyway, Ms. Arden. You sure you don't want to see a doctor? I know someone who is a nurse at the hospital in Leone who lives in the village," asked Juan, concerned.

"No, like you said, the fever is going away on its own. I feel fine now. Really," said Molly, who of course did not feel fine at all.

"Ok, you're the boss," said Juan, starting the truck and pulling back onto the highway. "Just let me know if you change your mind."

Rumbling along the long dark highway, they continued back to the hotel.

[PART II]

Chapter 12, SOTAR

Ananmaya took a glance at the little man with whom he would spend the next eight hours. Changing the man's seating arrangement was an easy trick, but the practical joke had backfired. He sat back, closed his eyes, and pretended to take a nap.

Ananmaya's gift gave him access to the molecular structure of anything he touched. He often read books without ever opening them. Finding this man's boarding pass and changing the position of a few million ink molecules had been an easy task.

Bhuvanesh had always warned against abuse of the gift. His time with his mentor had instilled in him a strong moral code, which he tried his best to live by. He gave people their privacy, and never looked deeper than what a normal person would see.

Bhuvanesh might have understood why he had to do what he did at the bank, but he would be scowling at what he did with this man's boarding pass. Abuse of power was a slippery slope. Once you started, it got easier and easier to do. He needed to have better restraint. He closed his eyes and tried to relax.

"Are they going to feed us or what on this flight?" sputtered the angry little man. "Where's that stewardess?" He hammered the attendant button.

The pretty stewardess arrived a few moments later with a smile. "Yes sir, may I help you?"

"Look, we're in the air now. Can you radio the airport or something and please correct this intolerable seating arrangement? I paid for a first-class ticket. I do not intend to spend my flight riding back here. You might as well put me in with the luggage," said the man.

The stewardess smiled and continued. "Sir, we discussed this already. Your boarding pass is not coded for first class. If there is a problem with your ticket, you may inquire at customer service, when we arrive in Miami. I'm sure if an error was made, they will refund your first class passage."

The little man glowered at her and fumed, "If you are not going handle this, I will."

He took the air phone out of its socket in the rear of the seat in front of him. He fumbled for his credit card.

"I'm sorry sir, but the air phones are not working right now. For some reason, they stopped working shortly after takeoff," said the stewardess.

The man's face went red and he unbuckled his seat belt. "I want to talk to the captain," he demanded, getting out of his seat.

The stewardess continued her relentless smiling. "Please return to your seat, sir. The captain has not turned off the REMAIN SEATED sign yet. And I'm sorry, but you can't speak to the captain, it is against regulations. I will however, relay to him your complaints. Now, please return to your seat."

The man's anger seemed not to recede so much as to burn itself out. He slumped back into his seat with a scowl on his face. "Can I at least get some dinner?"

"Yes sir, we will server your in-flight meal in about an hour. Would you like some peanuts in the meantime?" asked the smiling attendant.

He simply glared at her and did not say anything.

The stewardess turned and walked back up the aisle, completely unfazed. Ananmaya thought she was handling the man with a bureaucratic professionalism that she seemed to enjoy.

Although he had nothing to do with it, he smiled that the air phones were not working. This man was not used to not getting his way. Maybe the joke would teach him a lesson in humility.

Then again, maybe not, he thought, noticing the man busily trying to make his cell phone work.

"I don't think that is going to work at 30,000 feet," said Ananmaya.

"*Mercda,*" muttered the man under his breath, putting the phone back in his pocket. "Yes, I know. It was a ridiculous attempt. Look at this boarding pass! Do you see a seat 'Z' on this plane?"

"No, there's obviously been a mistake," said Ananmaya, glancing at the stub.

"My point exactly," said the man. "What I can't understand is how it got there. I know I purchased a first-class ticket. I was in seat *4B*. I saw it myself."

"It's definitely unusual," agreed Ananmaya. "They should give you the benefit of the doubt. It is very unfair."

"Yes. Quite correct! I'll have that woman's job before this is over. She doesn't know who she is dealing with," said the man. "I apologize. I have not introduced myself. My name is Pinotti," he said, holding out his hand.

"Ananmaya," he returned, shaking his hand. Something about the man's name rang a few warning bells in the back of his head. Where had he heard that name?

"I'm the assistant director at the Observatório Nacional. I'm on my way to New York on urgent business for the director, Dr. Mariconi. We have had an interesting last few days, and he has sent me to tie up a few loose ends," he said with obvious self-importance.

Ananmaya went pale and sank back into his seat. Ganesh obviously was a comedian. Now he knew where he knew that name. What were the chances that one of the men he had just stolen from would be seated next to him? Worse, it seemed as if they knew where he was going, although apparently, they did not know who he was.

Unbelievably, the stolen artifact was now less than three feet above the man's head in the overhead compartment. This must be the universe's way of punishing him for altering the man's boarding pass.

"Hey, are you feeling okay? You are looking a little pale," observed Pinotti.

"Um, yes, I'm fine. Just a little air sick I guess," said Ananmaya. He picked out a magazine and pretended to read it.

This misadventure had gone too far. The plan had been simple. He was supposed to have quietly broken into the bank, taken the artifact, and left the empty safe-deposit box behind. No one ever checked its contents, so no one would discover the missing artifact for some time. Because of sloppy timing, he had nearly been caught and advertised to the world his unique abilities.

In all his travels, Bhuvanesh had only found one person exceptionally gifted enough to become his student. Now, that person was hiding behind a magazine, in an airplane at 30,000 feet, feeling exceptionally stupid. He began to wish Bhuvanesh had never told him about shifters and Einstein's secret society.

Bhuvanesh said that the gift was a rarity. Few had it and even fewer knew how to use it. In all of history, only two or three times in a generation would someone be born with the gift.

Recently however, it was showing up in more and more people. It was also changing and manifesting itself in different ways. Abilities ranged from the mundane to the extraordinary. The extraordinary is what Bhuvanesh had looked for.

Because of their abilities, shifters had blazed brightly in human history. You would know them by their brilliant insights into science and the arts. Da Vinci, Newton, Copernicus, and in more recent times, Tesla and Einstein were all undoubtedly shifters.

Of course, there were also abusers of the gift who used it to manipulate others to gain power. Ghengis Khan,

Alexander the Great, Napolean, and Hitler were all aided by their shifter gifts.

This information had amazed young Ananmaya. Hitler? Tesla and Einstein? They were like him? How could this be? To be a part of such an infamous group of people did not seem possible. Bhuvanesh had presented a long list of famous names, which he easily recognized. But the one that fascinated him the most was Einstein.

"Einstein was a shifter, like me?" Ananmaya had asked.

"Quite. Except, he was not so prone to distraction," said Bhuvanesh trying to get the day's calculus lesson back on track.

"You're not implying that you actually knew him, are you?" asked Ananmaya.

"Of course I did. We spoke at length. Near the end of his life, we discussed his concern that he would leave *the Society* with no one at the helm. He had been looking for someone with a strong moral compass. At the time, I had to decline the offer. He was a great man, but a terrible judge of character," said Bhuvanesh.

"What society? What do you mean?" asked Ananmaya.

"I had hoped not to bring up *the Society* until you were older; however, I suppose now is as good a time as any," said Bhuvanesh. "I was once part of a secret shifter society known as *SOTAR*, the Society of Theosophy and Research.

"This secret group of very well connected individuals provides shifters with much needed guidance and resources. They found me, and taught me much of what I know."

"What did Einstein have to do with this?" asked Ananmaya.

Bhuvanesh sighed; he had hoped to keep this short.

"I see the lesson for today has been derailed yet again. Honestly, I do not know what is worse, your ability to change the subject, or my willingness to allow it to happen. Yes, Einstein and Nikola Tesla were the founders of the group." He adjusted his seating position and continued.

"Einstein was one of the world's most impressive shifters. At an early age, he realized what he could do, and being intensely curious, he dived deeply into studying the microverse around him. By dissecting matter at more and more fundamental levels, he slowly began to understand the fundamental rules governing matter and energy. This led to his legendary energy to mass equation, and to many other insights concerning gravity, matter, and light.

"He was well aware that his abilities could be abused. He often spoke of how he regretted releasing the secrets of the atom, only to find them used in the making of atom bombs, which killed thousands.

"With the *Pandora's Box* of atomic energy now open, shifters were probably the only hope we had to avoid destroying ourselves. Einstein wanted to provide that future shifters would understand the key role they would play in the future of mankind.

"Understanding the fundamentals of the universe obsessed Einstein. This included an understanding of the gift itself. His powers mystified him. Why these extraordinary abilities given only to a select few? Where did they come from? He began procuring as many records as he could about shifter history. Apparently, someone had attempted this before.

"Almost two hundred years before the birth of Einstein, a shifter astronomer named Christopher Wren helped to form the *Royal Society of London* in an effort to secretly attract people like himself. He had also seen the need to organize shifters. Unfortunately, not many gifted individuals appeared in the years that followed, and the focus of the organization changed. Einstein had gotten as much as he could from the group, but desperately needed other sources of information. He found what he had been looking for at the close of World War II in the 1940s."

Ananmaya knew a little world history and thought he knew where Bhuvanesh was heading. He excitedly interrupted, "He must have gotten help somehow from Hitler, right? You said he was a shifter too, wasn't he?"

"Yes, very good! Hitler was indeed a shifter. For opposite reasons, Hitler had also compiled an extensive shifter database. His Nazi scientists discovered a genetic commonality that showed Jewish descent had the highest potential for producing individuals with the gift—yet another reason to fuel Hitler's hatred of the Jews.

This discovery was not surprising, considering his greatest shifter adversary also had Jewish parents. Hitler had known for some time that Einstein was a shifter, and shortly after the Nazi rise to power in 1933, he sent his secret police, the *Sturm Abteilung,* to attack Einstein's home in Germany. Luckily, Einstein was in California at the time and managed to hide himself from further attempts.

"Hitler had millions of Jews murdered in the holocaust that followed, not only because of his hatred, but also to protect himself from future shifter rivals. The Nazi's performed experiments in genetics to enhance the gift in predictable and controllable ways. Hitler's dreams of a *super-race* were never realized, but the vast database of family histories and genetic experiments remained after his suicide in 1945. This is what Einstein found and added to his research much later in the group's history."

"So, Einstein formed a secret club for shifters, and you were there? What do they do? Is it still around?" asked Ananmaya.

"When I was a member, the Society's goal was to find and train shifters. They encouraged members to use their gifts to help humanity and make the world a better place. Nikola Tesla, also a founder, was an excellent example this philosophy in action. His indispensable innovations electrified the twentieth century, yet he never claimed fame or fortune. He died in poverty and his name is almost lost in oblivion.

"Although few in number, there are many shifters in key locations around the world. This gives the organization much power. Unfortunately, with much power also comes much corruption."

Bhuvanesh noticed the sun going down, and the evening light beginning to fade. "It's late, my friend. I think we will stop for now. I know you are wondering why I left, and sometimes I wonder if I did the right thing. But that is a discussion for another day. If we are to salvage anything of today's lesson, we had better get back to it."

Bhuvanesh had recommended for Ananmaya never to contact SOTAR. After Einstein had died, the Society's goals became more centered on themselves rather than what they could do for humanity. Apparently, Einstein's fears were not unfounded.

* * *

Ananmaya glanced from his magazine to the man next to him. If Pinotti was a sample of their current enrollment, Ananmaya now understood his teacher's willingness to leave the organization.

The man obviously had no shifter skills, or he would know who he was sitting next to by now. He must just be an underling in the group. Unfortunately, it also looked as if they were going to the same place. This at least was useful information; he knew they would be waiting for him there. Keeping your enemies close had some merit.

As of right now, the artifact was safely in his possession. Einstein had left it in the care of the observatory in Brazil for almost a century, nearly forgotten. Soon, it would be back in the United States, the home of Nikola Tesla, the man who lit not one, but *two* worlds.

Chapter 13, Messages From Mars

Nikola Tesla leaned closer to the receiver. Yes, there it was again, that strange sequence of pulses. The sequence kept on repeating like clockwork every few minutes; it never seemed to change. This was another radio message emanating from space, yet this one was not from Mars.

In 1899, Tesla was experimenting with a magnifying transmitter at his first laboratory at Pikes Peak, Colorado. Working late one night, he heard a repeating pattern of signals coming from the direction of Mars. He had even admitted as much to the press. "Collier's Weekly" had reported the discovery in an article entitled, "Talking with the Planets" in March of 1901.

Unfortunately for Tesla, further correspondence with Mars had been less than forthcoming, and people were questioning the man's sanity. Nevertheless, he continued to pursue his research with magnifying transmitters at his laboratories in New York and Canada over the next twenty years.

In late August of 1918, everything changed. Tesla was working at his privately funded, secret laboratory in Canada, where he had set up two gigantic *Teslascope* magnifying transmitters. And now, they were picking up transmissions again, this time not from Mars, but from the direction of the Sun. These transmissions were not as subtle as the ones he had heard before; they were quite clearly organized and much less sporadic.

They were easily discernible as a sort of Morse code. Feverishly recording the repeating series of pulses and pauses, he soon realized that the pattern repeated over and over. Expecting the message to be extraterrestrial, he did not think it would be possible to decode it quickly. However, the size and structure of the message looked very similar to a regular written language. On a whim, he tried to decode it using the English alphabet.

After only a few hours, Tesla had decoded the message. Much to his surprise, the message was in English, which was disappointing. This meant it was likely terrestrial in origin and probably a hoax. The message read:

OUR PLANET BROUGHT HERE
FROM A PARALLEL UNIVERSE
POWER FAILING. SUPPLIES LOW. NEED HELP
S. EDINGTON, ROYAL CHIEF ASTRONOMER

Nevertheless, the coded messages from the Sun intrigued Tesla. They changed little in their content or detail and were regular in schedule. From everything he knew about electricity and radio, the only way it would be possible to hoax this message would be for someone to put a transmitter in orbit. That would be altogether impossible, even for Tesla. After much testing and analysis, he finally decided that the message was indeed coming from deep space. But from where?

At this time of year, Mars was high in the sky, on the same side of the sun as the Earth. Also, neither Mercury or Venus were in the proper position, excluding them as well. Since the messages could not possibly be originating from the Sun itself, he concluded that the source must be from some point beyond the Sun, moving along, opposite the Earth.

The frequency of the signal proved as much. Radio waves at that frequency could easily traverse the ether unimpeded by the immense hydrogen fireball in the sky. Perhaps there was indeed a planet on the other side of the Sun as the messages implied.

After the world ridiculed him for announcing that radio waves were coming from Mars twenty years ago, he decided to keep the news to himself until he had more evidence. He would respond to the source of the transmissions with his new *Teslascopes,* which were very powerful and built for this purpose.

He tried for days, but was unsuccessful in eliciting a response. The message kept on repeating, apparently unaware or unable to respond to his attempts to communicate.

Frustrated, Tesla realized that he needed help. An unknown force had dragged a new planet into our solar system, and the people there were in trouble. He didn't exactly understand where they said they had come from. What had they called it? A parallel universe? This was thinking more along the lines of Albert's lunatic ideas.

Although usually at odds, the two scientists had a begrudging respect for one another. Yet Nikola had difficulty trusting Einstein's outlandish theories. How could gravity bend light? How could space and time be flexible? It simply defied common sense. Obviously, someone like Albert would find the message from the hidden world extremely interesting.

A few weeks after the transmissions started, he invited Albert to his lab in Canada to hear them for himself.

"You do realize there is a war on, don't you?" asked Einstein.

"For others, yes. For men like ourselves, I do not think so," said Tesla with a smile.

"Yes, but travel is getting difficult for me. You must know I cannot stay. They will miss me in Berlin if I stay away too long," said Einstein taking off his coat.

"This will be worth all the subterfuge it took to get here. You must hear this. Come, put your ear by the receiver."

Tesla led him to the workbench where a large box with dials and meters was humming softly to itself. Coils of wire ran from the device up and through the cracked plaster ceiling. Einstein looked dubiously at the device, but moved lowered his head to the circular opening Tesla was indicating.

"What have you been putting in your tea, Niko? All I hear is noise," said Albert doubtfully. "Please, tell me you are not hearing Martians again."

"You must be getting hard of hearing, old boy. Listen to the amplitude shifts!" said Tesla, annoyed at the use of his nickname.

"I will remind you, sir, that I am nearly twenty years your junior," said Einstein, putting his ear back to the receiver.

At first, all he heard was the pop and hiss of static, then he noticed something. The volume of the static was rising and lowering like a tide rapidly rolling in and away from the shore. It did so in a very discernible pattern.

"And you have been able to decode this?" asked Einstein.

"Quite. You have it transcribed there in front of you. The pattern repeats every fifteen minutes. It has been doing so for days."

Einstein read the message. The story it told was astonishing. A parallel universe? This was something Nikola would never have conceived of on his own. The man had made outlandish claims before, but this seemed beyond even his furtive imagination.

"Truly fascinating. I do not quite know what to say. I expect you should continue monitoring and hope for more information," said Einstein. "They do not seem to have much to say, do they?"

"I believe it is an automated beacon, set in motion, but now quite outside their reach. They must have put some sort device into orbit, so their planet's rotation doesn't interfere with the direction of the signal. They also seem to know where we are, as they have aimed the narrow beam directly at us," said Tesla.

"Yes, that theory very likely fits the evidence," said Einstein, bemused at his friend's unwavering confidence. "Niko, with all the projects you are working on, I'm surprised you have had time for this."

"I make the time. I can think of no greater thrill than when one of my inventions unfolds itself at my work bench," said Tesla.

"That is commendable," said Einstein, looking at his watch, "but I find myself quite pressed for time. I do apologize, my friend, but I have things on my agenda I must get to before I leave for Berlin."

"Ah yes, your relativity nonsense," said Tesla. "So much effort and expense for something so utterly unfounded. I do not know what you hope to prove."

"You will see, my friend. You will see," said Albert with a smile, putting on his coat and hat. He made for the door. "Good luck with your radio messages. You have made splendid progress. Do keep me informed of any changes. If you will excuse me, I have a boat to catch."

* * *

On Einstein's return to Berlin, there was a letter from London waiting for him. This was odd because any correspondence between London and Germany had ceased entirely because of the war. However, Einstein had a few high level friends at the academy, and they had seen to it that this letter from the *Royal Society of London* made its way to his desk. Einstein opened the letter as his sipped from a bowl of soup he had heated on the little stove in his apartment.

Apparently, they were forming expeditions to prove his theory of *General Relativity*. They would be sending two teams to view a rare solar eclipse, which they would use to prove his theory. Because of the rare opportunity the eclipse presented, the Royal Society was going to send two expeditions, one to Sobral in Brazil, and another to the African island of Principe. Both locations were equally inaccessible and difficult to reach. The expeditions would require strong leadership to succeed. There were many qualified people applying for the expedition, yet it was hard to find the right man among them. However, they did have one person in particular of whom they wanted his opinion.

When he saw the name Arthur Eddington on the list, he almost dropped the letter in his soup. *Hadn't that been the same name in Nikola's messages from space?* The spelling was different, and so were the first names, but both men were apparently distinguished astronomers. Also, the timing was spectacularly coincidental.

This was all very strange. The letter indicated that this Arthur Eddington was a staunch supporter of his theory and that he actually understood it.

He decided to correspond with the man in person. This would be difficult as he had just returned from an extended leave, and travel out of Germany was getting harder and harder to do, even for a shifter. But this would be worth the risk. He needed to speak with this man. The eclipse could serve two purposes.

Edington had been surprised to learn that, in a few days, the man behind general relativity was coming to meet him in person. Since the start of the war, the government had banned travel between the two countries. Not surprisingly, the celebrated scientist had requested that Edington not divulge his private visit.

A few days later, the two men were talking on a park bench, near the grounds of the Royal Society of London. Edington had kept his promise of confidentiality, but Einstein had taken time to know the astronomer better before bringing up the subject of Tesla's discovery and the other Edington. The two men had been talking for an hour, and Eddington's grasp on the nearly incomprehensible theory of relativity was astounding.

"You must understand that what I am about to tell you is rather, well, hard to believe," said Einstein to the surprisingly receptive man in front of him.

"Hard to believe? I thought we were discussing relativity," said Eddington with a smile.

"Yes, yes," said Einstein amused. "I expect once one accepts that, one can believe anything. I must congratulate you on your grasp of the subject. You are quite adept at clearly illustrating the obtuse. I see we have picked the right man for the job."

"Thank you, sir, I appreciate the opportunity. It is an honor," said Eddington, pleased with the confirmation from the celebrated scientist. This meeting with Einstein did not seem real to him. The man was larger than life. How could he be sitting here in the café discussing relativity with him now? How did he get here? It did not seem possible.

Einstein took a moment to sip at his tea, which he dropped four more lumps of sugar into.

"Speaking of the job, there is something I need you to do, and I need you to trust me. We are both men of science; we only seek the truth. Sometimes however, that search can lead us down some very strange paths. I need you to walk with me on one now."

"Yes, sir. What is it?" inquired Eddington.

Einstein paused, considering the best way to answer the question without sharing too many details. After a moment, he replied, "Mr. Eddington, I need you to find a planet, a planet that should not exist."

Chapter 14, Arrival Day

"*Oi mate!* You goin' to the party tonight?" asked Ayden, rapping his knuckles on the Chief Royal Astronomer's open door. Edington had relaxed the observatory rules governing access to this floor, after Almos had retired.

"No, I don't think so. I've got all this paperwork to finish," said Edington with a sigh. As Chief Royal Astronomer for the past ten years, he had to approve grants for research personally, even if the board had already given them the green light. The grant he had in his hands now was for a fascinating idea which used radiometric radiation, a phenomenon Quinn Mandic, the town engineer, had discovered ten years ago which also had inspired Edington's *Message in a Bottle* project.

Now, they wanted to resurrect the old beacon and make it into a sort of telescope. He smiled at the innovative idea. Apparently, the ether was alive with Quinn's radiometric radiation. Instead of transmitting an apparently useless distress call, they would recycle the defunct little satellite into a *radiometric telescope.* It would be able to detect faint objects, vastly beyond the visual range. He signed off on it, and dipped his pen in ink to ready for the next one.

"But it's *Arrival Day* Sam! And it's the twentieth anniversary! The whole town is going to be at the street party," said Ayden, not wanting to leave his friend in this stodgy office while he went off to have fun.

It had been twenty years since Philolaus was swept into a parallel universe. Now, for some reason Edington could not understand, they celebrated the event each year as Arrival Day.

"People will always find a reason to party," said Edington with a smirk.

To him, being yanked through space and time by an unknown force did not seem to be something to celebrate.

But for most of the colonists, they felt lucky to have survived it. Therefore, they celebrated with family and friends every year on the day it happened.

"Right then, have it your way. But if you're not out of this office by ten o'clock tonight, I'm coming to get you, and I'm bringing Eloisa," said Ayden.

"Fine, fine. I'll meet you at the pub in an hour. Good grief, Ayden, no need to bring her into this," said Edington.

That satisfied his friend. Ayden smiled, saluted stiffly with mock respect and bowed out of the room.

Neither one of them was getting any younger, but somehow Edington had managed to remain a bachelor even though women relentlessly pursued him. Ayden had gotten married five years ago to a local pretty girl named Amanda Cummings. They were expecting their first child soon.

They had introduced Amanda's best friend, Eloisa Dodds, to Edington around the same time, and although she was also quite attractive and obviously interested, Sam was not quite ready to settle down. For now, he was married to his work.

Twenty years. Had it truly been twenty years since we arrived in this universe? When Almos told the panicked colonists what had really happened to their world, life on Philolaus had gotten complicated. Although, he had to admit, the old codger had surprisingly come through in allaying their fears.

Assembling at the Calliope, Ayden and Sam had joined the other Parifeldie colonists who were waiting for Mayor Stanton to take the podium. Obviously shaken himself, the mayor did not quite know what to say. "Please everyone, remain calm. We are assessing the situation. The colonists in Madeley just reported that the phenomenon has been in their sky for over an hour. So far, other than the heat, there are no other adverse effects."

Madeley was farthest east of all the colonies. So distant, that their nearest neighbor, the town of Parifeldie, was an hour behind them for the morning sun. The previous night's windstorm had downed one of Madeley's telegraph lines, which had delayed their warning.

By now, all six colonies now knew the sun had a twin in the sky and evacuation alarms were blaring everywhere. All ships were being hurriedly prepared for liftoff. People were furiously stuffing their belongings into pillowcases and running to the ships. Children were crying. There were many injured in the confusion. No one knew what it all meant. No one, except for Professor Almos and Sam Edington.

Professor Almos and Mayor Stanton were speaking to each other away from the microphone, and the mayor was getting angrier by the moment. "What incomparable arrogance! Who do you think you are to have withheld the facts from me?"

"I have withheld no facts. I do not have any. I only have theories. Theories apparently with errors, as I did not expect this to happen so soon," said Almos.

"Regardless, you should have informed us. We could have done something," said the mayor incensed.

"No, we could not have. No one can. A power I do not understand is moving us, and there is nothing anyone can do about it. Why needlessly worry people about the inevitable?" advised Almos calmly.

The mayor sat down and wiped his brow with his handkerchief. He wanted to say that just because Almos did not have a solution, what made him think no one else would? But then, remembering who the intelligent man in front of him was, he added weakly, "It's just that we deserve to know how we're going to die."

"We're not going to die. I thought I explained all that," said Almos. "This movement process has been too precise, too surgical. There is intelligence behind it. If it wanted us dead, it would have let the tidal forces of having two suns rip us apart by now."

"Well then, please Professor Almos, by all means let's hear your theory. Please explain to everyone why we now have two suns," said the mayor tersely.

Almos took the podium and gave an eloquent speech that was telegraphed around the planet. In it, he explained his observations, why they had convinced him that there was no real danger, and that no one should panic, repeatedly reassuring everyone that there was nothing to fear. He reminded them that leaving the planet was not an option.

"As colonists, isolation is nothing new. We are accustomed to working together against impossible odds. This is our strength and our refuge. None of us had strong ties to Archænis, or we would not have volunteered to be here. We thrive on discovery and blazing new trails. This is simply an extension of that purpose; we are still pioneers and we will survive," Almos's words had calmed fears and stopped the people from rioting in the streets.

By that evening, the sky had utterly changed. The stars were in entirely new configurations. A wide band of stars and stellar gases stretched across the horizon, and strange constellations danced overhead. A full-time operator now manned the observatory telegraph, as astronomers across the planet made discovery after discovery.

The following morning passed as Almos said it would. Only one sun shown, and if it were not for the nightly stellar reminders, no one would know that they were in another universe. Like transplanting flowers, they had been very carefully uprooted and planted into their new home.

Old Almos had retired ten years later, and on his recommendation, the city council unanimously agreed to promote young Edington to take his place. At twenty-seven, he was the youngest person ever to hold the position of Chief Royal Astronomer.

Edington had kept extremely busy in his new office; after all, they had an entirely new universe to discover. Already, they had discovered five other planets in their new solar neighborhood, strangely similar in orbit and size to the ones they knew back home.

Both gas giants were here. They soon discovered *Kronos,* surrounded by her striking rings; only here, she was a yellowish-orange, not a pale blue. *Zeus* looked largely unchanged, with his giant red eye still a raging storm.

Concerning the inner rocky planets, hot little *Hermes* and crimson *Ares* still plied the heavens, but *Ares* was much smaller and tinted reddish orange across its entire surface, instead of just at the equator. Most astonishing was the discovery of another inner planet, much the same size as their home world.

At first, they thought they had found Archænis' complement in this universe. But too many factors did not match. For one, it was not opposite the sun nor was it in the same orbit. It was at a point between the orbits of Philolaus and Hermes. In addition, it did not have the same appearance. Gone were the blue and green jewel-like features of home, replaced by a dense, cloudy veil. They decided to call this mysterious planet Aphrodite, as she was quite beautiful, shimmering in the evening sky.

With the exception of Aphrodite, the similarities between the two solar systems could not be ignored. This meant there was still a chance of finding a parallel version of Archænis opposite the sun, hidden from their telescopes.

Edington signed the last provision request on his desk and put the lid on his inkwell. He could hear the Arrival Day celebrations starting outside in the village below. Edging closer to the large round window in his office, he saw colorful arc lamps lighting the faces of the partygoers as they laughed and danced in the street.

So much had changed, but then again, so little. Edington marveled at how adaptable the human race was. They had accepted as home this strange and alien new universe. Philolaus had seen several new generations of people since the move. These children, who had never known another sky, would be their legacy. Eventually, even Archænis would disappear into the past as a legend. A forgotten piece of history; a fantastic tale told over campfires.

He took his coat off the coat rack, locked, and sealed the door behind him. He had just reached the first flight of stairs when his apprentice, Orville Hopkins, caught up with him, quite out of breath.

"Sir! Mr. Edington! Please wait!" said his assistant, who had been running down the stairs from the observatory platform, two at a time.

"Yes, what is it Orville? What's the bother?" asked Edington.

"It's back, sir! The probe we sent…I just saw it pass overhead. At first, I thought it was an asteroid, but it came around for a second pass. It's apparently on the last stages of its re-entry vector," Orville's face had flushed with excitement. Orville reminded Edington of himself when he was just seventeen. Here, was a boy who chose to lose himself in the stars instead of carousing in the festivities below. His enthusiasm was boundless.

"Thank you, Orville. That is very exciting news. But what are you still doing here? No one has a night shift on Arrival Day. Go have yourself some fun. The probe will not land until tomorrow morning. I punched the landing sequence into the cylinder myself," said Edington. "When we retrieve it from the jungle tomorrow I will let you help us develop the film."

Against much resistance from Mayor Harold Hastings, the pompous son of the previous mayor, George Hastings, they had recently built and launched an unmanned ether probe to search for a planet on the other side of the sun. As soon as the probe returned with its reels of film, they would know with certainty if it existed.

Building and sending their own ether probe was a very complicated, very resource intensive undertaking. The mayor had opposed it from the start. For ten years, Edington's *Message in a Bottle* effort had returned little on the investment. Predictably, Hastings had been more than skeptical about building and sending an ether probe around the sun. However, the people understood the need; if they found a world like Archænis, populated with people like themselves, they might also find help. Eventually, popular opinion had swayed the council.

Even though the probes from Archænis had always proved themselves reliable, there was always the possibility of failure. Thus, they designed the probes to land in the jungle, rather than possibly endanger the colony if re-entry damaged the radium core. This one especially so, as its parts were of questionable integrity.

The probe would slow itself down by looping the planet several times, and then land slowly in the jungle, releasing a red smoke plume that the retrieval team could see for miles. The team would wear ether suits as they entered the vapor-laden jungle to bring the table-sized probe back up to the town. There, the town engineer would carefully disassemble the probe to recover the photographic film canisters, being careful not to disturb the radium power generator.

"Could I go with the retrieval team tomorrow?" asked Orville, against all hope.

"I'm not sending you into a toxic jungle to pick up an experimental, radioactive ether probe, Orville," said Edington amused. "Let the experts do their job. Besides, your mother would kill me."

Orville smiled. "Ok, but you will let me know the moment we get the film right?"

"Yes, Orville. The very moment. Now off you go. I'll close up the observatory dome," said Edington.

Edington smiled, as Orville ran down the hallway, riotous with excitement.

"Oh, to have the spirit of youth again," sighed Edington, turning to trundle back up the stairs to Platform B.

* * *

"Sir! Sir! It's me, Orville. Wake up!" said Orville as the morning sun poured in through the open slit in the dome.

"Stop bothering me, Juni. I don't have any bananas," murmured Edington in his sleep, his head resting on the wooden desk in Platform B. He had fallen asleep there.

"Please, sir. Wake up! The probe has landed. The retrieval crew is ready," said Orville shaking him.

He woke slowly. It had been a long night. He had only meant to close the dome and shut down the telescope, but the nebula in the hourglass constellation had beckoned to him. The easily recognizable constellation had been back in the sky for weeks. It was Edington's favorite ever since the rift had replaced the King's Crown so many years ago. He had even gotten to name the bright nebula the constellation contained, calling it the "Breach" as it looked as if someone had broken the hourglass at that point and all the sand had run out.

Coming up here last night, he had noticed young Orville had left the telescope trained on the object. *A boy after my own heart,* he had thought, well pleased. From then, until quite after midnight, Edington had been exploring the heavens with the huge telescope as he had done so many times before as a youth. It was a wonderful escape that he had not enjoyed in years. He never seemed to have the time anymore just to sit and marvel at the sky. He had fallen asleep up here, meaning only to rest for a moment. Apparently, Ayden had not followed through on his threat to exasperate him with Eloisa.

"Ok, ok, I'm up. I will need some coffee," said Edington, slowly getting to his feet.

Orville's expression of excitement quickly turned to one of horror.

"Don't worry, Orville, I'll get it myself. Good grief," said Edington, making his way to the maniacal coffee machine.

Almos's ancient coffee machine still sat in its place on Platform B. Edington kept it around to remind him of the old man, and somehow he had acquired a taste for the evil brew. The smelly, noisy, and somewhat dangerous coffee machine had not aged well over the years. Its cantankerous habit of producing coffee only when it felt like it had evolved to one of the *I will kill you if you turn me on* variety. After nearly losing a finger, the machine terrified the young assistant, and he would not go near it.

"That thing plain hates me," said Orville.

"No, no, she just greatly *dislikes* you. If you give her what she wants, most of the time, she will let you live. She hardly ever kills anyone anymore," said Edington jokingly, as he donned his safety goggles and leather gloves, before turning on the machine.

"I'll just be downstairs. I…um…forgot to seal my door," said Orville beating a hasty retreat as Edington threw the knife switch.

After the smoke had cleared, Orville returned to Platform B to find Edington reclining in his chair, feet on the desk, calmly finishing his morning coffee. Goggle-shaped circles around his eyes showed where they had protected him from the machine's wrath. The machine burbled and popped menacingly.

Handing him a towel, Orville said, "As I was saying sir, the retrieval team has assembled. They are waiting for you downstairs."

"Excellent. No time like the present. How far away is the probe?" asked Edington, wiping his face. He peered wistfully into his empty cup.

"Not far, about a mile or so. The smoke plume is quite visible. Take a look," said Orville, pointing out the window.

Edington peered through one of the eastern windows. Sure enough, a wide swath of red was spreading out in the light breeze. “It will keep releasing plumes like that every fifteen minutes. But they won’t last forever. Let's get going,” said Edington.

Wearing their protective gear, the retrieval team descended into the jungle on rappel lines attached to the cliff face. The whole town had shown up to see them go. The successful return of the town's first ether probe had everyone excited. Speculation as to what the probe had found ran rampant.

“Do you think it found anything out there, Mr. Edington?” asked Ettie Farlow, the teen-aged daughter of Amelia Farlow who had served on the town council for over twenty years.

“There is a very, very good possibility that it did indeed, Ettie,” said Edington. “I'm just happy that it made it back in one piece.” He watched as the retrieval team descended.

The retrieval team took the better part of the morning just to get down to ground level. Showing the thumbs up sign, the team disappeared into the wilderness to find the probe. Shortly after the expedition left, the support crew set up a winch at the cliff face. The winch would lift the heavy probe out of the jungle, as the makeshift satellite had no external controls to reactivate its lift engine.

Shortly after lunch, a cheer went up. The expedition had returned with a disk-shaped probe on their shoulders. It looked battered and tired, but intact. All the members of the team were accounted for, and Edington breathed a sigh of relief. The dangerous part of the project was over. They attached the probe to the winch and hauled it up the cliff face.

After getting the probe to the science lab on the lower level of the observatory tower, engineer Mandic dismantled the probe carefully. Radium power generators could be unexpectedly explosive under the right conditions which is why they were never used large scale. He brought the film canisters to the darkroom, where Edington, Orville, and a team of specialists waited in anticipation. The townspeople had crowded the observatory lobby that evening and Edington had never seen the place so alive with excitement.

The film negatives from the probe developed with agonizing slowness. But making a stupid mistake in the developing process would ruin the entire project, and be wholly unforgivable. Orville was uncharacteristically patient throughout the entire process. He carefully opened each canister and placed them in the agitators.

Ever so slowly, the last of the negatives came out of the chemical baths. Now, they could finally make the black and white photographic prints.

At first, the prints showed nothing but empty space. However, towards the end of the last batch, they found what they had been searching for. Floating in the black depths of the ether hung a glittering jewel of the planet hiding on the other side of the sun.

The darkroom erupted in exultations of excitement. It became alive with cheering and congratulations. However, in the commotion, someone knocked over a bottle of acid that reacted badly with the empty developer bath and the fumes nearly asphyxiated the distracted scientists.

Thinking quickly, Orville took the fuming bath outside where a barrage of townsfolk approached him, wondering what was going on.

He quickly disposed of the noxious chemicals and announced excitedly, "There's another planet on the other side of the sun!"

A cheer went up. The crowd picked up the boy and passed him around over their heads. Orville could not stop laughing.

Edington came out next, blinking in the light. He was holding up an enlarged print from the negative. The still wet photograph showed a planet decidedly like Archænis in size and appearance. Although only monochromatic, clearly visible were continents against what was most likely water as shown by the shape and brightness of the clouds suspended above them.

"It looks just like Archænis," said someone in the crowd.

"Is that the Georgian Republic?" asked someone else.

"No, it's the right shape, but the wrong size," a young boy corrected.

"Surely, that must be the Golden Straight," observed a man at the front of the crowd.

"Yes! Yes, I see it clearly! That means that the Northern and Southern Waylands are beneath those clouds," said an older gentleman with a foreign accent.

"Obviously, the mission was a complete success," said Mayor Hastings, reluctantly shaking Edington's hand. "I must admit, I had my doubts."

"Thank you, Mayor," said Edington suspiciously. "When can we talk about a manned mission to the planet?"

At this, the mayor began to stammer. "Well, that is a bit putting the cart before the horse, sir. We will need to discuss the proposal further. Put something together for me and I will look at it later this week. For now, let's celebrate!"

Everyone cheered and congratulated Edington and his team. Edington smiled and shook hands as people began leaving the observatory. The celebration was moving down the mountainside to the pub below.

"Bloody well amazing, mate," said Ayden. "Eloisa will be all over you, now that you are the big man around town. C'mon, let's grab a pint."

"Thanks. I'll be down in a second," said Edington.

For some reason, he did not feel much like celebrating. Publically, the mayor had praised Edington for his success, but his eyes had told quite a different story; he had seen hatred and jealousy in those eyes. Edington felt sure the mayor had no intention at all of supporting his idea for a manned mission.

He could only hope that the people of Philolaus would support him in this, as they had before. Because if they didn't, they were all very likely going to die.

Chapter 15, Mariconi

Ever since she had that nightmare on the ride back to Tierra Maya, Molly's headache wouldn't give her a break. Two days had passed since meeting Naomi, and no amount of aspirin or relaxing on the beach would relieve it. It wasn't so much a migraine as it was a persistent, annoying buzz in the back of her head. It was affecting her progress on the book.

At least that's why she assumed she could no longer write. Every time she would sit down at her laptop, nothing came to her. The spring of creativity she had been drinking from had thoroughly dried up in the heat of those two suns from her nightmare two days ago.

Now, instead of writing, she was reclining on the terrace, watching the reflection of the moon wavering on the ocean's surface, trying to get a grip on her life.

She was finding it difficult to remember what she had previously written. Looking back through her book, she found surprising details that she had no recollection of ever writing. It was as if she was reading words written by someone else. She felt as if she were reading words she somehow had written in her sleep.

Transcribing her handwritten notes from Chaccoben into her laptop had been especially surreal. She remembered having to write those notes in pencil because the laptop had died at the ruin, but she had no idea where or when she had scrawled all those glyphs in the margins. They looked like the ones she had seen on the walls of the hidden temple. For some reason, she had drawn the odd crown-shaped constellation on every page. *This was getting disturbing,* she thought. *Was she losing her mind?*

The little piece of paper Naomi had given her lay crumpled in her bag. She dug it out and unfolded it. The phone number on the paper was strange; it had too many digits. *It must be a foreign exchange,* she thought.

The number intrigued her. *Who were they?* She wondered why Naomi thought they could help. She picked up the hotel phone and dialed the front desk.

"*Ci?*" inquired the attendant. Juan apparently was off duty tonight.

"Oh, hello. This is Ms. Arden. I've got a phone number I need to call, and I was wondering if you could tell me if this is a local exchange."

"Sure thing, Ms. Arden, what's the number?" asked the clerk.

Molly read the long number to the clerk and waited.

"No, miss, that is an international number. I believe it is either Venezuela or Brazil. Let me check," There was a brief pause while she heard the clerk rummaging through some papers. At last he said, "Ok, it is a number in Brazil. Do you want me to put it through for you?"

Brazil? Was that even in the same time zone? It wasn't too late into the evening, so she doubted the call would greatly disturb anyone. Then again, Naomi had said not to waste their time. Really though, what was she going to say? "Excuse me, but who is this?"

She didn't even speak Spanish, or was it Portuguese they spoke in Brazil? She could not remember.

"Ms. Arden?" inquired the clerk.

"Yes, I'm sorry. I was wondering if you could do me a favor. I am not sure if I've got the right number. Would you know what language they speak in Brazil?" asked Molly.

"I believe they speak Portuguese, Ms. Arden. I cannot speak it, but sometimes Spanish is close enough to get by. Do you want me to call the number for you? Who should I ask for?" asked the clerk.

Molly wanted to say she didn't know, but that would just complicate things. She quickly thought up a name.

"Thanks, please do. Ask for Ellen. If it's a wrong number, ask them who you dialed by mistake."

"Sure thing, Ms. Arden. I'll call the number now and ring your room if I find out," said the clerk. "By the way Ms. Arden, I love your latest book!"

"Thanks. I really appreciate it," said Molly with a groan. Although she was sick and tired of hearing about the *Dragon's Keep* series, at least those books never gave her nightmares and pounding headaches when she wrote them.

She hung up the phone and wondered aimlessly what Edington was up to now that he was thirty-seven. A chill ran down her spine. *Thirty-seven? What the hell? When did he stop being a teenager?* The thought disappeared as fast as it came, like a melting snowflake. Intrigued, she waited to see if more *inspirational snowflakes* would appear. Before any more did, the phone rang.

"Hello, Ms. Arden? This is Eduardo from the front desk. I called that number you gave me. I got an answering machine from a place called the Observatório Nacional in Rio de Janeiro. I did not leave a message. Did you want me to call them back?"

"No. It must be a wrong number. But thanks for calling," said Molly, more confused than ever.

"No problem. Is there anything else I can get for you?" asked the clerk.

"Do you have anything for headaches?" asked Molly, noticing her aspirin had run out.

"Sure thing. I'll send up some ibuprofen," said the clerk.

Molly had him also send up some hot tea to help her sleep. It apparently was working. Also, the ibuprofen was doing a better job on her headache, or it was going away on its own. Either way, she felt better. Even so, writing was out of the question. It was the last thing she wanted to do. The book would have to wait. It had asked too much of her over the past week, and she needed some time to herself to recover. Now that the headache was finally ebbing, she wanted to take full advantage of it and rest as much as possible.

She turned off her phone and unplugged the alarm clock as well as the hotel phone. She even considered closing the double doors to the terrace to keep the morning beach noise at bay, but changed her mind. The soothing sounds of the ocean were too alluring. She fell fast asleep. *Nothing* would disturb her now.

A few hours later, a noise from the terrace disturbed her. It had sounded like a crash. Molly sat up with a start. It was still dark in the room, but in the moonlight, she could see the potted plant from the terrace lying in ruin at the foot of her bed. It looked as if someone had kicked it over. She leaned over to turn on the lamp but froze mid-way there after seeing a shadow move across the wall. *I'm not alone in the room*. Whispered voices in the dark set her heart pounding.

"Idiot!" whispered a voice.

"Get her!" intoned the other.

Molly saw one of two figures move toward her bed. The man yanked off her sheets. To her horror, she saw he had a strange, pen-sized gun in his hand. In the other, he held a rag probably meant to gag her.

"*Boa noite*, Ms. Arden. Please, don't make this difficult for us," said the man in the shadows.

Running on adrenaline, Molly kicked at the man as hard as she could. He doubled over with the unexpected blow. Molly rolled out of bed and scrambled for the door. The other man was waiting for her there with his gun drawn. "Ms. Arden, please. There are more of us downstairs. You do not want to do this."

Molly screamed as loud as she could. When she did, the man behind her cupped his hand over her mouth and pinned her against the wall. She bit down on his hand, hard as she could. She tasted blood in her mouth. The man let out a yelp and let her go.

"She bit me! She actually bit me!" he exclaimed.

Taking advantage of the reprieve, Molly ran for the terrace. It was only one floor up, and a jump from there to the soft sand below would probably only result in a bruise or two. At least that is what she hoped.

Before she reached it, however, she heard a crackle, and the terrace in front of her lit up, as if by a blast of sunlight passing through rippling water; a discharge of energy spider-webbed across the slate walls of the terrace. Thin filaments of lightning rippled over the cracks and grooves of the tile before finally dissipating to nothing.

What the hell was that? Who were these people? Molly skidded to a halt on the terrace, not sure what to do next.

"You fool! Don't shoot her! We need her alive!" yelled the man by the door.

Well, that was somewhat reassuring, thought Molly. She looked for help on the beach. There was someone there. Her heart raced with hope as she called out. The man looked up at her and smiled. He was holding a gun like the others, which he pointed directly at her.

It was then that she noticed the large, black, silent helicopter parked on the beach behind him. The rotors were spinning, but they weren't making a sound, no sound at all. It was the last thing she saw before the man behind her grabbed her and pressed a foul smelling rag over her face, causing her to pass out.

Molly woke in the seat of an airplane leaning against the window. Opening her eyes, she saw a rugged terrain of tree covered mountains beneath the clouds. Her head rang like it used to in college when she had woken after have a few too many drinks with her friends during their study groups.

"Gods. What did I drink last night? Where am I?" she asked to no one in particular.

"You are on final approach to Rio De Janeiro, Ms. Arden," said a thickly accented voice in the seat next to her. "Please, drink this. It will help with the effects of the neurotoxin." He handed her a glass of a thick red liquid. It looked like blood against his clean, white suit.

Neurotoxin? What? Suddenly, the events from the previous night all rushed back. She had been attacked in her room. They had knocked her out, and now she was being kidnapped. She tried not to panic, and failed. She screamed.

"No one can hear you at 15,000 feet, Ms. Arden. Besides the pilot and the stewardess, we are the only ones on the plane," said the man, gesturing to two other people glaring at her from the back. It was the men from last night. One had a bandage on his right hand.

Molly noticed that zip-ties bound her hands and feet. They had also buckled her seatbelt firmly across her lap. She wanted to cry. Why was this happening to her?

"Please, Ms. Arden. We are not going to hurt you. Trust me. I apologize for the rude way we have treated you, but this matter concerns us greatly, and we do not have time to dally. Tracking you down has been difficult, to say the least. We have wasted too much time. We need you at SOTAR headquarters—*immediately,*" said the dapper old man. She could not place his accent; it sounded Central American.

"What do you want? Why have you done this? I'm not rich. Lots of people have that impression about famous people, but really, I'm not, I mean, I do all right, but I'm not a billionaire like Steve Jobs or Bill Gates. I doubt I could be ransomed for anything that would justify all this expense," As she rambled, tears welled up in her eyes.

"Ms. Arden, drink your tomato juice. It will make you feel better. And you are right, you aren't nearly valuable enough to ransom," said her captor, dispassionately offering the glass.

She felt as if she was going to retch, and it was going to go into this man's lap, *damn him.* They had yanked her out of paradise in the middle of the night, and now this man had the nerve to insult her?

Furious, she swung her arms around to knock the glass out of his hand.

The tomato juice flew spectacularly all over the man's face and suit, the glass rolling somewhere beneath his seat. The man closed his eyes and sighed. Before she could gloat over the outcome, something extraordinary happened. The mess on his face and even the stains on his suit began to *glow.* That was the best way she could describe it. The splashes of red simply got brighter and brighter until they were almost a blinding white light. Then, in an instant, the light receded with a flash. When her eyes regained focus, the glass was back on the tray, and the tomato juice had somehow returned to the glass.

The men in the back of the aircraft had seen the incident and were laughing riotously. It was as if this sort of thing happened all the time.

"Ms. Arden, my colleagues were correct. You are quite a handful," said the man, raising the glass off the tray. He thought for a moment, and then decided to drink it himself.

Molly felt lightheaded. She could not believe what she had just seen. She looked at the glass in his hand, then at the man himself, then back at the glass. She backed away and wanted to scream again, unwilling to comprehend what she had just seen.

Surprised at her alarm, the man asked, "Are you expecting me to believe that you honestly do not know what just happened, Ms. Arden?"

She was starting to see spots, so she closed her eyes. She hoped when she opened them that she would be somewhere else. Surely, this was just another vivid nightmare. One that she would soon wake up from, in her room back at Tierra Maya.

"You're not dreaming," whispered a voice in her right ear.

She jumped with a start, startled that the strange man's face was so close to hers. She backed away even further.

Things like this just do not happen. It was as if she were in a movie. "How did you…what happened to the…" she stammered, eyes darting to the empty glass.

"Look, we've gotten off completely on the wrong foot. I admit it is our fault for using heavy-handed tactics to get you here. Nevertheless, you are an unknown quantity, and we must take certain *precautions*.

Now that things are somewhat under control, please let me explain. My name is Mariconi, Dr. Adolfo Mariconi," He held out his hand for her to shake.

Molly turned away and looked out the window in fear and disgust.

"Look, Ms. Arden, you called *us* from your hotel last night. You must have known we were looking for you. How else would you have known how to reach SOTAR headquarters in Rio?" asked Mariconi.

Molly did not say anything. She couldn't; she had no idea what they were talking about. Were they expecting her to believe that she asked for all this? How had that one phone call caused all this?

The man fumbled in his shirt pocket. "I have something for you, Ms. Arden. I think you lost this," He handed her something cool and metallic.

Molly looked at it. It was her lost necklace! The one she had lost in the hidden temple.

The military-looking people she saw after returning to the temple had been there for *her*. From there, they must have traced the phone call from Tierra Maya. She had stupidly sent them a homing beacon!

But why would Naomi have given her over to such dangerous people? Did she know the phone call would lead them to her? No, probably not. She could not believe that sweet old woman would have intentionally endangered her.

"This must all be a mistake, a misunderstanding. What do you want with me?" asked Molly.

"First, I want you to drink some tomato juice. It really will make you feel much better." The man pressed a button to call the flight attendant.

The stewardess had apparently anticipated this as she already had a tray with another glass. She smiled at her. It was as if she had seen the disappearing trick a thousand times. "It's just tomato juice, sweetie. I poured it myself from the can. It won't kill you," she said.

Molly reluctantly drank the concoction. It tasted awful, but it did make her feel a little better. Her headache was going away, and she only had a little airsickness.

"I will cut to the chase, Ms. Arden, as we haven't much time. Who is Edington?" asked Mariconi, staring directly into her eyes.

Edington? They must mean the character in her book. They must have raided her room when they took her hostage and read the book she was writing.

"He's a character in the book I'm writing," said Molly confused.

"Please, Ms. Arden. We know you have been in communication with the people of Philolaus. The book you are writing is simply an exploit of your involvement with them. Honestly, do you think me a fool? You should have stuck to your insipid dragons and princesses," said Mariconi, losing patience. "What we need to know is why they asked you to do what you did, and what their plans are."

"No, you've got it wrong. That's just a science fiction book I'm writing. Philolaus isn't a real place!" said Molly. "If you think otherwise, you're crazy!"

"No, just cautious," said Mariconi. "We have not been in contact with Philolaus since 1930, and now someone has stolen a precious artifact related to the planet. It was not in your room, and you do not fit the description of the man who took it, but it is obvious that you are involved somehow. We want to know what they are planning."

"Philolaus does not exist! It is a story, you imbecile!" said Molly angrily.

Mariconi looked a little perplexed, and then he relaxed. "You almost had me believing you just then, Ms. Arden. You do not actually expect me to believe you are innocent in all this, do you?"

"Edington and Philolaus are figments of my diseased imagination. If you think they are real, then you have worse issues than I do at the moment," said Molly tersely.

Mariconi sat back in his seat, finger tips pressed together, and thought for a moment. "Explain why you were in Chaccoben. How did you know about the transport chamber in the hidden ruin? We know you were there."

Transport chamber? What was he saying? Molly thought. "Look, that room found me! I was standing on top of a hill trying to get my bearings, when I fell into a hole. It almost all came toppling down on top of me." Molly was trying not to implicate Adrianna or Naomi in all this and hoped Mariconi would think she just stumbled onto it.

"A hill? You didn't know it was a Dzolob Temple?" asked Mariconi.

Dzolob? That name sounded familiar. Weren't they the mysterious and ancient invaders that Naomi had mentioned? How did these people know about that obscure race? Obviously her captors knew much more than she did. Maybe playing dumb would get her out of this. It would not be hard; she had no idea what in the hell this was all about.

"Look, are you going to let me go?" asked Molly, changing the subject.

Mariconi sighed. "We will be landing in Rio soon. You disappoint me with your lack of cooperation. I had hoped we could come to an agreement that would be mutually beneficial to both of us, but I see you have chosen otherwise. As you will not be forthcoming with me, I see no reason to do so with you."

"You've got the wrong person! You have gotten me confused with someone else. I'm just a writer. I don't know anything about ancient Mayan races or how imaginary people could be real. They are just stories!" said Molly, exasperated.

Dr. Mariconi opened a magazine and idly flipped through the pages, ignoring her. He knew she was hiding something, something she did not want to admit, even to herself.

Molly had already suspected Philolaus was more than a figment of her imagination. She had felt the heat from those two suns. She had experienced Edington's panic as he had run for the Calliope. From the beginning, the book had taken on a life of its own, practically writing itself, with her only as an observer and scribe.

Too many strange events had happened. Up until now, she had thought it was only in her head. Maybe she was having a nervous breakdown from the obligations and stress of being a popular writer. Maybe she was reading too much into the weird coincidences.

In light of recent events, it was hard to maintain that belief. She had seen with her own eyes what had happened to the tomato juice. She had not imagined it—or had she? Maybe the neurotoxin Mariconi spoke of had hallucinogenic side effects. No, it was real, she was sure of it. The men in the back had seen it and laughed.

Since going loopy was no longer an excuse, she had to face this strange reality. Things were going on she did not understand, and somehow she was in the middle of it all. She was neck deep in all this, and she knew it, regardless of how much it horrified her. Either that, or everyone in this plane was mad, herself included.

She hoped that could be true. She genuinely did.

Chapter 16, Sobral

Ananmaya's self-imposed layover in Miami gave him time to regroup. He had used his American passport to simplify things with customs. So, for now, he was just like any other American tourist returning from vacation. Exhausted by the long flight, he did not feel much like catching a connecting flight to New York tonight and instead bought a ticket for the following morning.

Pinotti apparently had other plans. He was fighting his way to the front of the queue, demanding satisfaction from the stunned clerk. "I just spent the worst eight hours of my life on that deathtrap of a machine you call an aircraft. I'm sure the luggage traveled better than I did," complained Pinotti to the clerk. "I paid for *first class*, and instead got hurled into the back of the plane with the riff-raff. None of the crew would take me seriously. I insist you correct this matter now. What are you going to do about it?"

An argument had ensued, eventually with the clerk relenting. She had apparently found the original invoice in the computer, which did indeed show his first class status. She could not explain the altered boarding pass. Victorious, Pinotti milked it for all it was worth.

"I insist to be refunded entirely for the flight. Such intolerable treatment should demand nothing less," said Pinotti.

What he got was a partial refund for the difference in cost for riding coach, and a free upgrade for his next flight. Not entirely satisfied, Pinotti angrily boarded the next leg of his connecting flight to New York, staring intently at his ticket, daring it to change. Ananmaya watched the ill-tempered little man go, knowing he might very well meet him again under quite different circumstances.

Ananmaya checked into a motel and put his new clothes in the closet. He had made a few purchases since arriving in Miami. It felt good to be back in the states; it was more of a melting-pot here, and he did not stand out so much.

He liked the food here too. Although not the healthiest of choices, the vegetarian burger and fries he had eaten tasted like nirvana. In the back of the taxi, he had wolfed the greasy meal down hungrily, as they drove through the streets of Miami looking for a hotel with vacancy.

The search had taken some time. NASCAR fans had booked most of the hotels in advance for the upcoming race that week. The only place he was able to find with an available room was the Motel Blu in a questionable part of town. Not the cleanest of places, but it was positively antiseptic, compared to the Brazilian favela.

He had needed to keep off the radar as much as possible in Brazil. He could not afford to be discovered there. SOTAR had eyes everywhere, especially in their home country. After all, finding shifters is what they did. If the student of a former member showed up on a hotel roster, it might have raised eyebrows. Those precautions had apparently paid off. He had avoided capture and made it successfully back to the United States with the artifact.

He took a shower and turned on the television. He clicked through the channels until he found a national news program. The reporter was following a breaking story.

"Molly Arden, author of the popular *Dragon's Keep* series, has disappeared in Mexico," intoned the reporter, as the words, *AUTHOR DISAPPEARS IN MEXICO* rolled across the screen. They flashed a recent photo of the famous writer. "Arden has been missing for over three days. Family and friends became concerned after losing contact with her, while she vacationed alone, in Costa Maya, Mexico."

Ananmaya had heard of Molly Arden, but had not read any of her books. He never seemed to have the time for the simple joy of sitting down to a good read. Her disappearance saddened him. The world had lost a valuable person, one who could give others an escape into the fantastic.

The reporter continued, "The Tierra Maya hotel manager contacted Arden's publicist after hotel staff failed to find her on the property. The local police have turned up no clues as to her whereabouts, but an investigation is still pending."

The reporter moved on to other breaking headlines, none of which had anything to do with him or the bank in Brazil. He needed to stop worrying. It was just a small bank, in a nondescript neighborhood in Rio. The heist had not even made the local papers. Only, he had never done anything like this before, and he kept expecting capture around every corner.

Ananmaya turned off the television and focused on the present; trying to calm his mind of any doubt. He brought out the artifact from inside his satchel and turned it around in his mind. Again, the enigmatic object remained stubbornly unperceivable.

He put the box in the room safe and tried to go to bed. After arriving in New York, he would be in Buffalo by tomorrow evening. Leaving early the next morning, he would make his way to the Toronto side of Niagara Falls. From there, he would have to be extremely careful as SOTAR would probably be expecting him. He had planned this mission for months, but he had not anticipated anyone being at the lab.

Besides occasional maintenance, SOTAR had largely abandoned the secret lab for almost nearly a decade; no one was supposed to be there. Well, he would just have to improvise.

He had been extremely fortunate, considering his mistakes. If luck continued to favor him, he might actually pull this off. Soon, he would be hurtling through space to a nearly forgotten world. That is, of course, if Tesla's reports could be trusted.

What he had read in the SOTAR records in Brazil had astounded him. At first, he could not believe what he was reading, and thought Tesla had been ranting in his old age.

Tesla had acted oddly near the end of his life, and some had called him a lunatic. However, there were also the notes from Einstein, which backed up the man's claims. Apparently, Einstein even had photographic evidence, taken by the astronomical expedition to Sobral, Brazil in 1919. Unfortunately, the project director had secreted the photos away to London.

What was the director's name again? Edwards? Ellington? Ananmaya could not remember. He decided to take another look at the Sobral reports. He unfolded the papers from the tin cookie box in his satchel.

They were all perfectly blank. This was because he had taken precautions to conceal their sensitive nature shortly after stealing them from the Observatório Nacional. If he were ever captured, no one would ever find the secrets these documents concealed.

Concentrating for a moment, he changed the state of the ink molecules back into a visible state. Slowly, black typewritten letters began to emerge. He read them as they appeared, impressed that something so utterly astounding could remain hidden for so long. The story these notes held could change the world.

* * *

Assisted by the director of the Observatório National in Rio, Henrique Morize, the Sobral expedition finally arrived at their campsite in northeastern Brazil. It was a remote part of the country, and travel there was difficult. Much of their equipment had become damaged or compromised. Setbacks aside, they were able to set up their equipment reasonably well, barely in time for the eclipse.

When the eclipse caused the sky to darken, it was possible to see stars in the area around the sun. If Einstein was correct, the sun's gravity should alter the position of those stars. They could check this by comparing that same part of the sky from a previous night when the sun was not there to influence the starlight. Unfortunately, due to problems with the telescope optics, they were unable to provide reliable data concerning the shifted starlight.

However, the three members of the Sobral team had seen something else—something no one ever expected to find—something kept quiet and never reported to the general public.

Instead of only detecting shifted stars, the telescopes at Sobral revealed something unbelievable. They showed a new planet, never before detected and apparently directly behind the Sun!

This planet had gone completely undetected because it followed an orbit exactly opposite that of the Earth. This kept it perpetually blocked from view. They had discovered nothing less than the Earth's twin sister!

In the darkness of the eclipse, they could now see the sunlight reflecting off the planet because of same gravitational effects that shifted the starlight. A thin, crescent-shaped umbra was peering out near the edge of the eclipsed sun. This stunned the small group of astronomers.

Even though Brazil was the ideal location for viewing the eclipse, the planet was only visible for a few moments before clouds obscured the view. At the Principe site, the project director, Arthur Eddington, was watching the eclipse with equal attention; however, he never spotted the planet. Visibility on the African island had been poor at the time. Only the team at Sobral had been able to see it, and capture its image on their photographic plates.

The excited researchers wired Eddington immediately with their incredible news. His strange response had been *unfathomable* to the men. He told them to tell no one of their startling discovery, and to secure the plates which showed the planet. All news of the planet was to be kept quiet until they could be debriefed on their return to London.

Shocked that Eddington was forcing them to cover up the discovery of the century, the three astronomers reluctantly agreed to wait until the man could explain himself. Only then did they discover the truth of what they had found and the true purpose of their mission to Sobral.

Eddington was furious at the turn of events. He had used a much higher quality telescope at the site in Principe and supposedly was better prepared. However, the weather on the tropic island had been less than cooperative, giving him just a few seconds between passing clouds. Although Eddington did bring back evidence of the shifted starlight that Einstein needed to prove relativity, the astronomer had not been able to detect the planet.

Considering the equipment he had given them, the Sobral team should not have been able to see the planet. He had been very lucky that they had wired him before going to the press.

Concerned about the turn of events, Eddington had wired Einstein immediately. Einstein had found the whole thing to be very amusing. He did not think that bringing the three more men of science into SOTAR would be any cause for alarm. He agreed to meet with them when they returned from Brazil.

After arriving in London, the group had convened with Einstein in a small office at the Royal Astronomical Society. There, he explained his reasons for concealing news of the planet. He told them about Tesla's messages from space and his ideas on parallel universes. He told them everything, including his nature as a shifter and his involvement in SOTAR. Lastly, he told them how Tesla was secretly planning to construct a ship in an effort to go to Philolaus in person.

At first, the three men had thought the celebrated German scientist had gone mad, even with reassurances of his sanity from Eddington. However, after Einstein demonstrated a few of his own shifter abilities to the dumbfounded men, they had no choice but to accept his fantastic stories.

Charles Davidson and Andrew Crommelin, the two English members of the team, had understandably switched their tea to brandy shortly after the revelation, as they tried to come to terms with what Einstein had told them in the cramped office.

Henrique Morize, the team's Brazilian representative from the Observatório Nacional in Rio de Janeiro, was utterly fascinated and spoke at length with Einstein on the nature of shifters. He was particularly intrigued by the society and the work they were doing.

During this conversation, Einstein had expressed the need for a secure center of operations for the rapidly expanding organization. Almost immediately, Morize offered his facility in Rio. Shortly thereafter, Einstein made him SOTAR's first director of operations.

Morize, Eddington, Davidson, and Crommelin had all unexpectedly become SOTAR's newest members. The men vowed to keep their secret until they knew more about the planet and its people. Besides, who would believe such an incredible story?

* * *

Ananmaya put the papers down for a moment and yawned. He was getting tired. Reading about the expedition had been entertaining, but the jet lag was getting to him. He tried to read a few more lines, but found himself curled up on the bed. It had been a long flight, and he had not gotten much rest, considering his who his companion was on the plane.

He wished he knew for sure why Pinotti was going to New York. Had SOTAR somehow known what he was up to and where he was going? If they knew so much, why was it that Pinotti had not recognized him?

He would have his answers tomorrow evening. Tomorrow would be a busy day indeed, especially if he needed to plan for *contingencies.*

Too tired to care about it anymore, his exhaustion won out, fighting down the annoying doubts trying to creep into his mind.

With an unclear conclusion of tomorrow's events on the horizon, Ananmaya fell into a fitful sleep, leaving the future to fend for itself.

Chapter 17, The Elektra

Tesla got up from his roll top desk. The letter from Albert had been quite clear, but he could not believe it. They had found something extraordinary in Siberia, which had not been reported in the newspapers. The New York Times had run an article just last week about the recent expedition to Tunguska. It had shown eerie photos of devastation from the incredible explosion over Siberia in 1908, nearly twenty years ago.

Thanks to Kulik and his team, the world had become humbled by revealing Earth's real vulnerability in a dynamic, changing universe. Unfortunately, with the photos had come more questions, not answers. Because of the lack of a crater, no one knew what had caused the explosion, that is, until now.

Incredibly, Einstein had somehow known gotten to the expedition before they returned to Moscow. He had convinced them to keep the discovery a secret, and now, according to the letter, he wanted to them all to meet at the underground lab at Niagara Falls in Toronto.

Although both Tesla and Einstein were principle founders of SOTAR, they rarely communicated except when it related to the *Elektra Project.* To ask Tesla to travel four-hundred miles to Niagara to meet in person showed either extreme urgency or extreme arrogance. He was on the fence as to which was the case here. Albert had an annoying habit of insisting on his own point of view. Unfortunately, he had an even more annoying habit of being right most of the time. Even so, the Elektra was Tesla's project, and without his expertise, she would never get off the ground.

After the Wardenclyffe debacle, powering the Elektra had become Tesla's primary goal over the past ten years. His experiments in antigravity engines showed promise, but the ship would require extreme amounts of energy. How to do this without significantly increasing the payload weight was a persistent problem.

Over the years, he had filed numerous patents for improved turbines and generators, but nothing was small and light enough to generate the power he needed.

The wireless power station at Wardenclyffe would not only have powered the ship all the way to the other side of the sun; it also could have powered most of Long Island.

That fool J. P. Morgan had ruined everything when he pulled his funding. Somehow Morgan had found out Wardenclyffe's true purpose was not for broadcasting radio, but for broadcasting power. Morgan, never much the humanitarian, had no interest in providing the world with *free* wireless energy. He bankrupted Tesla when he cut off his flow of money to the project.

SOTAR had tried to find funding elsewhere, but by now, Morgan had blacklisted Tesla and branded him a lunatic. No one wanted to work with the mad man, regardless of his achievements. He was now living almost in poverty at the Waldorf-Astoria mostly on credit. An unusually solitary man, his only companions were the pigeons he occasionally fed in the park. Funding or not, the Elektra Project must be completed. It would be his last, greatest achievement—if he could only get the beast off the ground.

The discovery at Tunguska must be related somehow to the Elektra. They would not be asking him to leave New York if it wasn't important. Albert knew his current financial situation and had included a train ticket to Toronto in the envelope.

Hmmm. There was only one ticket, he noticed. No return fare. What was Albert thinking? The letter had been vague in its intent; most SOTAR communication was. He wondered what could be so sensitive that it could not be discussed in detail in the letter. How long was he expecting him to be gone? He looked at the train schedule for further details.

Great Scott! The mail must have been late! The train was to leave for Toronto this very evening! Tesla put down the morning post and turned to pack. He had barely finished his meager breakfast. Damn that man. What could they possibly have found that was so important as to justify all this trouble?

Besides the obvious meteor impact theory, the news article offered a few other explanations for the event. Perhaps a tremendous release of natural gas had erupted and exploded. Maybe the Russians were experimenting with the atom bomb as suggested by Einstein's lunatic theories. And lastly, wasn't it odd that Mr. Tesla was testing his Wardenclyffe tower at exactly the same time the explosion happened?

Tesla smiled at that one. Of course, Wardenclyffe did not cause the explosion. That test signal sent a high-energy beam directly into deep space. There was absolutely no chance it could have curved around the North Pole to Siberia. Yet the timing of the beam and the explosion were disconcertingly close. Could they have been somehow related? Maybe this is why Albert needed to see him.

No point thinking too much about it now. He would know soon enough. He stuffed a few shirts into his travel bag. Since he had no idea how long he would be gone, there was no way to know how much to pack. *At seventy-two, I'm getting too old for this chicanery,* he thought with annoyance.

Deciding to travel light, he only packed enough for a few days. Now for the hard part. He had to decide which instruments to take, and which to leave behind. He chose a few of his most useful instruments and stuffed them into another bag; there would not be much left in the nearly abandoned lab.

He had not been down there in...what was it? Nearly five years? Had it actually been that long? It would be good to see the Elektra again. He missed her sleek lines and beautiful craftsmanship. So much potential just waiting there, deep underground in the dark. Waiting for him to feed her insatiable appetite for electricity.

He took one last look around to see if he had forgotten anything. He thought he was as ready as he needed to be. Suitcase in hand, he left his apartment and made for the elevators. It was only then that he realized he was still in his morning slippers. After only a few more return trips for forgotten materials, Tesla hailed a cab for Penn Station. He would have just enough time to catch the train to the Canadian side of Niagara Falls.

* * *

The train to Toronto had taken an indeterminable amount of time. Tesla had traveled for over ten hours and had not gotten much sleep. Apparently, the taxis in Canada were not much faster. This taxi was making the train ride look supersonic. *The Elektra would be able to cover distances such as these in only seconds,* he mused.

Finally, the beautiful renaissance and classical-style architecture of the Toronto Power Station appeared through the morning fog. The famous architect, E.J. Lennox, had designed the stunning building. This was the same man who had designed Toronto's magnificent castle, *Casa Loma.* Six Corinthian columns reached skyward in front of the ornate, multistory building, topping the entrance with a roman style piedmont. The building looked more like an art museum than a power plant.

Tesla climbed out of the cab, paid the driver, and walked up the wide stairs into the facility lobby with his suitcase. He enjoyed visiting the Niagara facility. He had designed most of the electrical works and along with Westinghouse, owned nearly all the patents the power plant employed.

A disheveled white-haired gentleman sat on a marble bench under some trees in the little park near the entrance. The man stood up and came towards him.

"It's good to see you my friend," said Einstein, shaking Nikola's hand. "How was your trip?" then, noticing Nikola's tired expression, he said, "I'm sorry for all this rush and secrecy, but you will soon understand. Please, let's go down to the lab. We have guests this afternoon."

The two old friends walked through the stone foyer, their feet echoing on the highly polished marble tiles. After passing by the mahogany trimmed administrative offices, they went down several flights of stairs and opened the door to the main wheel well. Here, all traces of classical elegance utterly disappeared. Huge, iron girders crisscrossed the cavernous room. Steel webbed catwalks with cast iron railing ran everywhere, seemingly suspended in space as they ran down into the darkness. Tall electrical boxes, conduits, and ductwork ran along the walls, following the catwalks down deep into the wheel pit.

The noise was deafening as tons of water from the Niagara River spilled down though an immense iron-plated pipe in the middle of the room. Supported by enormous girders, the penstock pipe dropped the water eight stories down to the turbines below. From the bottom of the well, the gigantic turbines spun immense greased shafts, which reached back up to the generators high above their heads. The whole place shook with the sheer power of it all.

Einstein turned to Tesla and shouted over the noise, "Do you have your key? I seem to have forgotten mine."

"Of course I do," retorted Tesla, annoyed. He took a brass key out of his jacket pocket and gave it to him with a grunt.

"Thank you," shouted Einstein. He inserted the key into a keyhole on the side of an old access panel with the word Electrical written on it. A myriad of meters and large switches dotted the panel. He pulled a large knife switch and with a snap of ozone, the tall panel vibrated, then swung open, revealing a long hallway lit by bulbs hanging from the ceiling.

They walked inside, and the disguised door closed behind them. The noise from the wheel well had quieted significantly. He returned the key to Tesla.

"What's the point of dragging me down here, Albert? I still do not have the answer to our power problem," said Tesla.

"You may no longer have a power problem to fix," said Albert with a grin. "Trust me. Soon you will see. You will see." Einstein was giddy as a schoolboy as he led him down the hall.

At the end of the cold, dimly lit hallway was a mine car lift. They climbed inside and closed the rusted gate in front of them. Tesla pressed the switch that started the electric winch high in the dark vertical shaft. With a rumble, they slowly descended into the dampening darkness.

"I haven't been here for ages," murmured Tesla, brushing some moisture off the sleeve of his suit jacket. "It's more humid than I remember."

"Well, we are nearly a hundred feet below ground and moisture is unavoidable with the tunnel being so close to the water," said Einstein.

"There's no danger of a collapse is there?" asked Tesla concerned as the old elevator stuttered, encountering some rusty resistance.

"Oh no, these tunnels will last a hundred years," said Einstein, as the lift passed down through the ceiling of a large underground vault. Arc lamps, bracketed to a catwalk that ran along the length of the ceiling, brightly lit the mostly cylindrical tunnel. The curved ceiling and floor shone brightly, reflecting moisture off the moldy, red brick-lined walls.

The iron girders of the elevator shaft protruded from the hole in the ceiling, down to where it anchored itself in the brick lined floor. From his high vantage point, Tesla easily made out the oblong, torpedo shape of the Elektra resting on her pylons near the back of the long tunnel, filling out most of its thirty-foot diameter. A multitude of thick wires and cables snaked out from the ship to massive transformers positioned on brackets along the curved walls. The scene reminded Tesla of Frankenstein on the operating table, about to be hit by lightning.

The lift came to an abrupt stop on the tunnel floor. They slid the guardrail back and stepped out. A thickly bearded man greeted them from behind round rimmed spectacles.

"Dobraye utro, comrade," said Kulik offering his hand to Tesla. "It is nice finally to meet the man behind the legend."

Tesla reluctantly took his hand. He had developed a nervous aversion to germs, and he found himself washing his hands more and more each day. Unfortunately, the Russian looked as if the dirt was wearing him. Because of the grime, he didn't recognize him at first. However, the man's accent, along with the distinctive beard and moustache gave him a fair idea with whom he was shaking hands.

"Dr. Kulik of the Tunguska expedition, I presume?" asked Tesla.

"*Da.* Excuse, please. I am not normally in such a state. Anya and I have been helping the professor to get the lights turned back on, and the water pumped out. I slipped and fell in the dark. These Niagara tunnels were never built for the comfort of scientists like ourselves eh?"

It was true; the tunnel they were in was once one of two horizontal shafts that evacuated the water from the penstock after it had spun through the huge turbines. The two shafts came together at the tailrace junction a few hundred feet past the Elektra. The long tailrace tunnel then emptied itself directly behind Horseshoe Falls.

Ten years ago, Einstein had SOTAR agents in the Canadian government declare one of the turbine shaft unsafe, citing obtuse reasons of tunnel instability. This gave them the excuse they needed to close off the shaft and construct the secret lab, which would house the space craft.

Giant floodgates on either end of the shaft sealed it off from the turbines and the tailrace junction. When the power plant reopened, no one except the chief operations manager was aware of the lab's existence—and he was a member of SOTAR.

When the ship would need to leave, the gates would open, the water would rush in, and the watertight, torpedo-shaped craft would float up towards the middle of the tunnel. The current would help to rapidly accelerate the Elektra, before she hurtled through the opening behind the falls. Once outside, the antigravity engines would activate and the ship would rocket into space.

The first few years of the Elektra project were exciting and SOTAR engineers had built the ship quickly to Tesla's specifications. However, there was a problem with his theoretical anti-gravity engines. They worked in the lab, but he would need an untethered power supply to raise the ship and her small crew. The wireless transmission tower at Wardenclyffe was supposed to have provided that wireless power.

Without Wardenclyffe, the power problem had proved insurmountable and had stalled the project indefinitely. Their chances of getting the ship off the ground were looking grim.

"I must say, *comrade,* the Elektra has exceeded my expectations. She is indeed very beautiful. It is a pity she sits here so long unappreciated, alone in the dark," Kulik walked them to the ship where his young assistant was waiting near a large wooden crate.

Kulik's assistant was just as dirty as he was. She was wearing a heavy rubber apron over her dress, which water had soaked almost up to the knees. But mostly what caught him off guard was that his assistant was female.

"Kulik, you do not mean to say you have brought a young lady down here into all this?" said Tesla with a start. He noted her ensemble also included heavy leather boots and goggles around her neck.

"*Da comrade.* Anya and I have been through much worse than this. She is an invaluable companion," said Kulik with a smile. "Spend a few winters in Siberia. You will find our women are hardier than the average man."

"Yes, but still it is all rather undignified for a lady of such obvious charm to be…well…to be rendered in such a manner," said Tesla, shocked.

"Would you rather I be dressed in petticoats and paraded about like the women in Paris?" asked Anya, offended. "I have other things to offer other than just my appearance."

"I…I…" stammered Tesla. Women always had a way of flummoxing him. Because of his work, he did not have much experience with the opposite sex. He had been in love only once, a very, very long time ago. However, he had willingly sacrificed that love on the altar of science, learning to bury his emotions and live the life of a recluse.

"I apologize, madam. I meant no disregard," said Tesla.

"Very well, sir," said Anya, offering her hand, which Tesla shook awkwardly.

Anya smiled. "Albert, you were right. He is like dinosaur, brought to present. I would think he has never seen a woman before. Still, he is charming."

Tesla reddened and took away his hand. He coughed and turned to Einstein who was smiling broadly.

"I say, Albert, what's all this about? From your letter, I understand these people found something unusual at Tunguska?"

Einstein continued to smile at him, not saying a word.

"Do grow up, Albert," sighed Tesla. The man could be infuriating at times. He took him aside, as Kulik and his assistant began unpacking a large wooden crate. In hushed tones, he asked, "Is it related somehow to Philolaus? How much do they know?"

"Niko, I have told them everything. They deserved as much. It was a small price to pay to keep the discovery from falling into the wrong hands," said Einstein.

"What is it? Are they…*like us?"* asked Tesla.

"Well, like us, they are seekers of knowledge and truth. But I think you mean, are they shifters? No, they are not. However, they have sacrificed much to be here now with the stone, and I for one trust them implicitly," said Einstein turning back to the Russians who had just retrieved a small black box from the crate.

"I believe this is what Professor Einstein wanted you to see," said Kulik, motioning for Anya to put the box on the workbench near the ship. She had assembled a complicated looking apparatus, which Tesla did not immediately recognize. Upon closer inspection, he thought it might be some sort of huge electromagnet.

She put the small box on a wide copper plate mounted between a large array of coiled devices. Heavy power cables snaked out into the darkness from the device. Anya put on her goggles. She closed a switch and with a crackle, the apparatus began to hum. She carefully opened the lid of the shiny black box.

Chapter 18, Hastings

Mayor Harold Hastings looked at the paintings lining the passage outside his open office door. The hallway was short, so the five large portraits were crowding the space. With a sigh, he noticed that his own portrait had apparently gone tilted again.

Readjusting the frame had become part of his daily routine; he would give it a little nudge every morning as he walked by. It was only a mild annoyance, but he had the impression that it was somehow reproaching him; marking its contempt of his somewhat perfidious term of office.

That's it! Tomorrow, I'm calling maintenance. You're getting nailed to the wall. He had a piercing headache, and was feeling exceptionally irritable this morning.

Of course, the other four mayors, including his father before him, seemed to be immune to this annoying form of portraiture puerility. Those paintings were always upright and upstanding as the mayors they portrayed.

Ha! What a joke. My father was an idiot, and so were the others. Even his father's predecessor, the honorable Mayor Stanton, had been involved in some sort of cover-up concerning the anomaly that had brought them here.

Harold clearly remembered that morning. He was only eight years old when the two suns had shone in the sky. His father, George Hastings, had rushed them all to the Calliope when the evacuation sirens had sounded. There, everyone waited in fear, not sure what was going to happen. Through sheer force of character, Professor Almos and Mayor Stanton had just barely been able to control the situation and avoid a planet-wide panic.

When things had calmed, and the sky had stopped changing, people started asking questions. Why hadn't someone warned them about the impending tragedy?

Why hadn't the council been better prepared? Rumors circulated that Almos and Stanton had known all along what was going to happen. Some even suggested that they had *wanted* it to happen. The council had even called that idealist fool Edington to testify in the inquiry that had followed.

Harold's father had led the inquisition, which did not turn up much. No one was formally charged, but because of the rumors, their stature in the town had diminished markedly.

Seizing the opportunity, Hastings Sr. had convinced the council to remove Stanton from office and have an early vote for a new mayor, with himself as a candidate. With the popularity he had gained bringing the scandal to light, he had won easily.

Harold glared at the painting of his father. The crafty old man had shoehorned himself into office but had squandered his position as mayor. He had been far too spineless to be an effective leader. He had left most of the decision making to the council and even let Almos continue to serve as advisor.

His father had grown fat and apathetic, and under his weak leadership, the town had lost two more generators. The TPA could no longer find the parts needed to sustain the town's needs, and they had gotten desperate. They proposed risky expeditions to find additional resources and raw materials, but Hastings Sr. had incredulously motioned for more rationing instead.

If Mandic, the town engineer, had not found a way to improve the efficiency of the thermopiles, the colonists would have hung Harold's father from the nearest Pomelo tree by his toes. His father had been a cowering fool, but somehow, he managed to complete his long, ten-year term.

Harold did not consider himself as cowardly as his father. He hated living in the shadow of his father's ineffectual leadership, and in what it had done to the office.

With the dismal apathy of his father, the position of mayor had become almost completely figurative. No one listened to the mayor anymore; they all turned to the Chief Royal Astronomer for council.

Up until he died, Almos had practically run the planet. He played the previous mayors like puppets on strings. Even worse, when Almos retired nearly ten years ago, he appointed his erstwhile apprentice, Sam Edington to the position of Chief Royal Astronomer. Young and inexperienced, Edington had not been half the man Almos was, and the council had floundered aimlessly during George Hasting's remaining time in office.

The town was looking for strong leadership in the mayoral election that followed his father's term. Harold had promised just that, firm, innovative leadership, and he would do it without the meddling of the Chief Royal Astronomer *or the council.* Over the years, he had collected embarrassing information on just about all of the council and he intended to use it. Once elected, he would be practically a dictator. To do what he wanted to do, he would need to be.

From his father, he had learned to recognize and seize opportunities where others saw none. He saw such an opportunity in the energy crisis and intended to use it. Becoming mayor would be the first step in a personal long-term plan to run the entire accursed planet.

He could see where Philolaus was heading. As the doomed people went to hell, only he would remain safe and protected. He had no intention of starving on insufficient rations, or having some desperate colonist murder him in his sleep for his resources.

Unfortunately, when Harold ran for mayor, he found himself fighting his father's poor reputation. It had been a constant struggle to distance himself from his father's poor policies. Even worse, the people had called for Sam Edington to run as well.

Fortunately, the fool would have none of it, and preferred instead to work away in his observatory, distancing himself from public service.

Surprisingly, Harold's only real competition had been fellow council members, Amelia Farlow and Philomena Forrestal, two of the most intractable women he had ever met. However, in the end, he had managed to bribe and blackmail his way into office and soon the town had its fifth mayor, whether they wanted him or not.

Harold considered himself the best mayor Parifeldie had ever seen. In truth, he was quite the opposite. What he felt were firm, well-balanced decisions were actually heavy-handed tactics with little to no compassion. He distrusted his advisors and ran the council with fear rather than respect.

He made rash decisions and coordinated many town projects himself, but always at a high price. More than once, his poor management had caused fatal accidents. However, he always managed to deflect the blame, something at which he was particularly adept.

He maintained a firm grip on his position and enjoyed the benefits the job offered. Over the last ten years, he had run the town dry by building a secret stockpile of food, equipment, and even weapons as per his long-term plan. This reserve gave him a considerably higher standard of living than the people he governed.

Soon, the stockpile would be large enough to take the next step. This world would not be able to sustain itself much longer, and the people would start becoming desperate. Soon they would do anything, agree to anything, if only it would put food on their table.

This dismal fate had finally arrived. He knew this because it had gotten harder and harder to get the things he would need, much less the things he wanted.

He eyed the empty little wooden box on his desk. It had been that way for over a week. How was he supposed to relax and think clearly without his daily cup of coffee? Grinding those aromatic beans every morning made life on Philolaus just barely tolerable. *Well, at least things seemed better,* he thought, and that's what was important. Most things usually took care of themselves in the end, didn't they?

Although the coffee here wasn't any different than it was on Archænis, it was not easy to obtain and was difficult to grow in the alien climate. Now that rationing was in effect, coffee had become the least of the town's concerns. To have enough to grind and prepare on a daily basis would be an incredible luxury, far outside the reach of the common person. Unfortunately for the town coffers, Mayor Hastings felt he was far from being *common.* He *deserved* these little indulgences. He would make another visit soon to old farmer Collins and see what was up with his private reserve.

I have to relax, he thought. The headache had gotten worse. He wondered if going so long without coffee had made him so pallid and irritable. *If that old farmer knows what is good for him, he'll get me what I need. Otherwise, he might find he no longer has a field to plow by the afternoon.*

"Did you want me to cancel your meeting today?" asked his attractive young secretary, standing by the door. "You look positively piqued."

"No, no, thank you, Ettie. I'm fine. What do you have for me?"

She brought in a sheaf of papers and laid them on his desk. "Just the usual paperwork, sir. Except for this, it is a request for additional funding from the observatory. Mr. Edington's new project sounds so exciting, don't you think?"

Exciting? Not exactly the word he would choose, he thought. That bastard Edington was getting to be as bad as his predecessor. The boy kept drumming up public support with his never-ending stream of ideas, and he was getting more and more control over the council. With the success of his recent ether probe, things were only going to get worse. The people practically idolized him now. Hastings was sick at the thought of losing his control at such a pivotal moment.

Hastings sighed. "Yes, Ettie. It will definitely stir things up. Is there anything more?"

"I do not think so. What else can I do for you, sir?" asked Ettie.

He eyed his lovely assistant bending over to pick up a dislodged paper off the floor. She certainly was quite attractive. *He could think of quite a few things she could do for him,* he thought salaciously, admiring her lithe form.

She stood up and turned unexpectedly, handing him the paper. Not to be caught leering, he pretended to fix his gaze on the clock on the wall behind her.

"Umm, no thank you, Ettie. Please do not let me keep you. It is getting late. You get home to that mother of yours. Please, give Amelia my regards."

As she left the room, Hastings pulled himself together and eyed the recent papers on his desk with disgust. That bastard was actually going to pull it off. He had been fighting it for months, but Edington had somehow swayed the council to vote in favor of the project, regardless of his threats. The council members were weak. They did not see the big picture as he did. Public opinion had swayed them on more than one occasion, and in his opinion, the public were complete idiots.

Why couldn't they see what was right in front of their noses? The photos from the ether probe had not just shown continents on the strangely similar planet. They had shown evidence of a prolific civilization. Obviously, there were many more of them than there was on Philolaus. What if that race also plied the heavens with ether ships? What would happen when they noticed the new planet in their skies, ripe for conquest? He knew exactly what they would do, because he would do it himself. They would invade. Why alert them to our presence and lose our only form of defense? Surely, it would be best to remain unseen and undetected.

However, Edington was unwilling to listen to reason. He wanted to revive one of the old ether ships and send a team to visit the planet and meet its inhabitants. That was insanity! Why did scientists always naively believe in the best in people?

He stared at the funding request on his desk. If he signed it, and things went badly, he would go down in history as the mayor that gave away the keys to the kingdom. Not signing it would cause a call for his resignation. He stared at the ceiling, thinking about what to do. The ancient ceiling fan creaked against its whirring fan belt. Like everything else, soon it would fail and they would have to scavenge to fix it. *Everything here is so old and unreliable,* he thought, watching the fan's erratic movements.

Just then, the seed of an idea began to take root in his mind. Hmmm, everything in town was falling apart, including the old ether ships. Therefore, it would not be outside the realm of possibility if the ship he gave Edington suddenly exploded or went off course. Accidents happened often in the interstellar ether, even with the best of equipment, and Hastings did not intend to give Edington anything close to the *best* equipment.

Publically, he had always denounced the mission as being too risky and a waste of resources. Therefore, if the ship never returned, the blame could hardly fall on him. *Yes, it might actually work.* This is just another opportunity in disguise; an opportunity that had many fringe benefits.

Smirking, he approved the funding and basic resource allocations for the manned trip to the new planet. Edington was going to have his ship, but the council would appoint the crew. Because Hastings controlled the council, this meant he would be the one doing the choosing. He had a long memory, and he could think of many individuals that he would consider expendable. They would be right there at the top of the roster, alongside the name of Samuel Edington.

* * *

"What do you mean he can't see me?" demanded Edington. "What has happened to my appointment?"

"Mayor Hastings is in an emergency session right now, Mr. Edington," said Ettie, with a worried look on her face. "Unfortunately, some of the requisitions for the Calliope are proving difficult to procure."

"Such as?"

"I really could not say, Mr. Edington, but Mr. Mandic is in there right now, and he is in a quite a state. They have been arguing for hours. I would guess it would have something to do with the ship or her engines," said Ettie.

"Really? I spoke to Quinn only yesterday, and he assured me the Calliope would be ready in a week or two. Surely, the council is going to give him what he needs, aren't they?" asked Edington.

"I really do not know, Mr. Edington," said Ettie. "I can get you a meeting with the mayor next week. Would that be alright?"

"Bollocks. I don't know why I even try. Sure, Ettie, pencil me in so that I can be pushed back a few more times. I was just going to complain about the ship's roster. I do not approve of sending young Orville into the depths of the ether. I agree with his mother that he is too young and inexperienced for ether travel. And besides, I need him here to watch the observatory while I'm gone. I do not understand why the council is conscripting the crew. There would be more than enough volunteers," said Edington.

Ettie blushed at the mention of Orville's name. She and Orville had an awkward fondness for each other. She would hate to think of hurtling poor Orville into space.

"Certainly, Mr. Edington, I will pass your concerns to the mayor. Did you still want your appointment?"

"Sure. By then I'm sure there will be even more to complain about," said Edington turning to leave.

"Um, Mr. Edington?"

"Yes, Ettie?"

"Do you think the people on that world will help us?" asked Ettie.

"I hope so. It might look like Archænis, but that planet is not home. We don't know what her people will be like. I hope that they will be like us, driven to understand their place in the cosmos. I'm sure both of our civilizations will learn a lot from each other," said Edington.

"What if they aren't, you know, friendly?" asked Ettie thinking of the mayor's point of view on the subject.

"Well, that is a possibility, but I do not see how we have any choice in the matter. We are out of resources, and we are out of time. We either take the risk or be starved out here in the ether. Power levels are so low that we can barely pump enough water to irrigate the crops. If we have another long windstorm, it is doubtful that the air pumps will give us enough air to breath. The supply tanks are below their minimum pressure levels as it is."

Ettie looked at Edington in horror, her hand covering her mouth. She apparently had not heard how grim things actually were.

"Don't worry Ettie; there hasn't been a severe windstorm for years," Edington said reassuringly.

He had not meant to scare the poor girl, but those were the facts. They were one bad storm away from death by asphyxiation. To make things worse, the Calliope would be taking several tanks of breathable air with it as well, a rather significant amount. It had surprised him that the mayor had not protested at that.

Maybe the man was so busy compromising other aspects of the project that it had somehow avoided his scrutiny. *Best not to question a favorable turn of luck,* thought Edington. But no, even if the mission failed, he would simply have accelerated an already inevitable end. The colonies were dying and there was nothing they could about it by staying here. They needed outside help.

"Thank you, Mr. Edington. I know you are doing your best," Then, looking down, she said in a quiet voice, "Please, tell Orville I said hello."

Edington smiled. "I will at that, Ettie. Oh yes, he asked me to give you his regards as well."

Ettie was beaming as Edington tipped his hat and left the mayor's office.

* * *

"With all due respect, Mayor, you are being a horse's ass," snapped Quinn Mandic, the town engineer.

"And you, sir, are not helping your case," said Hastings indignantly.

The two men had been arguing for hours. The aged town engineer was red faced with anger. His cool blue-grey eyes looked out under a wrinkled brow of almost eighty years. He had seen much in his lifetime, including the two previous administrations. This *prat,* however, was the worst of the lot.

"Why are you being difficult? Can't you see the whole planet is behind this?" asked the engineer.

"Mandic, you are a smart man. I would not have expected public opinion to have blinded you. If those people find us, they will destroy us. They are not our saviors; they are our enslavers. They will overrun this planet the moment they discover us. For now, their sun hides and protects us. Why alert them to our presence? We know absolutely nothing of them. I would expect you of all people to see through Edington's naiveté and understand the threat we are facing here."

"The only threat I see here is you," said Quinn grimly, arms crossed.

Mayor Hastings sighed and looked at the little box on his desk wistfully. It was still empty. Farmer Collins had promised him another two weeks supply, but it had not arrived. He would need to expand that man's motivation.

For now, he would have to suffer through this moron's tirade. He cheered himself with a happy thought. In just a few days, Quinn Mandic might not be coming back to this office again, ever.

"This entire project has been a fool's errand from the beginning. I am simply mitigating the damages the best way I can," said the mayor.

"By denying me the test equipment? How exactly does that do damage?"

"The people of Philolaus need the things you want. We require these tools to manage our power grid. I have told you this countless times. You may not take this irreplaceable equipment. You will only lose them out in the ether following this foolish scheme. I have seen to it that you personally will be on board to supervise any unexpected problems. I'm sure someone with your intellect can work without inductive resonators," said the mayor.

Mandic fumed. "It's not a matter of intelligence, and you know it. Do not patronage me, Mayor. Without the resonators, there is no way for me to monitor any defects in the magnetic field around the Leviton ore."

"Defects? Why should there be any defects? Instead of solving problems at home, we have the top minds on the planet winding those coils for you. Surely, they will perform as promised. Can't you test them here?" asked the mayor, smiling to himself.

"Of course not. You know very well that it is an ongoing process. The resonators need to monitor the fields throughout the entire flight. Even minor fluctuations in wire thickness and length during the coil construction can cause huge magnetic variants in the long term when dealing with Leviton ore. The ship could go tumbling out of control. It is lunacy to fly without them!"

"It's lunacy to fly at all, Mr. Mandic. I recommend that you uphold extremely high standards during the construction of the coils because you are not getting the resonators. We need them here," said Hastings, with finality. Looking up, he noticed the engineer was still glowering at him. "This conversation is over, Quinn. I have another appointment. Please, do have a nice day."

"Harold, you are just like your father," said Mandic, turning to leave, "a coward."

Hastings' smug attitude disappeared, and his vision went red with anger. No one called him a coward, no one. And now, the man had the audacity to turn his back on him!

He nearly launched himself at the old man leaving his office. Barely able to restrain himself, he clenched the sides of his chair and waited for his anger to subside.

Oh no, Mr. Mandic. You will not be coming back. None of you will.

Chapter 19, Archænis

Molly's head was about to explode. They had knocked her out again shortly before landing at a small private airstrip and she was just now coming out of it. The two large men from the plane had hauled her out of the car and now hustled her through a courtyard populated with strange round buildings with domed roofs.

What were those things? She squinted through the confusion in her eyes. They must be observatories. About four of them, varying in size, crowded the small field they were crossing. They were highly ornate, and looked positively ancient. Most were in various states of disrepair.

This must be the place she had called from Costa Maya, the National Observatory of Rio, or something. Mariconi had called it SOTAR headquarters. *What was SOTAR? Why am I here? What the hell is happening to me?* Her head pounded, and she moaned into the night.

"Quick, she's coming out of it. Get her inside," said Mariconi, unlocking the door as the two men dragged Molly up a short flight of stairs leading to the two double doors of the entrance. They hustled her inside, and she heard Mariconi lock the doors behind them.

The men dumped her semi-conscious body onto a sofa in a large room.

Mariconi studied her limp form. *Was she really the one? She certainly didn't look very powerful.* He needed to know, desperately.

Since 1908, men from Archænis, like himself, had been working to infiltrate the shifter society on Earth. They had plundered SOTAR's vast resources to find a very peculiar shifter with an unusual talent, a talent that could move worlds.

Shifters were rare on Archænis, as it was on Earth. When their governments discovered them, they exploited them for their abilities or simply had them killed. There also were no shifters on Philolaus, at least none of which the colonization initiative was aware. Lastly, Archænis' history had never shown a shifter of any such magnitude before. This is why they began their search on Earth shortly after the gateways had opened.

Ancient and forgotten gateways between the worlds had mysteriously reopened on Archænis after remaining silent for thousands of years. At the same time, a planet disappeared from their universe forever, taking with it the six colonies they had established. The war hungry hordes were demanding other worlds to conquer, and Philolaus had been their stepping-stone to the rest of the universe. They desperately wanted their world back.

The key to Philolaus' disappearance was the activation of the ancient gateways. They had ruptured the ground around them when it happened, uncovering lost stone temples deep in the southern Waylands and some even underwater. The pyramidal structures now glowed with pulsing energies. Ripples of tangible power had radiated to all points on the globe. For a few days, even the eastern arm radium wars had ceased as everyone observed the strange lights in the sky.

A few days later, the postal ether probes from Philolaus had stopped coming. An ether ship left Archænis to investigate. To their utter astonishment, they discovered the planet disappearing into a rift in space. Eventually, the rift itself had vanished. Fearing that the disappearance was related to the gateways, the major governments of Archænis decided to do something unheard of in their history. They decided to work together until the nature of recent events could be determined.

Archænis' historians brought to light ancient texts concerning the temples. Apparently, the Dzolob, a prehistoric race in the southern Waylands, discovered the existence of a parallel world in a desperate attempt to reach their God. These ancients had somehow bridged the narrow gap between worlds with their temples and human sacrifices.

Once they had opened the gateways, they had plundered and enslaved the other world for a millennium. For an unknown reason however, a great disaster had occurred, destroying most of the Dzolob population in the alternate universe. The surviving Dzolob were driven out, and the gateways had been closed forever. Now someone, or something, had reopened the ancient portals and used them to abduct their colony world.

This woman held the key, thought Mariconi, and soon he would have it. For now, he would play her game. He would trap her within her own lies. If she still failed to see reason, he could implement other methods.

Dizzy and disoriented, Molly tried to sit up. She almost rolled off the sofa and onto the floor. That was when she realized her hands were still tied.

"Marcio, please release Ms. Arden. I do no think she is going to give us any more trouble," said Mariconi.

The man with the bandaged hand grinned menacingly at Molly as he pulled out a nasty knife. For a moment, she thought he intended to release her from her *life,* but he just cut at the ropes binding her wrists.

Holding down her hands as he worked, he hissed, "I nearly lost a finger because of you. Maybe I should slip and even the score."

The knife got closer as he sawed away at the ropes. Finally, he finished. Molly pulled away from him as he put the knife back into his pocket.

Marcio chuckled. "Trust me, sweetheart, you would be better off with me than with the boss."

Molly looked around the ornate room. It was a large room with coffered walls and ancient battle weapons displayed on the walls. The room was an eclectic mix of many cultures, but foremost was an unmistakable Mayan influence. A large map of the Yucatan peninsula was right behind his desk. What was a room like this doing in a Brazilian observatory complex?

"You may leave us, gentlemen. I would like to have a private discussion with Ms. Arden," said Mariconi.

The two men left the room, leaving Molly alone with her captor. With that impeccable white suit and unusual accent, Mariconi looked like the guy from that old *Fantasy Island* television series. She almost expected to see Tattoo peeking out from behind his big wooden desk.

"What do you want with me?" asked Molly, still dazed.

"The truth, Ms. Arden. Simply the truth. Tell me how you know about Philolaus," demanded Mariconi.

"Please, I don't understand. Philolaus is not real. Why you are doing this to me?" pleaded Molly.

Mariconi sighed. This woman surely knew by now that she had no options. Why did she insist on pretending ignorance? Did she think him that naive? Her manuscript alone implicated her involvement.

Furthermore, there was the temple. They had been looking for a temple in that area for weeks. He had known that they were close, but it had remained elusive until she had led them to it. For her to insist she found it by accident bordered on the ludicrous.

She also must be connected to the theft of the artifact. The two events were too close simply to be a coincidence. The woman was obviously a shifter, but he needed to know the extent of her abilities. She might even be *THE* shifter, the one he was supposed to find. He was not about to let her go now, after waiting for nearly fifty years.

Her thieving accomplice had been able to phase matter—*a powerful gift indeed*. There had not been any prominent matter shifters since the death of Houdini in 1926. Why didn't SOTAR know about these two powerful shifters? How had they gone unnoticed until now? He needed to know her role in all this.

"Okay, Ms. Arden. Let's entertain your declaration of ignorance," said Mariconi. "Please, do tell me. Why were you in Costa Maya?"

"I'm on...*I was* on vacation," stammered Molly.

"Not exactly the vacation destination of choice for someone with your standing, is it, Ms. Arden?"

"My agent recommended the place to me. She said I wouldn't be bothered there." If she didn't feel so sick, she might have chuckled at that.

"Why did you go to Chaccoben?" asked Mariconi.

"I wanted a peaceful place to write," said Molly. "The beach was too crowded and noisy. I had a tourist map, and it sounded interesting," Molly was starting to see spots again. Where was that tomato juice when she needed it?

"Who told you about the hidden temple? Who were those people with you?"

Good, thought Molly. *He doesn't know about Juan and Adriana.* At least she would be able to keep her friends out of this mess.

"I've already told you. I had gotten lost in the woods. To get my bearings, I climbed to the top of the hill. The ground gave way, and I fell inside. I did not know what I had fallen into until the dust settled. No one was with me. I was by myself," said Molly.

"My people saw you and your two friends running from the site a little later. They called for you to stop," said Mariconi annoyed. "Who were you with?"

"I...I came back later with two park employees that I told about the find. I don't know where they went, and they never told me their names."

That was a lie. No one had been back to site since his team had cleared it. They had concealed the hole in the chamber ceiling, and were watching the temple. If park employees really had been with her, there would have been a score of archeologists at the location by now. She was not telling him everything; she was protecting her friends.

"Let's assume all this is true, Ms. Arden…" said Mariconi.

"It is. I swear it. Please let me go. I'm not feeling well," Molly's head was pounding again with the effects of the neurotoxin.

"Well then, please explain your new novel. Where did you get the idea for so fantastic a tale? You are a fantasy writer—dragons, princesses and such. This is a bit of a stretch for you, isn't it?" asked Mariconi.

Molly tried to pull herself together. She spoke softly, "Yes, I suppose so. I wanted to…needed to…to do something different. I don't know where I got the idea. The story started writing itself. That happens sometimes."

"So, it just came to you then? You honestly believe Philolaus is just a figment of your imagination?" asked Mariconi with quiet contempt. This was getting nowhere. He was tempted to pull out the historical record and confront her with Tesla's notes. Then the evidence would be overwhelming. However, he was not quite ready to divulge so sensitive a secret. There was always the outside chance she was telling the truth. He could not take the risk.

"How did you get our number, Ms. Arden? Why did you call us?" asked Mariconi.

"I did not call you. I don't know who did. Didn't you say you had been researching Chaccoben? Maybe you dropped a business card and some kid found it?" said Molly. This was a lame excuse, but it was all she could think of in the haze clouding her pounding head.

Another lie, thought Mariconi. *She is getting careless, and I am losing patience. It is time to end this.*

"Ms. Arden, I never told you we were doing research in the area. You are lying to protect someone. Who told you about the observatory and gave you our number?"

Molly's heart sank. She had just screwed up, and she knew it. She looked down at a spot on the floor. She suddenly felt like retching again.

"Ms. Arden, I'm though playing games with you. I can do things to you—*painful things.* This is your last chance to tell me everything you know."

"Please, I do not know anything. Just leave me alone. I won't tell anyone about this. Just let me go," pleaded Molly.

Mariconi's calm face twitched. I had hoped it would not come to this. She followed his gaze as his eyes moved along the wall of sinister weaponry. He slowly went from one sharp edged weapon to the next, as if choosing a fine wine.

"I do not think you fully understand how persuasive I can be," said Mariconi. He pulled a large curved blade out of a scabbard on the wall. It sang as it slid out of the metal holster.

Admiring the edge, Mariconi continued, "How would like to see your fingers removed one by one? Then, before you completely bleed to death, I will shift time back so that it never happened. But make no mistake, you will remember the pain; that is quite certain. We can do this over and over again. It is entirely up to you.

"What are you?" asked Molly dry mouthed, remembering the strange thing he had done with the tomato juice in the plane.

"I am a shifter, like you of course. My talents lie however, in the temporal realm. I am a shifter of *time,"* said Mariconi.

"But that's not…that's…" said Molly feeling faint. "I'm not…"

The gleam of the moon on the sword was the last thing she saw before the world around her collapsed in a swirling, black mist. The drugs and the interrogation had taken their final toll. Exhausted, she passed out.

Chapter 20, Maiden Voyage

A fist-sized black stone glistened in mid-air between two square copper plates, which were part of a strange apparatus Anya had constructed on Tesla's workbench. Kulik's assistant had enclosed the area between the plates by lowering four walls made of brass bars, trapping the hovering stone inside a cubical metal cage. Huge electromagnets above and below it hummed a low vibrato in the musty air of the underground chamber.

Anya stepped aside so that Tesla could examine the assembly closely. Both hands resting on the workbench, Tesla leaned his aged body closer. He stared at the stone for some time. Then, with a grunt and a sudden turn, he put on his hat and began walking toward the elevator.

"Niko! Wait! Where are you going?" asked Einstein.

Without looking back, he muttered, "Albert, I have better things to do than stare at a piece of magnetite in a magnetic field. I do not know what you hoped to achieve with this cut-rate, children's science-fair exhibit. This has been a waste of my time. Good day to you, sir."

Infuriated, Tesla had reached the elevator and turned around to shut the gate. At that moment, he caught the smile on Einstein's face. The man continued to mock him! This fool's errand simply had been a childish game him. He was just about to say something, when Einstein said something instead.

"Anya, turn down the top coil to about half power, will you?"

"But Professor, that will…" started Anya.

"It's fine. The apparatus can take the shock."

Anya tentatively turned one of the two grey Bakelite knobs on the device to 50% power. Immediately, something happened inside the metal cage.

From inside the elevator, Tesla could not see exactly what was happening in the cage, but he heard a *thunk* as if the stone had struck one of the copper plates. Then, miraculously, the entire apparatus, electromagnets and all, lifted off the workbench. The power cables trailed below it, looking like a tethered hot air balloon.

Soon, the clips holding the cables to the wall began to pop off one by one as the apparatus continued to rise. With a cry, Kulik ran to the workbench and turned the dial back up to 100% before the machine could pull itself free from its wired tether. It lowered back to the workbench with a heavy *thud.*

"Professor Einstein, in interest of science, I must protest. Very stupid, this thing you did. If something interfered with power, we could have lost artifact forever," complained the Russian.

"Agreed, I am an imbecile," said Einstein in good humor. "But it was an effective demonstration, no?"

Tesla did not exactly understand what he had just seen, but it got him out of the elevator. He walked back to the workbench.

"How powerful are those electromagnets?" asked Tesla.

"These large electromagnets are only ones we find in lab storage area," said Anya. "They are capable of much higher current than we currently use. We do not need anywhere near as much power to control artifact. Right now, we consume only 2,500 milliamps at 100%."

"That's impossible. There's no way 2,500 milliamps could generate enough work to lift that much weight," said Tesla.

Einstein grinned, "You are correct, Niko. However, the electromagnets are not doing the lifting. The *stone* is."

Tesla looked again at the shiny black stone floating inside the cage. It just hovered there, reflecting his confused face back at him. Testing a suspicion, he picked up the stone's sturdy black container and grabbed a screwdriver. He tapped the box with its metal blade. It stuck fast to one of the walls with a *clang*. As he suspected, the Russians had constructed the box out of *magnetite*. Thus, the electromagnets and the cage must be working the same way to contain the stone's innate ability to…to what…*fly?* This was preposterous.

"Albert, are you saying this stone can fly?" asked Tesla, handing Einstein the box.

"Not as such. More accurately, it repels gravity. Because of this, I do not think it belongs in this universe; perhaps has been mislaid, like your oddly displaced planet," said Einstein, practically jumping up and down with excitement.

"This is what landed in Tunguska, Kulik?" asked Tesla. "Why hadn't it simply floated away?"

"*Da, comrade.* At first, we do not understand this either. And we have a very difficult time moving it at all. But Anya found thousands of small, spherical magnetite fragments in ground as well. Apparently, entire region is rich with this ore. When she moved magnetite fragments, stone changed position. Once we understood connection of stone to magnetism, it was simple matter to construct magnetite box to contain artifact," said Kulik.

"Astounding," said Tesla. "Did you find anything else near the site? Any sign that this was of intelligent origin?"

"No, there was nothing, *comrade,* just artifact, and naturally occurring magnetite."

"What is its lifting force?" asked Tesla.

"So far, we have been able to raise about two tons," said Anya.

"Why only two tons?" asked Tesla.

"We run out of weights in lab," said Anya smiling. "For now, total potential is still unknown."

Tesla was dumbfounded. That something so small could lift so much was amazing. Even more astonishing was that a small magnetic field could mitigate this tremendous power. He did not quite know what to make of all this. This discovery would change *everything*.

"This is why we should return artifact to box. If we have a power outage, there is chance it could push its way up and out of here," said Kulik anxiously.

"Go ahead, Kulik. You may put your baby to sleep," said Einstein offering him the box.

"Spasiba, Professor," said Kulik gratefully, taking the magnetic container.

"Still worried about your antigravity engines, my friend?" asked Einstein, smiling at his friend.

"Engines?" asked Tesla, a new light gleaming in his eyes. "Who needs engines?"

* * *

Had it only been two weeks? So much had happened in such a short time, thought Tesla. He had made more progress on the ship in the last few days than he had made during its entire construction. It had all happened so quickly.

Structurally, the ship had always been ready to go. Air tanks and plumbing for maintaining air pressure, as well as other forms of life support, had already been installed nearly five years ago. So had a prodigious bank of batteries for powering the ship's electrical systems.

They had even completed construction on Tesla's original antigravity engines, which had patiently waited for an energy source that never came. Now, those engines were no longer needed. They were removed and replaced with something only a third their size, that used only a small fraction of their power draw.

A vertical copper cylinder about the width of a man now stretched from floor to ceiling near the middle of the ship. Inside the cylinder was a complex arrangement of electromagnets that surrounded the small stone that had made all this possible.

The design of the engine compartment had come to him in a flash. He had seen it, he had built it, and it had worked perfectly as he knew it would. Now, only two weeks later, the ship was floating free of her support blocks for the first time and they were about to make history, all thanks to a small black stone no bigger than an orange.

Tesla had insisted on making the dangerous maiden voyage alone, but Kulik's assistant Anya had been extraordinarily stubborn to the point of taking her stone back to mother Russia. Turning to Kulik for some assistance in the matter had not been much help at all. Kulik had agreed that the discovery had been hers, and she could do with it what she wanted. To make things worse, Albert had been on her side from the very beginning.

"Niko, please, forget for a moment that she is female. Like yourself, she is also a scientist. In the interest of public relations between our two countries..." said Einstein.

"Albert, I do not believe for a moment that you, of all people, can simply ignore that she is female. She reminds me of the fact every time I see her face. Those eyes...that smile. They remind me of someone, a girl I once knew," recalled Tesla. "I could not live with myself if something were to happen to that poor child," said Tesla.

"My friend, I believe you are smitten," said Einstein with a smile.

"Preposterous! I am seventy-two years old. I could be her grandfather. Besides, you know I've never had anything to do with women; they are a distraction and they cloud the mind. It is simply, it's just that, well, confound it, women should not be put in perilous situations, that's all."

"Have more faith in your abilities, Niko. I certainly do. I know just as well as you do that everything will go perfectly."

The compliment warmed him, but he was still nervous. They were about to fly at unheard of speeds to unheard of heights in an untested ship, powered by a stone that

Einstein proposed had come from another universe. He felt he would have her blood on his hands if any unforeseen circumstances occurred.

But he had relented, and now they were embarking on a voyage only dreamed of in human history—*a test flight to the moon.* He closed the round brass door in the ceiling of the Elektra and took his seat next to Anya. With a rumble he heard Einstein open the rear floodgates of the lab. Soon, nearly the entire chamber would be underwater.

"You understand that women are bad luck on ships," teased Tesla, making sure Anya's seat restraints were tight. The seats faced the forward window and tilted back at a forty-five degree angle. He reached over to turn on the forward lighting. It reflected off the surface of the choppy, rapidly rising water.

"Look! The water has reached the ship!" said Anya, ignoring his comment, watching in awe as the water quickly submerged them.

"Hull pressure is within parameters. As expected, the engine voltage spiked just slightly to negate buoyancy," said Tesla, carefully watching the gauges on the console in from of them. "We should be able to leave the moment Albert opens the forward floodgates."

The lights offered limited visibility underwater, but Tesla could still see the huge double doors still closed in front of them.

"Shall I contact them?" asked Anya, waiting to tap the all clear on the ship's Teslascope. The Teslascope was a miracle of technology in itself. The ability to send messages without wires over interplanetary distances had limitless applications. Anya was astounded to hear about Tesla's attempts to communicate across the void of space as early as 1908. Indeed, he had perfected this technology nearly ten years before the first short range radio broadcasts.

"Yes. I believe we are ready. Tell Albert to open the gates."

Kulik and Einstein stood on a catwalk suspended from the tunnel ceiling. The water had leveled off just a few feet below them and the ship was now fully submerged.

"Any moment now," said Einstein, watching the control panel in front of him. Because they were flooding the tunnel, they had removed all the equipment in the lab below and raised the lift. Now just this one control panel remained, hung from the catwalk railing. Heavy cables ran up through the ceiling to the main control room upstairs, giving him local control of the floodgates. During the lab's construction, they had altered the indicators in the main power plant control room, so no one would know what was going on below.

"Look comrade! The signal!" said Kulik pointing at an amber light flashing on the control panel.

The scientist quickly decoded the message.

ELEKTRA READY. OPEN GATE.
HAVE WINE ON RETURN. WE BRING CHEESE.

"Cheese indeed," Einstein laughed, remembering the old moon adage. "Okay, Kulik, here we go. I'm opening the forward floodgates."

The large double doors slowly opened. Tesla watched the voltage gauge spike as the ship fought to stay in place against the increased current of water escaping into the enormous tailrace tunnel beyond. He made a few last minutes measurements and reached for the brass slider that would alter the magnetic field and allow the ship to move into the flow.

"I apologize, madam. Would you like the honor?" asked Tesla, pulling his hand back.

Anya smiled and nodded her thanks. Taking the knob, she pressed it down to release the safety latch. Then, taking a deep breath, she slowly pushed the slider away from her along the groove in the console. At first, nothing seemed to be happening; she did not feel the vibration or acceleration she had expected. However, looking through the forward window she saw that the opened floodgate was getting bigger by the moment. They were indeed moving forward, and the speed seemed to be increasing even though she had taken her hand off the knob.

"I do not understand. Why is our speed increasing?" she asked.

"The Elektra's speed is deceptive. What we control is not the velocity, but the rate of acceleration. This is why your little stone is more powerful than you can imagine," said Tesla. "With this engine, we can maintain a constant level of acceleration without expending additional energy or resources. The longer we leave it running, the faster our velocity becomes. Thus, it is very important we maintain the controls at all times."

"But this is not possible. Could you not travel faster than the speed of light, given enough time?" asked Anya skeptically.

"If you believe such nonsense, then yes, you could. I do not subscribe to Albert's version of the universe. Maybe now he will rethink his idea of *light* having velocity at all, much less a speed limit."

The ship moved rapidly towards the main tailrace tunnel. Tesla adjusted the horizontal controls to manage the turn. The Elektra gracefully turned and increased her speed. Tesla flipped a switch and took his hands off the controls. The brick lined walls of the tunnel flashed past in a blur.

"Shouldn't we slow down? What if there is another turn? You have very little visibility," said Anya concerned.

Tesla smiled. "The tunnel is very straight and less than a mile long. We will be there in seconds. Even so, the Elektra uses its engine to detect the mass around it. We will stay centered in the tunnel as long as we keep this switch closed. He pointed to the switch on the console he had just flipped. Also, we must exit at speed to avoid the rather complicated timing needed to repel the force of the water coming over the falls."

Then casually, he added, "We should exit the falls at nearly four hundred miles per hour."

Before Anya could exclaim her surprise at this, the scene in the forward window changed dramatically. Suddenly, a grey wall appeared in front of them at the edge of visibility. It was coming at them entirely *too fast*. They were going to collide with a tunnel wall after all. She closed her eyes and braced for the impact. A thunderous wave of vibration filled the ship for a moment, and then it was gone, replaced with an eerie silence. She opened her eyes and saw stars in the forward window. She turned to Tesla, who had a pale, but stoic expression, as he adjusted the controls.

"Was that the falls?" speculated Anya.

"Yes, we are now entering the upper atmosphere." Tesla was visibly shaken. "We nearly clipped a few trees coming out of the tunnel on the other side of the bank. We will have to remove them to keep this from happening again. Luckily I managed to avoid them." Then mostly to himself he said, "Just barely."

They had timed the launch at night to best avoid detection, but the newly installed Niagara floodlights encouraged late night, romantically inclined visitors. Tesla hoped the couples would be more interested in each other, than in anything strange ejecting out of Horseshoe Falls.

They had thought of everything. They had been prepared for this moment for years and now it was finally happening. The Elektra was flying them higher and faster than man had ever gone before. In a few seconds, they would be outside the Earth's atmosphere and into the ether of space. With a ship like this, the possibilities were endless. The entire universe was now an open book, waiting to be read. His only regret is that this ultimate triumph had come so late in life.

"Why are you crying, my dear?" asked Tesla.

"It's just so beautiful," said Anya looking through the starboard portal down at the blue and white curvature of the Earth.

Tesla joined her at the window. The Earth was indeed extremely beautiful. From this height, none of the scars of humanity could be seen. Only a peaceful, silent jewel sparkling in the void. The easily recognizable continent of Africa quickly swung into view, pockmarked with clouds. As they were moving against the Earth's rotation, the Americas should have been next. Instead, the terminator horizon, which divided day from night, panned into view and the Earth went dark. Lightning flashed in strange glowing configurations, zigzagging across the storm fronts below. Then, quickly as the darkness came, it left, replaced with dawn over Australia and Asia. Quickly, the cycle began to repeat.

"We have gone around the Earth in less than thirty seconds," said Tesla. Then, after doing a little mental arithmetic, he said, "We must be moving over two thousand miles per hour. Twice more around. What do you say?"

"Certainly," said Anya, breathless.

By the time the Elektra had completed two more revolutions, the indicator light on the Teslascope blinked. Anya decoded the message.

WHAT IS STATUS?

She quickly tapped out their status and current course. The ship was now heading for the moon. Even at their tremendous speed, the moon stubbornly remained a distant disc, floating in space. Tesla was at the console monitoring the chronometer. The slowly rotating numbers indicated thirty minutes, five seconds until *AR*.

"What does *AR* stand for?" asked Anya.

"Acceleration Reversal," said Tesla. "It's the midway point in our voyage where we must turn and reverse our acceleration. Without doing so, we would overshoot the moon and head off into deep space."

"How fast will we be going when we reach that point?" she asked.

"Over two hundred and fifty thousand miles per hour," he said. "After reversal, I hope to orbit the moon at a much more leisurely pace."

"Any chance of landing on its surface?" she asked.

Tesla shot her an incredulous stare. "You still do not fully comprehend the dangerous position you currently occupy. You are traveling at unheard of speed, in an untested ship, in the most hostile environment possible, with less than a foot of protective shielding and insulation between ourselves and a very painful death. You are literally flying through space in a tin can!

"Going to the moon's surface would be foolhardy in the extreme. One puncture of our copper skin and the ride is quite sincerely over. At the speeds we are traveling, even something the size of a pea could burn a hole through the ship.

"Let's not get closer to the moon than we must. Soon man will walk on the moon, but let's take things one step at a time my dear, one step at a time."

His condescending tone had insulted her, and she remained silent throughout much of the rest of the voyage. After they reached the AR point, Tesla altered the magnetic fields surrounding the stone, and the ship spun around and began to slow. They would continue to fly backwards as they decelerated around the moon. This would insure they had a modicum of normal gravity in the ship. Tesla reset the chronometer. Anya's angry expression had not gone unnoticed.

"I apologize, madam. I have forgotten what it was like to be young and impetuous. The young think they will live forever. If you wish, we can drop to within a thousand feet of the surface. We should still be safe at that height, and you should get a remarkable view."

She gave him a hug and smiled broadly.

"I still think women are unlucky on ships," said Tesla embarrassed.

Soon, the moon filled the forward window and the details were fantastic. Huge craters, canyons, and ridges stood out in stark contrast to great grey plateaus stretching out to the moon's horizon.

The Elektra dropped lower, hugging the surface as they made an orbit over its features. They had answered many questions about the moon in their survey, including the one that men had wondered about since looking up at the night sky: was there life on the moon? Unfortunately, they could see nothing to support the old contention. The moon was beautiful, but utterly barren.

Soon, they reached the terminator where the far side of the moon began. Tesla raised their altitude. "We are going into uncharted territory. No one knows what lies behind the moon. Also, we need to return to the original flight plan and head back to Earth."

"If we must," Anya sighed. She gave a longing look back at the fantastic landscape as it disappeared into the darkness.

The far side of the moon had been featureless and oppressive. It was impossible to see anything in the pitch-black port side window. With nothing to guide them visually, Tesla anxiously hovered over his instruments as they passed through the depressing void. Eventually, a thin arc of light appeared on the horizon, and above that, the Earth shone out like a distant beacon.

Anya gasped. The Earth was so small and so very distant. She felt utterly homesick and suddenly afraid. The whole frightful impact of how incredibly far away they were, and how much faith they had put into this little craft, hit her at once, and she paled.

"It's not as if you can pull over and change a tire, can you?" asked Tesla, noticing her demeanor.

"No. I suppose not."

"Don't worry. I am about to rotate the ship and resume acceleration. The trip is halfway over and we will soon be on our way back. I just have to reset the chronometer again. I believe it will be another thirty more minutes until the next AR point," said Tesla.

However, before she could take comfort in this, a loud crash sounded near the rear of the ship, like someone hitting a kettle with a sledgehammer. Her stomach lurched as the ship shuddered to a stop.

"What the Christ?" exclaimed Tesla, fumbling at his seat restraint straps, which were now floating in mid-air in front of him. Apparently, the illusion of gravity had stopped with the ship.

Filled with dread, Anya could now hear a hissing sound coming from the rear of the ship. A hissing sound that was getting noticeably louder as the seconds ticked by.

Chapter 21, Bhuvanesh

The motel radio was blaring some inane nonsense from the local radio station morning show as Ananmaya woke. He slammed down the snooze bar for the third time, cutting off Bud and Holly's "Great Balls of Fire" early morning show. He groggily opened his eyes and looked around. The SOTAR records he had been reading last night were scattered over the bed, and he was lying on top of most of them. *I must have fallen asleep while reading,* he thought, as he wiped the sleep from his eyes.

He was awake, but he did not feel especially well rested. His disheveled bed, with the covers on the floor and the pillows flung around haphazardly, paid witness to a very restless night. The papers beneath him on the bed made little crinkling noises as he shifted his weight. He moved over and picked them up.

Oh yes, the Sobral expedition, thought Ananmaya for a moment, as he concentrated on the papers, shifting the ink back into an invisible state. The eclipse of 1919 had changed those men's lives forever.

The project director, Arthur Eddington, was not a shifter, and neither were the three men from Sobral. However, because of their newly discovered planet, they found themselves part of something much bigger than they ever expected.

He thought how strange it was that the name *Edington* had showed up on two planets from two different universes. Tesla's radio messages had said their planet was from a *parallel* universe. He wondered if the two men could have been quantum brothers across the gulf of intradimensional space.

From his own considerable expertise in quantum physics, he knew that parallel worlds were more than just a fictional concept. They did exist, at least mathematically.

But even to Ananmaya, the coincidences with Philolaus were so improbably as to be astounding.

He wished the records had contained more details about the planet, but he knew there were none. Since the inaugural flight of the Elektra in 1939, any further communication from the mysterious planet had ceased and Tesla never came back. Well, that was not entirely true.

Ananmaya rubbed his sore neck. The cheap motel bed had left a lot to be desired. He double-checked the time on the clock radio. 6 a.m. He had plenty of time to catch his flight to New York.

For his entire life, it seemed like he was always traveling, never putting down roots. He wondered what it would be like to own a home and live in one place. Was there another version of himself on some parallel world living a quiet, sedate, perfectly normal life? Did he have a regular job? A wife? Kids?

If this alternate version of himself did exist, he obviously would not be a shifter. Shifters could never be happy in such a life; they required a much wider view. For Ananmaya, the entire world had become his home. He had passports in many countries and bank accounts in several others. He spoke several languages. Travel broadened the mind, and for Ananmaya, this was everything.

His childhood in India with Bhuvanesh had been instrumental in training his mind to handle the fearsome power he possessed. His teacher had opened doorways in his mind that he did not even know existed. Now he wanted to see everything; he wanted to know everything. He wanted to experience it all.

He owed more to his friend and mentor than he could ever repay. When Bhuvanesh died, his death took a long time for Ananmaya to put behind him. He had felt so many things on that day, betrayal, anger, grief, and fear.

At the time, he could not have imagined how his life would change in so many remarkable ways.

* * *

"I know you want to see the world, my young friend. But know that you are not ready," whispered Bhuvanesh in the few minutes they had left, once his life support had been turned off.

Through a tear-stained face, Ananmaya held tightly to his mentor's hand as he listened to his last words. Normally an impetuous teenager, this time, he chose not argue and let his mentor speak.

"But that is as it should be. You will never be ready. You will never be worthy of attaining everything you seek. No one ever is. But know that even in the face of this truth, what is important is that you never stop trying. Never lose hope," said Bhuvanesh, his voice starting to falter.

"But you've lost hope!" said Ananmaya tearfully. "You want to die and leave me! You could have let me remove the cancer that is killing you. I can see it in your body, destroying you from inside. Why do you continue to shield yourself from my help?"

Bhuvanesh took in a deep, rasping breath; it would probably be almost his last.

"I have lived much longer than most, and I have seen many beautiful things. However, I also have seen much anguish and pain. I am tired, my friend. I no longer wish to bear my burdens."

Bhuvanesh stared up at him with blank eyes that no longer saw into this world. Death was close now, too close, and coming too fast.

"I have given all I can in this life. I want to see what the next life offers, I want to follow those I have lost."

Grief stricken, Ananmaya asked, "Who will teach me now? What am I to do?"

"Everything teaches," said Bhuvanesh with a smile. Then with barely a whisper, "even failure and loss."

And with that, his friend and mentor left this life, leaving Ananmaya alone in the cold hospital room with only sorrow as his companion. For the second time, Ananmaya found himself alone and on his own.

A week after burying his friend, Ananmaya had a certified letter waiting for him at the front desk of the small, run-down apartment complex he had been living at in India. The message was in English and was from a law firm in the United States. It stated that they were very interested in speaking with Ananmaya, and could he call on them immediately upon receipt of the letter. There was a business card stapled to the letter. It read:

The Law Offices of Thompson, Hayes and Simms
E.J. Simms, Attorney at Law

There was a California address and phone number. He stared at in fascination. *California?* What could this possibly be about? He did not know anyone in the United States, much less California.

It was too early to call overseas now; it would have to wait until later that evening. This was fine, as he had planned to spend the day in quiet meditation. It would be difficult now with this distraction bouncing around in his head.

Bhuvanesh had taught him an old style of yoga, which he found excellent in focusing the mind and body. He employed it now, going through his routine slowly. He focused on his teacher, trying desperately to find him in the void, calling out to him with his mind.

Nothing came to him. No one called back; Bhuvanesh was truly gone. He continued to try for a long time afterwards, until he lay exhausted on his mat, sobbing himself to sleep again.

He awoke to rain pelting his window. It was dark outside, but he could see it was coming down hard. He went into the kitchen and fixed himself something to eat. The strange letter from earlier that day was still waiting for him on the table. He pulled off the business card and dialed the number.

"Thompson, Hayes, and Simms. May I help you?" inquired the receptionist on the other end of the line.

"Um, yes, I am calling from India. Please excuse my English. I am not very…"

"Excuse me, did you say India? Please hold on, " said the woman in a rather excited voice. For a few moments, the line was silent, then a man spoke on the line.

"Hello, this is E.J. Simms. Am I speaking to Mr. Ananmaya Gujarati?"

"Yes, yes sir," said Ananmaya nearly speechless. He had not used his last name in years. It was a surprise to hear it from a complete stranger.

"Mr. Gujarati, we have been trying to reach you for days. I assume you received our letter?"

"Yes, yes, I did. What's all this about?"

"First off, Mr. Gujarati, I am sorry for your loss. Mr. Sharma was an old friend of mine. He will be sorely missed."

Mr. Sharma? Who was Mr. Sharma? Ananmaya did not remember anyone named *Sharma.*

"Mr. Sharma? I'm sorry, but I don't know anyone by that name."

"Ah, I think I understand. I think perhaps you might have known him only by his first name, Bhuvanesh."

Bhuvanesh Sharma? How did this American know Bhuvanesh? More importantly, how did he know his last name? He hadn't shared it with him it in the ten years they had traveled together. Bhuvanesh kept much of his past in shadow, his family name especially so.

Why did this lawyer know so much? Was he also a shifter? Was this some sort of condolence call from another member of the Society that Bhuvanesh was once part of? What was this?

"Yes. Bhuvanesh was like a father to me. But Mr. Simms, I am at a disadvantage here. Who are you?"

"I apologize. I would have thought he would have told you about our firm, *considering his last wishes,"* said Mr. Simms. "I represent Mr. Sharma's estate and handle his affairs in the United States."

"What estate? What does this have to do with me?" asked Ananmaya.

The line went silent for a few seconds.

"Hmmm, I suspect he hasn't discussed any of this with you. This is very strange. He has told me much about you, however. I think you may need to sit down, son," said Mr. Simms.

Ananmaya's heart was thumping. Could it be? Could Bhuvanesh, the street magician be leading some secret double life? They had been traveling together for years. When had he found the time?

"Bhuvanesh has entrusted me with his will. He gave us specific instructions to follow on the day of his death. Frankly, I am amazed how he knew exactly when and where he was going to die. You will have to tell me how he did that someday. His will clearly states that all his assets and interests now belong to you. You are a rich man, Mr. Gujarati."

Ananmaya sat in stunned silence for a moment. He looked over at his mentor's old sleeping cot and bag. As far as he knew, those were Bhuvanesh's only possessions. Bhuvanesh was a rich man? This was insane!

"I'm sorry, but I think I lost something in the translation. Did you say Bhuvanesh was *rich?"*

"Well yes, to put it mildly. Over the years, Mr. Sharma made several very wise investments in technology futures. Have you heard of a little dot com called Google?"

"Yes, but surely…"

"Bhuvanesh Sharma is one of only a few major stockholders in the company. There are a few other stocks he owns that I am sure you would recognize. His portfolio is performing quite nicely if I do say so myself.

"Through our partners, we have managed the portfolio on his behalf for some time now. With your permission, we would like to continue servicing the account. Based on current performance indexes, you could retire now with a life of luxury," said Mr. Simms.

"What are you talking about?" asked Ananmaya incredulously. "He would have told me about this."

Bhuvanesh would be the last person he would think of as a stock market mogul. If he had all this money, why hadn't he used it to find more shifters? Why had they led such a meager a life? It didn't make any sense.

"Please, Mr. Gujarati, don't take this the wrong way. I can see you don't believe me; however, that doesn't change the fact that you are now the beneficiary of Mr. Sharma's estate, which is worth millions. Frankly, I'm at a loss myself as to why he did not tell you about his will.

"Are you certain he never mentioned any of this to you? If not spoken, maybe a document? Did he leave a copy of the will somewhere perhaps?"

"Mr. Simms. I am going to have to call you back. I need to think about this," said Ananmaya, as if in a dream. He hung up the phone and looked towards the cot. Bhuvanesh's satchel still rested at its foot where he had left it after insisting that he go to the hospital. It was all he had left to remind him of the wise, kind, and stubborn man that had been his friend.

He had planned on emptying the satchel and packing up the cot, but he could not bring himself to do it. His loss was still too near and too acute. Now however, he opened the bag and looked inside. To his surprise, there were many documents in the bag. Could this insanity be true? Was there possibly a will in the old satchel?

He pulled out a folder of papers, which Bhuvanesh had bound with string. Beneath the string, he had affixed a piece of notepad paper with just one word, Ananmaya.

He pulled out the card and flipped it over. On the back, it read:

Ananmaya,

My friend, I am truly sorry for the grief you must feel. But all books run out of chapters, and even my story must eventually come to an end. I have done many things in my past which I regret. I have worked hard to teach you not to make the same mistakes.

I regret that this is now a path you must walk alone. In time, I hope you will understand why I have kept some things hidden from you.

Please know that I loved you as if you were my own,

- Bhuvanesh

Tears running down his face, Ananmaya tore the string off the folder of papers. Pain and confusion ran through his mind as he opened it. He looked down at the first page, not believing his eyes. Staring back up at him was the last will and testament of Bhuvanesh Sharma.

* * *

Standing up to stretch in the dim light of the motel room, Ananmaya prepared for his morning rituals. It was nice to have time for yoga again. He would need to be focused today, and the Raja exercises relaxed him.

He ran through his routine, taking his time, finding his center, and clearing his thoughts. He had gotten through several asanas when the alarm clock sounded, announcing that it was time to leave. With a sigh, he let reality slowly reassert itself.

He felt something cool and heavy in his hands. Somehow, the little black magnetite box had made its way out of the room safe and into his lap. He looked down at it quizzically; he only had a vague recollection of retrieving it.

It stared back up at him as if daring him to open it. He smiled. He had gotten the box between one of the asanas and forgotten that he had mediated on it. That was proof enough that the Raja had worked. He no longer felt worried about the box or its enigmatic contents. He knew the artifact inside would work as expected. Indeed, many of the previous day's doubts about his mission had dropped away from him like leaves in autumn.

He shoved the box and the last of his clothes into his satchel and picked up the phone to call for a cab to the airport. The blank SOTAR papers were still in a pile on the bed. He was sorting the papers back into his bag, when the sound of a car horn got his attention. The cab had arrived. He hurriedly finished packing and opened the door of his murky motel room. The bright morning sunshine temporarily blinded him; it was going to be a great day to fly.

* * *

The flight to New York had gone smoothly, and his plane arrived at the Buffalo Niagara International Airport later that afternoon. One of the oldest airports in the country, it was also one of the busiest. Ananmaya had gratefully left behind the noisy, rushing crowd when he stepped outside of the stylistic airport. Its gently sloping roofline cast long shadows behind him in the afternoon sun. It was unseasonably warmer than usual, which was fine, as he had not had time yet to purchase heavier clothing.

For Ananmaya, traveling light was an understatement. As he had gotten older, the life lessons he had learned from Bhuvanesh became more and more apparent. Bhuvanesh had them live a life of poverty to teach him exactly how little one needed to be happy. He taught how fleeting the pleasures of wealth could be. Like a fish in an aquarium, human greed grew in proportion to the limits of wealth.

He now saw the wisdom in why Bhuvanesh had hidden his considerable wealth during that stage of his young life. Having that much money would have been all too easy to exploit and misuse. It also would have brought to them too much attention. Most importantly, it would have been robbed him of a vital life lesson in humility.

Meanwhile, the money had silently grown in America, waiting to finance the mission Bhuvanesh had planned for him. Yes, money was a deceiver and the root of all evil, but it sure came in handy when you didn't want to swim thousands of miles across the Atlantic ocean.

Over the years, he had only used a small portion of the immense fortune as he continued to live modestly. Because he wished to remain inconspicuous, the adventure in Brazil had barely put a dent in his resources. He doubted that even Bhuvanesh had expected his investments to perform so exceedingly well. After all this was over, he would find a way to put the money to good use.

It was going to be dark soon, and if he wanted to make it to the Canadian border, he needed to get going. He hailed a taxi. He had considered renting a car, but this would be, after all, a one-way trip.

A yellow cab pulled up to the curb. Ananmaya spoke to the driver as he got inside the back seat.

"I need to get to the Rainbow Bridge. I'm trying to make it to Toronto this evening."

"The Rainbow Bridge? You sure, boss? It's going to be plenty backed up today. I mean, it's your nickel, but you would do better with the Peace Bridge," said the driver in a thick Mediterranean accent. "Either way, the fare is still pretty high. You sure you want to take a cab? Most take the bus."

Ananmaya smiled to himself. He liked the man's honesty. He opened his satchel and dug inside.

"Would $300 cover it?" he asked, handing the driver the bills. "You can keep the change."

"You serious, boss?" asked the driver, pocketing the money. "Brother, you got yourself a cab! What part of Toronto do you want to go to?"

"Queen Victoria Park near the falls. I'm looking for the old Toronto Power station."

The driver looked confused for a moment, and then he thought for a moment.

"Yeah, I think I know the place. It's that old, abandoned place that looks sorta like a castle, right?"

"Yes, that's the place."

"Hmmm, I think they closed that place back in the late sixties. It's all boarded up. Kids sometimes break in to go exploring. I have heard that it's haunted. People keep seeing strange lights and hearing some really *weird* shit coming from underground. You a ghost hunter or something?" asked the driver.

Actually, that was closer to the truth than the man could have known. This whole adventure had been about chasing ghosts from the past. He had been putting faith in wispy promises from what could easily have been the ravings of a lunatic. Still, he had to believe the stories were true. Why else would he be doing all this?

"Um, no, I'm a photographer," said Ananmaya, thinking quickly. He patted his satchel to suggest there was a camera inside. "I like to photograph old buildings and things like that."

"It's creepy if you ask me, but OK. You da boss," said the driver, glancing at his watch. "With the time it will take to get there, I don't think you will have much light left. But we'll see. I'll get you there plenty fast."

With that, he put the car in gear and the bright yellow cab pulled away from the curb.

[PART III]

Chapter 22, Rescue

Carvalho's investment was paying off. After what he had heard at Pinotti's door, he wanted to know who was frequenting the building's main office. For a few reals, he had convinced a few of the local street kids to keep an eye on the Observatório Nacional, and one of them had seen something.

"Sim, Corporal. I saw four people go inside tonight. Two big men, a woman, and the man you told us to look out for," said Felipe, the ten-year-old boy Carvalho had enlisted to watch the building over the past few days.

Hmmm, so Mariconi had finally returned from his mysterious trip abroad. He wondered who the others could be. He would need to go there in person to find out.

"Who's watching the building now, Felipe?" asked Carvalho.

"My sister, Mariana. But she's not as brave as me. She's just a girl," said the little boy with pride.

"Great work, Felipe. You will make a great police detective someday," He gave him two reals and patted him on the back. "Go find your sister and make sure to give her one of these. Can I count on you?"

"Sim! Sim!" said Felipe while hurrying off, shoving the money in his pocket, and beaming with pride.

He's a good kid, thought Carvalho, motioning for the bartender to bring the tab. Felipe reminded him of himself at that age.

At only eight years old, Carvalho had worked the streets for money as well. It was the only way families could survive in the favelas. Everyone worked, begged, or stole what they could to survive. Times were hard then and now. He had known no other life until enlisting in the *Policia Militar* on his eighteenth birthday.

For a little less than twenty years, the military police had been his family as well as his career. Now, because of the incident at the bank, his career had been put on temporary leave.

Too many of these temporary leaves can easily lead to a permanent one. He had to get to the bottom of this and clear his name. He would find the thief and make him explain to his sergeant how he had gotten away. There was no such thing as magic.

Pinotti had not told him the whole truth. Mariconi was the key to this mess, and he intended to get some answers. He paid his tab and left the bar. He had work to do.

* * *

Molly woke in a small room on a cot. Pipes lined the ceiling. The place had a mildewed, disused smell to it. She quickly took an inventory of her fingers. All ten digits were there. Somehow, she did not feel relieved.

Her head had cleared; she had apparently slept off the neurotoxin's effects. *That stuff really packs a wallop,* she thought. Lucky thing too; it had saved her some grief last night and bought her some time. She wondered how long she had been asleep.

She knew she was still in a bad situation, but she was resolved to it. Somehow, the experiences of the past two days had woken up something inside her. She was feeling more like her old college self, the one that used to throw caution to the wind and damn the consequences. The one that didn't have meet deadlines and the expectations of millions of fans. She felt more alive than she had in a long time.

She looked around. The room she was in appeared to be a basement maintenance room with cinder block walls, no windows, and a single metal door. She tried it, but it was locked from the outside. No surprise there.

Think Molly, think. Mariconi had called me a shifter. What did he mean by that? Did he think I could manipulate time like him? No, he said that he was a time shifter, but that did not imply the same about me. So what was my power supposed to be? She was more confused than ever.

Molly looked for a way out of this. Besides the pipes and ventilation shafts high in the ceiling, there was nothing else in the room. She looked at the rectangular vent six feet over her head. It was completely inaccessible.

How come in movies, ventilation shafts are always conveniently within reach and able to accommodate fully grown adults? I mean honestly, who needs to have that much air conditioning.

She considered banging on the door, but something stopped her. Above her head, she heard a scurrying sound. Something was moving in the ventilation shaft.

Ugh. This old place must have armies of rats. Sure, why not? Let's add rabies on top of everything else.

As if her worse fears were being realized, the vent's grill suddenly swung down, creaking on heavily painted hinges. But instead of flooding the room with vermin, a rope snaked its way down to her. Molly yelped in surprise, thinking at first it was a snake.

"Lady, take rope. *Vai!*" whispered a soft voice in the ceiling.

Molly looked up and saw the sweetest face she ever saw. A little round-eyed girl was in the ventilation shaft smiling down at her. Short black hair framed her tanned face. She was motioning for her to climb the rope quickly into the shaft.

"You must be kidding," whispered Molly to her little rescuer. She had never been able to climb the rope in high school gym. But then again, she never had a psychopathic Mr. Rourke wanting to chop off her money makers before. It was a good incentive to try.

"Lady, take rope. *Vai! Rapido!*" whispered the little girl more insistently.

Molly did as she asked and started to climb. She had gotten only one foot off the ground when she noticed the little girl had left. Now what? This was not going to work. She knew it immediately. She just was not strong enough. She hung there motionless, feeling stupid, promising she would work out more if she ever got out of this alive.

With a jerk, the rope suddenly moved. Unbelievably, she was being pulled upwards into the ventilation shaft. Someone strong at the other end was hoisting her up. As she neared the edge of the shaft, she got a foothold on a pipe. This allowed her to crawl inside the narrow cavity.

The little girl's face poked down through a square opening in the shaft about ten feet in front of her. "Lady, come! *Rapido!*" whispered the little girl.

Molly clambered inside and slid on her stomach along the narrow ventilation shaft. At last she reached a beam of light coming through the opening in its ceiling. She turned and poked her head inside. The little girl stood in a very small room that housed the large ventilation fans. *If those fans turned on now, she would be pureed,* Molly thought grimly.

The girl pointed to a small access panel in one of the walls. The rope was holding the hatch slightly ajar. The little girl kicked it open, and they clambered into the room beyond.

"Ms. Arden? Are you okay?" asked a man in military fatigues, helping her to her feet as she stumbled out. Dust covered her from head to toe.

"Yes, as well as could be expected. Thank you. Where am I? Who are you?" asked Molly while brushing herself off.

"My name is Carvalho. We are in the maintenance shed outside the building where you they were holding you. This is Mariana. She is the one that found you. It's her you should thank. It is a miracle we were able to get you out at all. This place is more heavily guarded than the presidential palace. We still need to get off the grounds. Please, put this on."

He handed her a lab coat and finished spooling up the rope. "Also, tie up your hair. I apologize, but this is the best disguise I could come up with on short notice."

Molly put on the coat and tied her hair with a bit of string from the rope. "How do I look?"

The burly man smiled. "Like someone trying to escape by wearing a bad disguise. But it will have to do. Let's go."

"What about Mariana?" said Molly looking around for the cute little girl who had somehow disappeared.

"Oh, she can find her own way out," said Caravalho disinterested.

"She can't be more than six years old!" exclaimed Molly. "Where are her parents?"

Carvalho looked at her as if she had lobsters crawling out of her ears. "Ms. Arden, she will be fine, really. We need to go now before they discover you are missing."

They joined a group of tourists leaving the observatory museum. Amazingly, no one stared at Carvalho. Molly thought for sure a man in military fatigues would stand out at a public facility, but then she noticed that armed men were everywhere. They were also carrying high powered rifles. Was this common in Brazil? She vaguely remembered something about Brazil having a military police force, so maybe it was. She really did need to get out more.

They made it to the front entrance and took the elevator down to the street. A ridiculously small car was parked at the curb. Carvalho put his gear in the back seat and quickly got them both inside. Molly fumbled for the seat belt, but gave up when she realized they didn't work. Carvalho started the car and drove off into the congested streets of Rio.

Carvalho seemed unconcerned about the whole affair. He even turned on the radio. Unexpectedly, the station was playing American rock and roll.

"So, do this often, do you?" asked Molly.

"*Que?* Uh, what?" asked Carvalho, turning the radio down.

"Rescue women in distress, I mean?"

"Well, not before lunch, in broad daylight, if that's what you mean," said Carvalho smiling.

"What's going on?" asked Molly. "Things are moving so fast, I don't know what to expect next. For example, where the hell are we going?"

Carvalho was swerving in and out of the traffic, moving quickly through the crowded street. Strangely, no one seemed to be bothered by his insane driving.

"As far from those people as we can get right now. I am taking you to a place we can talk. Somewhere public, but quiet. Have you ever been to *Pau d'Acurar*? It is a popular tourist attraction, and there's only one way up there," said Carvalho.

"You're taking me sightseeing? Well this is turning out to be one hell of a first date," smirked Molly.

"I just want to talk, Ms. Arden," said Carvalho still smiling. "The mountain is a very public, but quiet place. We need to compare notes. I think you may be involved in something I am working to understand."

As they sped through the city, Carvalho explained about the theft and why he, or rather his two young *deputies,* had been watching the observatory.

"After Felipe told me Mariconi had returned, I drove to the observatory to speak with him. The guard insisted he was not there, and he would not take a bribe, so I left. That's how I knew something was up. Sometime later, Felipe's sister Mariana, who was still watching the complex, found me. She told me she saw the man in white tell the two bigger men to come back inside. She told me they carried you unconscious into the maintenance tunnel."

Carvalho paused a moment to shout out of his window at someone on the street. The pedestrian was apparently oblivious to the effect half a ton of metal careening at sixty kilometers per hour could have on his body.

"Mariana is a brave little girl. She followed them as far as she could and saw where they put you. They put a padlock on the door. She almost got caught trying to open it. She told me where you were, and had even found a way to get you out. We waited until the observatory opened in the morning, and the tourists showed up. That's when we busted you out."

"Tell her I am forever grateful to her. Where does she live? Can I thank her myself?" asked Molly.

Again, Carvalho looked at her strangely. "Ms. Arden, you do not know much about this part of Brazil do you? Trust me, you don't want to know where she lives. These kids do not have what you would call a home. But Mariana and her brother are smart. They will be fine. I'm more worried about you. Did you know the whole world is looking for you?"

"What?"

"Ever since you went missing in Costa Maya a few days ago, the world's been in an uproar looking for the famous Ms. Molly Arden," said Carvalho pulling into a circular parking area.

"Look, you can just call me Molly," she replied. But suddenly a vagrant walked up to the car. He spoke to Carvalho and a brief argument ensued. The man wanted money to watch the car while they were gone. Carvalho briefly showed his badge and the man walked away briskly.

"Look, we can talk more up there," Carvalho pointed to the bay where the peaks of two towering mountains that looked like oversized footballs shoved in the dirt on their ends. "Let's go."

"What?!" Molly exclaimed again. She didn't have so much a fear of heights. Just a fear of hitting the ground.

The shadow of something moving fast passed over the car and Molly looked up. A large cable car packed with people was zipping directly overhead in the direction of the mountains. It hung from nearly invisible cables extending from the depot behind them to the tops of the mountains hundreds of feet up in the air. With all that weight, it looked extraordinarily unsafe. Was she expected to ride this deathtrap?

"I don't do well with heights," she pleaded.

"Come on Molly. You will be fine. You're with me after all," Carvalho said and smiled. He took her arm in his and led her to the depot.

Chapter 23, The Calliope

"I think we've been struck by a meteor!" shouted Orville, his voice rising in panic.

"Bloody friggin' hell!" cursed Edington to the universe in general. "Now this happens? *Now?*"

The ship had been acting erratically since passing the midway point in her long journey, and it had only gotten worse. By the time they passed the second inner planet, the Calliope had begun spinning out of control.

Mandic and Edington worked miracles for hours trying to stabilize her and, in the meantime, the other five members of the crew tried hard not to be sick as they managed their jobs.

Every time Mandic corrected one axis of rotation, she would start spinning along another. The manual controls on the ship were simply not up to the level of precision they needed to keep the flight straight and level without the aid of the automatic compensators. It was a miracle they remained more or less on course at all. However, things had gotten much worse on their final approach to the planet.

Its large moon was twice the size of the one that circled Archænis, and much closer than they had expected. Its gravitational pull had wreaked havoc with the complicated course projections Edington had pre-prepared for them.

Normally, Mandic could have adjusted for this, but without the compensators, they were flying by the seat of their pants.

They had just barely managed to escape the moon's gravity well, and had regained some notion of control when suddenly, something slammed into the ship's cargo hold with a resounding crash. The collision had been had been enough to send them once again tumbling end over end.

Unfortunately, the stress of the flight had taken its toll on the elderly engineer. He had taken a few bumps trying to maintain his position near the radium powered magnetron, and had a pallid expression.

"We need to stabilize this velocity so that we can reorient ourselves," coughed Mandic.

Edington noticed his friend's composure and feared the courageous man had radiation exposure sickness. He nodded and turned to his apprentice who was piloting the ship, "Orville, cut all acceleration again. We need time to level out from this latest injustice."

Orville readjusted the controls and began to implement the trimming circuits, trying to predict what was coming next.

"On my mark, use one-third power on the port coil for three seconds, then one-fourth power on the forward coil for two. Ready…set…*mark!*"

Orville already had his hand on the controls he needed. He quickly applied the corrections.

Edington noticed, however, that he had only applied the last correction for one second rather than the two he had asked for.

"Orville! What are you doing?" exclaimed Edington.

If this first adjustment did not put them in precisely the right rotation, the rest of his prepared corrections would be pointless.

"I believe you might not have compensated for our additional forward momentum from the collision, sir. If you look out the window, you will see the correction was accurate," said Orville sheepishly.

Edington and Mandic looked out the window. Sure enough, the moon was rotating slowly before them, at exactly the right interval.

"Ahem, yes, quite right, Orville. Excellent work. Prepare for the next set of corrections," said Edington.

"Aye sir," said Orville.

"And Orville..."

"Yes sir?"

"Don't do that again without checking with me first."

"Aye sir," said Orville smiling, taking the controls again.

Surprisingly, his apprentice had turned out to be one hell of a pilot. He had come through when they needed him. Edington and Mandic had needed time to calculate their course corrections to compensate for the large moon. Orville had managed to give them the time they needed, by instinctively flying the ship in a series of dizzying loops, flying in and out of the gravity well. If it had not been for his quick thinking they would have been another impact crater on the scarred and pitted satellite.

"I don't like the inductance readings on the port coil," said Mandic, half-buckled in, hunched over the glowing magnetron indicators.

"Harland, Meriwether, unbuckle yourselves and go below. Check the shielding on the port coil," said Edington.

"Calvin and Philomena, put on your ether suit helmets and then take a look at the impact damage in the cargo hold. Be careful at the airlock. It might be jammed. Don't get yourselves locked in there."

What a crew, thought Edington. Four astronomers, a city engineer, and two council members were hardly the ether-hardened stock of their forefathers. *What had the mayor been thinking?*

Himself and Quinn Mandic he could understand, but Harland and Philomena? The two popular council members were just as surprised as Edington when their names had made the roster. The mayor had argued that he needed them on the voyage for diplomatic relations with the new planet. And although the two had no great love for the mayor, they were pleased to be part of the crew.

They had been surprisingly quick studies for having no previous interest in science, and Edington had assigned them to life support and solar radiation monitoring. They had done a remarkably competent job of it.

Lastly, no matter how hard he tried to get them off the list, Orville, Calvin, and Meriwether had be conscripted as well. Why the Calliope needed the apprentice to the Chief Royal Astronomer and both his research assistants on this trip was beyond him. That left no one in charge at the observatory. Also, at the time, Edington would have preferred older navigators with more experience.

However, the two astronomers' adeptness at mathematics had proven invaluable in the astronavigation of this strange, unknown universe. Their young minds reacted quickly to unexpected challenges, and Edington doubted senior navigators could have done any better with this unfamiliar part of space

Edington smiled. He was proud of his crew.

The mayor had wanted this trip to fail. He had not given them the tools they needed, and probably had seeded the crew with people he thought would not be up to the task. Nevertheless, he had inadvertently given Edington exactly the people he needed to survive as much of the mission as they had.

They had made it this far, and he would be damned if he'd let the ship crack up on the moon because of some random meteor impact.

Unfortunately, what he was *not* telling them is that they no longer had the power to return home. All the course corrections had consumed so much radium that their supply was nearly exhausted. Their only hope was that the people on the planet below could somehow help them.

"It looks like Harland and Meriwether fixed the shielding on the coil," said Mandic, watching the needle rise. "We're almost ready to proceed."

The two men glided up through the round door in the floor of the bridge and closed the bulkhead door. They pulled themselves along the console and made their way back to their seats. Harland looked green because of the lack of gravity in the ship.

"Harland, if you are going to be sick…" began Edington, but suddenly Harland pulled out a paper bag from the receptacle in front of him and heaved his lunch into it.

"I was going to say use the bag, but I see you have remembered your training," said Edington with a smile.

"I'm okay. It's just my stomach. All this spinning…" said Harland hoarsely, folding the bag shut and fitting it into the disposal.

"I know. It won't be long. When Calvin and Philomena get back we'll start the counter rotation," said Edington.

Where were they, he thought? They had been gone for too long. Edington was getting an unpleasant feeling in the pit of his stomach.

"Did you want me to go after them sir?" asked Meriwether. The stocky, well-built young man was positively thriving in the low-gravity environment. He started unbuckling his seat again.

"No, not yet. Let's give them a few more minutes, and then I will…" Edington paused as he noticed the airlock indicator flash from red to green. They had returned to the airlock from the cargo hold.

As soon as the air pressure equalized inside, the large brass handle would start to turn. Then the heavy, cast iron hemispherical door would open into the control room.

"Ah, here they are now," Said Edington, turning to face the door. "Let's see how much damage we have."

The door hissed open, and Philomena came out first, her helmet already off, and a surprising smile on her face. She was quickly followed into the control room by Calvin who was having trouble removing his helmet.

Philomena turned and looked past him into the airlock expectantly. Astonished, Edington saw another set of arms reach out from behind the airlock door to help Calvin with his helmet. With a small twist, it was free.

The arms belonged to a beautiful woman in a strange ether suit. She handed Calvin his helmet as she floated in behind him. She looked around in rapt astonishment as she floated halfway into the control room.

Then, startled as if she had forgotten something, she turned back towards the airlock. She reached out a hand to help yet another person pass through the bulkhead opening.

Mandic's mouth dropped as he saw whom the young woman was pulling through the airlock. Edington and the others gasped as well. An elderly man in the same strange ether suit as the woman floated into the room. His arms and legs began flailing wildly, utterly unaccustomed to the lack of gravity. Besides his animated appearance, what struck the occupants the most was that the man looked exactly like Mandic*!* All eyes were now on the elderly stranger.

"Unhand me!" said Tesla to Meriwether who had come to his rescue.

He even sounds like me, thought Quinn, who had put the present crisis on hold. He unbuckled his restraints.

"I am perfectly capable of finding my own way, young man," said Tesla shaking off Meriwether's hand. Tesla took hold of a clamp on the wall.

"Why are these people looking at you in such a way?" asked Anya.

Chagrined, he hadn't noticed that everyone was staring at him, until now. He suddenly felt very self-conscious and stopped flailing so much. It didn't help; they continued to stare.

Tesla saw one of the men in the room, an older man, pulling himself closer to them.

"Quinn Mandic," said the man, looking up at them, offering his hand.

"Great Scott!" Tesla exclaimed. "But that is, I mean, we look, I mean to say, you look just like me!"

"Yes, but I believe, more to the point, that we look like each other," said Mandic. "This is peculiar, is it not?"

"Strange indeed, good sir, strange indeed," Tesla said over his initial surprise. "My name is Tesla. Nikola Tesla, and this is my assistant, Anya."

Anya greeted Tesla's twin, studying him carefully. She compared him with her comrade.

"This is astounding. You two could be brothers," she said. Both men smiled at her. It was uncanny; it was as if Tesla was looking in a mirror.

"If that were true, our mother would probably have some serious explaining to do," said Tesla smiling.

Mandic laughed, which then turned into a hacking cough. He bent over for a moment and covered his mouth until the fit subsided.

"I'm sorry. I have not had a very good trip. I am rather out of sorts. Please excuse me."

Mandic let Meriwether help him back into his seat as Edington floated up to the new arrivals.

"I take it then that you two must be from the planet?" asked Edington, pointing through the starboard window at the blue-green orb of Earth slowly drifting through space.

Tesla and Anya nodded.

"Why did you ram us? Calvin and Philomena tell me that your ship has buried itself halfway into our cargo hold."

"Yes, we seem to have crossed paths. Rather bad form on my part, I must say," said Tesla, bemused by the ridiculous situation. "Smaller ships should always give way to the larger, no?"

"Well, we were not exactly flying in a predictable manner either," said Edington. "We didn't expect to find other ether ships. We were not even aware that your people possessed ether travel."

"We don't. Not yet," said Anya. "The Elektra is experimental craft. We were on test flight."

"A test flight? Do you mean to tell me that your ether ship is one of a kind?" asked Edington.

"Quite. After many unsuccessful years trying to develop an antigravity engine, we recently uncovered a completely new form of propulsion," said Tesla. "More specifically, my lovely colleague here was the one who actually discovered it."

Anya blushed as she spoke, "Twenty years ago something crashed into planet and left behind rather remarkable stone. It has given us power to leave our world."

"Do you mean *Leviton ore?*" asked Mandic.

"Excuse, please?" asked Anya.

"Naturally occurring, antigravity ore," said Mandic. "Do you mean to say this element is unknown on your planet?"

"Except for stone we find at the impact site, we had no idea something like this could even exist," said Anya.

"Did you say you found it twenty years ago?" asked Edington.

"Yes. In northern Siberia, near top of world," said Anya.

Edington thought for a moment. "I believe you are using the same element that moves this ship. It is extremely rare in our universe, but it exists in enough quantity to build ships like these. We use it in all of our ether crafts, including our unmanned probes. From what you are telling me, Philolaus arrived in this universe at the same time your meteorite appeared. The two events cannot simply be coincidental."

"What do you suggest?" asked Tesla.

"The postal ether probe!" interrupted Orville excitedly.

"What?" asked Edington.

"The missing postal ether probe, Mr. Edington! It must have been within the event horizon when we fell into the rift," said Orville.

"I see where the young man is going." said Mandic. "The ether probe must have been on its way and had succumbed to the same force that had pulled us here. Undoubtedly, its mechanics got confused by the new orbital geometry and crashed into Archænis's twin here. Thus, what you found was the only surviving part of the probe—her Leviton ore. It is strange that it did not escape back into space."

"I can answer that," said Anya. "The area it crashed in is rich in naturally occurring magnetite spheroids. At first, we thought it was material from the explosion, but later geological testing showed the magnetite was indigenous to the area. After studying the properties of the floating stone, we knew it was highly receptive to magnetic influence. The magnetite must have kept it trapped where it impacted."

Mandic nodded his head in agreement.

"Absolutely fascinating," said Tesla amazed. Then, he had a sudden realization. "You must be the people we are trying to find. Over ten years ago, I received a radioscopic message from a planet on the opposite side of the sun which requested our help. We built the Elektra in response to that call. Are you from that planet?"

"Yes! Yes, we are. I sent that message. My name is Samuel Edington. I hadn't realized that anyone had heard our call. As such, we have come to you in this ship. You are aboard her majesty's research vessel, the Calliope. "

Tesla and Anya shook his hand.

"I do not understand. If you have ether travel, why send us message?" asked Anya.

"We did have ships, but over the years we have gutted them for parts. Their coils, mechanics, and Leviton ore have all been stripped away and repurposed," said Mandic.

"The colonies sacrificed much to give us the parts needed to resurrect this one craft. It is likely the only journey she will ever make and she is our last hope for survival," added Edington.

"Once we knew our planet was in a parallel universe, we soon realized we would not be able to sustain ourselves without help from our home world, Archænis. The striking similarities between our solar systems gave us hope that there may be another planet opposite the sun as well. We sent an autonomous probe to detect and photograph the planet if it existed."

"And it worked! It really did," said Orville excitedly. "The photos showed your world was almost an exact duplicate of Archænis."

"But there were still confounding mysteries. Since a parallel planet like Archænis exists in this solar system, why didn't we find a planet like Philolaus as well? We were very concerned at the prospect of another world becoming displaced because of us," said Meriwether.

"But then Mr. Edington remembered Aphrodite," said Orville.

"Aphrodite?" asked Anya.

"Yes. We had also found an additional world between our orbit and that of Hermes, your innermost planet. We called her Aphrodite. With the same mass and size, she would be the parallel to Philolaus if not for her tighter orbit," said Edington.

"Ah, I am beginning to see," said Anya. "You must mean Mercury and Venus. How strange it is that you chose of the Greek names and we the Roman."

"Do you?" said Edington. "How very interesting. And your home world, what do you call her?"

"Earth," said Anya. "It is neither Greek nor Roman."

The odd name rang a bell in the back of Edington's mind. It must have been in a story he had read once, long ago. Some tribal legend or such from one of the southern countries. It was a familiar name, but he could not quite place it. Interesting as it was, the little etymology discussion would have to wait; there were more pressing matters.

"Unfortunately, I'm afraid our people have become uninvited guests in your universe, guests who are deeply in need of assistance. We have come to plead our case," said Edington.

"Excuse me, Mr. Edington, but more specifically to the immediate, we need to get the Calliope under control," said Mandic, making another adjustment. "The collision with Mr. Tesla's ship has not exactly improved matters. I could use another set of hands over here."

"Quite right, Quinn, first things first. Mr. Tesla, if you would, please assist Mr. Mandic at his station," said Edington.

"Certainly," said Tesla. As he groped his way to the engineer, he tried to comprehend the highly improbable series of coincidences that had recently occurred. Both his ship and Edington's had collided at the same point in space and time, under entirely different circumstances. If that fact alone were not enough, he had found a duplicate of himself on that ship. Incredible, just incredible.

"I'm sorry, did you say your name was Mandic?" asked Tesla moving over to help Quinn at the controls.

"Yes. My father was George Mandic," said Quinn. "Does that mean something to you?"

Tesla wavered at the name. He did not quite know how to respond without sounding awkward.

"I believe sir, that your father, well, was my mother," said Tesla.

Quinn gave him a blank, incomprehensive look.

"Let me explain. My mother's maiden name was Djuka Georgina Mandic. There are similarities in our universes, but apparently rather striking differences. The sexes of our parents apparently are one of them. Who was your mother?"

"Anise Kalinic, named after my grandfather, Ananias Kalinic," said Quinn. "Are you suggesting that your father was also my mother?"

"Not at all. My father's name was Milutin Tesla. Kalinic was my grandmother's name, which she lost when she married my grandfather. These two gender reversals caused your family line to be Mandic and mine to be Tesla, yet we share similar progenitors. Fascinating, don't you think?"

"Yes, but genealogy is not the science we need to employ at this time," said Quinn. "Are you familiar with resonant electromagnetic theory? We need to get the ship righted and pointed in the right direction. Orville cannot hold her here much longer."

"Why don't you simply let my ship's engine tow you to a safe harbor? My engines and controls are still functional, and we could do so by leaving the Elektra embedded in your flank," asked Tesla.

"Unless you can hold your breath a really long time, I don't think that's going to work," said Harland, sitting next to Mandic. "Because of the damage to the hull, all the air in both your ship and the cargo hold has escaped."

"We patched what we could, but accident has even depleted the air reserves in that part of the ship," said Philomena.

"They could wear the ether suits and attach an air hose to the control room airlock," said Harland. "There's extra tubing in the supply closet."

Until hearing Harland's suggestion, a young man seated next to the pilot had quietly been watching the events of the last fifteen minutes. He now spoke. "Mr. Edington, just because this man looks like Mr. Mandic, and says he is willing to help us, doesn't mean he is trustworthy. No offense meant to our visitors sir, but he did ram us. With all this space around us, it is a rather odd coincidence wouldn't you say? How do we know we can trust them?"

"Honestly, Calvin, have you no manners?" asked Philomena.

"No, he is simply voicing an obvious question. One that I may have the answer to," said Edington.

"Before his death, Professor Almos had been working on a theory to explain the phenomenon that brought us here. In his notes, he went into great detail on the nature of parallelism between the worlds. In simple terms, we are like someone looking at his reflection in a carnival mirror. When he raises his hand, a corresponding hand rises in the reflection, but because of the distortion in the glass, it is not exactly the same effect, but it is a reflection nonetheless. This elegant description shows how parallel universes can be different, but related."

"Yes, but what about meeting in the deeps of the ether, at the same time and place? How do you explain that?" insisted Calvin.

"Because Mr. Mandic was on our ship and Mr. Tesla was on his. Consider the illustration once more. Imagine that the viewer is Quinn and the reflection is Mr. Tesla. Even though they knew nothing of each other, each man had a desire to visit the other's world. In our case, Quinn wanted to go the Earth and worked towards doing so on Philolaus. In Mr. Tesla's case, he wanted to visit Philolaus and worked towards doing so on Earth. In both cases, the impetus to journey was the same, but each man's path to achieve this goal was different, as would be their distorted hypothetical reflections. As in the mirror, when you step closer to the glass, the reflection steps closer as well. Eventually, both will touch the glass at some point at precisely the same moment. Thus, the fates of these two men guided our two ships and everyone in them."

"That's a bit too esoteric for me," said Calvin doubtfully.

"Please, we mean no harm. We are only trying to help," said Anya.

Mandic began another coughing fit, doubling over. Philomena and Harland rushed to his side.

"He needs a doctor," said Philomena wiping his sweating forehead.

"Can you help him?" asked Harland, looking at the newcomers.

"We need to get him to Earth," said Tesla. "I would suggest that we land your ship on the far side of the moon so you can make repairs. There are, well, politics involved in landing a ship this large on Earth. We are not accustomed to visitors from other planets and, as much as I would enjoy the satisfaction of proving life exists somewhere other than on Earth, I doubt you and your crew would enjoy the attention you would get from our governments. How are you with your provisions?"

"We have more than enough food, water and air to last for another two weeks," said Philomena.

"That's not the real problem," said Edington. "The main issue is the radium supply. We'll be out of power in just a few days."

Tesla saw the look of shock on the crew's faces. Apparently, they had not known about this.

"I can help with that. For now, we can use part of the power stored in the batteries on my ship. They should sustain you while we go back to Earth with Mr. Mandic, and you make repairs," said Tesla.

"You can store power?" asked Edington, surprised.

"Yes. Why?" asked Tesla.

"I can see we have a lot we can learn from each other Mr. Tesla. I will accept your offer to tow us to the far side of your moon as well as the balance of your assistance. Thank you," said Edington.

"Harland, Philomena, please see to it that Mr. Edington and his lovely assistant get everything they need."

"So you are going to let them take our engineer and maroon us on their moon?" asked Calvin.

"You're welcome to come with us," said Tesla. "My ship can carry four."

"And we can use the help with Mr. Mandic," said Anya.

"An excellent idea indeed, Ms. Anya," said Edington. "Calvin, after we set the ship on the far side of the moon I want you to brief Mr. Tesla on our planet's history and its problems. When Quinn has recovered, he can fill in the technical details. We will begin repairs here. The damage to the cargo hold will take a week or more to repair. Also, I'd like to get the coil's automatic compensators working. See if Mr. Tesla has any ideas concerning that."

"There's no need for all of you to remain up here. We can take shifts and take turns during return trips. Would this be possible, Mr. Tesla?" asked Calvin.

"Of course. It is a matter of a few hours to travel to the moon and back. And as my ship is small, there will be many trips needed to bring the supplies you need for repairs," said Tesla.

"The problems your planet is facing are matters we will need to discuss in detail. We have no space fleet. We have no cargo ships. But we do have a private group of very talented individuals, the same powerful organization that helped me build the Elektra, our planet's first space craft."

"Well, unless they can do things beyond the reach of us mere mortals, I won't believe it," said Calvin.

"Don't worry. We can," said Tesla, "and we do."

Chapter 24, Pursuit

Molly and Carvalho waited in the queue for the gondola. Carvalho had brought a change of clothes from the car and was now wearing jeans, a black t-shirt, and a light jacket which covered the butt of a handgun holstered at his waist.

"I like the shirt," said Molly amused.

"We need to fit in with the other tourists here."

"Yeah, but *'Weapon of Mass Seduction?'* "

"It was the only thing I had that wasn't in Portuguese." said Carvalho.

They stepped into a gondola already crowded with tourists. To her horror, Molly realized that some idiot chose to make the entire cabin out of *glass,* including most of the floor as well as the door sliding shut behind them. As the gondola lurched forward, she gripped Carvalho's arm tightly, trying hard not to look down.

"Why are we doing this again?" she asked.

"You will see. Do not worry, the ride isn't long, and we're only going to the first landing," he said, pointing to the top of the football-shaped mountain that they were fast approaching.

They were now hundreds of feet up, suspended over the steep jungle mountainside, but it wasn't as frightening as she had thought. The ride was incredibly quiet and smooth. For Pete's sake, there were children and babies in the cabin with them; none of their parents seemed overly concerned. Everyone was taking pictures and pointing out landmarks in the sprawling city below.

There seemed to be people of every nationality in the gondola with them, excitedly speaking to one another in their native languages. This mountain was a popular tourist attraction indeed.

"Look, there's the beach!" said a little boy behind her, tugging on his mother's dress.

Surprised to hear someone speaking English, she turned to find an Australian family behind her. They were trying to see over her shoulder. She smiled and moved over, letting them have her spot.

"Cheers, love," said the mother to Molly as she raised her son to the railing to get a better view. "It's a right beaut, orright?"

"Yes, yes it is," agreed Molly. The beach stretched for miles forming a long, thin crescent against the ocean.

"That's *Praia do Flamengo.* It is one of our best beaches," said Carvalho proudly.

"Do us a favor, would you mate?" asked the husband, offering Carvalho his camera. He squeezed in next to his family at the rail, and they smiled for the photo.

Carvalho took the picture and handed the man his camera back.

"Good onya!" said the man. "Nice place you folks have here. You two from around these parts?"

Molly started to say they were not a couple, but Carvalho interrupted her.

"Yes, we live in Copa Grande, in the south of Brazil. We're on our honeymoon. My wife has never been to Pau d'Acucar," said Carvalho, taking Molly's hand in his, covering her bare ring finger.

"Oh, that is lovely," said the woman, smiling at Molly. "Do I know you, love? You have a familiar face. You're an American, right?"

"Canadian, actually," lied Molly, getting into the act. She hoped the gondola would dock soon. She did not know how long they could keep up the ruse if these people continued asking questions. Luckily, she had a flash of inspiration. "I met Miguel when I was in college. He was a foreign exchange student, and he swept me off my feet. We've been together ever since."

"Well, I'll be stuffed! That is just so romantic," the woman cooed.

"Mummy, look! There's people on the mountain!" said the little boy.

Everyone looked at the now vertical slope of the approaching mountain. Sure enough, there were some intrepid thrill seekers steadily climbing ropes attached to pitons that had already been setup for the purpose.

"Blimey. Aren't they hot enough as it is?" said the man, noticing their black fatigues and shirts.

"It looks like a military exercise," said the woman, taking her son off the rail, as the gondola pulled into the depot at the top of the mountain. "They are probably Brazilian military in training or something."

"Or something," said Carvalho, cursing under his breath, as he exited.

"Well, anyhow, pleased to meet ya," said the man, shaking Carvalho's hand. "You and the little woman have a great time. You fellas going up to the next mountain?"

"I think we'll enjoy the view here. My wife is not very fond of heights," said Carvalho.

"No worries mate! See ya," said the cheerful man taking his little boy's hand.

"I saw ninjas climbing the mountain!" said the boy to his parents as they walked off.

Molly looked at Carvalho and did not like what she saw. He didn't look so much anxious as he did annoyed. Something had riled him.

"Let's go. Our talk is going to have to wait," said Carvalho, hurrying her up the cobblestone mountain path. "We've been followed."

"You don't mean the ninjas, do you?" asked Molly.

"Of course I mean them. Who are these people?" demanded Carvalho, rapidly moving her along a route that overlooked an astoundingly beautiful vista. They must be more than a thousand feet up.

"You wouldn't believe me if I told you. I thought you knew more than I did. Where are we going?"

"I have a friend that works for Helisul Turistico, a touring company. He owes me a favor. I only hope he is working today," said Carvalho.

They ran down a path that led to a small building with a helipad behind it. A helicopter with the words "Helisul Panoramic Flights" emblazoned on the tail sat waiting there.

Molly stopped running. "No! No! No! This is where I draw the line. I'm not getting into one of those!"

Carvalho looked at her with surprise. "You'd prefer to go back to the observatory?"

Molly looked back up the hill at the depot. "Ok, even if those men were from the observatory, they won't be here for at least an hour. They were moving fast, but I seriously doubt they were really ninjas. We can just take the gondola back down, can't we?"

"And do you honestly think no one will be waiting for us down there? I'm surprised no one was already up here to rush us. Those two on the mountain are probably just there to keep an eye on us. They want to make sure we do not do something unexpected, something like that," said Carvalho, motioning towards the helicopter.

Molly had to admit that her options were limited.

"Let's just go inside and see if Marceau is here," said Carvalho opening the door for her. "And you are right; we have a little time until they get here. We can talk."

* * *

"Enrico!" said a thin, middle-aged man with a thick black moustache facing them from behind the counter.

Travel posters and brochures littered the small room. The posters showed Brazil from a dizzying height, portraying sprawling panoramic scenes of mountains and beaches. Helisul had stamped their logo in the bottom right corner of each poster. A list of the sights to see was on the counter with the duration and cost of each flight.

Molly noticed there was a special package today for flying over Ipanema, Copacabana, and Corcovado—the famous, one hundred, thirty-foot statue of Jesus with his hands outstretched. It featured prominently on the ad.

"Bom dia. Tudo bom?" greeted Marceau.

"Tudo…e você?" replied Carvalho, exchanging the greeting.

"Mais ou menos. Você me trouxe uma tarifa?" asked the man in indecipherable Portuguese. He motioned towards Molly who didn't understand any of this. She looked at Carvalho questioningly. They could be discussing her bra size for all she knew.

Carvalho apologized and switched to English. "Actually Marceau, I've brought you *two* customers. We need to ask you a favor. How soon can you get the helicopter ready?"

"Well, as soon as someone else shows up. We only fly with three or more passengers," said Marceau. "Have you seen the special today?" He motioned towards the advertisement.

"Marceau, please. You need to get the helicopter ready *now*. We need to get off the mountain as soon as possible. It's important. You owe me."

The man's eyes turned towards Molly, then back at Carvalho. "What's going on, my friend? Is everything okay?"

"No, it's not. And for your own sake, I suggest you not ask any more questions. Also, I'll need to pilot the helicopter myself."

Marceau's eyes widened. *"Meu Deus!* Are you insane? I would lose my job if they found out! Worse, I could lose my license!"

"I can't let anyone know where we're going. It is for your own protection, Marceau. There are some very bad people after us," said Carvalho.

"What have you done now?" asked Marceau annoyed. "*Amigo,* I do owe you, but I can't let you take the helicopter. Let me fly you. I'll take you where you want to go."

"Okay, but you are taking a pretty big risk."

"It's no problem, but we're even now, right?"

"*Sim,*" said Carvalho giving the man a brotherly embrace.

"Just hurry and get it ready," said Carvalho.

Marceau left to outfit the helicopter. Molly turned to Carvalho.

"Just a minute, *En-ri-co,* " said Molly, comically pronouncing each syllable of what she now knew as his first name. "I don't remember saying I would get into one of those. And what's this about your being a pilot? You know how to fly helicopters too?"

"Yes. I trained for several years with GRPAe, the aerial patrol in São Paulo. These commercial helicopters are much the same, only without the infrared sensors, searchlights, and heavy artillery," he said.

"Somehow, this information does not make me feel any safer," said Molly. "Are you sure we need to do this?"

"You tell me. Who are these people? Why are they after you?" asked Carvalho.

Molly recalled the last two days. It had all gone by so quickly. Only two days ago, she had been in an altogether different hemisphere, sipping margueritas on the beach. Now, somehow she had traded one tropical paradise for another. She didn't know if she could tell him the fantastic tale without thinking her insane. She trusted him, but who was this man? Why was he helping her? She needed to find out his part in all this.

"First, tell me why you were watching the observatory," she said.

Carvalho took a moment deciding how much to tell her before he spoke. "Four days ago, there was a theft in downtown Rio. Someone broke into a bank and stole something that apparently belonged to the observatory. My men and I responded to the call and chased the suspect down an alley, but he, well, he got away," said Carvalho hesitantly.

"I went to the observatory to find out more about the theft, but they told me nothing I didn't already know. Only that the object was valuable and irreplaceable."

"So, you're a detective in your spare time as well, Corporal?" asked Molly.

"Only when I'm not rescuing beautiful women," said Carvalho with a smile.

Molly blushed at the compliment. She had not been called beautiful since…gods…how long had it been? She could not remember. It felt nice. "So anyway, why did you keep a watch on them? Weren't they victims?"

"Yes, but I had a feeling they were not telling me everything they knew. Dr. Mariconi, the observatory director, was out on business and would not be back for a few days. However, I still wanted to speak with him. His assistant, a difficult little man named Pinotti, told me he was unreachable. However, after he thought I had left, I overheard him speaking to Mariconi on the phone. Although I didn't hear all of the conversation, they were talking about something called a *shifter* being involved in the theft. My gut instinct told me to keep an eye on them. Apparently, it paid off," said Carvalho while looking at Molly.

Molly stiffened. A *shifter?* That was what Mariconi had called her, and himself. Now there was another one on the loose, and apparently, he was a thief.

"Yes, I know Dr. Mariconi," said Molly. "He is not what he seems. He's not a mild-mannered observatory director. He's insane and dangerous. He's got it into his head that I'm one of those shifter people you heard them speak about. But what's weird is that he thinks the story I'm writing is actually real."

"You are writing another book? I thought you were on vacation," asked Carvalho, surprised.

"Look, you're as bad as my agent. She is always on me to take a break, but I'm sorry, it's what I do. I enjoy writing. I'm pretty miserable when I'm not doing it."

"What's the book about?" asked Carvalho. "Why did he think it was real?"

At first, Molly thought she would only tell him about the book, but after looking into those sincere eyes, she decided to tell him everything. She only hoped he wouldn't fly her straight to an insane asylum when they finally took off out of here.

She started with the hidden chamber she had found in Costa Maya, and then her discussions with Naum, and finally how Mariconi had tracked her down, captured her, and brought her here against her will. Carvalho's eyes widened at the mention of the energy weapons they had used in her room. Besides one or two other clarifying questions, he had remained silent throughout her dissertation. Now he was gazing at her with a curious fascination, as if she were a rare animal in a cage.

"Well? Does any of this make any sense to you?" she asked, irritated at his lack of a reaction.

"None whatsoever. You have no idea why Mariconi thought you were one of these shifter people?"

"Other than that they were the insane ravings of a mad man? No, not really."

"Have you ever moved things through time or walked through walls?" he asked rather bluntly.

"No! Of course not. And who said anything about walking through walls?" she asked.

"I've seen it happen, with my own eyes. Remember the suspect we were chasing?"

"What, the thief?"

"Yes, he ran down a dead-end alley and simply passed into the mountainside, like a ghost. It scared the hell out of all of us. I think your Dr. Mariconi and my robbery suspect are both people with extraordinary abilities. For Mariconi to say you are one of them, implies you have some abilities as well. You have no idea what they could be?"

Molly remembered how she had felt about the story she had been writing. How vivid and tangible it had seemed. She remembered how painful and frightening that final moment had been when Edington's planet had what…arrived? Yes, that was it. They had arrived in a new universe. Which universe? This one? It didn't make sense. Mariconi had said they had known about the planet for almost a hundred years. The timing was all wrong. How could she possibly have had anything to do with it?

"Ok. Enrico, she is good to go," said Marceau coming back inside.

Carvalho got up, shook his hand, and then sucker punched him in the stomach.

"Oooh," exclaimed Marceau, doubling over in pain.

"I'm sorry, my friend," said Carvalho. "It's for your own good. Don't worry. You can tell anyone that asks that I threatened you and stole the helicopter. When we are clear, I will report its position to the Policia Militar so that Helisul can recover it. I'll take good care of your baby. This way you will have the proof you need to say I overpowered you. This should leave a pretty convincing bruise." And with that, he knocked him out with a right cross.

Marceau slumped to the floor next to a horrified Molly.

"Come on, let's go," said Carvalho, taking her hand.

They climbed into the helicopter, and Carvalho passed her a set of headphones. He flipped a few switches and started the turbines. The blades slowly rotated to speed as the engines whined loudly. Molly's heart was racing as the little helicopter lifted a few feet off the ground. She had never been in a helicopter before, and the experience was not one she was enjoying. There was so little between her and the outside. Even through her headphones, the noise and vibration in the cockpit surprised her as the blades above made their characteristic whup, whup sound. Suddenly, the little craft rocketed skyward, the little helipad shrinking fast below them.

She gasped, "What did you do that for?"

Carvalho pointed at the gondola depot, now at a dizzying angle below them. She saw the two climbers in black fatigues standing on a ledge near the top. One held a phone to his ear and had binoculars pointed at them, the other man held something that looked like a laser pointer. Both were staring directly at the helicopter as it passed overhead. Suddenly, the man with the phone pointed skyward and motioned to the other. The other man aimed the pointer.

A voice sounded in her headphone. "We need to get to the other side of the mountain fast. Hold on!"

The helicopter banked quickly and tilted forward at an extreme angle, just missing a bluish white flash of plasma and electricity coiling out of the tiny device the man held. It was so close that the hairs on Molly's arm stood up like with a static charge. The quick change in direction made her feel so heavy in her seat that she was sure she was going to pass out. After a few seconds, however, the helicopter leveled out and the ledge was behind them, obscured by the mountaintop. The city was insanely far below them. She closed her eyes.

"Are you okay?" asked Carvalho concerned, his voice followed by a crunch of static.

"No, not really," said Molly, shaken.

"Was that one of the guns you were talking about?" he asked.

"Something like it, yes."

"That was close," he said. "But I think we're safe now."

Molly just kept her eyes closed; she certainly did not feel safe. She felt as if she were soaring through the air on nothing more than a lawn chair and a prayer. She would only feel safe when she had the ground firmly planted beneath her feet.

"I think our next step would be to find this other shifter. It's what I've been trying to do all along. He's got the answers we need. Do you have any idea who he might be?" asked Carvalho.

"I want to land. I want to land now," said Molly softly, feeling sick.

"Oh, okay. I'm going to set her down in the Tijuca National Forest. There are miles and miles of wild jungle there, and although they may see the helicopter go in, they will not be able to continue following her from the ground. From there, I'll commandeer a vehicle and return us back into town."

She probably did not want to know what he meant by commandeer, but landing sounded wonderful. She nodded her agreement and tried not to think about her queasy stomach.

* * *

"You didn't have to just leave him there!" said Molly, upset about the way Carvalho had procured their most recent method of transport. They were rambling along in an old white minibus, which the owner had modified for handicap access.

"Yes, I did. We can't let anyone know which way we're going. Don't worry. It's only a kilometer or so to the next bus stop. He will be fine."

"He was in a wheelchair!"

"It's a downhill street. What's your point?"

Molly fumed. She could not believe his nonchalance. "Do you always just take what you want, when you want it?"

"Only when I'm being chased by ninjas with ray guns, *minha namorada,*" said Carvalho.

"I suppose *minha namorada* means nagging bitch, right?" asked Molly angrily.

"Oh no, it means 'my girl' Oh wait. I guess it does mean that," said Carvalho amused.

"I'm glad you find our situation so funny."

"Molly, you really need to relax. I'm going to drive up to the *favela* to find Philippe and his sister, and then we're going into town to get some dinner. This will all look better in the morning."

Her eyes brightened at the chance to see Mariana again. "What's a *favela?*"

"It's what you Americans might call a slum, I suppose. Although, I use the term somewhat loosely. Look over there at that mountainside. Do you see all those little buildings bunched together? That's one of the favelas. They build on land owned by the government that nobody wants. You find them along busy highways or high up on rocky mountainsides. Most of them come from up the northern countryside looking for a better life in the big cities. However, they mostly end up in the favelas, barely scraping out a living doing jobs no one else will do. There are also a lot of drugs and prostitution up there, but many decent people too. They do what they can."

"And those two kids live up there?" asked Molly horrified.

"Sure. I've never met their mother, but she lives somewhere up there. I think she is a cleaning woman for one of the hotels."

"We're not going up there are we?" asked Molly as they pulled into a cobblestone road leading up the mountainside.

"Oh no, at least not all the way. You would stand out like a light bulb. I'm just going up to the local bar to ask about Felipe. He will come and find us later."

They pulled the car in close to a small brick and corrugated tin roof structure with an open front. Cardboard windows flapped in the warm breeze. Little round tables and chairs were setup outside, where men of varying sizes and willingness to wear shirts had congregated. Soccer was playing on a small television on the bar. They were all talking loudly and drinking beer.

Molly cringed into her seat, but Carvalho seemed to fit right in. He leaned out of the minibus and motioned for a young boy to come over. After a brief exchange in rapid Portuguese, the boy nodded and held out his hand. Carvalho gave him a few bills. The boy smiled and went back into the bar.

"Ok, that's it. Let's go get some food. Those were my last few reals. You're buying."

"What? Enrico, those people took me in my nightshirt! They were decent enough to give me these clothes before I got off the plane, but other than what I'm wearing, this is all I own at the moment!" said Molly.

"Well, that is a problem. Now that we've attracted these people's attention, they will not stop until they get their hands on us. Neither of us has a home to go to until we clear this up. They will expect us to start looking for help. The police will be monitoring any family you have back in the states, and Mariconi certainly has someone watching my apartment. Besides family, do you know anyone you can call that you can trust?"

Molly thought about it. The only person that came to mind was her agent, Ellen. She was a dear friend, and she would be worried sick about her.

"I might know someone. My agent, Ellen."

"Hmmm." Carvalho thought about it. "Still a little risky, but we're going to need the money. We can use one of the old public phones, and you can call her collect."

"What about you? Don't you have friends in the police?" she asked.

Carvalho laughed. "I'm a bit of a black sheep in the family. I'm not very popular, especially with recent events. You must understand that there is a system of corruption in the military police. It's not pretty, but it is necessary.

The government severely underfunds many departments of the military police. We have to take bribes and sometimes look the other way for minor offenses, just to get what we need to operate. I'm not saying it's the best solution, but it keeps squad cars running and families fed. Unfortunately, some people take advantage of the system more than they should. I am not one of those people. I've pissed off a lot of people by not always towing the line. I'm on two weeks leave as it is for letting that shifter escape."

Molly was amused at Carvalho's easy use of the new word. "Well, you let one shifter escape, but you've captured another," she said with a smile.

Carvalho nodded with a grin as he drove them down the twisting streets, into the crowded city of Rio.

Chapter 25, Pinotti

The Toronto Power Station sat in stately silence, silhouetted against the evening sky. Although abandoned for nearly forty years, the bold edifice still commanded a dignified and regal presence. However, an air of loss permeated the building now as she sat in the dark, unmaintained and discarded. She had once been one of the most ornate and beautiful buildings in Canada in sharp contrast with her much appreciated, but rather industrial purpose.

As an engineering wonder, the power station was not only extraordinarily beautiful, she was also the most ambitious complex ever built to harness the immense power of Niagara. She was the largest and most powerful hydroelectric power plant in the world and supplied Tesla's new alternating current as far as New York City.

Oh yes, "the war of the currents," thought Ananmaya as he approached the stately multi-columned front entrance of the building. Tesla and Westinghouse had fought a bitter campaign promoting Tesla's alternating current over Edison's direct current. Eventually Tesla and Westinghouse had won out. Even now, Tesla's alternating current generators continued to power the world, long after this power station became obsolete and was shut down. Edison had thoroughly misjudged Tesla's abilities, calling his ideas splendid, but utterly impractical. Winning the war of the currents had been welcome poetic justice for Tesla, who was not used to coming out on top in affairs of business.

Now, Ananmaya sought to uncover another of this utterly impractical scientist's inventions. If Bhuvanesh's notes were accurate, Tesla's ship still sat buried and forgotten beneath this sad, abandoned building. He just needed to find his way inside.

So far, there had been no sign of Pinotti, nor anyone else for that matter. Apparently, the cabbie had been right; no one came here anymore. Besides the sound of rushing water at some distance behind the building, there was little else in the eerie silence. A full moon was rising above the fir trees behind the building.

He scouted around the building looking for signs of entry, but none presented themselves. Weathered plywood boards covered the windows and the doors were chained and locked. He inspected the padlock on the front door. It looked rusted shut and probably would not open even if he had the key. If Pinotti was here, he had not used this entrance.

Could he be wrong about Pinotti? Maybe Pinotti hadn't come here. The irate little man might just as well be back in Buffalo on altogether different business. Perhaps they weren't concerned at all about the ship.

Suddenly, Ananmaya had an appalling thought. *What if the Elektra had been moved? What if there was nothing down there but empty, stale air?* No, it couldn't be. Einstein had given Bhuvanesh documents that showed detailed plans of maintenance for the facility. Furthermore, Bhuvanesh had found evidence that SOTAR was still allocating funds to Canada, nearly thirty years later. Ananmaya had spent much of his time in Brazil secretly going through the SOTAR archives to verify its current location, which he thought he had done. Surely, everything pointed to it still being here at the old abandoned power plant.

He sat down on one of the concrete benches near the front entrance to think. The Niagara River rumbled powerfully in the distance behind the building, so much so that he could feel it is vibration as he sat on the bench. He closed his eyes and concentrated. A few moments later, he smiled, leaned over, and put his ear to the ground. The austere marble entranceway was shockingly cold, but as he listened, he heard a faint, regular hum emanating from beneath him. It was the sixty-cycle hum of high power electricity cycling far below him.

Ananmaya jumped to his feet. *It's here! It's actually here,* he thought excitedly, all doubt emptying from his mind. *Now I just need to get down there and find it.*

He reached into his bag, took out his flashlight and turned it on as he approached the front door again. "Well, here goes nothing," he said to no one in particular, as he touched the broad paneled double door and closed his eyes. His hand slid easily through the heavy wooden door as if through water. The rest of him soon followed, and in a few seconds, he vanished into the dark building.

The interior was a complete mess. As he swung his flashlight around, he saw that graffiti and trash littered the once prestigious halls. Apparently, this place had seen its share of vandalism over the years. As he walked past the ancient offices towards the towering wheel-pit, he saw that everything not nailed down had been either stolen or removed. Even the half-opened, rusty fuse boxes had been relieved of their fuses, leaving oddly colored rectangular imprints behind. Beer cans and other trash littered the area, but some of the graffiti had been useful. Urban explorers had left arrows pointing the way through the building down to the wheel-pit in an effort to help others find their way to the vast tailrace tunnel below. He followed them now.

In recent years, the Toronto Power Station tailrace tunnel had become a holy grail to urban explorers for its extreme inaccessibility and the spectacular exit of its tailrace behind the falls. This invasive activity had worried Ananmaya when he saw detailed photos of the tailrace someone had posted on the Internet. Luckily, no one had gone deep into the twin feeder tunnels before the tailrace where the underground lab was hidden. Yet, it would be just a matter of time before SOTAR decided the risk of discovery was too great and decided to move the ship. What he saw now made him smile with relief.

The arrows had stopped at what now appeared to be an iron stairwell disappearing into a solid concrete floor. Apparently, SOTAR had filled in the openings and grate work that led down into the lower recesses of the power plant making it impossible to reach the tailrace deep below. This explained why no new photos had appeared in recent years. Along with the boarded up windows and doors, this last obstacle would hold even the most determined urban explorer at bay. Fortunately, Ananmaya would be using another way down.

He walked slowly down a corroded iron catwalk a few feet over the silent, tomb-like wheel-pit. The occasional drip of water broke the gloomy silence. At last, he found the panel box he had been looking for. His flashlight illuminated one barely legible word, ELECTRICAL.

The humming was much more pronounced here than it was outside. Behind the panel was a concrete wall that marked the end of the catwalk. The gauges, dials, and knife switches on the panel were all corroded and dead as the air in this forgotten room. Looking closer, he noticed a small area near the bottom right where the dust had been recently disturbed. On the side of the panel, he found a small keyhole. In addition, one of the knife switches seemed a bit less corroded than the others; its shiny Bakelite handle glistened in the beam of his flashlight, showing signs of recent use.

The panel was exactly as the notes had described it, he mused. *This must be the secret entrance to the SOTAR lab.* That someone had used it recently was evident, but he had no idea whether or not anyone was still inside.

Cautiously, Ananmaya turned off his flashlight and shifted his way through the disguised doorway. He found himself in an empty, dimly lit hallway. Ancient bulbs hung from the ceiling from old cloth-covered wires. At the end of the corridor was the electric lift that descended almost a hundred feet to the tunnel below. The whole scene looked frozen in time. Apparently, the maintenance budget had not extended to this part of the facility.

Looking down the open elevator shaft, he could see a brightly lit chamber below. He could not detect any movement or activity from this vantage point, but that did not mean they were not waiting for him down there. He held on to the wrought iron girders that supported the lift in an effort to scan the lower room with his mind before he descended. Unfortunately, he did not learn much; the room was too deep for him to get an accurate impression of its contents. Even so, he should have been able to detect if it contained something as large as the Elektra, which it didn't. This was very disconcerting. *Well, there is only one way to know for sure,* he thought. He slid open the gate, got inside the lift, and pressed the button marked DESCEND. Slowly, the lift moved down into the dark shaft.

As he finally passed through the ceiling of an immense underground tunnel, he saw the entire chamber easily. What he saw disheartened him greatly. The brightly lit lab certainly did not look as forgotten as the rest of the building above, but the Elektra was nowhere to be seen. Cables ran the length of the room, but stopped short near the paddock where the Elektra was kept. Nothing stood there now, except for the concrete support blocks and a tangle of wires and disconnected piping. Just as he had feared, the Elektra had been moved.

He was so shocked by this discovery that he didn't notice that his lift had landed, and its gate was open.

"Step outside and turn around," said a man stepping out of the shadows behind him.

Ananmaya wheeled around to see the angry little man from the plane. Pinotti's face scowled with recognition.

"YOU!" screamed the man from behind a strange-looking gun. "You were the one on the plane! I don't believe this. You are the shifter?"

"What? I don't know what you are talking about," said Ananmaya, stalling for time.

Pinotti thought for a moment, caught off guard. Then, coming to a realization, he regained his livid expression.

"I said move away from the lift, you bastard."

Ananmaya stayed where he was, his hand resting on the gate of the elevator door.

"Please, do give me a reason to kill you. I should shoot you now for that stunt you pulled at the airport," Pinotti said as he rubbed his neck with his free hand. It had been annoyingly stiff after the long, uncomfortable flight.

"Where is the ship, Pinotti?" asked Ananmaya calmly.

"Like it matters to you, shifter. You're not going to need it where you are going."

"And where is that?" asked Ananmaya. "I know you're not going to kill me. That gun can only stun."

Pinotti's face had become beet red. "And exactly how would you know that shifter? What other secrets have you stolen from us?"

Ananmaya smiled. He had seen working drawings of Tesla's death ray before, but he could only guess that this handheld version Pinotti was waving at him would be of the less lethal variety. However, he knew it was likely that they would be curious about him and his abilities. To have such a powerful shifter showing up unexpectedly on the society's radar would be like having an elephant appear in a bathroom. He stepped carefully out of the elevator, still holding on to the gate.

"Hold it right there. I would prefer not to have to drag your unconscious body out of here. You are correct. The plasma energy from this gun will not kill you, but nor can you avoid its effects through your shifter trickery. It is designed to stop rouge shifters like you," Pinotti held out his free hand, "Now, give me your satchel."

Ananmaya passed him the bag.

Pinotti rifled through it, the gun still trained on him.

"Aha! I have it!" said Pinotti triumphantly, holding up the black box to study it more closely. It gleamed in the bright lights of the room.

"I wouldn't play with that if I were you."

"Why not?" asked Pinotti smugly. "This artifact is SOTAR property. What could be so important that Einstein would hide this from us?"

So they don't know what the box contains. Ananmaya now understood why Einstein had hidden the stone in plain sight, among the hundreds of other treasures SOTAR had accumulated over the years. It would easily become lost in paperwork and forgotten, until now.

"Never mind me then, Pinotti. By all means, go ahead. Blow us all to hell. See if I care."

Pinotti hesitated, but then thought better of the matter. He returned the box to the satchel resting on the workbench.

"This is for Dr. Mariconi to inspect anyhow. You and your accomplice are going to suffer greatly for what you have done."

"Accomplice? What accomplice?" asked Ananmaya.

"Don't play me for a fool. You have no idea what you are up against," said Pinotti. "We caught your little girlfriend in Mexico. She has led us on quite the chase, but soon she will tell us everything she knows. It is only a matter of time."

"You have found another shifter?" asked Ananmaya, confused.

"Not just another shifter, *the shifter,* the one that caused the rupture in space. The one we have been searching for, for over a hundred years. We have her now, and it's all over. You can stop pretending you know nothing about it. We know what you were planning to do."

Ananmaya stiffened. This was extremely distressing news. If it was true, his mission had ended before it had even begun. It couldn't be true, how could it be? He had not believed such a person could exist, but apparently the speculation had all been true. When Philolaus appeared, many had theorized that only a powerful, intelligent force could have positioned it so precisely in our solar system.

After Tesla had established contact, both worlds had discussed the matter at length. As the colonies had no great love for their home world, they suspected one of their own had been responsible for the shift. No one came forward however, and the hypothesis became unprovable.

With this new information, not only had the planet been brought through interdimensional space, but it had moved through time as well. That would mean that the shifter had caused events to unfold in the past! Ananmaya's mind reeled with the unbelievable power that this unknown shifter wielded. How had they caught her? Why didn't she use her gifts to escape? Surely, she was more than a match for such as these. How could they possibly bind such a person? If this shifter was indeed under their control, his mission was more urgent than ever.

Bhuvanesh knew that an outside influence had irrevocably corrupted SOTAR after Einstein died. He had been convinced that a foreign power was exploiting the organization's resources. Ananmaya's research had only recently discovered the *alien* nature of this power.

The people that now controlled SOTAR were not from Earth, nor were they from Philolaus; this much he was certain. Appearing at nearly the same time, they had somehow breached the same rift that had brought the planet into this universe. These people were bent on world domination and had both Earth and Philolaus in their sights. They seemed to come and go, never appearing in large numbers. They were ruthless and cruel, yet seemed to be biding their time, waiting for the right moment to strike.

To Ananmaya, that moment had seemed imminent. He knew they were hunting down shifters, desperately looking for something or someone. Now he knew what they had been looking and waiting for. *But how? How had they known the shifter would be on Earth? How did they know she would be from the future?* He desperately needed some answers.

"So this shifter, what's her name?" asked Ananmaya, trying to hide his growing despair.

"Even now, you continue to pretend your ignorance?" Pinotti sighed. "Very well, I will amuse you. She was hiding under one of the most famous names in the world. The shifter's name was Molly Arden," said Pinotti. "She's being held for questioning at SOTAR headquarters right now. She professes innocence and insists that she knows nothing about being a shifter. That will change soon. Dr. Mariconi is personally handling the interrogation."

Ananmaya took a step back. Of course he recognized the name; it had been on the front page of every newspaper from Miami to Buffalo. Molly Arden had been the young woman that had gone missing in Mexico a few days ago. How could she be the one that could shift worlds? They must have made a mistake. Nothing made sense, yet in the back of his mind, something clicked. Unfortunately, he did not have time to put the pieces together. For now, he had to get out of this mess and concentrate. He gripped the elevator framework tightly as an idea came to him.

"I have him. I'm coming up," said Pinotti into a radio. He returned it to a clip on his belt and motioned for Ananmaya to turn around. "Get back inside. We're going for a little ride."

As he did so, Pinotti came behind him, putting the muzzle of the cylindrical gun against the small of his back. "Don't try anything stupid, thief."

"Wouldn't dream of it," said Ananmaya.

Pinotti press the button that raised the lift, but nothing happened. He pressed it again. Still nothing. He cursed loudly.

"Looks like the maintenance funds have not been spent very wisely," said Ananmaya.

"It's no matter. We'll take the blasted ladder," fumed Pinotti, as he slammed the gate open. Surprisingly, it fell off its hinges and shattered as it hit the floor. The pieces began to shimmer. Suddenly, they turned into puddles of water. The transformation had so mesmerized Pinotti that he failed to notice Ananmaya come up quickly behind him and wrench the gun out of his hand, sending it spinning across the red, brick-lined floor. The gun shattered like glass as it hit the curved wall, each piece melting away into the clear liquid. At the same time, a loud whump sounded as the lift car, pulleys, and cables fell apart and transformed into a glowing rain, creating a deluge of water in the lab as if a bathtub had been overturned.

"What are you doing? Stop this at once. You cannot escape. I have two helicopters waiting above us now. My people will be down here in an instant," exclaimed Pinotti.

"In that case, you are right. I have very little time. Where have you moved the ship, Pinotti?" demanded Ananmaya menacingly as he towered over the little man.

Pinotti spit in his face. "Your little shifter tricks don't scare me. I've seen things more frightening than you can imagine."

Ananmaya looked at the immense double doors at both ends of the chamber, and then at the lift, finally his eyes rested on the concrete blocks where the Elektra had sat. His mind raced. Where was the ship? How had they had time to move it out of the lab? It simply had to be here—*somewhere.* He returned his attention to Pinotti who was sidestepping a rivulet of water. He suddenly had a daring idea. Picking up his satchel off the workbench, Ananmaya turned to climb a ladder attached to the framework of the iron elevator.

"Pinotti, can you swim?" he asked, quickly scaling the ladder.

"Swim? What do you mean? Where are you going? Stop that!" shouted Pinotti. He tried to follow him, but the ladder was melting into water as Ananmaya climbed. Was the fool going to make a run for it? Apparently he wasn't, for instead of continuing up through the shaft, Ananmaya stopped and walked along a catwalk suspended from the ceiling.

"This is your last chance Pinotti. Where is the ship?"

"Go to hell!" shouted Pinotti, as he looked around nervously. The thief was up to something; he just didn't know what. He glanced at the large double doors of the floodgate at the back of the chamber. Surely, he did not mean to…

Suddenly, a siren sounded, and a red light strobed. The lights dimmed. A deep rumbling sound came from the back of the chamber. Pinotti screamed in horror and tried to clamber up the elevator framework, looking for a way out.

Water poured in a torrent as the large flood gate opened in the back of the lab, knocking Pinotti off his feet as he held on to the iron girders for support. The water was filling the lab, knocking over workbenches and shorting out equipment. It was rising extremely quickly. The current threatened to pull Pinotti from his tenacious perch.

"Stop! Stop! Close the gate! Please!" plead Pinotti, trying to stay above the frigid, tumultuous swells.

"Where's the ship?" replied Ananmaya.

"I can't swim! Please, stop!" exclaimed Pinotti.

"I suggest you tell me where the ship is. You do know it is also a submarine, don't you? A nice, dry, waterproof submarine. You could use one of those right now, couldn't you?"

"Please. You don't know…you can't…" Pinotti's trousers had become caught on a something just below the catwalk, and he could no longer pull himself ahead of the rising water.

"Tell me where the ship is, and I'll help you," offered Ananmaya.

"It's here. It's still on its moorings! Mariconi sent it perpetually a few seconds into the future. Please! I…" Pinotti's head went under the waves, one of his arms flailing about wildly.

Interesting, thought Ananmaya as he pressed the button which opened the flood gates on the other side of the lab.

Instantly, the water level began dropping as the water emptied out through them into the main tailrace tunnel beyond. Pinotti coughed and sputtered as his head once again appeared above water. He looked like a drowned rat.

"So, Mariconi is a shifter as well?" asked Ananmaya.

"Yes," sputtered Pinotti. "He's a time shifter."

That *was* impressive. Time shifters were rare indeed, rare, and very dangerous. Shifting along that dimensional axis drove most men mad. It was no surprise that such person was running this operation. Ananmaya could bend time as well, but he had only done a few experiments with quantum time dilation effects. He had never attempted something on such a large scale. He knew he could never force something the size of the Elektra into the future, much less keep it there in perpetuity. However, he might be able to get it back. He had a good idea of how Mariconi had done the trick, and he thought he might be able to reverse it.

"Little good it will do you, thief. No one but Mariconi can bring the Elektra back," said Pinotti smugly.

Ananmaya had not heard this. He was reaching out through space and time with his mind. He was tracking the ship through time by tracing its graviton particles, which were independent of time and space. Yes, there it was, he could see its outline in his mind. Mariconi had held the ship forward in time using graviton particles. Like a donkey chasing a carrot held out in front of it, the ship moved forward through time attracted by the gravitons. When it did so, the gravitons moved forward as well; thus the ship would never stop moving through time. It was a brilliant idea, one he would have to remember. It was also going to be difficult to diffuse without ripping holes in the fabric of space-time. He set to work for he had very little time left.

The water had leveled off and now filled the tunnel about halfway up. Pinotti still clung to the lift's framework, as the current was still very strong. He wondered where those jarhead idiots were. SOTAR maintained high-level contacts in the American military and had even sequestered a stealth Comanche helicopter for this operation. He fumbled for his radio, but discovered that the deluge had flushed it away. They would be here soon enough, and that bastard was going to pay. Everyone was going to pay for this. He looked up at Ananmaya on the catwalk. He had gotten quiet all of a sudden and was staring down at the water. Pinotti followed his gaze, but only saw the empty paddock beneath the flowing water.

"I don't know what you are trying to pull thief, but when my associates get here, you're…" Pinotti was cut off in mid-sentence as the water exploded beneath him. A hot spray of nearly boiling water showered him, and he screamed in pain. Was the shifter trying to blast his way out of here?

"Sorry about that, my friend," said Ananmaya, making his way back down what remained of the ladder. "The water was trying to occupy the same space as the ship, and the ship won."

"What are you talking about?" asked Pinotti, wiping his eyes.

He looked to where Ananmaya was pointing. There, rolling gently up to the water's surface was the long, cigar-shaped form of the Elektra. The gleaming copper craft had somehow returned from the limbo where Mariconi had sent it.

His jaw dropped. "How did you…but only Dr. Mariconi could…"

"Riveting isn't it?" interrupted Ananmaya, as he climbed down past him to the hatch on the top of the ship, which had just broken through the water's surface.

Shaken from the explosive arrival of the Elektra, but more concerned about what Mariconi would do to him if he failed, Pinotti knew he had to find a way to stop this powerful shifter. He gripped the steel girder and tried to regain his footing, but a rivet had caught his pants. He tugged and pulled, but could not free himself. He looked closer. He wasn't just stuck; he was actually riveted to the structure in several places! The heads of large rusty rivets were now poking through the wet fabric as if his pants had always been a part of the framework.

So that's what the smug bastard meant when he passed by, fumed Pinotti. He had been toying with him.

"You won't escape! That ship has not moved in almost a hundred years! Don't you think if it worked we would have used it ourselves by now?" shouted Pinotti angrily.

Ananmaya waved a free hand as he climbed inside the ship. "You take care now," he said, smiling.

As Pinotti shouted obscenities, Ananmaya closed the hatch and screwed it shut. For being so old, the ship was in excellent shape. She had hardly changed over the years. Besides the new batteries and glowing LED strips along the ceiling, she was still the same complicated copper and brass machine from the diagrams he had studied. The indicator panel and controls were the same now as they had been when Tesla flew her so long ago. Everything was exactly as he had hoped it would be.

Ananmaya sighed with relief, took the artifact out of his satchel, and turned towards the engine bay. The hard part of his mission was just about over.

Chapter 26, Eddington

Arthur Eddington walked along the close-cropped lawn of Fenner's cricket ground in London. He regarded the moonlit field with fondness; he had enjoyed many a match at Fenner's during his fifteen years at Cambridge after accepting the position of observatory director in 1914. This evening however, the field was quiet, damp, and dark, except for the rustling of the leaves in the trees surrounding it. A thin fog hung low in the air, blurring the crescent moon hanging low in the night sky.

A man with bushy sideburns and a cane walked beside him. Except for himself and this old friend, not a soul stirred in the wide, hallowed sporting grounds.

How long had it been since the Sobral team had last been together? It must be at least what? Ten years? Poor Morize had taken Einstein's secret to his grave in Brazil just last month, as would have the others he was sure. Luckily, it did not seem as it would come to that for the rest of them. Finally, they were going to get some answers after all this time.

"So, we are once again to meet with Mr. Einstein," said Crommelin. "Where is the old codger hiding now?"

"I do not expect he has arrived quite yet," said Eddington. "I'm sure he will be here soon."

"It's been a long time. I expect I can wait a few more minutes," said Crommelin. "How have you been old sport? You still have your head in the stars from what I've seen of you in the papers."

"Yes, Cambridge has been most suitable. My tenure as director and my endeavors in fundamental theory has kept my hands far from being idle," said Eddington.

"Quite, quite," said Crommelin. "Have you had much correspondence with Mr. Einstein in that regard?"

"Actually, no. He has become quite the celebrity since the eclipse, hasn't he? Even now, everyone still beckons for the man's time. We do send the occasional letter, but mostly we keep up with each other's work in the scientific papers we write. Morize was the only one that kept up a regular correspondence with the man," said Eddington. "The only recent contact I've had with Albert was the telegram he sent last month. I assume you received one as well, which read the same?"

"Yes, I did. We were all to meet here this evening at Fenner's. But where is Davidson?" asked Crommelin.

"I haven't heard from him at all. I was hoping we would find him when we arrived. So far, you and I are the only ones here," said Eddington.

"That is rather tragic about Morize, wouldn't you say? I heard of his passing just recently. If only he had only held out a few months longer," said Crommelin.

"Strange that you bring that up. There was something peculiar about his death," said Eddington. Just then, a movement at the west end of the field caught his eye. At first he thought it might be Einstein, but soon realized his mistake. There was someone approaching, but it wasn't Einstein. A tall man in a bowler cap walked towards them quickly out of the darkness.

"G'day chaps. What'av I missed?" asked Davidson smiling, hand outstretched.

"Davidson! You old charlatan! How have you been?" said Crommelin shaking his hand. Eddington followed suit.

"It's been a bit of an adventure getting here, and make no mistake," said Davidson. "I was in New Zealand when I received the telegram. I've been traveling for over six weeks! The bloody ship sank in Melbourne, and I had to go by freighter the rest of the way. I've only just arrived off the train from the port."

"That explains the luggage then," said Eddington looking at the tattered bags the man was carrying.

Davidson looked sheepish. "Right mate. Um, I'm a little in the dongers right now. I was hoping you could put me up for the night?"

"Certainly. Of course, but let's wait to hear what Einstein has to say first. I'm sure he will be here soon."

"You mean he's still not here?" asked Davidson looking around. "So it's just us then? Where's that Brazilian bloke, Morize?"

"Unfortunately, Henrique won't be making it here tonight. He passed away just last March. Natural causes," said Crommelin.

"Oh, that's rather, well, it's rather depressing idn't it? If Einstein had put this little reunion together just a few months earlier..."

"Actually, I was just starting to tell Crommelin about that before you arrived," said Eddington. "From what I've heard from others in the society, someone in SOTAR may have poisoned him."

"Murdered by one of us? Surely not," sputtered Crommelin.

"I thought Morize said the observatory would be safe," exclaimed Davidson.

"Albert had thought that Morize's idea of headquartering SOTAR at the National Observatory in Rio was a good one as well," said Eddington. "No one would suspect the quiet facility being the seat of SOTAR operations much less guess that Morize was SOTAR's director. I don't even think Morize's wife Rosa knew."

"Then how...who?" asked Crommelin.

"Einstein has suspected for some time that SOTAR is being corrupted from within. He feels like he is losing control of the organization. Morize's death is further proof of those suspicions. As director of operations, Morize had been investigating strange discrepancies in funding and personnel before he died."

"Well crikey," said Davidson shaking his head. Then, typical of Davidson's optimistic nature, he brightened.

"On the other hand, it is right good seein' you gents though. What's it been? Ten years?"

"At least," said Eddington.

"In all that time, have you heard anything about what this is all about? You're Einstein's man, Arthur. Surely you must have heard something more about the planet."

"All I know is that the telegram called for everyone to meet in the cricket field at Fenner's in Cambridge at ten o'clock on Sunday, May 11th. We were to tell no one. He said that the promise he made to us ten years ago was about to be fulfilled," said Eddington.

Crommelin nodded in agreement.

"Mine says the same," said Davidson. "It's just that I've had a long trip with a lot of time to think about it, and I've had an idea. Maybe he chose to meet at night because something might be happening, you know, up there, that he wants us to see. What do you think, Andy? You're the comet man in these parts. Anything interesting happening tonight?"

"Not that I know of. Besides, he could not have picked a worse night for it. This fog would be blasted inconvenient for viewing the heavens tonight," said Crommelin.

"Also, why would he have us meet in the field instead of the observatory?" interjected Eddington.

"Too right, mate. I was hoping I didn't just travel half way around the world to look at shooting stars," said Davidson. "I must say, I was a little worried. The man has a wicked sense of humor."

"This is no joke. Ten years ago, when we returned from Sobral, Einstein promised we'd be the first to know when they established communication with the planet," said Crommelin.

"He also said we'd finally get recognition for the discovery as well. Don't forget that," said Davidson.

"Yes, that too. But we all agreed that as the planet might be populated with people much like ourselves, we would maintain its secrecy until we could discern its true nature.

I can only guess that Mr. Tesla has finally bridged the gap and established communications with…"

Eddington beckoned Crommelin to stop speaking for a moment, "Excuse me, gentlemen, but do you hear that?"

The three men stood still in the quiet, foggy night. The wind was starting to pick up. Soon, they heard what Eddington had noticed. A low hum was coming out of the air above them, more felt than heard. The sound reminded Eddington of the high-voltage transformers the college used in its new power plant.

There was a steady breeze now, sending the fog into spiraling eddies, which began clearing a hole high above their heads in the center of the field. They could see the night sky quite plainly through the new cylindrical opening. The humming grew much louder and the breeze became a light gale.

Davidson saw something and shouted. "Bloody hell! Get down. Take cover!"

Eddington and Crommelin back looked up instinctively. What they saw astounded them. They ran for the trees as something immense blotted out the starry sky.

"What is it?" asked Davidson.

"A Zeppelin, perhaps?" suggested Crommelin from behind a chestnut tree.

"It's unlike any airship I've ever seen. It's nearly as long as the field!" said Eddington astonished.

The ship came down quickly but silently, filling the air with an odd, vibrating sensation. As the ship approached the ground it slowed, and the hum became more subdued. Eventually it stopped entirely, and the ship hovered just a few feet above the close-cropped lawn, motionless.

"Was this worth your trip here, Davidson?" asked Eddington dumbstruck.

Davidson was speechless, staring in awe at the magnificent ship towering into the sky. It must have been nearly five-hundred feet long and nearly a hundred feet in height and width. It was as if the Titanic had been dropped into Fenner's field. Like the Titanic, it resembled more that of a stout sailing ship than a dirigible. Polished wood with brass fittings decorated a hull which shimmered with frost that hissed and popped as it thawed. Large iron gratings along her sides were venting what he thought must be steam. Running in parallel lines, row after row of round portal windows ran along her length like on a cruising steamer. She had no masts or steam funnels, but instead had strange piping and machinery on her decks. Three large tanks were securely fastened in a recess in her rear flank, which looked as if they contained pressurized gas or liquid.

Eddington noticed the ship was deliberately running dark. He could see many arc lamps mounted in pockets along her hull, but none were lit. The ship was the most remarkable, yet disconcerting thing he had ever seen. It just hung there in space, seemingly immune to the force of gravity.

"Um, now what? Was this supposed to happen?" asked Crommelin.

"Your guess is as good as mine," said Eddington, taking a timid step forward now that the ship had landed.

"Bloody hell, Arthur! What are you doing?" asked Davidson from behind a bush.

Eddington ignored him and continued towards the ship, which was hovering quiet as a balloon in the center of the field.

She holds her position without a sound—none at all, he thought, his scientific curiosity outweighing his fear.

Now he was closer, he could see a large rectangular outline near the ship's forward, which he thought must be a loading bay door. He walked towards in an effort to justify his suspicion.

To his surprise, the door began to open slowly. Its nearly twenty-foot width was folding downward like a drawbridge, facilitated by huge hydraulic pistons on either side that hissed with released pressure. It completed its slow downward arc and rested on the ground, forming a gangplank leading into the opening some ten feet above it. Steam from the hydraulics had obscured the entrance, but now that the door had stopped moving, the view was clearing rapidly. Through the dim opening, he could make out movement inside. Three men walked out into the moonlight and descended the gangplank.

"Albert!" cried Eddington. Then, recognizing one of his companions, "and, Mr. Tesla, I presume?"

"Arthur, my friend, how have you been?" said Einstein giving him a bear hug.

"Never mind that. What is all this?" asked Eddington indicating the ship. By now, the others had caught up and were exchanging greetings with the outlandish arrivals.

"This is the Calliope. She is an ether ship," said Tesla.

"An ether-ship? As in a ship that plies the ether?" asked Eddington staring in disbelief at the floating behemoth.

"Yes, but her captain can explain her arrangement better than I," sad Tesla, turning to the third member of the party.

"Arthur Eddington of Earth, I would like you to meet Samuel Edington, of Philolaus," said Tesla smiling.

It was like looking into a mirror. Both men had the same astonished look on their faces as they stared at each other. Arthur saw that they were identical except for their clothing. This man was wearing a strange uniform, very utilitarian in design, whereas he was wearing his usual evening cardigan and slacks. As he stared, he noticed that even the thin wire frames of their eyeglasses had the same oblong shape. *Astounding.*

"Pleased to meet you," they both said simultaneously, as they shook hands.

"I know how awkward this feels," said Tesla amused. "It happened to me as well. Anya and I were on the Elektra at the time."

"Anya? The Elektra?" asked Eddington. "I don't follow."

"Albert, have you told them nothing?" asked Tesla, chastising the man. "I see I will need to explain. The Elektra is my ship."

"We have been a little busy after all, Niko," said Einstein. "And besides, you know how I like surprises."

Tesla sighed and turned back to the group. "We will fill you in soon enough. In a moment, all of you will meet Kulik and Anya, our Soviet friends who made the Elektra possible. They are up their now, assisting the crew."

"So this, this thing, is from the *planet?*" asked Davidson.

Einstein nodded vigorously, giddy as a schoolboy. "Yes. This magnificent ship belongs to the Philolans. Well gentlemen, do I know how to make an entrance or what?"

Sam Edington stepped forward, "The Calliope is one of several colonial ether ships in her majesty's fleet."

"One of several? You mean there's more like this?" asked Crommelin.

"There are five others on Philolaus right now, in various states of disrepair," he replied.

"Gentlemen, we can talk more on the journey. We should probably be going," said Einstein. "I see Mr. Davidson has his bags, but where are yours?"

The three stunned men looked at each other utterly confused, and then returned their gaze to Einstein.

"Journey?" asked Eddington.

"Luggage?" asked Crommelin.

"Oh dear, another detail I forgot to mention in my telegram. I do apologize. Things have been happening so fast. We quite literally *ran* into the Calliope with the Elektra over a month ago and we've been working quickly to facilitate repairs," said Einstein.

"Not to mention working out how we can best assist Philolaus without bringing her to the attention of the world," added Tesla.

"You drop the bloomin' Titanic on Fenner's and you're worried about drawing too much attention to yourself?" asked Davidson incredulously.

"I quite agree. I would feel better if we could all please board the Calliope as soon as possible," said Tesla, turning to go. "I'm sure the crew can supply your accommodations."

"Where are we going?" asked Eddington as he led his two bewildered colleagues up the gangplank. He feared he already knew the answer.

"To Philolaus of course!" laughed Einstein stepping inside.

"My friends, we must come to a decision," continued Mayor Hastings, halfway through his speech. He looked over the crowd assembled before the podium. They looked frightened and not sure what to do. Exactly how he wanted them.

"These are hard times. Hard times demand tough solutions. Resources are scarce, as we all know. I have discussed the situation with the city council, and we are considering the formation of a militia," said the mayor. "We must do this to protect ourselves from the other colonies, should it come to that."

The crowd grew restless. They barely had a police force, and their ten or so unarmed volunteers were law enforcement only in the figurative sense. The idea of a militia, however small, reminded them of the old days on their war torn home planet of Archænis. No one wanted to bring that nightmare here.

"But we're the capital city! Would they really attack us?" asked someone in the audience.

"Ms. Kavanaugh, we are the largest, oldest, and most organized township on Philolaus, but do not think for a moment that we dictate policy to the other colonies. They look to us often for advice and help, but as you know, there is no centralized government on this outpost of a planet. We govern ourselves individually, and as such, we must protect our own interests. A militia will help in that regard," said Mayor Hastings.

"Won't the other colonies see this as a threat and build their own militias? Is such provocative action absolutely necessary at this point?" asked a young man near the front.

Hasting recognized him as Thomas Haynes, a journalist for their small, weekly newsletter. He had his infernal pad and pencil in his hand.

"They are free to do as they will. I wouldn't be surprised if the other colonies were doing the same thing already," said Hastings to the little man, who was scribbling it all down.

There was more murmuring in the crowd. It continued to surprise him just how naive people could be. When the storehouses started running out of food, did they think that families were just going to sit back and watch their sons and daughters slowly die of starvation? No, there would be a war of survival and the militia was only the beginning. He would soon be building an army.

"What about the Calliope? Shouldn't we wait for them a bit longer?" asked an older gentleman.

"Sir, we must put away the foolhardy belief that help will come to us from outside. We are, and always have been, on our own. Wasting time and expense on more dangerous and risked ventures will only accelerate our end. The Calliope is not going to return. I fear the ship and her crew are lost to us forever, a tragedy we could have avoided, if the council would have listened to me," said Mayor Hastings somberly.

"But Mr. Edington said…"

"Edington was a fool. I have always maintained that the enterprise was doomed from the start, and now you see the proof. It has been almost two months, and there has not been any sign of the Calliope's return. As the ship was only outfitted for only half that time, I'm afraid they are not coming back," said the mayor, trying to hold back a smile.

He loved this. Finally, everything had gone his way; his plan had worked flawlessly. He had personally sabotaged the Calliope's control coils during their construction to ensure their failure. With Edington, Quinn, Harland, and Philomena out of the way, he would have little opposition when he declared martial law.

Suddenly there was a gasp from the crowd. People were turning to face the same direction, squinting upwards into the sunlight.

Hastings saw that many of them were pointing at him, no, wait, they were pointing *behind* him. He turned to look, just as the wind began to pick up. Dry sand blew across the raised platform. Oh no, not a windstorm, not after he had called everyone outside for his speech! He was just about to bolt down the stairs and seal himself in his office, when his gaze fell on the large object dropping out of the sky. Suddenly, the fear of a windstorm seemed negligible to the dread he felt now.

Quietly descending into the commons square behind the platform was the very large and very much *intact* Calliope. She drifted gently down in full view of the crowd and nestled into her moorings.

A cheer went up in the crowd. They rushed past Hastings and the stage to the commons area to greet the returning heroes. The mayor, slowly followed behind them, stunned into silence by the turn of events. How had they survived? It didn't seem possible. How could his perfect plan have turned upside down in just a few minutes?

The wide bay door lowered and revealed many people in the loading dock. The council had only sent seven people with the Calliope, but now nearly double that number stood by the gangplank waiting to descend.

"They've done it!" said someone in the crowd.

"And they've brought help!" shouted another.

"I hope they've brought more than that," replied a third.

A little girl spoke, "Look! There are two Mr. Edingtons!"

The mayor shielded his eyes and looked closer at the new arrivals. The two men standing side by side did look strikingly similar, too similar. In fact, they were identical! Unbelievable! There were two of them now! What cruel joke was fate playing on him now? Two Edingtons? As if one wasn't hard enough to deal with already. What was going on? Apparently, Edington had found more than he bargained for on the strange parallel world.

His head was reeling on how he was going to contain this situation. Why hadn't the coils failed as they were supposed to? No one, not even Quinn, could have controlled the ship after the way he had misaligned them. Without the inductive resonators, they should have spun off into the ether. What had happened? How had they done it? His perfect plan was crashing down on top of him.

Hastings looked at the people coming down the ramp. Quinn was in the front, but he looked different. Besides his outlandish clothing, he now presented a commanding countenance, quite out of place on the man's normally tired face.

"Mr. Mandic, wonderful to see you back, sir," lied the mayor, holding out his hand.

Instead of taking his hand, the man simply stood before him with his arms crossed. "Mr. Mandic has remained behind. My name is Tesla. I'm from the planet which we call Earth. From what Mr. Edington has told me, you must be the mayor."

"Um," said the mayor not sure how to respond. What was this? Another double? Who was this man? Where was Quinn?

Edington had joined the group and he did not look happy.

"Ah, I see you have returned to us in one piece," said the mayor.

Before he could finish, Edington punched him square in the jaw, catching him completely off guard, spinning him to the ground.

"Bloody nice right cross," said Davidson smiling.

"You bastard! You fat, pompous, cowardly bastard," stammered Edington, livid, as he stood over the mayor who was scrambling away from the irate astronomer.

"We almost died out there because of you! Quinn still might. We left him there, half out of his mind from radiation poisoning," said Edington.

"What are you talking about?" asked the mayor, rubbing his jaw and trying to hide a growing anxiety.

"I don't need to explain anything to you. You're the one with explaining to do. We know you had something to do with damaging our control coils. If it were not for Mr. Tesla, we never would have made it back. As you were the only one against this enterprise, we have all the proof we need of your meddling," said Edington.

The mayor looked around at the murmuring crowd. Any minute now and they would be come to the same conclusion. The situation was looking grim. Perhaps a strategic retreat would be in order. "I don't need to stand for this. I'm got more important things to do than go fisticuffs with you."

"And where do you think you're going, mate?" asked Davidson, collaring the man.

"Unhand me!" said the mayor, trying to shake off him off.

"Not bloody likely, you cocker. From what Mr. Edington says, you sent them out there completely unprepared. You wanted their mission to fail."

"You can't prove any of these outrageous accusations!" the mayor snarled. "None of you can."

An older man with unkept white hair and a ridiculous moustache stepped forward off the ramp and approached him.

"I believe that would be for an official inquiry to prove," said Einstein. "For now, I suggest we focus on your planet's more pressing needs."

"What? We don't need your help. Not from any of you. I *know* why you are here," said the mayor glowering at the strangers. "You're planning a full-scale invasion."

"Really? All six of us?" guffawed Crommelin. "Kulik, were you aware of this invasion plan?"

The Russian looked perplexed for a moment, and then smiled. "Sorry, Comrade, your humor is wasted on me. Anya and I are more comfortable with machines in engine room."

"I assure you this is no joke. You are agents from Earth, sent to gather information before you invade our planet. And I will not allow it," said the mayor angrily.

"They are here to help, *you idiot*," said Edington.

"I suggest you let your own people decide," said his twin from Earth.

"Yes, by all means. Let your people decide if we shall stay," concurred Einstein.

The crowd around them had heard and seen everything that had transpired. A call went up, demanding a public vote.

"We might be a small town, but we do have rules," said the mayor. "The council will need to convene a special session to decide the matter. Until then, Edington, his crew, and the off-worlders are under arrest."

A few of the security volunteers had already pushed their way forward when Edington had slugged the mayor. They looked quite out of their league and not sure what to do next.

"Arrest these people," said the mayor.

No one moved. It was ridiculous to ask five unarmed volunteers to arrest such a large group of people forcibly. People were laughing at them. They stared back at the mayor questioningly.

Edington sighed. "We have been traveling for a long time. My crew wants to return to their homes. Orville's mother must be out of her mind with worry by now. Also, I fully intend on showing our guests a greater level of hospitality than you have. I will find Mr. Einstein and his friends quarters in the dormitories at the observatory. Just try and arrest us, you pompous ass."

The mayor fumed, but there was little he could do. The people were against him, rules or no rules.

"I must insist that you return the Leviton ore you have on board the Calliope. Until the council decides on the matter, we need assurance that these people cannot leave the planet. Surely, even you can see this as a necessary precaution," said the mayor.

"Crikey! He's a lovely one, idn't he?" exclaimed Davidson.

"It is fair request," said Kulik. "With Mr. Edington's permission, I will retrieve core."

"It most certainly is not fair. We will need the ship in a few days to return Mr. Einstein, Mr. Eddington, and his two colleagues back to Earth. They must return to their lives on Earth. As Quinn's health is poor and we needed Mr. Tesla here, Quinn agreed to act as his replacement. As Mr. Tesla had led a very reclusive life, it is doubtful many will notice the change," said Edington.

"Preposterous! We must decommission the ship immediately. We need the parts. Much has changed since you left," stammered the mayor.

The rest of Edington's crew had also been speaking with to people in the crowd. Two of the crew, Harland and Philomena, were speaking with fellow members of the council.

"I'll say things have changed," exclaimed Philomena. "I just learned he was just about to form an army."

"Not an army, a *militia,*" said the mayor. "We need to defend ourselves."

Unbelievable, thought Edington. What had happened over the last two months? Had things gotten so severe that the colonies were going to fight each other like hungry animals over a carcass? Didn't the mistakes of the past have any bearing on the present?

"We have much to discuss, Mayor. Rest assured, no one will leave without my approval. For now, you will simply have to trust me," said Edington.

The mayor had no choice. The people were clearly on Edington's side. Red-faced and steaming with anger, he broke free of Davidson's grip and pushed through the crowd in a huff.

As the mayor left, most of the crowd began to disperse. Talk circulated about a party in the pub to receive the heroes. Apparently, the discussions were to continue in a more informal venue.

As they walked through cheering streets, Edington noticed how run down the buildings had become. Many of the shops had closed entirely. As the sun set, he noticed the windows were balefully illuminated by candlelight instead of the bright white of arc lamps. All the streetlights were off, casting the city in a foreboding gloom. Things certainly had changed. Was it like this on all the colonies now? Had things gone too far to bring them back from the brink?

The pub seemed to be the only building in town with a cheerful disposition. Warm firelight poured through the open door as the crowd led the group inside. Bright eyed, happy people packed the small pub. Members of Edington's group were pulled aside and had beers pushed into their hands. Kulik found a spot at the bar and began drinking like a camel. Anya laughed as young men separated her from the rest and fought for her attention. Curious patrons had cornered Crommelin and Davidson by the fireplace; their coats and top hats were the subject of much fascination. Orville had found his mother waiting for him by the door and she was now hugging him to death, much to his embarrassment. Edington's two astronomers, Calvin and Meriwether, found themselves at the bar recounting their recent adventures. Harland and Philomena were involved in a more serious conversation with their fellow councilmen. The two Eddingtons had caused quite a stir. They spent much of the night explaining their identical appearances, which they barely understood themselves. Even Tesla had been cajoled by Einstein into accepting a beer, and was enjoying the celebration.

There was so much attention and excitement that Edington could almost forget the dismal state of things outside.

Well, no matter, things would turn around soon. With the return of the Calliope, there had also come hope. It was in everyone's faces. The mayor would not be able to stand in his way now. Finally, they had a real chance for survival. If just one of the fantastic new ideas proposed by Mr. Tesla worked, their energy problems would be over forever.

Chapter 27, Dinner and a Show

"What did she say?" asked Carvalho, as Molly got into the passenger seat of the van.

"She didn't so much say, as yell," said Molly, ears still ringing. "She said she has been worried sick, and that the whole world was looking for me. Then she asked what the hell was I doing in Rio de Janeiro?"

"What did you tell her?"

"I told her I was all right for the moment, but I was in trouble and needed help. As I didn't have time to go into details, I promised to call her again soon when we were safe, but for now I just needed some money. That's when she screamed for me to go to the police or the American consulate."

"We?"

"Um, I sort of mentioned I was already with a police officer to put her mind at ease. I said your name was Miguel Sanchez."

"But Sanchez is not even a Brazilian name," said Carvalho.

"I was in a hurry, ok? You kept making those 'wrap-it-up' motions with your finger to get off the phone!"

"Ok, ok, so did you get what we need?"

"Yeah, but I don't think she is very happy about it. She gave me her bank's routing and checking account number and even her private PIN. But she made me promise to call her back as soon as I could. Are you sure your friend at the bank can make an international money transfer like this without an ID?"

"If he wants his twenty-six parking tickets to go away, he will," said Carvalho, starting the van.

They made the short trip downtown easily. The van pulled up to the sidewalk near a small building with the words *Banco Bradesco* on the back-lit sign above the doors.

Carvalho opened the door for Molly as she went inside. After a brief conversation with the security guard, Carvalho led her to an office cubical where they could wait for the clerk.

"You've got lots of friends," commented Molly.

"I've done lots of favors." Carvalho grinned.

The clerk showed up after a few minutes and cast a nervous glance at Carvalho. However, after a brief exchange in rapid Portuguese, he took Ellen's information and left the cubicle. A short time later, he returned with an envelope full of reals.

"Won't he get in trouble for this?" asked Molly, shielding her eyes, as they walked back into the evening sunshine. It was almost five o'clock, yet the sun was still intense as ever.

"Only if your friend reports it. No one checks the details of every single transaction every day. I suppose a random audit might turn something up, but he's one of those smart computer guys, and I don't think this is the first time he has done this for someone," said Carvalho shutting the van door.

"Oh, right."

Carvalho looked at his watch. "We're doing well. We need to be at the restaurant by nine o'clock. That's when we're supposed to be meeting Felipe and Mariana."

"Sounds great, but can we get a snack or something? I'm starving. Also, can I get some new clothes and change before we do anything else? I'd kill for a shower right now."

"I was thinking the same thing," said Carvalho. "Ah ha! I think we have discovered your power; you can read minds! Can you guess what I'm thinking now?"

Molly jabbed him in the side. "I don't need to be a mind reader to know what you are thinking of, bucko."

Carvalho face turned beet-red.

"No, no, I wasn't thinking that. I was only…" he stammered.

Was he blushing? That was just too cute, she thought.

"At least not on the first date, big guy," she said, kissing him lightly on the cheek.

Carvalho relaxed a little and smiled. "So we're dating now, is it?"

"Just keep your eyes on the road," said Molly, her turn to redden.

"We'll need a place to sleep. I know of a quiet motel that doesn't ask any questions. We shouldn't be bothered there." Then, adding quickly, he said, "Relax, I'll get double beds."

"Oh, you are just a pillar of chivalry," said Molly amused.

"We can get clothes and things in the street market next to the motel. I'll help you find what you need," said Carvalho.

"Enrico?" inquired Molly quietly.

"Yes?"

"I don't think I've had a chance to properly thank you."

"What do you mean?"

"You saved my life and put yours at stake in the process. I don't know how I'll ever repay you."

"*De nada,*" said Carvalho. "I was involved in this before I met you. Finding you has been the only pleasant part of this whole messed up thing."

Molly took his hand in hers and put her head on his shoulder. "Gods. I'm just so tired. Why are these things happening to me?"

"I don't know. I think we'll find that out when we find that other shifter."

"How are you going to find him?"

"Whatever this shifter took from the observatory, they desperately want it back. They know more than they are letting on. I think they know exactly where he was heading," said Carvalho.

"How do you know that?"

"During my interview with Mariconi's assistant, Pinotti, I explained my encounter with the thief. Later the next morning, Pinotti rushed off to New York on *business.*

"I don't remember meeting anyone named Pinotti," yawned Molly.

"Lucky you. He is a real *babaca,* um, sorry, I mean *asshole*. He must have been out of town when they brought you here. I am hoping Philippe or his sister can tell me if they've seen him return. If he has, then we might have a chance at finding out who is behind all this and what they want. When we find Pinotti, we'll probably find our shifter as well."

Carvalho looked down. "Molly?"

Apparently, the pretty, young American had fallen asleep on his arm. She was sleeping soundly, but he relaxed his arm a little to make her more comfortable. She really was quite attractive. In the short time he had known her, he had come to like her quite a lot. With so much going on in her life, she somehow had kept her head and her wry sense of humor. He admired that.

Alone with his thoughts, Carvalho marveled at how quickly his life had changed over the past eight days. Just a little over a week ago he had seen something that he should have just pretended never had happened. Now, because of his stubbornness, he had this woman, one of the most famous writers in the world, sleeping on his shoulder, expecting him to keep her safe from lunatics with ray guns. His life had become as unreal as one of her fantasy novels. He wondered just what had he gotten himself into, as the van rattled along the winding streets into the Brazilian sunset.

Getting out of the tailrace tunnel had been tricky. No one had inspected the abandoned tunnel for almost fifty years, and Ananmaya was not entirely sure that it hadn't collapsed somewhere. Those intrepid urban explorers had made it to the end however, and even posted photographs on their website. This was somewhat reassuring, but he reached out with his mind anyway to check for any recent developments. He would need to proceed slowly, so exiting through the falls at speed would be impossible.

Reaching the torrent of water passing over the tunnel's exit, he was glad he had taken the precautions. Because of constant erosion from the water outside, he saw debris filling the lower half of the exit. Large boulders along with masses of concrete and brick were piled high beneath the water. There was enough room to leave, but only by going slowly and carefully. He trusted Tesla's assurances concerning the little craft's integrity, but that was *a lot* of water out there. He had an idea. Surely, Tesla would forgive a little shifting for the sake of precaution.

As the ship maneuvered over the debris and through the last few feet of the tailrace, he closed his eyes and concentrated. This would be much more difficult than what he did in the mountain. As he couldn't phase shift the large ship all at once, he would only shift the part of it directly under the falls.

There was a deafening rumble as the cockpit passed through the falls. Ananmaya felt the chill of the water as it passed harmlessly through his vibrating atoms. When he opened his eyes, the ship had emerged and was rising slowly towards the top of the "C" shaped gorge, turning slowly clockwise in the cold night air. The Elektra was once again free of its earthly tomb. It rose silently above the thundering falls.

As it was well past midnight, the park had turned off the brilliant and colorful lights illuminating the falls; only the lights of a few buildings on Goat Island were visible. As he approached the narrow stretch of land separating the American and Canadian falls, something caught his eye. Near the ridge was a tall bronze statue, lit from below. A man in an evening coat and cane stood on top of a large generator, looking forward over the falls. Ananmaya smiled as he recognized what it was. In 2006, the Canadians had finally erected a statue to the mad genius that had lit the world. The monument was a long overdue dedication to the nearly forgotten scientist. How fitting that this statue would see the Elektra off for her last flight.

"Thank you sir. Thank you for everything," said Ananmaya, turning the ship south. He pushed the accelerometer to three gravities and the ship rocketed away under the somber, bronze gaze of Nikola Tesla.

* * *

Ananmaya overshot Brazil by a few thousand miles, putting him somewhere in Antarctica. He had frantically slowed the Elektra to a stop, and now the ship was hovering above a featureless, windswept icy plateau. This wasn't going to be like flying an airplane. There were no automatic controls. Tesla had designed the ship to cover vast distances, not to puddle-jump continents. Pushing her to three gravities had been a big mistake; he had gone nearly halfway around the world in only a few seconds. Getting the hang of the Elektra was going to take some time. *Still, I should be able to work out the math and timing to do what I need to do.*

His travel plans had changed dramatically since his little chat with Pinotti back in the tunnel. His itinerary now included a quick stop in Brazil. Originally, he planned to visit the Philolans in person to warn them about an imminent invasion from Archænis that threatened both their worlds. He knew that only a personal visit would get their attention.

* * *

Shortly after their arrival on Philolaus, Tesla and Einstein decided to cease further communication with Earth and have the Elektra destroyed upon her return. The Earth wasn't ready to find out about her twin sister just yet. Besides the years of war both men had personally experienced, Einstein also feared the dark presence infiltrating SOTAR. Until he knew more about its nature, he agreed it would be necessary to keep the planet veiled in secrecy. At the time, Einstein had not realized that the dark influence already knew more about the world than he did.

Upon his return to Earth, Einstein had Mandic destroy Tesla's work on the interplanetary transmitters, but had hesitated at dismantling the Elektra. Instead of destroying the beautiful ship, he decided to disable her by secreting away her Leviton core to a private vault in Brazil over 4,000 miles away during a visit to the observatory in 1930.

Mandic would keep an eye on the ship from New York as he played the role of Tesla on Earth, while Tesla, Kulik and Anya stayed behind on Philolaus to oversee the work that would help the world to survive. With the lines of communication broken, Einstein never saw or heard from Tesla or the two Russians again. He could only hope that the seeds of change they had planted would grow and bear fruit.

It was at this point that Einstein's private journal had ended. In the eighty years that had passed, no more broadcasts were forthcoming from the strange world. She had remained hidden, even with significant advances in technology over the years. When a space probe showed possible evidence of the planet, SOTAR agents in NASA had quickly suppressed it. Ananmaya had found records showing how they had altered photos and data from both the Voyager 1 probe in 1990 and the STEREO solar probes in 2006. Apparently, Mariconi's people had found it in their best interest to continue SOTAR's mandate to keep the planet hidden.

No longer trusting his organization, Einstein gave his journal along with Tesla's notes to Bhuvanesh. Years later and nearing death, Bhuvanesh put his life's work in his satchel and left it with a note for his young apprentice to find. In addition to the papers, Bhuvanesh left his will, which would provide Ananmaya with all the financial resources he would need to complete his mission.

Ananmaya's life had come into clear focus when he discovered what his mentor had left him. He suddenly saw what he had been preparing for all those years and why Bhuvanesh had waited to tell him until he was ready. Bhuvanesh's letter had moved him greatly, and he eagerly embraced the mission set before him.

The months of tedious searching through ancient filing cabinets at the observatory in Brazil had paid off. He knew that Mariconi and his people had somehow used the ancient Mayan temples to travel to our universe. For hundreds of years, the portals had remained sealed, but with the appearance of Philolaus, nearly a hundred years ago, the forgotten portals had reopened rather dramatically on their world. They found that each Dzolob temple on their world led to a corresponding gateway on ours. Many of the gateways on Earth were destroyed or under tons of rubble, but they had found several to be intact. Mariconi had been trying to locate one in Costa Maya when Ananmaya had stolen the artifact in Brazil. Knowing that the powerful shifter would be out of town is why he had chosen that day to break into the bank.

Costa Maya. Of course! Why hadn't he seen it before? That was where that writer, Molly Arden, had been vacationing before she disappeared. With Mariconi there, she had been exactly in the wrong place at the wrong time. He could see why the man felt it so unbelievable that she knew nothing about the temple or being a shifter. The odds were, well, impossible to calculate.

Nevertheless, Mariconi believed she held the key to the Dzolob portals. And right now, that key was totally in the wrong hands. He would need to rescue Ms. Arden before he did anything else.

Ananmaya looked out the forward window of the ship and saw only a cold, white vastness. It was starting to snow furiously. He needed to work out his trajectory quickly; hanging around with the penguins was getting him nowhere. He quickly ran the figures through his head, and used the ship's instruments to chart the course manually. It was surprising how much you could do with such basic equipment. As soon as he was ready, he pushed the brass slider forward and the ship darted forward, leaving spinning circular eddies in its snow filled wake.

"That dress suits you," said Carvalho over the hubbub of the busy restaurant.

"Thank you. How did you know my size?" asked Molly, trying to read the menu. So far, only the words *La Mole Restaurante* were making any sense to her. She put it down.

"I guessed. You were very tired. I did not want to wake you until we had to leave."

"Well, it's very nice," said Molly, fidgeting with the light fabric of her blouse. She had seen many women wearing the same breezy style of clothing. It made sense in this climate.

"You talk in your sleep. Did you know that?" asked Carvalho.

"I do not! I know because I stayed up all night once to find out," joked Molly.

"Very funny. But seriously, you said some really weird things."

"Really? I don't remember. I must have been dreaming again. What did I say?"

"You kept saying you had to close a door. You needed to close *Edington's door,*" said Carvalho, motioning for a waiter.

The hair on the back of Molly's neck stood up at the mention of the name. She felt a shiver run down her spine. She remembered with frightening clarity how real her last dream about Edington had been. She hoped never to go through that experience again. Since leaving Costa Maya, she had thought little about the book. She had been too busy trying to stay alive. She took a sip from the glass in front of her.

"Sim, senhor?" inquired the waiter, surprising Molly as he came up behind her. She choked a little on her drink.

"Desculpa Mausso. Um momento," said Carvalho, surprised. "Molly, are you ok?"

"Yes, I'm fine. I'm sorry. I was in a world of my own and he surprised me, that's all. Go ahead and order for me. I'm too hungry to be picky."

"Okay then," said Carvalho picking up the menu. He placed the order and sent the waiter on his way. He looked at his watch.

"Philippe is late. I was going to get him some dinner. I guess I'll get him something to go when he shows up."

Halfway through their meal, Molly noticed Carvalho peering over her shoulder. She turned around in her seat. A little boy was walking through the restaurant towards them. *That must be Philippe.* She could see his sister's resemblance in his tear stained face. Apparently, he had been crying. He walked up to Carvalho as if in a trance.

"*Que, Felipe?* What's the matter?" asked Carvalho.

"*Desculpe, Corporal. Desculpe.* I am so sorry. But they…they have her," stammered Philippe.

"Who? Who do they have, Philippe?"

"Mariana! They have my sister. They said they would kill her if I did not cooperate," he bawled.

Carvalho's eyes darted upward towards the door, then back at Philippe.

"What do you mean? What…"

Molly saw Carvalho's face tighten as two men approached them from either side. Carvalho slowly reached for his gun.

"I wouldn't do that if I were you," said one of the large men. He had a bandage on his right hand. In his other hand was a small, silver device that looked like a laser pointer wrapped in fine wire. Molly immediately recognized the man and his dreadful weapon. Why wouldn't they just leave her alone? It was all happening again.

"Marcio, put away your toy. I don't think we need to make a scene here," said the other man reaching into Carvalho's jacket. He deftly removed the gun and put it in his coat pocket.

"Geez, Andre, you take all the fun out of everything," complained Marcio, putting the device in his pocket.

"What about me? Where is my sister? Where is Mariana?" pleaded Philippe.

"Run along, little boy," smirked Andre. "If you keep being good, maybe we'll let her go."

Philippe looked horrified, *"Por favor, senhor! Por favor!"*

"It'll be okay, Felipe. Do what they say. I'll watch out for Mariana," said Carvalho.

The little boy just stood there and stared, not sure what to do.

"*Vai!* Leave now!" insisted Carvalho.

Philippe reluctantly backed away from them looking miserable, repeatedly looking over his shoulder as he left.

"You'd be better off watching out for yourself," said Andre, taking Carvalho's arm. *"Seu bastardo filho da puta."*

Carvalho tensed and his fists clenched at what Molly thought must have been a personal insult. Was he going actually going to fight these two thugs?

"I wouldn't try any heroics, my friend. You'll do exactly as we say or we will send your little spy home one piece at a time," whispered the man. "Now get up, both of you."

Molly and Carvalho stood up slowly from the table.

"Let's go, nice and easy," said Marcio nudging Molly forward. "Dr. Mariconi doesn't like to be kept waiting."

Chapter 28, An Explosive Discovery

There had to be something, somewhere. Everyone had skeletons in their closet, including the illustrious Mr. Edington. Hastings rifled through the filing cabinet in the Chief Royal Astronomer's private office. Once he found what he was searching for, he would be able to force Edington and his friends into voluntary exile. There was no way they were going to have their way, particularly about returning to—what did they call their planet—Earth? The resource crisis had positioned him to rule this planet, and he did not intend to lose his control, much less be dominated by another world.

To make matters worse, Edington and his friends were out at the thermopile farm with half the town watching. The fools actually thought they could solve the power issues. They were about to test an invention from that Tesla fellow, which undoubtedly would fail. Their own planetary scientists had designed those thermopiles, and there simply was no way to replace or improve them further. Nor did Hastings want to do so. His plans relied on keeping the power levels where they were.

Power would be available only for those who could pay. Those unable to afford it would no longer be a problem after the first windstorm. The population would decline to fit the available resources, leaving him dictator over who remained. He already controlled the Town Power Authority and had stockpiles of food and supplies. No one was going to upset his control of resources.

How could these meddling Earth people be smarter than the greatest minds on Archænis? It didn't seem likely. Yet, improbable as it was, he still harbored concerns. Edington's little group needed to be discredited and disposed of before they could do serious damage to his plans.

While everyone was watching the demonstration, Hastings had let himself into the observatory complex using a city maintenance key ring. As he suspected, the place was completely deserted. Even the afternoon security guards had joined the other spectators at the farm far below. With no one to stop him, he easily made his way through the high-security levels of the complex, unlocking and opening the bulkheads as he went.

Unfortunately, he found some difficulty getting into Edington's hermetically sealed private office. The heavy brass portal required a private key he did not have. This was odd because the maintenance ring should have had keys for every sealed door in the observatory, but none of them seemed to work here.

What secrets are you hiding, Mr. Edington? thought Hastings, returning the key ring to his belt.

He reached inside the inside breast pocket of his suit and pulled out a curious looking copper card. It was pockmarked with tiny square holes in seemingly random places. Feeling along the hydraulic piping surrounding the door, he found the emergency pressure release valve. The valve would only open when the slot above it received the proper key card. This allowed rescue personnel to open jammed doors in the event of an emergency.

How clever I was to bring one along. He inserted the card and with a hiss, the hydraulic fluid drained out of the mechanism. The door gave way just enough to get his pudgy fingers enough room to pry it open.

He had been searching the eclectic office for about an hour when he looked through the large round window. Something was happening at the thermopile farm near the town's southern border. The crowd of people assembled there was cheering; he could hear it even from inside the office. To his chagrin, he realized that Tesla's experiment must have been a success.

Hastings was getting desperate. Soon, they would be returning, undoubtedly to rub his face in their latest victory. He quickly returned things more or less to their original state; it was hard to tell in the disheveled office. As he did so, he accidentally knocked a large wooden drawer off the desk he had pulled it out of earlier. It flipped upside down and landed on the floor with a crash. The rock samples it contained scattered everywhere.

"Bollocks!" cursed the mayor under his breath. He bent over to collect the rocks into a pile so he could put them back in the drawer. As he flipped the wooden box over, bits of wood and some papers he hadn't noticed before fluttered to the ground. Apparently, the drawer had a false bottom, which the crash had dislodged. He quickly folded the documents and put them in his suit's breast pocket since he didn't have time to read them now. He put the drawer and its other contents back into the desk and hid the broken bits of wood that had concealed the false bottom.

By now, the hydraulics had recycled, and the door resealed easily as he left the office. His heart was beating wildly. He was sure he had something important. Why else was it hidden? Much as he wanted to leave this accursed place, he paused for a moment, noticing a familiar smell in the air. He sniffed again. "Was that coffee?" he scoffed incredulously. How was it that these astronomers had their own personal supply, but the mayor of the town could not acquire so much as one bean?

He followed his nose to a short staircase leading to a sign that read PORTER OBSERVATORY—PLATFORM B. He pushed open the door marked for *Authorized Personnel Only* and went inside the dimly lit room. He was inside an immense domed chamber ringed with circular windows. A huge telescope sat motionless in the center. Workbenches and various equipment lined the walls. The smell of coffee permeated the air.

The others would be back soon. I shouldn't be lingering here. Nevertheless, the idea that these common people had a luxury he had been denied infuriated him. Edington would pay for this insult.

He soon found the source of the strong aroma. A pile of empty coffee bean sacks rested next to a behemoth of a machine. It was about as large a writing desk and had pipes radiating out of it in all directions. It looked ancient and seemed to be steam powered. A large rectangular box at the top held a large quantity of beans; he could see them though a vertical window in its side. The rest of the machine seemed dedicated to crushing and filtering the result into something resembling coffee. Near the bottom, a recessed orifice held a large, tarnished, vessel of glass and brass. Its base looked disastrously burned. Hastings surmised that this must be where the coffee was collected.

The machine looked frighteningly beautiful in its complexity, and he had to admire it. Until now, he had no idea that such a contraption ever existed. This would be one of the first things he would confiscate after he took care of Edington and his cronies. For now, he would just take a handful of beans out of the canister at the top, just for spite.

As he moved closer to the menacing looking machine, he saw welding goggles and gloves resting on the soot covered table next to it. *That's strange. I don't see a welding torch. Why would those be there?*

He shrugged and looked up at it again. He didn't know why, but he got the impression it was glaring at him somehow. He tried to raise the lid of the bean receptacle, but it was latched shut.

There must be a release mechanis. He looked for a lever. *Perhaps this will do it.* He pressed a conspicuous looking button.

CLICK. WHIRR. To his surprise, the machine turned on and began to vibrate.

THUD. GROAN. To his horror, it began to bellow black clouds of smoke, which started filling the room. He frantically tried to return the little lever back to its previous position, but it would not budge. It had stuck fast.

FZZZZ. THUD. THUD. THUD. The machine was practically dancing now, hopping up and down, pulling pipes out of the walls. Water sprayed everywhere. Scalding, high-pressure steam jetted out of the machine as it bounced around the room.

BOOM! The machine exploded, sending coffee beans in every direction like shrapnel. The glass carafe caught the mayor in the temple, knocking him to the floor unconscious. The carafe shattered on the floor next to him as he fell.

* * *

"It works! It works!" shouted Einstein happily, clapping Tesla on the back.

"Did you have any doubt?" calmly inquired Tesla as he inspected the power readings.

His resonant oscillator was working exactly as he had imagined it would. Converting the direct current output of the thermopiles into a high frequency, triple-phase alternating current showed significantly less power loss as it traveled the long copper wires into town. Ultimately, with his plan to build a power transmitter, they would not need the wires at all.

"I had one or two doubts," said both Eddingtons nearly simultaneously.

"You two really need to stop doing that! It's confoundedly nerve-wracking," said Crommelin.

"Yes, the sooner I return to Earth, the better," said Eddington. "I've found the whole experience rather unsettling."

"We keep meeting each other and getting in each other's way," continued the other.

"It's like fighting your reflection," they both said at the same time. They sighed and turned away from each other.

Tesla also understood the uneasy feeling of talking to oneself. On Earth, he had the same difficulties as Mandic described his planet's power problems. The two men kept interrupting each other. Eventually, Tesla was able to suggest several solutions to the power issues. Power transmission would be the easiest hurdle to overcome as he had just fought and won the battle to use alternating current at Niagara. To implement the same on Philolaus, Einstein had SOTAR fund the construction of over two hundred resonant oscillators. This was only one of the many innovations they had brought with them.

Crommelin was talking to Thomas Haynes, the town reporter, about their recent success. Now that the experiment had worked, everyone was talking excitedly about the amazing people from Earth.

Edington cleared his voice, "Thank you all for coming. Yes, we have made a significant advance this afternoon. But this is only the first stepping stone in a long list of projects Mr. Tesla has in store for us. Our next step is to work with the TPA to get as many of these oscillators installed as possible. This one innovation alone will not solve our problems, but it will give us the breathing room we need to take the next step."

A cheer went up in the crowd. The scientists were bowled over by an outpouring of congratulations. Kulik and Davidson had rejoined their new friends from the pub and were well on their way back into town. They were soon followed by the others.

As they left, Einstein turned to Tesla. "You have done a great thing this day."

"Bah. Alternating current is nothing new. I have invented nothing."

"You are wrong, my friend. You have invented hope."

* * *

"Mr. Edington! Mr. Edington! Come quick!" said Orville, panic-stricken and out of breath.

"What is it Orville? Can't it wait?" asked Edington, excusing himself. He had been catching up with his mate Ayden, who had infuriatingly brought Eloisa to the pub with him.

"No sir, it's the observatory! *It's on fire!"*

"What?" shouted Edington and Ayden.

"I don't know. I was on my way up the mountain when I saw the smoke."

"Ayden, get the fire brigade. I'm going up there," said Edington.

"Eloisa can do that. I'm coming with you, mate."

"Fine, fine, let's go," said Edington, running out of the pub.

As they ran up the mountain path to the observatory, he could see the pillar of black smoke rising over the ridge. His heart sank. He could only hope the fire was localized in one of the sealed rooms and had not spread.

Out of breath, and panting fiercely, Ayden fumbled with his keys. His efforts were in vain as the door pushed open easily.

"Someone's been in here. I know I locked it behind me when I left," said Ayden.

"It wasn't me," said Orville. "I never got this far up. I turned around when I saw the smoke."

"You wouldn't have been able to reach it anyhow. Your keys only get you as far as the dormitories. That fire is up on Platform B," said Edington looking up. Smoke was pouring out from under its domed roof. He felt sick at the damage it must be causing to the equipment.

"Let's go," said Ayden. He had retrieved his revolver and was edging up the stairs to the higher levels.

"I think a bucket of water might make more sense than a gun," said Edington, grabbing a fire pail.

"Better safe than sorry, mate," said Ayden as they hastened through the building to the Observatory Platform.

Water was running down the final set of stairs leading up to Platform B. The hatch was open and black smoke filled the space above. Edington poked his head inside but the room was black as pitch. The only light was coming from a small fire near the back of the room where the coffee machine was kept. Was that what all this smoke was about?

"I think the coffee machine developed a short or something in its electric burner. That is probably what started the fire. The rubber tubing must have caught next, which set the rest into flames and made all this smoke. It's not a big fire, but I think we should put it out before I open the dome," said Edington.

He took out a handkerchief, covered his mouth and nose, and ran into the blackened room, followed by the others. Water was spewing from exposed pipes in the wall. He filled the pail and proceeded to extinguish the fire. After about the third time refilling the pail, he tripped over something large and heavy on the floor.

"Quick, Orville, I've pretty much doused the fire. Open the dome. I need some light. I think there's someone in here."

With a greased whine, the dome slowly cracked open. A sliver of light shafted into the room. It steadily grew in size until a large rectangle of light filled the room. The smoke began to clear through the opening, and Edington could breathe more easily.

"What is he doing in here?" asked Ayden, noticing the body first.

The three of them stood near the prone, unconscious form of the mayor, lying in a pile of coffee beans near the wall. He was sopping wet from head to toe. A bloody gash on his temple gleamed red in the sunlight. Black soot covered his expensive suit, which hung loosely on his limp form.

"Is he alive?" asked Orville, turning off the water.

Edington kneeled down and felt for a pulse. "Yes, he's just unconscious. I think he took something to the head. He will probably come around soon, but he'll have one hell of a headache."

Edington and Ayden propped the mayor against the wall to get his face off the floor. As they remove his wet and constricted jacket, something fell out of an inside pocket.

"What's that?" asked Ayden.

Edington saw the folded up sheaf of papers, which had been insulated from the effects of the water and fire. He took them out and unfolded them. He gasped at what he saw.

"It's on the Chief Royal Astronomer's personal stationary, but I've never seen this before. He must have found it stashed away somewhere in my office," said Edington, scanning the documents rapidly.

"Crikey! Your eyes are like dinner plates," said Ayden, watching his friend. "What's it say?"

"It's utterly fantastic. It's about Professor Almos. I need to show this to Mr. Einstein." Edington got up to leave.

"What about the mayor?" asked Ayden.

"When the fire brigade gets here, have him arrested. Most those men are on the volunteer security detachment. Also, I expect you should have Dr. Panavi look at his head injury. Hastings will have much to answer for when he wakes up. For now, I have to get this to Mr. Einstein. It's *much* more important."

Before Ayden or Orville could ask any more questions, Edington had disappeared down the wet stairs.

"What was all that about?" asked Ayden.

Orville just shrugged. "We're not allowed on that floor, much less in his office. I've never been there."

"Well, if it's about Almos, I'm sure it's something odd. He was a queer bird," said Ayden.

"What do you think the mayor was doing up here?" asked Orville, taking inventory of the waterlogged, smoke-damaged equipment.

"Getting himself impeached, I shouldn't wonder," said Ayden. "Breaking and entering, stealing documents, blowing up the observatory. No mate, it doesn't look good for the likes of him."

"Just look at what he has done to this equipment. These were the last few boxes of photographic plates on Philolaus," said Orville despondently. "Now they are ruined."

"Go have a talk with that chap Tesla. He seems to have the answer for everything in that bag of tricks of his."

Orville smiled. "You're probably right. I wonder what he would think of all this."

"Core, blimey! I've just had an idea. We're gonna need a new mayor soon, right? What about that Tesla bloke?"

Orville thought for a moment, "You know, I think you've got something there."

Chapter 29, Recaptured

Skirting the southeastern coast of Brazil, Ananmaya slowed and dropped the Elektra to within a few hundred feet above Guanabara Bay. Just ahead lay the small, uninhabited island of Pombeba about half a mile from São Cristóvão. Brazil had many of these tiny islands, which were too rugged or too remote for habitation, yet were close to the shore. He had been buzzing the islands near the coast for hours, and it was already late into the afternoon. Finally, it seemed this isolated island had the best chance to hide the ship while he went to look for Ms. Arden.

He was getting better at controlling the amazingly agile craft. He circled the small island, looking for signs of life. It looked deserted except for one small fishing boat moored off a small inland cove.

This will do just fine. He brought the Elektra down into the thick jungle, just a few hundred yards inside the cove, and lowered her gently until her skids touched the ground. After shutting down the equipment, he carefully returned the artifact to its magnetite box and put it back in his satchel. After exiting through the portal in the ceiling, he lowered a rope ladder along the side and climbed down.

A short distance away, Ananmaya dug a shallow hole near an outcropping of rock, removed the box from his satchel and buried it. Covering the ship with banana fronds the best he could, he hiked down the rocky slope to the tiny cove where he had seen the little boat.

The fishing boat could not have been much longer than twenty feet and looked heavily used and smelled of diesel. Fishing nets were hauled up along a hull that was once white with red trim, but now was peeling and covered in barnacles. No one seemed to be on board the gently bobbing scow. He waded into the water towards the little vessel.

"Para ai!" shouted someone behind him.

Ananmaya wheeled around to see two men walking quickly towards him. He raised his hands in friendship, *"Ta bom*. It's okay. I'm a friend."

The two fishermen had just returned from drying more nets on the rocks to find a stranger regarding their boat. He could see why they would be upset. He tried to reassure them of his intentions but his Portuguese wasn't very good. Luckily, they spoke English.

"What are you doing? Who are you?" asked the first man to reach him. His dark, sun-tanned skin looked like taut leather over his muscular, but aged frame.

Ananmaya thought up a story quickly. "Please, I'm a tourist. I've been stranded here. I saw your boat from where they left me and hoped you would give me ride back to shore."

"Who left you?" asked the other balding man, most likely his older brother.

"Those idiots on the tour group. I had paid to visit Rio's more remote beaches, and fell asleep on the sand while watching the surf. When I woke up, I found that everyone had left. I guess they forgot about me. I've been stuck here for hours."

The brothers smiled at each other, then they laughed out loud.

"Amigo, you need a beer. Sevastao, get our friend a *cervaja.* I'll finish with the nets," said Severino, the elder brother.

"Obrigado muinto," said Ananmaya, getting on board.

"We were just heading back ourselves. You are lucky to have caught us when you did. Not many people come to Pombeba," said Sevastao returning with the drinks. His brother went into the little cabin and started the engine which rumbled loudly and bellowed a thick plume of smoke.

"Thanks, I really appreciate it. Is there some way I can repay you?" asked Ananmaya.

"Well, if you've got any money, you can pay for our gas and we'll call it even," said Severino eyeing his satchel.

"And for the beer, and for our time. After all, this isn't a pleasure cruise," added Sevastao.

Ananmaya was glad he had decided to leave the magnetite box behind.

"Sounds fair to me. I've only got about fifty dollars. Would that cover it?"

"If that is all you've got, then that is all we can take," said Sevastao as Ananmaya handed him the money.

"We should be at the port in a few minutes. Enjoy the ride," said Severino, turning the boat toward the mainland.

Mariconi wanted them separated when they reached the observatory, but Carvalho had other intentions. He twisted out of Marcio's grasp and lunged for Molly; only he didn't get far. With a crackling flash, Marcio shot him from behind with his energy weapon.

Molly screamed as he fell to the floor in a crumpled heap, electric static arcing along his twitching back.

"*Murderers!*" she cried.

"Relax, Ms. Arden," said Mariconi. "He is only stunned. For now, I need you both alive."

He turned to his large associate. "Marcio, put him with the little girl. Maybe when he wakes up he can stop her incessant sobbing."

Shouldering Carvalho's limp form easily as a sack of potatoes, he took the corporal out of the room. Once again, Molly found herself facing the redoubtable man in the white suit, alone in his office.

"Are you having a nice vacation, Ms. Arden?" asked Mariconi.

"Go to hell," she said defiantly.

"I've already been there," said Mariconi, folding his hands. "If you knew the world I was from you would know that."

"I don't give a rat's ass about where you come from."

"My, my, we have gotten bolder since our later encounter, haven't we? I suggest you mind your manners. Where I come from we respect our superiors."

"Why don't you go back there if you don't like it?" she asked, glaring at him.

"Archænis is nearing its end of usefulness. It is a bleak, desolate, and dying place. To my people, your world is a paradise, a sweet, ripe fruit, ready to be picked, as was our stolen world. Now, we intend to take them both. But to do this, we need you."

"You can't be serious. What do you expect me to do?"

"I expect you to do exactly what we tell you, or your friends will die a painful death, *repeatedly,*" said Mariconi.

Molly remembered the extraordinary power this man wielded. Could he even roll back death with his little undo button? Surely not.

"Where is Carvalho? What have you done with him and the little girl?"

"Corporal Carvalho and Mariana are safe. They will remain so, unless you persist in your arrogance."

Mariconi stood up and walked to the large map of the Yucatan hanging on the wall.

"Ms. Arden, I will tell you exactly what we know and how we want you to perform for us. I will speak plainly, so there is no further misunderstanding. I expect you to do the same. I tire of playing games."

Molly dropped her head. There was no way out of this. He genuinely believed the things he was saying. The last time they spoke, Mariconi insisted Philolaus was a real place and implied she had something to do with bringing it here. It was all madness, but she would need to pretend to be who they thought she was, or her friends would suffer. He was probably going to kill them all anyway, but she might be able to buy some time. Carvalho was resourceful; he might find a way to save them.

"Do you see these locations marked in red?" asked Mariconi, pointing to several markings on the large Central American map.

"They represent the Dzolob temples we have found on your world that still have traversable portals."

Molly counted about seventeen of them. She also noticed a large, red circle around the marker in Costa Maya, which marked the hidden temple she fell into at Chaccoben. It also marked where fate had so unexpectedly turned her life upside down.

"We have found over three-hundred of these on Archænis. As most of our planet is barren, we no longer have dense jungles like you have on Earth. Our temples were mostly intact and uncovered. Your world is lucky that the jungle has overrun and destroyed so many of your portals. Otherwise, we would have arrived in force and taken your planet over a hundred years ago."

"I don't understand. You're from another planet?"

Mariconi sighed. "No, Ms. Arden. I am from a parallel universe, nearly identical to this one. We share many of the same planets you have in your solar system, with one important exception. Early in both our planets' histories, a large object collided with our worlds, spewing out debris that formed our moons. For one reason or another, your moon retained more of its mass and expanded to nearly twice the size of ours. We suspect that our lack of a large moon caused our world to fall into a binary system with the planet you call Venus at what's called the *L3 Lagrange point* in space."

Molly wondered what this astronomy lesson had to do with her. "Fascinating, I'm sure. I can see why you enjoy playing in an observatory," she quipped.

Mariconi glowered, and then continued. "In our universe, our parallel of Earth, which we call Archænis, formed a shared orbit with our version of Venus, the planet we call Philolaus. The two planets were exactly 180 degrees apart from each other, putting them in the same orbit, but on opposite sides of the sun. We had just begun colonizing the newly discovered world when she was stolen away from us."

Molly's headache was coming back. How did he know that Philolaus was Venus in a parallel universe? She hadn't written that into her story, and had only vaguely played with it as an idea for later in the book. Also, the rest of what he said matched up perfectly. She had given the people on Philolaus exactly the same past: a war-torn world, on the verge of collapse, colonizes a newly discovered planet, which mysteriously disappears. Lastly, Mariconi certainly looked and acted like someone from that evil world. What was going on here? Did she really have some sort of ability to see into a parallel universe? Had she inadvertently moved an entire world? If so, how had she done it? Why hadn't she done something like this before?

"We know you brought Philolaus here, into your past, but what we cannot understand is how precisely you placed her. The orbit has not decayed in the hundred years she has been here. Your solar system now has an additional planet, yet it has had little impact on the Earth other than what your people call global warming. It would take an amazing amount of planning and calculation for someone to place her so perfectly. Please forgive me, Ms. Arden, but I do not believe you possess such skills."

"Yet you think I can teleport entire worlds," she said incredulously.

"Yes, I do," said Mariconi smiling. "However, in the case of Philolaus I believe you had help, most likely, from the shifter that stole our artifact. He was very skilled and powerful. He left my assistant in an awkward predicament, to say the least. It took hours to reach him and cut him free."

"If I'm so powerful, why haven't I used my powers to escape?"

"I'm not entirely certain that you haven't. You have eluded us on more than one occasion, and I cannot put it all on the shoulders of your rather vigorous new boyfriend. Chance seems to favor you rather more than normal."

Molly tried to keep him talking longer. This wouldn't be difficult as he seemed to enjoy the sound of his own voice. "So what do the temples have to do with all this?"

"They have everything to do with it! Our universes have always been close. Our ancestors knew this and built portals between our worlds. They did this using human sacrifice and arcane rituals. The Dzolob tore holes in space-time that never sealed completely. These ruptures are strongest in the sacrificial chambers near the top of their temples. I believe you activated these ruptures to enhance your shifter power to bring the planet here."

Molly remembered the odd sensation she felt in that strange, dark room at the temple in Chaccoben. She felt as if she were in the engine room of a ship. It was very quiet there, but she could feel intense vibration all around her. Crazy as it sounded, there may be some truth in what he was saying. Hell, she had even been writing the story near one of them. She remembered how strong the urge to write had been; it had felt as if the story was writing itself. Even after her laptop had died, she had switched to pencil and paper, which she hadn't used in years. If the pencil had broken, she probably would have used a rock in the dirt.

However, now that she was out of Costa Maya, she hardly even thought about the book. It was like a dream, fading away quietly.

Mariconi continued, "Until you activated the portals, the temples had been forgotten in history, quietly hiding the power they possessed. The Dzolob had destroyed themselves in their never-ending thirst for blood and power on both our worlds. We are all their descendants, but your planet has had a very different history from that point forward. Our people have embraced the same ideals as our ancestors, while your world has not. We have become the wolf, while you are the lamb ready for the slaughter."

Molly tried to ignore the vile comment, "So, I assume your people followed the planet here?"

"Of course we did. When you pulled Philolaus into your universe, all the portals on Archænis exploded with energy. They glowed and pulsed for weeks, sending the entire planet into turmoil. Even the constant, infernal warfare ceased until the local governments could figure out what was happening.

"Once we discovered Philolaus had disappeared, we knew the two events were related. We dug into our history and rediscovered what the temples were and how their gateways worked."

"Let me guess, you sent human guinea pigs through the portals?"

"Volunteers, Ms. Arden. We call them volunteers. But yes, our explorers went through the gateways, but only sixteen portals allowed them to return. Some of the portals exited under the water, into the earth, or simply went nowhere. Traveling through the working portals, we found that your world had a secret organization of shifters who had discovered the planet's existence and was actively trying to communicate with it. They had even sent a delegation of scientists to the planet. You might recognize two of the men sent. They were shifters by the names of Albert Einstein and Nikola Tesla."

Molly sat in stunned silence. Einstein did what…with whom? Surely, this must be more crazy nonsense. "Excuse me? Did you say Albert Einstein was one of those shifter people?"

"Yes, Ms. Arden," sighed Mariconi. "As you well know, shifters are everywhere. Most everyone that blazes brightly in your history has had the gift in one form or the other. Oddly enough, shifters are not as common on our world as they are on yours, but they do exist."

"Okay, but what makes you think a shifter brought it here?"

"The shifting of Philolaus to your universe was so well orchestrated that it could only be the work of a powerful, intelligent shifter. Where better to look than the secret SOTAR organization founded by two of your most powerful shifters? After fifty years of my predecessors infiltrating SOTAR on every level, we were frustrated to find no one on your world could have accomplished such a feat. Then, a young, ambitious *time shifter* on Archænis discovered evidence of temporal manipulation in that part of space and insisted that Philolaus had not only moved across universes, but across time as well. He insisted that the person we were looking for would appear in the Earth's near future. They sent him to find the shifter, or face certain death on his return for being one himself."

"Let me guess. That was you?" asked Molly.

Mariconi smiled. "I have waited nearly fifty years trying to find you. It has not been easy. But recent activity on Archænis changed all that. You might have noticed there are seventeen portals listed on this map. Yet I said only sixteen portals were active when Philolaus was shifted. The seventeenth portal activated over a week ago in a desolate region on our world corresponding to Costa Maya in yours. I knew the time had come, and better, I knew where to look."

Things were starting to make sense to Molly now, frighteningly so. She could no longer believe this whole thing was just a horrible misunderstanding. She had played a role, even if she had done so unwittingly.

"Ms. Arden, let us examine the evidence. We found you near the portal when it activated. Your book is a history of

Philolaus. Your accomplice is a powerful shifter who has stolen artifacts related to the planet. Everything points to you. Do you still deny what you have done?" demanded Mariconi.

Molly fidgeted with her necklace as she always did when she was frightened; it calmed her. "No answer I can give you honestly will suit you. Just tell me what you want me to do."

Mariconi returned to his chair and looked pleased.

"I am a reasonable man, Ms. Arden. My terms are simple. You have my word that we will release your friends unharmed as long as everything goes as planned. Tomorrow morning, you and I will fly back to Costa Maya, and you will return to the temple at Chaccoben. I do not understand how you used the Dzolob portals for the Philolans, but you will use them again, only this time for us."

"What do you mean?"

"A fleet of warships is waiting in orbit around Archænis. You will bring that fleet here. The ships will easily destroy your planet's defenses and soon this world will be ours. We will also send a detachment to investigate any remnants of our colonies, although I doubt they even exist anymore. We have not heard from them in almost a decade."

"You expect me to open a door to invaders?" asked Molly incredulously. "And what if I can't do it?"

"Then we all die, Ms. Arden. My government has put much faith in my plan, and will not take kindly to mobilizing the fleet for nothing. But make no mistake, you and your friends will be quite dead before they execute me."

Molly was speechless. She simply nodded her head.

"Very well then, we have a deal. I will release your friends once the ships have arrived. You and I will return through the portal to Archænis where they will welcome me as a hero. I'm afraid you will never see your friends or your world again."

"Are you done with me?" asked Molly angrily.

"We are quite finished. I believe you are familiar with your previous quarters." Mariconi motioned for one of the guards to come inside. A stocky man named Dimetri entered the office, gripped her firmly by the arm, and escorted her out of his office.

Mariconi called out to her as they left. "Good night, Ms. Arden. Sleep well. You have a very busy day tomorrow."

There was a rustle of leaves in the tree near where Ananmaya was hiding. After arriving at the port, he had made his way to the observatory, where he was certain they were keeping Ms. Arden.

Finding a quiet alcove overlooking the entrance, he waited until nightfall to make his move. Although he knew the observatory well and had several methods of breaking in, doing so during working hours would be foolhardy in the extreme. He could not afford any more mistakes like what happened at the bank.

He watched the traffic going in and out of the observatory. Suddenly, something moved in the branches of the large mango tree overhanging his hiding spot. He looked up and saw a pair of legs dangling above him. A very frightened looking little boy was climbing out of the tree. Ananmaya would have assumed he was after the fruit, if it were not for the dire expression on his face.

"Pssst," whispered Ananmaya as the boy dropped to the ground.

Startled, Felipe turned towards the sound with wide eyes.

"Esta tudo bem, amigo. I'm a friend. My name is Ananmaya. What's yours?" asked Ananmaya smiling.

"My name is Felipe," said the boy cautiously. "Are you with the *Policia?*"

"No, no. But there are bad men in there I am trying to stop," said Ananmaya. "What were you doing up there?"

The boy glanced at the tree Ananmaya was pointing at, and then looked critically at Ananmaya.

"Do you work for the observatory?" asked the boy.

"No."

The boy smiled at Ananmaya, "So you are hiding from them too?"

"Yes, I am. I don't want them to see me either. They have a friend of mine in there. I'm trying to save her."

Felipe's eyes widened, he began speaking all at once in rapid Portuguese.

"Slow down, Felipe," said Ananmaya. "So, they not only have Ms. Arden, but your sister as well?"

"Yes, and Corporal Carvalho too. We've been helping Ms. Arden. We helped her to escape once already, but now…" His voice faltered.

"It's okay, Felipe; it's not your fault. I know you must be doing your best. Where is she being kept?"

"I overheard one of the guards talking about the new prisoners this morning. She's in the same place as last time. The others are in a cell down the hall from her."

"How did you get her out last time?"

His face brightened. "It was Mariana's idea. We used the vents. Just like in the movies!"

"Could we do so again?"

"I don't think so. They have locked the maintenance sheds with pad locks. Also, they posted a new sentry in the courtyard. He doesn't talk much and has a big scar on his cheek. Unless you can walk through walls, I don't think you're getting in there."

Ananmaya grinned. "Felipe, do you want to see some *magic?*"

Chapter 30, Farshift

Tesla looked pale, shaken to the core. Einstein had never seen him like this. "Are you okay, Niko?"

"I think I need a glass of water," said Tesla, sitting down. He continued looking off into space.

"What's wrong with Mr. Tesla?" asked Edington. He had just finished showing the two men the documents he found in the mayor's pocket, and something in them had stunned the gaunt man into silence. Certainly, the information was astounding and tragic, but he could not understand Mr. Tesla's forlorn reaction to the news.

"I don't know. Let's give him a little time with his thoughts. He will come back to us," said Einstein. "Personally, I don't know whether to laugh or cry. Your Professor Almos seems to have left us with a paper time bomb."

"Well, I just felt that, considering what you two represent, that you should have seen this," said Edington.

During their discussions on Earth, Einstein had disclosed the nature of the SOTAR organization to Edington. The man was so much like the Eddington from Earth that he had immediately trusted him. Unlike his counterpart, this Edington had not been surprised in the least to hear about shifters. Apparently, the existence of shifters on Archænis was not secret, although though they were extraordinarily rare and usually murdered if they exhibited their powers.

Einstein returned the documents. "Yes, thank you for sharing this with us. It is quite a lot to think about."

"Professor Almos went to his grave concealing this information. But after everything that has happened, I think that the people should know," said Edington.

"You were his friend," said Einstein returning the papers. "Do what you think is best."

How little must he have known about his old mentor, considered Edington. The professor's irritable, cynical demeanor, his fanatical obsession with his work, and his general detachment from the human race all had their roots from one tragic event in Almos's sad, sad past. A past that drove him to become the larger than life man that everyone remembered. A past when Almos had a wife, a burgeoning career, and a daughter.

* * *

Almos Kasonovic was in love, both with his research and his lovely new wife, Lisset.

As a reward for his invaluable assistance in turning the tide of the war, the government had given Almos funding for his research as well as a license to marry the young woman he had bestowed his affections on over the past five years.

Lisset was a beautiful, talented artist with deep blue eyes and flowing blonde hair. The couple was very much in love, but the ban on children, and more recently, the ban on marriage had been absolute. Until Archænis could get a control on its extreme population growth, the governments of the world had taken equally extreme measures on relations with the opposite sex. If a woman was found to be pregnant, she and with her unborn child were executed summarily. To become pregnant on Archænis meant signing your death warrant.

Almos had only been able to marry because he had supplied valuable information concerning the Slavetic Federation troop movements in a war that was tearing his country apart. His valuable intelligence had turned the tide of the war, and he had become a national hero.

He had not done it alone; he had help from a decidedly unusual source. All of his information had come from Viktor Kasonovic, his strange identical twin. He had never met the man in person, but it hardly mattered as Viktor was not exactly his brother. He was, in fact, a version of himself in an alternate universe.

As early as he could remember, the two men had shared their thoughts across the void. Both men had discovered this wondrous ability at an early age. Not surprisingly, their parents told them to speak of it to no one. Individuals on Archænis who exhibited any sort of shifter gift were either imprisoned or executed. Shifters were not tolerated in the cruelly competitive world they lived in. Although Viktor's world had no such extreme bias, his family felt it would help socially not to mention his not-so-imaginary twin.

Thus Almos and Viktor went through their lives irrevocably connected to each other, sharing each other's experiences. Almos observed the beautiful place his twin called Serbia, and his twin witnessed the constant battles and congested streets of the Georgian Empire that Almos called home.

Often, events would occur in both their universes that were remarkably similar. When this occurred, the men could literally be in two places at once, experiencing it from different perspectives.

Most of the time, events would play out at different speeds in each universe. Often, a resolution would appear in Viktor's world first. Other times, the similarity would end in Almos's world. They found these pockets of similarity to be wondrous opportunities to capitalize on predicting the future.

Recently, the Crimean war in Viktor's world was playing out identically to the Slavetic invasion from the north on Archænis. At the time, both men had been scientists working for their governments. Because the war was advancing more rapidly in Viktor's universe, he had been able to tell Almos where the next attack would take place. Almos would then relay this information to his superiors. With each successful report, his stature with the emperor grew. Eventually, the wars ended in both universes with vastly different results. Viktor's Serbia was on the verge of revolution, yet Almos's Georgian Empire had nearly won the eastern war.

When questioned by his superiors about his uncanny ability to predict enemy troop movements, Almos had obtusely referred to something he called his *Farshift Project.* He spoke about the project in terms deliberately designed to confuse the emperor's agents so that they never understood its true nature. They really didn't care how it worked, just as long as kept them one step ahead of their enemies. Support for his Farshift project became a priority and the emperor himself made certain Almos received all the funding he needed.

Farshift was actually something Almos and his brother had been working on for years. They were trying to build a device that would use their interdimensional link to open a physical portal between their universes.

A few years after the close of the war, Almos had nearly completed the complex project, but now faced an even greater trial. He had been married to his lovely wife Lisset for nearly four years. His brother had also taken a wife, yet she and her unborn daughter had died during childbirth. Almos had felt the heartbreak and remorse of his brother intensely; a pain he feared he would soon experience himself as well because his wife Lisset was also pregnant.

He feared his wife and child would share the same fate, not because of some complication in childbirth, but because of his planet's ruthless ban on children. Horrified at what the government would do if they discovered Lisset's condition, Almos and Viktor rushed through the construction of the gateway devices on both sides of the divide.

Early in their research, they discovered a method to locate areas of natural weakness between their worlds. Strangely enough, these locations were usually at ancient sacred sites. For their best chance of success, they chose to operate the portals in a place called Mexico on Viktor's side and a place corresponding to the southern Waylands on Archænis.

Almos originally intended to send his family as well as himself to the alternate universe, but tragically, he soon realized that he would need to remain behind. Without a shifter as an anchor on both sides, his family could become lost between worlds. He could not take that risk. Lisset would go alone.

With his heart breaking, Almos explained the horrible limitations of the dangerous transit to his beloved wife. She also would not be able to return. This would be a one-way trip. Experiments had proven that repeated travel between the universes was not going to be possible.

Unable to hide from the authorities much longer, Almos tearfully kissed his wife goodbye, and gave her the pendant he made for her during their courtship. She would wear it always to remember him.

Commiting to the most difficult decision of his life, Almos concentrated into the Farshift device, opening the portal and sending his pregnant wife to the only place he knew they would be safe—to his counterpart on Earth.

He would be with her remotely through Viktor, but she would have no such direct connection. Viktor would be the one to tell her of Almos's descent into depression, his anger against the government, and his fanatical obsession with science and his withdrawal from society. As time passed, Almos grew cynical and callous but was never jealous of his twin. He was happy that he had given Viktor back the family that fate had so cruelly stolen from him.

He watched Viktor and Lisset marry. He saw them raise his little girl who they named Anna. He saw her grow into a young woman and marry. Through his brother, he met his grandchildren and watched them grow: Alexander, a young man who wanted to become a boxer and Veve, a spirited young girl with dark brown hair and her mother's intense blue eyes.

Almos saw all these things, until forty-five years later, when he found himself on Philolaus, a world being pulled inexplicably into an alternate universe. The anomaly had thrown the entire planet into confusing turmoil, but secretly, Almos had known what was happening.

When the rift of strange stars had appeared in Philolaus' sky, he had recognized the constellation of Orion, the Hunter, glowing brightly inside it. How could he miss it? His twin from Earth had looked upon it often, rising in the Siberian night sky.

Like himself, his twin had also been an avid astronomer. Both men had found distinguished tenures as professors in the west. Viktor, in a place called England, and Almos in the country of Valencia. Both men had successful careers as astrophysicists, but Viktor had retired whereas Almos had gone to another planet. Now, that planet that was moving, and was going to be in Viktor's universe very, very soon.

The two scientists had worked furiously to understand what was happening with Viktor working from Earth and Almos from Philolaus. Both men saw a shifter influence in the move, but the scale was, to put it bluntly, astronomical. What kind of a shifter could do such a thing? Why were they doing it?

Putting the source of the anomaly aside, Almos tried to work out where the planet would appear and what kind of havoc it would cause in the orbits of their planets. Even if the two men were unable to do anything to save their worlds, at least they would know how much time they had left.

To his surprise, his calculations showed the planet ending up exactly in the only place where another world could possibly exist in this universe—the *L3 Lagrange point.* In 1772, Joseph Lagrange had proposed that planetary bodies would have five possible positions where another body could maintain a stable orbit in relation to the planet as it went around the sun. The L3 point was found within the same orbital path as the Earth, but 180 degrees on the opposite side of the sun. This was exactly the same binary alignment the planet Philolaus had shared with Archænis.

Also surprising was that the shift was not an instantaneous event. Almos was amazed to find that over the course of the transition, the planet's arrival destination continued to track along its proposed orbital path. It was as if something were guiding the planet as it transitioned, locking it to where it needed to be.

It was Viktor who figured it out first. "It is us, brother. We have become lodestones."

"What do you mean?" Almos asked.

"We are the centers of attraction. Our shared abilities are being used to choreograph the transition. Whoever is doing this has somehow tapped into our link and is using it to lock on to you and your people. Philolaus is being brought here with you as the focal point. I have become the reference point from which the orbit is scaled. This has had an effect both on us. Haven't you not noticed how tired you've been since this started?"

"I assumed it was just old age and stress."

"I don't think so. I think that as the universe sorts itself out we're being used as human guide posts."

"But what is causing this? Why is it happening?"

"I don't know for sure. Perhaps the Farshift project could have something to do with it?" Viktor proposed.

"What? Farshift was almost fifty years ago! We had nowhere near the power to do something like this!"

"I mean simply that the tear we opened might have left a scar on space-time. Something could have found and used that predefined route."

Almos thought the idea made sense. Using their gateway devices, they had clear-cut a wide pathway indeed. Given enough power, someone could theoretically send an entire planet spiraling down the tunnel; size was irrelevant. But how could this be done? Where could such a power be found? There were many questions that neither man was ever able to answer.

Viktor died of a heart condition ten years later, wife and family at his side. Almos following him in death nearly to the second. Lisset wept over both men's passing. She had seen them live long, interesting lives and had loved them both. She turned to her now middle-aged daughter Anna, and took her hand.

"I know you have seen more than your fair share of loss, my dearest," she began to explain.

Anna's husband had been lost in the war, and her son Andrew had been killed in an accident during a boxing match in New York, three days before his eighteenth birthday. His younger sister Veve, was all Anna had left. She was in the parlor, waiting for her mother to pay her last respects.

"Never lose hope, Anna. Always know there are other worlds than these," she said cryptically, almost a whisper.

Lisset had never spoken of the other universe, or of her husbands' strange powers, to her family. Other than being highly intelligent, neither her daughter Anna, nor her granddaughter Veve had inherited her husbands' uncanny abilities. The shifter gene apparently skipped a few generations. To give them as normal a life as possible, she felt it best not to tell them about Archænis or Philolaus, worlds so close, yet so very far away.

A little confused by the comment, Anna watched with further surprise as her mother removed the ever-present pendant from around her neck and pressed it into her palm.

"This was given to me long ago by someone I dearly loved and lost before I met your father. I keep it to remember his tragic sacrifice. It comes from a place that truly knows the meaning of despair. Looking upon it sometimes makes my own troubles seem less significant. May it now give you strength."

Speechless, Anna took the pendant. Until now, she had never held it before. Turning it over, she noticed an odd inscription on the back.

"Mother, I don't know what to say. I will keep it always. But, whose initials are these?"

Lisset sighed, her head bowed over her husband. To Anna she seemed so tired, so old and frail.

"I'm sorry, Anna. I haven't been completely honest with you. We had hoped to insulate you, to give you a normal life."

"What truth? Mother, what's all this about?"

This was it. Lisset decided to tell her everything. She knew that her daughter had wrestled with a similar problem concerning Veve.

Long ago, Anna had confided that there was a chance the man she married wasn't the biological father of her children. Deciding whether or not to tell them had weighed heavy on her. Before she could make up her mind, she had lost her son, Andrew. His death had compelled her finally to tell Veve the truth, much as Viktor's death was now persuading Lisset.

With a heavy heart, she began, "The initials are those of the man who gave me the pendant, your real father, Almos Kasonovic."

* * *

"I knew Anna Kasonovic," whispered Tesla, eyes downcast.

The man had spoken suddenly, catching Edington and Einstein off guard. Einstein turned to his friend and caught his face. Had he been crying? Actually crying? This was so unlike Niko. The man prided himself on his mastery of emotion.

"The story is true. I knew Anna when I was a student. We were very much in love," said Tesla with a sigh.

Edington and Einstein looked at each other for a moment stunned, then back to Tesla.

"From your expressions, I can see you don't believe me," Tesla straightened up and regained some of his composure. "Confound it! If you must know, I sometimes indulged my passions in my youth. I had not learned the self-control I have now. Also, she had the most understandable eyes I have ever seen. I fell madly in love with her from the moment I saw her."

"I must say, my friend, this is very refreshing to hear. Why haven't you spoken of her to me?" asked Einstein.

"She was the only woman I ever loved. Unfortunately, it was not meant to be. I wished to pursue the acetic life of an inventor, and she wanted a family. The roles were incompatible."

"You chose science over a woman?" asked Edington. He had often found himself in the same predicament.

"Yes. After we had parted, I vowed celibacy and have had no relations with any other women since. However, Anna and I kept in touch. Often, her two children visited me, whom I loved as my own. When her son, Andrew died, I was hard pressed to repress the anger and sadness I felt. My connection to the children was very strong. I often wonder if possibly they were mine."

Einstein's eyes bulged. "Niko! You don't mean to say…you rascal!"

Tesla sighed. "It was a single moment of passion. We had been fighting the same old fight. She simply could not fathom why I would spend so much time inventing, and so little time with her. She was often rather put off when I failed to show for an engagement, even when the sacrifice meant a great advance in my research. The girl could be so selfish at times."

"Yes, women do have the most unreasonable expectations. Do continue," said Einstein.

"Well, we were in my lab and she threw things at me. A large capacitor caught me rather neatly on the side of the head, knocking me to the floor. When I came to a few seconds later, she was sobbing over me, trying to wake me up. We made up, kissed and well, nature took its course. I left for America two few weeks later. We had agreed to put the encounter behind us."

"Niko, you were quite the scamp!" clapped Einstein.

"I would prefer this story not leave this room, if you don't mind," said Tesla.

"No one would believe it!" laughed Einstein.

"I have not dredged up this sordid tale for your amusement, Albert," said Tesla seriously.

"Then why?" asked Edington.

"Because of Anna's daughter, Veve. Veve is the granddaughter of Almos Kasonovic. Although neither Veve nor her mother have ever demonstrated any shifter abilities, in her veins runs the blood of not one, but perhaps two of the most powerful shifters in two universes. Eventually, one of her progeny will turn out to be a shifter with unimaginable power. We may find out sooner than later. Veve is pregnant with children of her own.

Chapter 31, Rescued...again!

A loud explosion on the street had Demetri automatically pulling out the stupid little weapon they had given him. What was he supposed to do with this thing anyway? He had nearly broken the little toy of a gun with his thick fingers the first time he handled it. Still, the two Italian heavies seemed to like it, and he had seen what it could do. Even so, he would have preferred his reliable Glock 33 pistol. At least it never needed charging. Holding the cylindrical weapon in front of him, he carefully approached the top of the wall that overlooked the street below.

Just some dumb kid, he saw, looking down. Someone was down there throwing fireworks in the street. Probably leftovers from New Year's Eve.

The city had changed dramatically in the last two hundred years. A residential neighborhood now surrounded the hill the old observatory had been built on, and the local kids were always up to something. Usually, they would break into one of the old disused observatory domes to get drunk or make out.

"*Para!* Get outta here," yelled Demetri to the boy, using one of the only Portuguese words he knew. The boy did not look up, but instead, ran off into the dark.

Demetri grunted. Stupid kid. He looked down the otherwise quiet street and put the absurd weapon into his back pocket. To hell with Mariconi, he cursed, pulling the Glock from the small of his back and putting it in the holster instead. At little more at ease, he returned to his watch in the courtyard.

* * *

Felipe's distraction had given Ananmaya all the time he needed to cross the courtyard to the back of the maintenance shed. The boy had been right; the door was padlocked shut with a heavy chain. It would only take a moment's concentration to spring the lock, but opening the door would be a noisy enterprise. It would be easier simply to pass through the wall.

Like a ghost, Ananmaya disappeared into the shed and let his eyes adjust to the dark. He found his way to the air conditioning intake vent that Felipe had described. Not surprisingly, the access panel was now welded shut. Mariconi was not taking any chances. He ran his hand along the welds and concentrated. They rapidly rusted over and disintegrated into a fine red powder. He removed the panel and let himself into the small, dark chamber.

Before he could locate the ventilation shaft that led to the underground holding cell, a large fan above him suddenly spun to life with a whine. He frantically reached for something to hold on to, jamming his feet into the walls of the chamber to fight the upward tug. He wouldn't be able to do this for long.

Using his mind, he reached into the motor driving the fan and saw it would take too long to stop; his grip was starting to slip. He needed to do something uncomplicated and fast. He focused on the spinning blades, which was a challenge as they were moving fast. Once he his mind had a fix on the central hub, he twisted all four blades flat. The wind died down, and Ananmaya caught his breath.

That was close, he thought, lowering himself into the shaft below. With the fan now useless, he would have little time to facilitate a rescue before someone complained of the increasing heat. He let the shaft lead him to Molly's room. The grating here had been welded shut as well. Looking down, he saw the famous writer sleeping fitfully on a cot in the darkened room below him. Apparently, Mariconi had posted a guard outside her room as well. He could easily see the guard's shadow moving in the thin line of light under the door.

He would have to be very quiet. Now that he could now see where he was going, he shifted through the grating, letting gravity drop him to the floor, solidifying slowly as he fell. Molly woke with a start as he landed with a faint thump next to her bed. She couldn't see who the shadowy figure was in the dark room, but it looked like a man. She inhaled, getting ready to scream. The figure lunged at her.

Ananmaya as he held his hand over her mouth and whispered, "I'm a friend. Please, Ms. Arden, don't scream! I'm here to rescue you." Molly's eyes searched his frantically as he kept his hand over her mouth. "Please, you have to trust me. I am a shifter, like you."

Molly stopped struggling, and her eyes went from fear to something like desperation.

"I'm going to remove my hand now, ok?"

Molly nodded. Ananmaya pulled away his hand and stepped back from her.

"Who are you? How did you…"

"My name is Ananmaya. We need to get out of here. Do you know where Carvalho and the little girl are?"

"Yes, they are in the room next to mine, but it's guarded."

"One moment, please," said Ananmaya walking toward the wall she indicated.

To her surprise, he didn't stop. In fact, he passed right through! A short time later, the strange visitor came back to Molly's room through the wall with two very surprised looking people, one under each arm. They stumbled into the room.

"Carvalho, Mariana!" said Molly as quietly as she could. She hugged Carvalho tightly.

"Please, we must be very quiet. There are guards everywhere. Mariconi is taking no chances," said Ananmaya.

"You must be the shifter that Mariconi keeps calling my accomplice," said Molly. "They said you could walk through walls, but I didn't know you could bring people with you as well."

"Actually, I didn't know it either. It was a good test for what we need to do next."

"And what is that, thief?" asked Carvalho tersely. "I'm not sure we should be going anywhere with you."

When Ananmaya appeared in his room, Carvalho had immediately recognized him as the shifter from the bank theft. Mariana had yelped with surprise, but Ananmaya put his finger to his lips, motioning them to be quiet. Carvalho didn't know whether to shake the man's hand or punch him in the gut. After all, he had been the one that had cost him two weeks' pay, and sent him on this little adventure.

"You're welcome to stay here, Corporal, but Ms. Arden and the little girl are coming with me."

Carvalho growled. "Molly, I don't know if we can trust him."

Molly thought for a moment, "How does that saying go? The enemy of my enemy is my friend?"

"You have a point. I suppose we don't have a choice," he said, turning back to Ananmaya. "What's the plan?"

Ananmaya walked around the room, trying to get his bearings. He faced the door and looked to be doing some mental arithmetic. "We need to exit in that direction. Luckily, the hallway will give us the distance we need to pick up speed."

"That hallway goes up a flight of stairs into the main lobby which is crawling with Mariconi's private police force," said Carvalho.

"We won't be going up the stairs. We're going *through* them," said Ananmaya. "A short distance through the bedrock at the back of the stairs should put us near the middle of the retaining wall, about two or three feet above the street outside."

"What about the guard outside my door?" asked Molly.

"Leave that to me," said Carvalho. "I assume you can do something about this door?"

Ananmaya smiled. "Of course," He pressed his palm to the doorframe. The door shimmered for a moment then turned into something resembling baked clay. Cracks began to spider web along its surface.

The guard outside fell into the room as the door he had been leaning on crumbled to the floor. He wiped the dust from his eyes with his bandaged hand. To his amazement, the small room had filled with people. Before he could use his radio to call for backup, Carvalho spun the man around with a jab to his jaw, flinging the radio onto the bed.

"I don't know what just happened, or how you got in here, but you're not leaving," growled Marcio rubbing his chin.

"He's going for his gun!" exclaimed Molly.

Carvalho bear hugged the large Italian, pinning his arms to his sides. Marcio stood up to his full height, picking Carvalho up off the floor, backing him into the wall hard. Carvalho groaned, temporarily winded, but still held on. When the large brute reared up to repeat the barrage, Carvalho kicked the back of the big man's knee, sending them both toppling over the bed, breaking it into pieces as it ripped away from the concrete wall. Carvalho fell hard with his opponent on top of him, flinging Marcio's weapon to the back of the room. Dazed, both men scrambled to regain their feet, but Carvalho was quicker. He stomped on Marcio's injured hand as he used it to rise.

The man howled in pain, just before Carvalho's knee caught him under the chin. Marcio fell over backwards onto the remains of the bed.

Carvalho turned to his companions, wiping blood off his lip, "You see, no problem..."

"Look out!" shouted Molly.

Marcio had staggered to his feet. He picked up a piece of pipe that had been part of the bed and raised it to crush Carvalho's head.

Suddenly, a bright flash of light appeared behind the man, casting him in a dark silhouette. Marcio's face contorted in agony as his eyes rolled back in his head. He fell to the ground unconscious. Behind him, Mariana held a small device in her hand, which emitted a dying whine. She was still pointing it when Ananmaya walked up to her.

"Give me the gun, *menina."*

Instead, she dropped it to the floor and ran to Molly, hugged her leg and sobbed, "The corporal...I..."

"It's okay, Mariana. You did the right thing," comforted Molly. "You're a very brave little girl."

Carvalho picked up the weapon and examined it. It was the same one they had used to knock him out when they had arrived. Evidently, it had several different intensity settings. He put it in his pocket along with the radio. They could come in handy.

"Don't worry, Mariana, he's only stunned, but he'll feel like shit in the morning. Thank you, *namarada,*" he tousled her hair.

"I thought I was your girlfriend," said Molly amused.

"Get in line," said Carvalho with a smirk.

"Well this was all a bit more violent than I would have liked, but ludicrously effective," said Ananmaya surveying the destroyed room.

"So what's your plan, shifter? Are we just going to walk out of here?" asked Carvalho.

"No, we're going to run. The observatory is built on a rise about twenty feet above street level. As we are in a basement, I expect the street is just outside the retaining wall which I estimate must be a few yards past the end of this hallway."

"But that's solid rock," said Molly.

"Which is why we need to run. As you have seen, I can pass us through solid matter. Unfortunately, I find it rather difficult to maneuver in such a state. We will need to get up enough momentum to cross through the retaining wall to the street outside. I think I can shift all the way through if we stay together."

"You think?" asked Carvalho. "It felt like I passed through a cheese grater the last time."

"It's either that, or wait for him to wake up," said Ananmaya pointing to Marcio.

"Let's go," said Molly, picking up Mariana.

"Mercda," cursed Carvalho as Ananmaya gripped the backs of their shirts and pushed them into a running gait. They cannonballed into the stairwell at the end of the hall.

BWWWAAAANNN!!! The bus driver blasted his horn at the *idiotas* that had come out of nowhere in front of him on the dark street. He had been able to swerve out of the way just in time. *"Filhos da puta!"* he shouted out of the window as he drove off.

A little boy stepped out of his hiding place and ran to the people that had suddenly appeared in the street.

"Opa! You are a magician!" exclaimed Felipe, helping Ananmaya to his feet.

"Felipe!" cried Mariana, untangling herself from the trash pile where she and Molly had landed in a heap. She jumped on her older brother, knocking him to the ground.

"Mariana, I'm so glad you are safe. I was so worried," said her brother as he hugged her and laughed.

"All of you just came out of nowhere. I was waiting by the car as Mr. Ananmaya said, when suddenly you were all tumbling into the street. Did you fall off the wall? You just missed getting hit by a bus."

"Oops. I hadn't considered that," said Ananmaya. "Being hit by a bus could have been somewhat inconvenient."

"I should say so," said Carvalho dusting himself off. As he bent over, a bullet whizzed past his ear. Two more exploded the concrete by his feet.

"Get in the car! All of you! Now!" shouted Carvalho, rushing them out of the street. He took cover behind the open passenger-side door and fumbled for the strange weapon in his pocket.

Three bullet holes appeared in the door he was hiding behind as everyone piled into the vehicle. Carvalho cursed under his breath. The bus must have alerted the guard in the observatory courtyard and now he was shooting at them. So much for a quiet getaway.

He looked up at the retaining wall and thought he saw a glint of light from the shooter's gun. Carvalho stood up, took aim and pressed the trigger on the unusual weapon. It clicked, but did nothing else.

"Mercda!" he felt a jarring sensation in his right arm as a bullet tore through it. He collapsed into the passenger seat, slamming the door behind him.

"Vai! Vai! Get us out of here!" shouted Carvalho to Ananmaya. Molly and the two children ducked down in the backseat. Carvalho gripped his arm. Blood was gushing out of the wound, too much blood. The bullet must have hit an artery.

"We need to get to the port. I have a boat waiting for me. Do you think we can…" Ananmaya paused, noticing a pool of blood forming on the floorboard. "Corporal, you've been hit!"

"So I've noticed," said Carvalho through clenched teeth. He was starting to feel faint.

"What?" exclaimed Molly, leaning forward to look at his bloodied arm. "This is really bad. We need to get him to a hospital."

"No."

Ananmaya pulled the car over, reached over and touched Carvalho's arm. To Molly's amazement, the blood stopped flowing, then actually reversed. As the last of it drained back into the wound, the opening closed, leaving only smooth skin. Carvalho's eyes rolled up, and his body went limp.

"Enrico! Enrico! What have you done to him?" demanded Molly.

"I've healed the wound, but he lost a lot of blood. I recovered what I could, but I can't replace all that he's lost," said Ananmaya.

Tears rolled down Molly's face as she shook him. "Enrico! Wake up. We need you. I need you. Wake up! Don't you dare leave me!"

A thin whisper escaped his lips. Molly leaned closer to hear.

"*Namarada,* " murmured Carvalho, "you really are a nagging bitch."

Molly wrapped her arms around him and kissed his cheek. She laughed in sobbing waves of relief as he hugged her back.

"Corporal, are you okay?" asked Felipe from the back seat. He sister held his hand and looked at them nervously.

"Yes, Felipe. I'm just a little weak. Listen to me carefully. I don't want you or your sister to ever return to this part of town again. These are very bad men. When we stop, I want both of you to go straight home to your mother. Lay low for a while, then disappear. That is an order. You understand?"

"Yes, Corporal," Felipe saluted.

"We're almost there," Said Ananmaya. "Guanabara Bay is just a few miles ahead. I don't think we've been followed."

"Guanabara Bay?" asked Molly. "Is that where you said you had a ship waiting?"

"In more ways than one," said Ananmaya cryptically. "What time is it?"

"It's nearly seven in the morning," said Molly looking at her watch.

"Good. My friends will be waiting for me. That is if they don't have a hangover."

* * *

The bullet-riddled sedan pulled into the busy port. The place was already buzzing with activity. The smell of fish and diesel permeated the air. Molly could see pier after pier containing boats of all shapes and sizes. They walked to where several small fishing boats were moored. Walking quickly along the pier, Ananmaya found the one he was looking for. Two men were in the process of loading the boat for the day's outing. He spoke with them in Portuguese.

"Like I promised, I've brought my friends. They are really looking forward to seeing Pombeba."

"I would have thought you'd had your fill of that place by now," said Severino.

"Well, the beaches are very private, and my friend here doesn't exactly enjoy wearing a swimsuit," he said, indicating Molly.

Severino poked at his brother and pointed towards Molly. They snickered and leered at her.

"What are they saying?" asked Molly.

"They are negotiating a ride to Pombeba," said Carvalho. "It's that small island in the bay. There is nothing out there. I don't know what he is planning."

Ananmaya rejoined them. "It's all set. Let's go. I hope you don't get seasick. It's a choppy ride."

"Why are we going to Pombeba? We can't hide there indefinitely," said Carvalho, following Molly into the gently bobbing boat.

"My ship is waiting for us there. It's only a stopping point," said Ananmaya.

The small boat pulled out the dock a short time later and began motoring towards Pombeba.

"Mercda!" said Carvalho squinting at the receding shore of São Cristóvão. Two black dots were in the sky above the wake the little boat was leaving behind. They were getting larger.

"I hate it when you say that," said Molly. "Something bad is usually not very far behind."

The two black helicopters swooped over the boat, silent as the wind. Severino and Sevastao poked their heads out of the open cabin as the shadows passed over the boat. "BOPE! BOPE!" they exclaimed. They began rummaging frantically for something under the bench in the cabin.

"What's a *Boppey*?" asked Molly, amused at the word that sounded like a baby toy. Then her face fell as she recognized the helicopters turning around to face them over the island. They were the same type SOTAR had used at her beach in Costa Maya the night they took her.

"The BOPE is our special division task force. I guess they are what you get if you crossed your SWAT team with your Navy Seals. But I don't think they have equipment like that. I've never seen helicopters like that before."

"I have. They belong to our friends at the observatory. Somehow, they have found us," said Molly.

"How? I doubt they could have found the car so quickly," said Carvalho.

"The radio! Do you still have the radio?" asked Ananmaya.

Carvalho pulled it out of his pocket and handed it to him. Ananmaya closed his eyes for a moment and scanned its construction. "Yep. As I suspected, there's a tracking locator inside." He threw it overboard.

Severino and Sevastao came out of the cabins with what looked like machine guns and fired at the approaching aircraft.

"These are your *friends*?" exclaimed Carvalho to Ananmaya who was taking cover.

Sizzling explosions in the water on both sides rocked the boat. The men in the helicopters were shooting back. Blue-white plasma arcs streamed out the helicopters as they strafed the water near the boat with their energy weapons.

The two brothers looked desperately at each other. It was obvious that they had never seen anything like this. Not sure what else to do, they leapt overboard, leaving Molly and her friends alone with the speeding boat. The two men swam for a small spit of land adjoining the island.

"Your friends were drug runners," said Carvalho removing a large bag of *Ganga* from the concealed compartment under the bench.

"I had no idea," said Ananmaya astounded.

"Live here long enough, and you'll find grandmothers growing this shit in their backyard," said Carvalho.

The black helicopters had circled around for another pass.

"Here, take the wheel. Get us into that cove," said Carvalho.

He took out Marcio's weapon and studied it closely. A little green light on the barrel now indicated a full charge. He also noticed that the back end of the copper tube had small numbers on it. They were marked one through five; currently, the setting was on two. He took a wild guess that bigger was better, and put it all the way to five. He hoped the little weapon had recharged itself enough to work this time. He took careful aim and fired at one of the approaching craft.

The gun whined and got so hot he nearly dropped it. An immense burst of energy shot out of the tube, sending Carvalho reeling backwards. He caught himself with his free hand and looked over the rail at the sky. There was now only one helicopter in the sky, and it was moving away rapidly. The other had disappeared entirely.

"What happened? Did it crash into the bay?" asked Carvalho, looking at his friends. They were staring at the spot where the helicopter had just recently been.

"No, not exactly," said Molly. "It just kind of went."

"That's a pretty powerful little laser pointer. I would like to study it sometime," said Ananmaya.

"Be my guest," Carvalho gave him the charred, smoking remains of the gun. "I don't think it's going to be of much more use to us. I probably should have used the three or four setting. Five seems to be a one-shot deal."

Ananmaya steered the boat into the cove and beached it. "This is our stop. Everybody out."

They hopped out of the boat into the shallow surf. Ananmaya led them up the beach to the tree line.

"Where's your boat?" asked Molly scanning the horizon.

"I never said I had a boat," said Ananmaya.

"Yes, you did," argued Carvalho, as he picked his way through the jungle.

"I said I had a *ship*," said Ananmaya.

"What's the difference?" exclaimed Carvalho. "Look, they know where we are now. If you don't have a boat, how do you expect us to leave?"

"In this," said Ananmaya. He removed the banana fronds from the Elektra, and she gleamed in the sunlight.

For a while, neither of them said anything. Molly's mouth had gaped wide open. "Is that a space ship?"

Ananmaya had not heard her. He had walked a short distance away and was digging something up near a boulder. He returned with a small black box.

Carvalho still could not believe what he was seeing, "So I'm guessing this isn't a submarine?"

"No. It's not a submarine," he said. "This, my friends, is the Elektra. Please follow me inside. We need to get out of here before they come back with reinforcements."

They followed Ananmaya up the rope ladder to the top of the ship and clambered inside. He shut the portal and it sealed with a hiss. Molly watched as he took the black box to the rear of the ship, where he opened it inside a small chamber. She heard a clang and felt a queer sensation of movement. They were rising!

"Ladies and gentlemen, please take your seat and fasten your seat belt. Also, make sure your seat back and folding trays are in their full upright position. Lastly, please make sure any electronic equipment has been turned off. Thank you, for flying Ananmaya Airlines."

Carvalho looked quizzically at Molly. She groaned and explained the joke.

"I'm sorry," said Ananmaya. "I'm not normally a comedian, but I've always wanted to say that."

"Will there be snacks on this flight?" asked Molly.

"Sorry, besides water and bananas, there isn't much in the larder. I haven't had much time to stock her with supplies."

The ship was picking up speed and soon they would be over the mountains. The sensation of movement had evaporated; they did not feel as if they were moving at all. It was unnerving to watch the ground disappear beneath them as the ship rocketed skyward.

"We won't need many supplies though as we won't be in space terribly long," said Ananmaya, adjusting the controls.

"Space?" asked Carvalho, raising an eyebrow.

"Yes. I intend to find the Philolans," said Ananmaya.

"We're going to Philolaus? Who are you and what is going on? Why did you save us?" asked Molly. Her senses had finally caught up to her and she had a million questions.

The scene outside had gone from a pale blue to a deep purple. Carvalho could see the curvature of the Earth from his window. They were moving incredibly fast.

Ananmaya turned to face them. “Okay, I've plotted our course. We will be in space for about sixteen hours. I suppose now would be a good time to introduce myself and tell you what this is all about. My name is Ananmaya Gujarati, and I am a shifter.”

Chapter 32, Between Worlds

They had been talking for hours. Eventually Carvalho had become lost in the conversation and decided to catch up on a little sleep while his two companions continued their banter.

Ananmaya wasn't surprised to hear that Molly hadn't known she was a shifter. "Most people have shifter gifts in various small degrees and don't even realize it. With these weakly gifted individuals, the true depth of the gift is unreachable, except for the minimal access providing the mechanism behind what you would call an everyday talent. The only difference between a shifter and a regular person is that a shifter has direct access to this mechanism and can fully exploit its immense power."

Molly thought about this. *So, shifters were really just ridiculously talented individuals? That gave a whole new meaning to the word "gifted."*

"So, someone that who was really good at, I don't know, let's say running. What would she be if she were a shifter?"

"Shifter gifts tend to fall along the core physical rules of the universe. So, for your runner, her gift would be either strength or speed, more precisely, velocity and acceleration. If she were a shifter, she would very likely be able to impart incredible speed to herself or other objects. The Roman god, Mercury, may have been such an individual. Some of our earliest religions could easily have been based on shifters setting themselves up as gods."

"But what about individuals that don't have physical gifts? What about painters, musicians, and sculptors? And more to the point, what about writers?"

"Those talents are all based on access to creativity and inspiration, two traits which really don't exist, at least not the way people think they do."

"What? I beg to differ," said Molly a little insulted.

"I thought you might take exception at that," said Ananmaya. "But hear me out. Quantum theory provides for an infinite number of universes containing every potential outcome over the eternity of time. In short, everything that could have happened has happened and is happening simultaneously across the multiverse. Still with me so far?"

Molly nodded. You don't attend as many sci-fi and fantasy conventions as she had, and not know about multiple universes.

"So, anything you could possibly imagine has already happened in some universe, no matter how improbable it is. Thus, when you imagine something for your *Dragon's Keep* books, you are actually tapping into a very real universe where dragons exist and are simply reporting on what you have seen. You didn't invent any of those worlds or characters. You saw them and reported on their lives. That's where imagination comes from—real places."

Molly laughed. This was all too preposterous.

"Laugh if you wish, but the fantastic worlds you write about really do exist, Ms. Arden. All the stories, written by all the writers that have ever existed, are real places in the multiverse and everyone has some degree of access to them."

That simply couldn't be true. She thought of a ludicrous example. "So, what about *The Wizard of Oz?"*

"Yep. Toto, Munchkins and all," said Ananmaya. "Somewhere a universe has a set of physical rules that allow such a thing to happen. I have no doubt that Frank L Baum was a powerful shifter, even if he didn't know it himself. Successful writers have clearer insight into the multiverse; thus, their stories ring more true. It's why their books are so popular. You are one of the most popular writers on the planet. Your books have broken all the bestseller lists. What does that say about your shifter gift of seeing into alternate universes?"

Molly had to admit, it was an attractive theory. Every writer secretly wished that their worlds actually existed somewhere. After all, wasn't that the point of writing? To tell the story of another place, a place you would like to be a part of, a place you could maybe someday escape to?

"So what happened to change all that? How did I go from simply seeing a world, to actually bringing it here?"

"Well, I actually agree with Mariconi on that. I think that when you were in Costa Maya, the Dzolob chamber you were close to enhanced your abilities. His ancestors opened a gateway between our universes. Those temples are still immensely powerful."

"Ok, now I'm confused," said Molly. "The temples only open to that one specific universe, right?"

"As far as we know."

"Yet my imagination can get stuff from any random universe I chose to write about, correct?"

"Yes."

"So, of all the universes I could have written about, why did I choose the only one those temples are connected to?"

Ananmaya thought for a moment. "When did you first get the idea for your story?"

"In the plane, shortly before landing in Mexico. I started writing the story that evening."

"There's your answer. Because of the temple in Chaccoben, the barrier between our worlds is very thin. As you got nearer to Mexico, that universe would have dominated your mind for attention."

Molly thought about the odd book she had been writing. It was so different from anything she had done before. And he was right, she had started writing it the day she arrived in Costa Maya. Also, what about all the other experiences she had while she was there, the vivid dreams, the headaches, and the exhaustion?

"Why did I write about its past, instead of its present?" asked Molly.

"That, I don't know quite yet. But time is not as

straightforward as you might think. It is just another dimension, as valid as height and width, and you can alter it just as easily. Well at least on paper.

"I do know that something ties you to the planet's history. I knew it the moment we escaped. When I passed us through the wall at the observatory, I almost lost you. I had a similar problem before with the artifact driving this ship. It didn't like to be phase shifted either. Both of you seem to share the same quantum signature."

"Sorry to disappoint you, but I was born on Earth. So were both of my parents. I'm certain of that."

"Well, whatever it is, it would probably explain how you found Costa Maya in the first place."

"Oh that's easy. My agent Ellen recommended it to me. Are you saying she's mixed up in all this?"

"Not directly. Something directed you to Costa Maya the same way pressurized water will find its way out of a maze of tubing, no matter how complex. You were meant to be there; make no mistake."

"No, you don't understand, I hadn't even heard of the place until…"

"Until what?"

"Until she said I was working myself to death and I needed a vacation all to myself."

"Exactly my point. Over your lifetime, you've made thousands and thousands of decisions, which all led to that one critical choice. From your decision to become a writer, to what you chose as your first book, to finding your agent, to writing more books, to burning yourself out and needing a vacation and finally to taking your friend's recommendation and traveling to Costa Maya."

"It's all been planned? By who?"

"It could have been planned, but I don't think so. That's like saying two pieces of magnetite in a pile of rocks coming together was somehow planned. It is simple physics. The universe sorts itself out at the most fundamental level. With people, this shows up in the choices they make, choices based on the options presented by the universe.

"Like the magnets, that world is pulling you. Your choices inevitably lead you to Costa Maya whether you were aware of it or not. Costa Maya was simply the path of least resistance to restore the balance between universes."

"Why now? Why not when I was a teenager or something?"

"I expect your power hadn't fully developed. Arriving early there with no ability would not have brought the two universes together. You weren't ready until now. The universe was patiently waiting to let you to be at the right place at the right time."

That felt right as well. She had been at the top of her game when she had left. Her books had been selling extremely well. He had an answer for everything.

"So, let me see if I've got all this straight. There are two very closely linked universes. Something ties me to a certain time and place in the other one. This is a bit of a mess, and the two universes want to sort it all out. The easiest way to do this was for me to use the power of the Dzolob temples to bring Philolaus here. Doesn't that seem a bit extreme of a resolution to you?"

"That's small-scale stuff compared to the universe in general, but it's too early to judge. You are still on that journey."

"Huh?"

"Aren't you in a spaceship on the way to the planet you called here?"

"Yes, but this was your mission, not mine."

"Obviously, our destinies have intertwined. It is apparent you need to be on Philolaus. I have done this under the pretense of keeping you out of Mariconi's hands. Whatever larger goal our fates hold can only by hypothetical. I think we'll have more answers when we arrive."

"When do we get there? I'm starving," said Carvalho yawning. He rubbed his eyes. "You two are still talking? Molly, you should really get some rest. You look like shit."

Molly glared at him. "You don't smell like a bunch of roses either, bucko."

"I just meant that you needed to rest. Actually, you're as ravishing as ever," said Carvalho, kissing her hand.

Ananmaya looked at his watch. "We have about twenty more minutes until we reach the RA point. That is when we turn the ship around and begin the deceleration through the remaining half of our trip. There will a period of weightlessness, which will be unsettling during the rotation. I would wait until after then to rest."

"I was wondering about that. How come we're not weightless right now?" asked Carvalho.

"The gravity you currently feel is close to Earth normal even though we have been constantly accelerating at nearly twenty times that for almost eight hours. This is because I've shifted your mass into a quantum space independent of the ship's acceleration, which is why we're all not flat as pancakes by now. It's the same trick I use to keep from sinking into the ground when I pass through walls."

"Twenty Gs for eight hours? How fast is this thing moving?" asked Molly.

Ananmaya checked his instruments. "I'd say a little less than twice the speed of light."

"What? Isn't that impossible or something?" asked Carvalho.

"Ask the Elektra," said Ananmaya smiling.

"But stuff can't go past the speed of light. Einstein said…" said Molly.

"I don't think Einstein compensated for strange little antigravity rocks from alternate universes in his field equations."

"Well, even so, if we're nearly halfway there, we should be close to the sun. Why aren't we burning up?" asked Carvalho looking out the window.

"The sun is below the ship. I took us on a high arc to maintain a safe distance. Nevertheless, the ship has several layers of thermal protection. Also, they have installed some impressive heating and cooling systems over the years. She has waited at Niagara a long time for this return flight. I believe SOTAR had been preparing her for a trip as soon as someone could discover how to get her off the ground."

"Mariconi must have been planning to visit himself at some point," suggested Molly.

"Maybe, but I don't even think Mariconi knows what we'll find there. Tesla broke all communication with the Earth almost eighty years ago. The planet has been masked in silence ever since. They were in a bad state when Einstein entered the last few lines in his journal, but he was certain their plans for reconstruction would succeed. I hope they've done well, because we are going to need their help. Archænis is planning a full-scale invasion and I don't think you were their only solution for getting their ships here."

"That might be so, but Mariconi's going to be in some serious trouble in the morning, regardless," said Molly.

"That is a comforting thought," replied Ananmaya, preparing to rotate the ship for turn around. "Everyone buckle yourselves back in. After the turn, we really should get some sleep, but one of us should take turns keeping a lookout. It will be another eight hours before we arrive at our destination."

"I'll take the first shift," said Carvalho. He reached over and tested Molly's restraints before checking his own.

"Ok, everyone ready? Here we go. Three…two…one!" The ship spun around with a disorienting jolt. After a few minutes of queasiness, Molly felt the pull of something resembling normal gravity. It had been a very long morning, so it didn't take long for her to drift off to sleep.

* * *

Tap. Tap. Tap. The little bronze telegraph key on the console beat out a staccato rhythm. Carvalho woke Ananmaya.

"What is it?" asked Ananmaya, looking around. Are we already there?

"Nearly there, but that key on the console is moving. Is it supposed to do that?" asked Carvalho.

"What?!"

Sure enough, the ancient telegraph key was tapping out a message in Morse code. Incredible. He had no idea that it was still functional. He decoded the message:

UNIDENTIFIED CRAFT APPROACHING PHILOLAN SPACE. PLEASE IDENTIFY.

Ananmaya couldn't believe his eyes. There were people still on Philolaus and they had technology advanced enough to detect them this far out in space. He checked the distance gauge. It showed them a little less than two million miles from the planet. At that distance, they would arrive in about fifteen minutes. He excitedly gave the message to his companions and tapped out a response.

THIS IS THE ELEKTRA. PLEASE ADVISE.

A few moments later, the telegraph tapped again.

DO NOT APPROACH.
HOLD YOUR POSITION OR BE DESTROYED.

Ananmaya immediately slowed the ship to a stop, its frame shuddering as he applied an alarming amount of reverse thrust.

"What was that about?" demanded Carvalho.

Ananmaya handed him the message.

"Oh."

"They don't seem very friendly," said Molly.

"What do you expect from a planet that wants to stay hidden?" said Ananmaya.

They waited in silence for half an hour, unsure of what to do next. Suddenly, the Elektra rocked backwards, then lurched forward. The hull began to vibrate.

"Are they shooting at us?" asked Carvalho.

"I don't think so. I think we've been harpooned *by that!"*

Molly looked out the window and saw a long silver cord extending from the Elektra to a silver disk with pulsing lights. It looked just like the stereotypical flying saucers you got in old 1950s B-movies. It looked almost comical as it dragged the Elektra through space by its tether. The telegraph beat again.

ELEKTRA. AWAIT INSTRUCTIONS. DO NOT RESIST.

"I think it's best we obey their wishes," said Ananmaya. "We're not exactly invited guests."

The strange craft had been towing them for nearly an hour when suddenly the brilliant green and white arc of the planet's curvature rolled up into the window. They had arrived at Philolaus. Four other craft had joined the flying saucer as they settled into a slow orbit around the planet."

It's real! It's really there!" gasped Molly, looking at the strange, emerald-colored world."

"It's quite beautiful," said Ananmaya.

"What do they intend to do with us?" asked Carvalho.

As if in answer, the telegraph started up again.

ELEKTRA. FOLLOW SCOUT SHIP
TO LANDING PAD C.
DO NOT DEVIATE COURSE

The tether detached and retracted into the scout ship. Ananmaya adjusted the sliders to maneuver the ship. The saucer dropped into the atmosphere at a horrifyingly fast pace and dipped into a small cloudbank. He had a hard time keeping up with it in the haze. Eventually, the cloud fell behind them revealing a vast landscape of high, broken plateaus separated by a dense, foggy jungle. Here and there, tall trees rose above the mist.

As they got nearer to the largest of these plateaus, Molly saw it contained a vast, bustling city. In the center, four tall white structures with domed roofs reached high into the sky, their nearly translucent sides glittering in the evening sunlight. Multiple archways joined them hundreds of feet above their bases. Smaller buildings crowded below them, some clinging to the edges and sides of the plateau like creeping vines. This city bore no resemblance to the small, struggling outpost colonies she had written about. There must have been half a million people down there.

"Look there!" said Carvalho.

Everywhere, long streams of vehicles raced between the buildings on invisible roads high above the ground. The scout ship in front of them merged into one of these lines and proceeded toward the tall towers.

Now that they were closer, Molly could see that one of the towers had large rectangular openings cut into its surface. Bluish-white translucent force fields flickered and crackled in each opening which held more of the ubiquitous flying saucers. *It's like a pigeon roost.*

The scout ship led them to one of these openings. The force field shut off, and it and went inside. Ananmaya guided the Elektra into the roost, taking a position next to the saucer as the force field flickered back on behind them. The scout ship lowered its three legs. Its running lights dimmed and pulsed, waiting for the Elektra to power down.

"Well, we're here. I suppose we should introduce ourselves," said Ananmaya. He lowered the craft to the floor where she rested on her landing skids.

"Here comes the welcoming committee," said Carvalho, looking out the window.

A group of about twenty officers in black and green uniforms lined up around the Elektra. They pointed strange looking rifles at the ship. None of them looked particularly pleased to meet their new guests.

Chapter 33, The Philolans

"Please tell me why I shouldn't have all three of you killed on the spot," demanded commander Nolan.

He was furious to find that actual outworlders were waiting for him in his office. Real people from Earth, in his office! Why hadn't that idiot on the scout ship followed procedure the moment they failed to identify themselves properly? For some reason, the young cadet had spoken directly to the Chief Royal Astronomer who incomprehensibly had gotten authority to bring them directly to Farshift Command. He would have that boy's stripes for making him deal with this mess.

"I'm sorry, did you say killed?" asked Ananmaya, not sure he heard the man properly.

"Yes, killed, more specifically, vaporized," said Nolan. "What were you thinking coming out here? I thought we had an agreement with your world."

"An agreement?" asked Carvalho. "What kind of agreement?"

"The one your United Nations signed with us back in the late forties. Don't play stupid with me. You know exactly what I'm talking about."

"Honestly, we don't. Please, give us a moment to explain," said Molly.

"Oh, you'll have plenty of time to explain, rotting in the brig."

Nolan hated dealing with politics. Now, he had a full-scale interplanetary incident to deal with. Damn that man. It would have been so much easier if the cadet had simply blown them out of the sky.

He was well within his rights to do so. About twenty years after both sides signed the treaty, the outworlders broke it by attempting to leave their planet with conventional rockets. During the Apollo moon program, three Philolan cruisers arrived in force to remind them to go no further with their idiotic manned space programs.

Nolan looked at his watch. The intricate brass instrument showed the time to be fifteen minutes past three o'clock. Professor Martin was late. For now, he would have to keep talking with these people.

"Are you telling me you don't know about your own UN Office for Outer Space Affairs?" asked Nolan.

"I know about the UN, I just don't know about any type of agreement between our worlds," said Ananmaya. "I wasn't aware anyone besides a handful of people even knew you were out here."

"We'd like to keep it that way, and so would your governments," argued Nolan. "Which one sent you?"

"We're not with any government," insisted Carvalho.

"Look, private space exploration on your world is naive and infantile. There is no way you could have come here in anything less than a government-funded space program. Frankly, I was surprised to hear how fast you were moving. We haven't heard of any covert programs on your world developing ships with anything near such speed."

"The Elektra is NOT a government space craft," said Ananmaya.

"I'll say she's not," said an old man bustling into the room. I apologize for being late, Commander, but I just had to see the ship for myself. "It's *her!* It's really *her!*"

"What are you talking about, Martin?" asked Nolan.

"That ship in your landing bay is a historic relic. You've never heard the story of the Elektra?"

Nolan thought for a moment. The name did ring a bell, something from their history before the city of Farshift was founded. But that was over a hundred years ago. It couldn't be.

"Are you telling me that's Tesla's ship? The prototype?" asked Nolan.

"Yes!" exclaimed Martin.

"But she was supposed to be destroyed along with her plans. Are you certain?

Martin nodded. "I inspected the ship myself. It's in wonderful condition. It will be a stunning addition to the museum."

Nolan snapped around to face his unwelcome guests. "What's that ship doing in my landing bay?"

Ananmaya ignored the Commander and turned to the old man. "I'm sorry sir, we haven't been properly introduced. My name is Ananmaya Gujarati, and these are my companions, Molly Arden and Enrico Carvalho."

"Professor Orville Martin, Chief Royal Astronomer at Farshift," said Martin shaking their hands. "Very pleased to meet you."

"Now that the pleasantries are over, can you please tell me why that ship still exists?" demanded Nolan.

"Einstein kept the Elektra intact at Niagara. He couldn't bring himself to destroy her," said Ananmaya. "The ship sat waiting underground for nearly fifty years. I was entrusted by my mentor with information given to him by Einstein before he died. Your commander has them on his desk. These papers tell your history as well as mine."

"This is a wonderful artifact, but I fail to see how it pertains to you," said Martin looking at the journal.

"It tells of Einstein's fear of corruption in his shifter organization. Neither Ms. Arden nor I have ever been part of SOTAR. Until recently, they didn't even know about us, although we are both shifters with quite extraordinary gifts.

Nolan pulled out his gun. "Shifters? You're shifters?"

Ananmaya nodded.

"Don't move," Nolan pressed a button on the console on his desk. The lights in the room flickered and Ananmaya fell back into a chair, feeling very light headed. Molly was affected much more dramatically. She fainted and fell to the floor unconscious. Carvalho rushed to her side.

"What have you done to them?" he demanded.

"I've nullified their power. This security field will effectively keep any shifter at bay. I must admit though, I've never seen it affect someone like that before," said Nolan.

Martin checked Molly's pulse. "She's unconscious, but she's alive and breathing. Honestly, Commander, is the security field really necessary?"

"It's protocol. We don't know what powers these two possess. This whole time they could have been running around in our minds, spying for their governments. Maybe now you'll reconsider the wisdom of having them removed to a more secure location."

Carvalho lifted Molly into a chair next to Ananmaya. She was beginning to stir.

"Can she have some water?"

Martin nodded and took a cup off the commander's desk. He glowered at him as he left the room to get some water from down the hall.

"Molly? Can you hear me? Are you ok?" asked Carvalho.

"Uh huh," said Molly. She felt like a pile of elephants was sitting on top of her. A droning buzzing sound filled her ears. She couldn't think straight.

Nolan took the time Martin was gone to interrogate them some more.

"Now that you know you can't possibly escape, tell me exactly who you are and why you are here."

"I understand your fear, Commander, and I don't hold any of this against you. But you must believe me, we are not part of any government on Earth," said Ananmaya.

"If she's harmed in any way, I will hold all of it against him," growled Carvalho.

"We, um, actually, I stole the Elektra from SOTAR so that I could bring you a message and offer my help," said Ananmaya.

"What kind of help could a self-proclaimed thieving outworlder possibly offer us?"

"I have information. There is…there will be an invasion. It threatens both our worlds," added Ananmaya. The buzzing in his ears was making it difficult to think.

"An invasion? What kind of invasion? From where?" asked Nolan.

"From Archænis."

Nolan's eyes widened. "What?"

Professor Martin came in with the cup of water, which he offered to Molly.

"Thanks," she said. She felt a little better. Now, only one elephant was sitting on her.

Unexpectedly, the professor leaned in close towards her, making her feel awkwardly uncomfortable. He seemed to be unabashedly staring at her chest.

"Enjoying the view?" snapped Carvalho.

"What? Oh, no. It's the necklace! Ms. Arden, may I see it?" asked Martin.

She let him hold the pendant in his shaking hand. He turned it around and inspected the fading inscription on the back. It read: TO MY DARLING LISSET - AK.

"I don't believe this! Where did you get this pendant?"

"I've always had it. It's been passed down in my family for generations," said Molly.

"Are you sure? Are you *absolutely* sure?" asked Martin stunned.

"Yes, from mother to daughter," said Molly. "I'm sorry, I can't think of how many generations back grandma Lisset was with all this buzzing in my head."

"Commander Nolan. Turn off the security field immediately," demanded Martin.

"I will do nothing of the sort. You might have the president's ear sir, but this is my base and I will protect it the best way I see fit."

"You'll do it now, or I'll see to it that you'll be commanding sheep on Madeley by the end of the week."

"You've got no authority," asserted Nolan.

"Oh, it won't be me calling for your resignation," said Martin. "It'll be the public. Just wait until they find out how poorly you treated the great, great, great, great granddaughter of Almos Kasonovic."

* * *

The aircar zipped through the sky, protected by a small convey of security vehicles. Two small one-man fliers led the procession, flashing their warning lights, clearing the traffic before them as they went. The glossy, semi-translucent walls of the buildings reflected the sleek form of the aircar as it flashed by. Martin had been asking questions ever since they had left Farshift Command.

"This is really quite extraordinary!" he exclaimed. "What you've been saying has explained everything."

"Would you mind explaining it to us?" asked Molly.

"Of course. Over eighty years ago, my predecessor, the late Professor Edington, released private documents describing in detail what our revered Professor Almos had called his Farshift Project. Farshift was an experiment to augment his shifter gift to a level where he might force a bridge between our universes. He used it to send his pregnant wife Lisset to Earth to escape a death sentence on Archænis. Have I said that children were a crime on Archænis?"

"Yes, we know. You've told us all this already," said Carvalho.

"Anyhow, Lisset had her baby, and they formed a new family with Almos's twin on Earth, Viktor. The little girl's name was Anna Kasonovic, Ms. Arden's great, great, great, great grandmother. But I have already said all this, please excuse me. What you may not know is that Anna fell in love with someone from both our histories. A gentleman named Nikola Tesla, the savior of Philolaus and the founder of our great republic which he named in Almos's honor."

Molly saw where this was going, and she gasped. "Are you saying I'm related to Nikola Tesla as well?"

"Yes, he would be your great, great, great, great grandfather if they had married," said Martin, beaming.

Molly turned to Ananmaya. "You said there was something odd about me which was drawing me here. Could it be that I have blood from an alternate universe running through me?"

"It's very likely," said Ananmaya. "It's like that little piece of Leviton ore in the Elektra. It keeps wanting to return here as well."

"Ms. Arden, you are the answer to a question that has puzzled us for over a hundred years. Now we finally know how and why we were brought here," said Martin.

"We already knew that when Almos and Viktor weakened the barrier with the Farshift project and sent someone through, they reopened a scar on the universe that had never healed. But we know now that it was you, because of your link back through time to Professor Almos, who pulled him and the planet sustaining him, into this universe. You were the first descendent of his who had the power to do so.

"Also, it had to happen at a time when both Almos and Viktor were alive so that they could be used as anchors as the planet shifted. Deciding to write that book was culmination of several lifetimes of decisions you and your family made in assisting the universes to sort themselves out."

"Oh yes, things are much better now," said Molly sarcastically. "We've now got this extra planet in our solar system, which is good because the invaders from another universe will need lots of room to…um…*invade.* Also, I just found out that I'm part alien as well. You're right, things are so much less complicated now that I'm here. The universe has an odd notion of what sorted-out means."

"Yes it does," said Ananmaya. "Look down there."

Molly and Carvalho looked out the side window. Were those cows down there? What were they wearing on their heads?

"We're passing over some agricultural areas. Our cattle are free to roam the plateaus. They are wearing control helmets. When we need one of them to return for slaughter or milking, we can simply call them with the push of a button. It's a painless form of mind control. As far as they are concerned, returning to the stock pen is their idea."

"I didn't realize you had animals from Earth here. Don't you take advantage of the indigenous animals?"

"Unfortunately, there are not many large animals to speak of. We have to import most of our livestock," He laughed, "In fact, that's what caused the incident in 1947 that led to the treaty."

"What incident?" asked Ananmaya.

"One of our scout ships had an electrical malfunction and crashed in Roswell, New Mexico on a cattle run. Your government captured two of our agents and debris from the ship. It was the first time our people had any contact with yours since 1930."

Molly, Carvalho, and Ananmaya looked at each other with wide eyes. They each knew something about the famous Roswell flying saucer conspiracy.

"They were never really in any kind of danger. Three other ships were in orbit above your planet at the time. We negotiated their release in exchange for a slow release of technology over the next fifty years. Your planet would agree not to pursue space travel or alert the media to our existence, and we would in exchange give you things like Velcro, transistors, microchips, piezoelectrics, and a whole host of other core technological advanced in agriculture, medicine, and other sciences. It's all in a secret international treaty filed at the UN Office for Outer Space Affairs."

"So you've been behind all those UFO sightings?" exclaimed Molly. "I thought aliens were little green men with big black almond shaped eyes."

"...with a penchant for anal probes," added Carvalho wryly.

"That's all part of your government keeping its end of the bargain. They perpetuate the myth of aliens from outer space to hide the truth of who we really are. Unfortunately, your government has found the myth to be convenient in other ways."

"What do you mean?" asked Ananmaya.

"Suppose you wanted to do experiments with live human subjects and not get caught? What better way than to hang a fake flying saucer beneath a stealth helicopter, dress up like an alien, then abduct some poor farm boy and get him high on hallucinogenics. Then, they could do whatever they wanted without fear of reprisal. Because, when he woke up back on the farm, he'd tell everyone he had been abducted by a UFO. He probably wouldn't even file a police report."

"Our government does that?" asked Molly.

"Your entire planet uses the myth of UFOs to hide their secrets in plain sight. Want to test secret government aircraft in public? Make it look like a UFO. Want to covertly buzz secret foreign government installations? Make it look like a UFO. No one can trace a UFO to its source, and worse, no one believes you anyway. Get the picture?"

"That actually makes sense," commented Ananmaya, horrifically amused.

"So, how do you know so much about us?" asked Carvalho.

"We have been watching your planet for a very long time. We even have a base on the far side..."

"Ahem," interrupted Commander Nolan from the front seat, next to the driver. "I think Professor Martin has said quite enough."

"We're on final approach to the capital building, sir," said the driver.

"Excellent. The president will be pleased at the time we've made."

Molly looked out the window at the large building they were approaching. It was octagonal and multi-tiered like a wedding cake. Massive buttresses fanned out radially to eight tall towers on each corner. It looked older and softer than the buildings in the city somehow. Wood and sandstone looked like the primary building materials. Unlike the tall tower near the center of the city, this building had been located near the edge of town. Vast landscaped courtyards surrounded the complex, blending into the countryside of the wide plateau.

"That is the Presidential Palace," said Martin. "It's very old. It was the last project Tesla had personally overseen. Unfortunately, he never saw it completed. Three years into its construction, he passed away at eighty-seven years old. He's buried down there, in the Presidential Memorial Gardens."

"The president? I didn't think Philolaus had a centralized government," asked Molly.

"Tesla changed all that. With each new, amazing innovation, he gained more and more respect and admiration. The Parifeldie Council unanimously elected him mayor shortly after Hasting's impeachment.

"He resisted the position at first, but soon saw its advantages. He proposed a new capital city where the people of Philolaus could all live and grow. He called this visionary new city Farshift, in honor of the brilliant Professor Almos."

"The people agreed to this plan?" asked Molly.

"Not at first. They thought he was crazy. They could barely support themselves as it was; it was preposterous even to consider founding a new city. But, he unveiled plans for an amazing new power plant, which could tap energy from the air itself, and transmit it hundreds of miles in any direction. Such a power plant would run this ambitious new city as well as supply power to the other struggling colonies. They built the power plant at Parifeldie, and it delivered on its promises. Soon, the city sprung up around it, and it was renamed Farshift. You've already been there. The command center is located in one of the power plant's transmission towers."

"That structure was a power plant? But, it's huge," said Molly.

"It had to be. It supports our entire civilization. It gives us the power to mine ore and refine raw materials into the things we need. Because of the power plant, we have made great advancements in agriculture, manufacturing, medicine, and science."

"That's another thing. How did there come to be so many people here?" asked Molly.

"As resources became abundant, a state-wide mandate on high birth rates was agreed upon. We are advancing technologically much faster than your people, but we are still woefully outnumbered. We know it will only be a matter of time before your technology catches up with ours."

"How many people are there on your planet?" asked Molly.

In only one hundred years, we now boast a population of nearly five-hundred thousand. We are still just a kingdom of small territories, but having an elected president was part of the ideals set forth in the Farshift's constitution. Having royalty reminded people too much of the tyrannical rule back home."

"Have you had many presidents?" asked Carvalho.

"They serve five-year terms, so I believe there have been thirteen," said Martin, doing a little mental math.

"Fourteen," corrected Nolan. "You're forgetting about President Kulik."

"He only lasted a month and he was drunk half the time. I hardly think he counts," said Martin.

"Do you mean Leonid Kulik?" asked Ananmaya. "Didn't he and his assistant stay on Philolaus with Tesla?"

"Yes, and because of that, he easily followed Tesla as our next president. Unfortunately, he got himself into a bit of scandal shortly after taking office. One morning, he was found in the city square, nearly frozen to death, next to a paint bucket, a length of rope and half a pound of cheese."

"Nearly frozen to death?" asked Carvalho. "Cheese?"

"Oh, did I mention he was completely naked? We have no idea what he had been up to the previous night, but neither did he."

"Sounds like he had a wild night," said Carvalho.

"Well, it was the last straw, and it got him impeached. Fortunately, his assistant Anya had a much more productive career as a research scientist. Her work led to the development of an anti-toxin to gases in our deadly windstorms," said Martin. "She's buried in the memorial gardens with her husband, Samuel Edington."

"Edington got married?" exclaimed Molly.

"Yes, they had several children, one of which was the grandfather of the pilot flying the scout ship that found you. He's the one that contacted me when you identified yourselves as being on the Elektra."

"Now, I'll have to pin a medal on that boy," growled Nolan.

"Indeed you shall," said Professor Martin. "There's going to be an announcement of our friends' arrival in a few days. I believe there will be a worldwide telecast of the event and festivities."

"Festivities?" asked Ananmaya.

"Yes. Didn't you know what the day after tomorrow is?"

"No."

"It's Arrival Day," grinned Martin.

* * *

Molly walked out on the veranda that overlooked the beautifully manicured lawns below. From this height, she could see over the edge of the plateau all the way down to the steaming jungle below. It stretched all the way to the horizon, turning orange, then crimson, colored by the setting sun. Just three short weeks ago, she had watched the same sun set on a beach at Costa Maya. She could not believe how strange her life had become in so short a time.

"They're going to want us at the press conference soon, Molly," said Carvalho softly behind her, putting his hands on her shoulders.

She relaxed into his arms.

"Yes, I know," she sighed. "Ananmaya is already there. He left some time ago to speak with the commander again. They wanted more information on the threat from Archænis. Gods, we've been here for two days and I feel like a caged animal. I want to get out. I want to see this world."

"He's just doing his job," said Carvalho. "Take it easy. It hasn't been so bad. There's the celebration afterward you know."

"That's easy for you to say. How would you feel if you wrote a book that came to life, but then instead of being able to enjoy it, you had it just dangled in front of you?"

"*Namarada,* you are full of worlds. For now, just enjoy the one you are in," soothed Carvalho, as they watched the sun drop below the horizon.

"Night falls so quickly here," said Molly, starting to shiver. Carvalho wrapped his arms around here and held her close.

Just then, there was an explosion overhead. They both turned to see what it was. Up above them, hundreds of sparkling lights glittered in the darkening sky. They were soon joined by another explosion of light, then another, and then another. The Arrival Day celebrations had started.

"Fireworks on another world. Would you look at that?" remarked Molly, with shining eyes.

"Beautiful," said Carvalho.

"Yes, they really are," said Molly.

"I wasn't talking about the fireworks," said Carvalho, brushing a loose strand of hair out of her face and caressing the side of her cheek. He looked deeply into her eyes and drew her face closer to his.

"I never really thanked you for saving me."

"Yes, you did."

"No, not from Marconi…from *myself*. It's nice to have something to care about other than my books, I feel…"

Carvalho silenced her with a kiss as they embraced under the canopy of a spectacularly shifting sky.

Epilogue

Mariconi wiped the sweat off his forehead with his handkerchief as he stepped over a thick vine across the jungle path. He heard a wheeze behind him as his twin tried to keep up.

His twin had always been a pale, wretch of a man, a mere shadow of his more vigorous counterpart. Mariconi had kept him buried in paperwork at the observatory, mostly out of embarrassment should someone notice the slight resemblance. The only person he could totally trust, he had given him an important task, which he had failed miserably to perform. Soon however, the annoying little man would finally be of some use.

As did most of the agents from Archænis, Mariconi and his twin had found each other within weeks of his arrival on Earth. Appalled, he found his twin a short, pudgy, balding man, only vaguely reminiscent of himself. Not surprisingly, the man had no shifter ability to speak of. Nevertheless, the pallid, wretch of a man seemed to worship the ground he walked on, so he had given him a job at the observatory where he could keep an eye on him.

"Please…wait," wheezed the red-faced man, stopping to rest on a log.

Two of Mariconi's security team gave him a questioning look.

"It's no matter. We are almost there. The sun will not set for an hour or so. We have some time."

"I don't understand. Why are we going to the temple? The shifters have escaped."

The idiot actually ventured to remind him of this. What remarkable stupidity.

"I have a backup plan," he scowled in disgust.

In actuality, his backup plan had little chance of working and he knew it. However, he was desperate enough to try anything, and there was a small chance of success. It would be dangerous, but he was going to die anyway if those ships did not arrive as planned. He had bet his life on that commitment and soon he would have to show his cards.

In the fifty years he had exiled himself to Earth, he had been researching the Mayan temples and the Dzolob people. There was strikingly little information on the Dzolob here, much, much less than on Archænis. In this universe, the Mayan people had somehow taken their planet back from the Dzolob and driven them back. On his world, they had thrived. They were the progenitors of his race, not a defeated enemy.

The Maya had also destroyed all the records of their existence. *All except this,* he thought, looking at the hill where he knew a temple lay hidden beneath all that mud and rock. This temple at Chaccoben had been the key gateway. Its activation had caused a chain reaction with the rest, harnessing their combined power, and channeling it here. How had the Arden woman done it? Could he do it again?

He had read the nearly flawless hieroglyphics inside the chamber after she had discovered its location. The story they told was a blueprint of murder and bloodshed. The releasing of souls on the sacrificial altar released tremendous amounts of energy, which somehow, the temple channeled and distributed to the other fifteen gateways. The sacrifices had to be voluntary, acutely painful, and there would have to be many of them.

He interpreted the sacrificial voluntary requirement as suicide, a desire to murder oneself. Rather than sacrifice himself, he would sacrifice his quantum counterpart on the altar. With any luck, this would fulfill the requirement and allow him to remain alive. This way, if the death of his twin had an effect, he could turn back time, and repeat the bloody act as many times as was required. He would repeat the process until all the portals were functional and the ships could come through the rift.

Looking at the hill, he hesitated for a moment. He had turned death backwards only once before, and he had nearly gone mad. He didn't know what nightmares he would face with his current course of action. Regrettably, he knew exactly what nightmares he would face from Archænis' shifter interrogation squads.

"That's enough. Follow me," commanded Mariconi. They climbed the hill.

Halogen lights brightly lit small room. All the equipment he would need was here. He peeled off his damp white suit and stood naked in the small room. He commanded his twin to do the same as he put on the sacrificial robes of his ancestors.

"What? Dr. Mariconi, I don't understand."

Mariconi turned away from him and looked at the setting sun. Soon it would be time. He began to perform the ancient ritual described on the walls of the chamber. He could feel it began to vibrate sympathetically to his pulse. He turned to one of the guards, "Take him."

One of the large thugs put a gun in the man's face. "Do as he says. Then get on the table."

"No! You do not mean to…you're mad! You are all mad!" screamed the little man, trying desperately to free himself.

Dimetri pinned him to the wall by the neck, choking him. He made little gurgling sounds as Andre removed his clothing.

"Stop it! Please. Why are you doing this?" he gasped as Dimetri repositioned his grip.

Mariconi began humming a deep monotone as he removed an ancient artifact from its cloth wrapping. An ebony dagger with an evil, twisted looking blade caught the last glimpses of the receding sunlight. He picked it up and offered it to the retreating sun. "It's time."

Hurling the squirming man to the table, the two men held pinned him to the altar by his hands and feet, exposing the white skin of his hairless chest that lurched with each thump of his pounding heart.

"No!"

As the last shaft of light moved to the crown of stars on the far wall, Mariconi's voice became louder and more insistent as he recited the ancient language of his ancestors. Raising the black dagger above his head he waited until the sun fully illuminated the lapis lazuli gem in the center of the constellation. Then he plunged down the dagger, deep into Pinotti's heart.

www.ingramcontent.com/pod-product-compliance
Lightning Source LLC
Chambersburg PA
CBHW070200120726
47909CB00001B/193

* 9 7 8 0 6 1 5 3 7 8 9 3 0 *